THE
WEDDING

Also by Danielle Steel

IRRESISTIBLE FORCES

GRANNY DAN

BITTERSWEET

MIRROR IMAGE

HIS BRIGHT LIGHT: THE
STORY OF NICK TRAINA

THE KLONE AND I

THE LONG ROAD HOME

THE GHOST

SPECIAL DELIVERY

THE RANCH

SILENT HONOR

MALICE

FIVE DAYS IN PARIS

LIGHTNING

WINGS

THE GIFT

ACCIDENT

VANISHED

MIXED BLESSINGS

JEWELS

NO GREATER LOVE

HEARTBEAT

MESSAGE FROM NAM

DADDY

STAR

ZOYA

KALEIDOSCOPE

FINE THINGS

WANDERLUST

SECRETS

FAMILY ALBUM

FULL CIRCLE

CHANGES

THURSTON HOUSE

CROSSINGS

ONCE IN A LIFETIME

A PERFECT STRANGER

REMEMBRANCE

PALOMINO

LOVE: POEMS

THE RING

LOVING

TO LOVE AGAIN

SUMMER'S END

SEASON OF PASSION

THE PROMISE

NOW AND FOREVER

PASSION'S PROMISE

GOING HOME

DANIELLE STEEL

THE WEDDING

Delacorte Press

Published by
Delacorte Press
Random House, Inc.
1540 Broadway
New York, New York 10036

Delacorte Press® is a registered trademark of Random House, Inc., and the
colophon is a trademark of Random House, Inc.

The jacket format and design of this book are protected trade dresses and
trademarks of Dell Publishing, a division of Random House, Inc.

Library of Congress Cataloging in Publication Data

Steel, Danielle.
    The wedding / Danielle Steel.
        p.   cm.
    ISBN 0-385-31437-X
    ISBN 0-385-31830-8 (limited ed.)
    I. Title.
    PS3569.T33828W43   1997
    813'.54—dc20   94-44391
                                                CIP

Manufactured in the United States of America
Published simultaneously in Canada

April 2000

10 9 8 7 6 5 4 3 2 1

BVG

To Beatie,
My first and much-loved bride,
May you be happy forever!

with all my heart
and love,
d.s.

CHAPTER I

The traffic moved along the Santa Monica Freeway at a snail's pace, as Allegra Steinberg lay her head back against the seat of the midnight blue Mercedes 300. At this rate, it was going to take forever. She had nothing particular to do on the way home, but it always seemed such an incredible waste of time just sitting there in traffic.

She stretched her long legs, sighed, and flicked on the radio, and she smiled as they started playing Bram Morrison's latest single. He was one of her clients at the law firm. She had represented him for over a year. She had a number of important clients. At twenty-nine, four years out of Yale law school, she was a junior partner at Fisch, Herzog, and Freeman. They were one of the most important firms in L.A., and entertainment law had always been her passion.

Allegra had known years before that she wanted to go into law, and it had only been for a brief, little while, after two years of summer stock in New Haven during her sophomore and junior years at Yale, that she had thought she might want to be an actress. It wouldn't have surprised anyone in her family, but it wouldn't necessarily have pleased them. Her mother, Blaire Scott, had written and produced one of the most successful shows on television for nine years. It was a comedy, well peppered with serious moments, and some occasional real-life drama. They had

had the highest possible ratings for seven of their nine years, and it had earned her mother seven Emmies. Her father, Simon Steinberg, was a major movie producer, and had made some of Hollywood's most important movies. He had won three Academy Awards over the years, and his reputation for box office successes was legend. More importantly, he was that rarest of commodities in Hollywood, a nice man, a gentleman, a truly decent human being. He and Blaire were among the industry's most unusual, and most respected couples. They worked hard, and had a real family, which they devoted a lot of their time to. Allegra had a seventeen-year-old sister, Samantha, "Sam," who was a senior in high school and a model, and who, unlike Allegra, did want to be an actress. Only their brother, Scott, a junior at Stanford, seemed to have escaped show business entirely. He was in pre-med, and all he wanted in life was to be a doctor. Hollywood and its alleged magic held no lure for Scott Steinberg.

Scott had seen enough of show business in his twenty years. And he even thought Allegra was crazy to be an entertainment lawyer. He didn't want to spend the rest of his life worrying about the "box office," or the gross, or the ratings. He wanted to specialize in sports medicine, and be an orthopedic surgeon. Nice and sensible and down-to-earth. When the bone breaks, you fix it. He had seen enough of the agonies the rest of his family went through, dealing with spoiled, erratic stars, unreliable actors, dishonest network people who disappeared in six months, and quixotic investors. There were highs certainly, and perks admittedly, and they all seemed to love what they did. His mother derived tremendous satisfaction from her show, and his father had produced some great movies. And Allegra liked being an attorney for the stars and Sam wanted to be an actress. But as far as Scott was concerned, they could have it.

Allegra smiled to herself, thinking of him, and listening to the last of Bram's song. Even Scott had been impressed when she was able to tell him that Bram was one of her clients. He was a hero. She never said who her clients were, but Bram had mentioned her on a special with Barbara Walters. Carmen Connors was one of her clients too, the Marilyn Monroe look-alike who was the decade's new blond bombshell. She was twenty-three years old, from a town in Oregon the size of a dinner plate, and she was an ardent Christian. She had started out as a singer, and recently she'd done two movies back to back, and it turned out she was a sensational actress. She'd been referred to the firm by CAA, and one of the senior partners had introduced her to Allegra. They had hit it off instantly, and now she was Allegra's baby, literally sometimes, but Allegra didn't mind it.

Unlike Bram, who was in his late thirties and had been around the music business for twenty years, Carmen was still fairly new to Hollywood, and seemed to be constantly beset by problems. Trouble with boyfriends, men who were in love with her and she insisted she barely knew, stalkers, publicists, hairdressers, tabloids, paparazzi, would-be agents. She was never sure how to handle any of them, and Allegra was used to getting calls from her anytime, day or night, usually starting at two in the morning. The young beauty was often terrified at night, and she was always afraid that someone would break in and hurt her. Allegra had been able to control some of the terror for her with a security company that patrolled her house from dusk to dawn, a state-of-the-art alarm, and a pair of incredibly unnerving guard dogs. They were rottweilers and Carmen was afraid of them, but so were her would-be attackers and stalkers. But in spite of all that, she still called Allegra in the middle of the night, just to talk out problems she was having on the set, or sometimes just for comfort. It didn't bother Allegra; she was used to it. But her friends commented that she was as much baby-sitter as lawyer. Allegra knew it was part of the job with celebrity clients. She had seen what her parents went through with their stars, and nothing surprised her. Despite everything, she loved practicing law, and she particularly enjoyed the field of entertainment.

As she sat and waited for the traffic to move again, she pressed another button on her radio, and then thought about Brandon, as the traffic finally began to edge forward. Sometimes it took her an hour to crawl ten miles on the way home from a meeting or seeing a client at their home, but she was used to that too. She loved living in L.A., and most of the time she didn't mind the traffic. She had the top down on her car, it was a warm January afternoon and her long blond hair shimmered in the last of the winter sunlight. It was a perfect southern California day, the kind of weather she had longed for during her seven long New Haven winters while she was at Yale, first for undergraduate, and then for law school. After Beverly Hills High, most of her friends had gone to UCLA, but her father had wanted her to go to Harvard. Allegra had preferred Yale, but she had never been tempted to stay in the East after she graduated. Her whole life was based in California.

She thought of calling Brandon at the office as she picked up speed again, but she decided to wait until she got home. She returned some of her business calls from the car sometimes on the way home, but she wanted to get home and relax for a few minutes before she called him. Like her own, his workday stayed hectic right until the bitter end, sometimes even more so at the end of the day, as he met with clients he had to go to court with the next day, or arranged conferences with other attorneys or judges. He was a defense attorney, a litigator, specializing in white-collar crime, mostly federal offenses involving banks, embezzlement, and extortion. "Real law," as he called it, not like what she did, he said blithely. But even Allegra had to agree that his work was as far as you could get from her practice. His personality was just as different too, he was far more tightly coiled, much more serious, and had a more intense view of life. In the two years she'd been dating him, more than once her family had accused Brandon Edwards of not having much of a sense of humor. To them, it was a definite deficiency in his character, since most of her family was capable of being somewhat outrageous.

There were a lot of things about Brandon that Allegra liked, their common interest in the law, the fact that he was both reliable and solid. She liked the fact that he had a family. He had been married for ten years to a girl he'd married while he was in law school. He had gone to Boalt at UC Berkeley, and Joanie had gotten pregnant. He had been forced to marry her, he said, and he still had feelings of resentment about it. But in some ways Joanie was still very close to him, after ten years of marriage and two children. Yet at times, Brandon still talked about how much he had hated being married to her, how confined he felt, and how much he had resented their shotgun wedding because she was pregnant. They'd had two little girls, and after law school he had gone to work for the most conservative law firm in San Francisco. It had only been by chance that they had transferred him to their L.A. office, just after he and Joanie had agreed to a trial separation. He had met Allegra the third week he'd been in town, through a mutual friend, and they had been going out for two years now. She loved him, and she loved his kids. Joanie didn't like letting them come to L.A., so usually Brandon went to San Francisco to see them, and whenever she could, Allegra went with him. The only problem was that in two years, Joanie had still not been able to find work, and she claimed it would be too traumatic for the girls for her not to be at home for them. So she was completely dependent on Brandon. And they were still arguing about their house, and their condo near Tahoe. In fact, in two years, very little had been resolved, the divorce had not yet been filed, and the financial arrangements never completed. Allegra teased him about it from time to time, about being a lawyer who couldn't get his own wife to sign a contract. But she didn't want to push him. For the moment, it meant that their relationship had to stay where it was, comfortable, but on hold, and it could go no further until he tied up all the loose ends with Joanie.

As she thought about him, and took the turnoff for Beverly Hills, she wondered if he'd be in the mood to go out to dinner. She knew he was preparing for a trial, and more than likely it would mean that he'd have to stay at the office until late that night. But she was hardly in a position to complain. Allegra had to work many nights, though usually not preparing trials. Her clients were writers, producers, directors, actors and actresses, and she did everything for them from contracts to wills, to negotiating deals for them, and handling their money or their divorces. The legal component of her activities interested her the most, but Allegra recognized better than most attorneys that with celebrity clients, or at least clients in show business, you had to be willing to handle every aspect of their complicated lives, not just their contracts. And there were times when Brandon seemed not to understand that. The field of entertainment had remained a mystery to him, despite all of the times when Allegra had tried to explain it to him. But he said that he preferred to practice law with and for "normal people" and in legal circumstances he understood, like a federal courtroom. He hoped to become a federal judge one day, and at thirty-six that already appeared to be a reasonable aspiration.

The phone rang in the car as Allegra made a turn, and for a minute she hoped that it would be Brandon, but it wasn't. It was her secretary, Alice. She had worked at the firm for fifteen years, and she was a lifesaver for Allegra. She had lots of common sense, a bright mind, and a soothing, maternal way of handling their more irascible clients.

"Hi, Alice, what's up?" Allegra asked, keeping her eyes on the road and flipping the phone on speaker.

"Carmen Connors just called. I thought you'd want to know. She's very upset. She's on the cover of *Chatter*." It was one of the nastiest tabloids around, and they'd been eating Carmen alive for months, despite repeated warnings and threats from Allegra. But they knew just how far to go, and they were masters at going no further. They always stopped just shy of libel.

"What now?" Allegra asked, frowning, as she rapidly approached the little house her parents had helped her buy when she finished law school. She'd paid them back since, and she loved her little cottage, tucked away off Doheny.

"The article said something about going to an orgy with one of her doctors, her plastic surgeon, I think." Poor Carmen had been foolish enough to date him once. They'd had dinner at Chasen's, and according to what she'd told Allegra, there hadn't even been sex, let alone an orgy.

"Oh, for chrissake," Allegra muttered, as she pulled into her driveway with a look of annoyance. "Do you have a copy there?"

"I'll get one on the way home. Do you want me to drop it off?"

"That's all right. I'll take a look at it tomorrow. I'm home. I'll give her a call right now. Thanks. Anything else?"

"Your mother called. She wanted to know if you can make it to dinner on Friday and she wanted to be sure you're coming to the Golden Globes on Saturday. She said she hoped you'd be there."

"Of course." Allegra smiled as she sat in the stopped car, talking to Alice on the speaker. "She knows that." Both of her parents were nominees this year, and she wouldn't miss being there for anything. She had invited Brandon to it more than a month ago, before Christmas.

"I think she just wanted to be sure you were coming."

"I'll call her too. Is that it?"

"That's it." It was six-fifteen. She'd left the office at five-thirty, which was early for her. But she was taking work home, and if she didn't see Brandon, she'd have time to do it.

"See you tomorrow, Alice. Good night," Allegra said, and took the key out of the ignition. She grabbed her briefcase, locked the car, and hurried inside. The house seemed dark and empty, and as she walked in and tossed her briefcase on the couch, she switched on the lights and strode into the kitchen.

She had a spectacular view of the city below. It was dark by then, and the lights were twinkling like jewels, as she helped herself to an Evian and sifted through her mail. A few bills, a letter from Jessica Farnsworth, an old friend from school, a handful of catalogs, a lot of junk, and a postcard from another friend, Nancy Towers, skiing in St. Moritz. She threw most of it away, and as she sipped the Evian, she noticed Brandon's running shoes, and she smiled. The house always seemed more lived in when he left his things there. He kept his own apartment too, but he spent a fair amount of time with her. He liked being with her, and he told her so, but he was equally clear about not being ready to make a commitment. Marriage had just been too confining and too traumatic. And he was afraid to make another mistake, which was probably why he was taking so long to divorce Joanie. But Allegra had everything she wanted anyway. She had told that to her therapist, as well as her parents. And she was only twenty-nine. She was in no hurry to get married.

As she put her mail aside, she pushed her long blond hair back and flipped the switch on her answering machine, then she sat down on a bar stool at the kitchen counter. Her kitchen was impeccably neat, and everything was done in white marble and black granite. The floor was black-and-white check, and she stared absently at it as she listened to her messages. Predictably, the first one was from Carmen, and she sounded as though she'd been crying. She said something incoherent about the article, and how unfair it was, and how upset her grandmother had been. She had called Carmen that afternoon from Portland. She didn't know if Allegra would want to sue this time, but she thought they should talk about it, and she asked Allegra to call her as soon as she got home, or had a free moment. It never occurred to Carmen that Allegra had a right to her own time. Carmen needed her for her own affairs, and that was all she ever thought of, but that didn't make her a bad person.

Allegra's mother had called again, inviting her to dinner on Friday night just as Alice had said, and reminding her of the Golden Globe Awards ceremony that weekend. Allegra smiled as she listened to her. Her mother sounded really excited. Probably because Allegra's father was nominated too, but in any case, she said Scott was coming down from Stanford to watch with Sam, and she hoped Allegra would go to the ceremony with her parents.

The next message was from a tennis pro Allegra had been dodging for weeks. She had started lessons several times, but she just didn't have time to pursue it. She jotted down his name, and made a note to remind herself to call him and at least explain that she couldn't.

After that there was a message from a man she'd met over

the holidays. He'd been attractive and worked for an important studio, but he wasn't playing fair. She had met him when she was with Brandon. She smiled and listened to the husky voice as he left his name and said he hoped that she would call him. But there was no question of it in her mind. She had no interest in going out with anyone but Brandon. He was the third important love affair in her life. The previous one had lasted for almost four years, through the last half of law school, and for her first two years in L.A. as an attorney. He had gone to graduate school at Yale too, and he was a director. But after four years, he had been no closer to making a commitment to her, and in the end he had moved to London. He had asked her to come too, but she was up to her neck in clients at Fisch, Herzog, and Freeman by then, and there was no way she could join him in London. Or that was what she had said anyway. But even she had figured out that there was no point giving up a great job and following him to the ends of the earth, when he simply refused to make any promises about, or even discuss, the future. Roger had lived "for today, in the moment." He talked a lot about karma, and chi, and freedom. And after two years in therapy, Allegra had finally gotten smart enough not to follow him to London. So she had stayed in L.A., and had met Brandon two months later.

And even before that, Roger had been preceded by a married professor at Yale. Allegra had gotten involved with him during her senior year, and it had been an affair filled with lust and excitement and passion. She had never known anyone like him, and the only way they had been able to end it was when Tom went on sabbatical, and hiked through Nepal for a year. He had taken his wife, and their infant son, and when they'd finally returned, she was once again pregnant. By then, Allegra was seeing Roger. But there had always been some powerful electricity between them whenever their paths crossed. Eventually, she'd been relieved when he went to teach at Northwestern. He had had overwhelming feelings of desire for her, but he had never been able to translate them into any kind of clear-cut vision about their future. All he could see, when he looked down the long road ahead of them, was Mithra, his wife, and their son, Euclid. He was something of a vestige of her past now, and her therapist rarely brought him up, except to illustrate the fact that she had never had a relationship that included any kind of promises involving her future.

"I'm not sure, at twenty-nine, I should have had that anyway," she had responded more than once. "I've never really *wanted* to get married."

"That's not the point, Allegra," Dr. Green always said firmly. She was from New York, and she had big dark eyes that sometimes haunted Allegra after their sessions. They had been seeing each other off and on for four years now. Allegra was comfortable with her life, it was just that there was a lot of pressure on her, a lot of expectations from her family and her law firm, and she was very busy. "Has anyone ever wanted to marry *you*?" Dr. Green honed in more than once on what Allegra always insisted was a meaningless question.

"What difference does that make, if I don't want to get married?"

"Why don't you? Why don't you want a man who wants to marry you, Allegra? What's that all about?" She was relentless.

"That's just stupid. Roger would have married me, if I'd gone to London with him. I just didn't want to. I had too much going on here."

"What makes you think he'd have married you?" Dr. Green was like a little ferret, she got into every corner, and sniffed out every possible lead, particle of harmless-looking dust, or insect. "Did he ever say so?"

"We never talked about it."

"Doesn't that make you wonder, Allegra?"

"What difference does it make? That was two years ago," she would say irritably. She hated it when Dr. Green would press a point till she wore it out with her questions. "This is silly." She was too young to get married anyway, and too involved in her career at the moment to think of marriage.

"And what about Brandon?" Dr. Green loved harping on

him. Sometimes Allegra hated discussing him with her. She just didn't understand his motivations, or how traumatized he had been by having to get married when his wife was pregnant. "When is he going to file?"

"When they settle the questions about the property and the money," Allegra always explained sensibly, speaking as an attorney.

"Why don't they bifurcate the financial issues, and just get a divorce? Then they can spend as long as they like resolving the property issues."

"Why? What's the point of bifurcating? It's not like we *have* to get married."

"No. But does he *want* to? Do *you*, Allegra? Do you ever discuss it?"

"We don't need to discuss it. We understand each other perfectly. We're both busy, we both have major careers. We've only gone out for two years."

"Some people get married a lot faster than that, or a lot slower. The point is"—she aimed her sharp brown eyes into Allegra's green ones—"have you gotten yourself involved yet again with a man who cannot make a commitment?"

"Of course not," Allegra answered, trying to avoid the laser gaze, but never quite succeeding. "It just isn't time yet." And then Dr. Green would nod, and wait to hear what Allegra would say after.

The exchanges were almost always the same. They had been for two years, except that Allegra was no longer twenty-seven, or twenty-eight, but twenty-nine, and Brandon had been only separated for two years now. His daughters, Nicole and Stephanie, were eleven and nine, and Joanie still hadn't succeeded in securing employment. She was still dependent on Brandon for everything she needed. And like Brandon, Allegra explained it by saying Joanie had no training. She had given up college to have Nicky.

In fact, Nicole's voice was the next one on Allegra's answering machine, telling her that she hoped that Allegra was coming to San Francisco with her dad that weekend. She said she missed her, and that she hoped everything was okay, and she hoped they'd have time to go skating. "And oh . . . that's right . . . I love the jacket you sent me for Christmas. . . . I was going to write a note, but I forgot, and Mom said . . ." There was an embarrassed silence as the eleven-year-old voice tried to regain her composure. "I'll give you the letter this weekend. Bye . . . I love you. . . . Oh . . . this is Nicky. Bye." She hung up, and Allegra was still smiling, when she heard Brandon's message that he was working late, and was still at the office when he called her. His message was the last one.

She turned off the machine, finished the Evian, dropped it in the garbage, and picked up the phone to call his office.

She was sitting on the kitchen stool with her long legs wrapped around it as she dialed. She looked long and lean and beautiful, and she was totally unaware of her looks as she called him. She had lived in a world of extraordinary-looking people for so long, and hers was a life of the mind rather than the beauty of face and body. She never thought about it, which somehow made her even more attractive. One easily sensed about her that she didn't even care how she looked, she was totally focused on the people around her.

Brandon answered his private line on the second ring, and he sounded busy and distracted. It was easy to believe he was working. "Brandon Edwards," he said, and she smiled. He had a deep, sexy voice, and she particularly liked the way he sounded. He was tall, and blond, and clean-cut, and preppy, and perhaps a little too conservative in the way he dressed, but she didn't mind that. There was something very wholesome about him, and very honest.

"Hi there, I got your message," she said cryptically, and he knew who it was the moment he heard her. "How was your day?"

"Endless," he said, still sounding frazzled. She didn't tell him about hers. He had very little interest in the clients of her law firm, and he always acted as though he thought her field of law was really more nonsense than legal. "I'm going to trial next week. And I'm having a hell of a time with some of the research. I'll be lucky if I get out of here before midnight." He really sounded exhausted.

"Do you want me to bring you something to eat?" she asked with a small smile. "I could come by with a pizza."

"I'd rather wait. I've got a sandwich here now, and I don't want to stop. I'll pick something up on the way over, if it's not too late, and you still want me." She could hear something warm in his voice as she smiled in answer.

"I always want you. Come as late as you want. I brought some work home too." She had the papers for Bram Morrison's next concert tour in her briefcase. "I've got plenty to do to keep me busy."

"Good, I'll see you later."

And then she remembered. "Oh, by the way, Brandon, I got a call today from Nicky. She must have gotten mixed up on the dates, she thought we were coming to San Francisco. That's next week, isn't it?" The coming weekend, he was going to the Golden Globes with her, and the following weekend they were going to San Francisco to see the children.

"Actually, I . . . I might have told her something about . . . I thought it might make some sense to go up before the trial starts. After that, I really can't get away for a while, or at least I shouldn't." He sounded awkward as he tried to explain, and Allegra frowned as she sat looking at the view from her kitchen.

"But we can't go this week. Mom and Dad are both nominated for awards, and so are three of my clients." Among them Carmen Connors. "Did you forget?" She couldn't believe he'd changed his mind. She'd been talking about it since before Christmas.

"No, I just thought . . . I don't have time to discuss this with you now, Allie, or I'll be stuck here all night. Why don't we talk about it later?" His answer didn't put her mind to rest, and she was vague a little while later when she called her mother.

Blaire was shooting her series all week, as usual, and she was tired at night, after hours on the set, but she was always happy to hear from her older daughter. They saw each other frequently, although less so now that Allegra was so involved with Brandon.

Blaire reiterated the dinner invitation for Friday night, and told her that her brother, Scott, would be there. His homecomings were important to all of them, and Blaire liked nothing better than an evening with all her children.

"Is he coming to the Golden Globes too?" Allegra asked, always happy to see him.

"He's going to stay home with Sam. He says award ceremonies are more fun on TV. At least he gets to see everyone he wants to, instead of being trampled by the crowd, unable to figure out who the reporters are running after."

"Maybe he's right." Allegra laughed at the description. She knew that Sam would have been thrilled to go, but her parents never wanted her in the public eye, or as seldom as possible, and certainly not at the Golden Globes or the Academy Awards. Every starlet in Hollywood would be there, and every possible reporter. The only reason they had ever agreed to her modeling career was because no one knew who she was when they saw her pictures. She modeled under the name of Samantha Scott, her mother's maiden name, and although her mother was well-known, it seemed less conspicuous than Steinberg. Everyone in Hollywood knew who Simon Steinberg was, and they would have done anything to take pictures of his daughter. "Anyway, I'll be there," Allegra reassured her. She was no longer quite as sure that Brandon would be there, though she didn't say anything about that to her mother. But eventually Blaire asked her. It was no secret between them that Brandon was not one of Blaire's favorite people, nor Simon's. They were both concerned that Brandon had gone out with her for two years, but still hadn't divorced his wife yet.

"Will Prince Brandon be with us too?" Blaire asked with an obvious edge to her voice, and Allegra hesitated for a long moment. She didn't want to get into a fight with her, but she didn't like what her mother had said, or the way she'd said it.

"I'm not sure yet," Allegra said quietly, which spoke volumes to her mother. She was always defending him, and as far as Blaire was concerned, she shouldn't have to. "He's preparing for trial, and he may have to work this weekend." She didn't think it was any of her mother's business that he might be going to San Francisco to see his children.

"Don't you think he could break away for one night?" Blaire asked skeptically, and the tone of her voice grated on Allegra like fingernails on a blackboard.

"Why don't you just let it go, Mom? I'm sure he'll do his best, and if he can, he'll join us."

"Maybe you should ask someone else. There's no reason for you to go alone, that's not much fun for you." It always annoyed Blaire that he left Allegra in the lurch whenever he had other plans, or too much work, or wasn't in the mood. He always did what suited him. She was always a good sport about it, and Blaire didn't see why she should be.

"I'll enjoy it either way," Allegra said comfortably. "I just want to be there to see you and Daddy get the awards," she said proudly.

"Don't say that," Blaire said superstitiously, "you'll jinx us." But there was very little that could jinx either Blaire Scott or Simon Steinberg. They had each won a Golden Globe Award several times before, and it was both prestigious and exciting, and in recent years, it often foretold how the Academy Awards would go in April. It was a night that meant a lot in Hollywood, and the Steinbergs were all excited about it.

"You'll win it, Mom, I know you will. You always do." The Golden Globe was unusual because it was awarded for television as well as for movies, so it was an award which both Steinbergs could win, and had. It made Allegra very proud of her parents.

"Never mind the flattery." Her mother smiled, proud of her daughter too. Allegra was a terrific girl, and she and Blaire shared a special bond, which had always kept them close together. "What about Friday night? Can you come to dinner?"

"I'll have to let you know tomorrow, if that's all right." She wanted to discuss Brandon's plans with him, and see what he wanted to do about San Francisco. If he stayed, then she wanted him to join them for dinner at her parents', but she thought it might be easier to negotiate all at once, so she put the conversation off till morning, and they chatted for a few minutes about Scott and Sam, and her father. Blaire explained after that that she was introducing a new character on the show, and the idea had been very well received by the network. At fifty-four, she was still beautiful, and full of exciting new ideas. She loved what she did, and she had had another show before this one on the same network. And for the past nine years, she had had incredible success with her current show, called *Buddies*. But the ratings had wavered a little that year, and there was no doubt in anyone's mind how much the Golden Globes would help them. This time, Blaire really wanted to win it.

Blaire Scott had Allegra's long, lean looks, and a model's body, and her hair had been naturally red, but it had long since faded to a warm strawberry-blond that actually needed very little help from the bottle. She had had her eyes done once, and her neck tightened a few years before, but she had never had her face lifted. She was the envy of all her friends, and watching her age so gracefully gave Allegra a lot of hope for the future. "The secret is not doing too much," she always said matter-of-factly to her daughters about plastic surgery. But Allegra always swore she'd never do it. She thought it was a waste of time to try and tackle nature. "Wait a few years, you'll feel differently," Blaire said wisely. She'd said the same thing, but finally at forty-three, in the public eye more than she'd planned, she'd done the eyes, and then the neck at fifty. And as a result, she looked barely more than forty-five now. "It ruins everything when people know how old you are," she teased Allegra at times, but she had no real desire to conceal her age, just to remain attractive to Simon. At sixty, he was still the handsome man he had always been. If anything he looked better now, she said, than he did when they were married.

"You lie," he always grinned winningly when she said that. Allegra loved being with them. They were kind, intelligent, happy people, and they made everyone around them feel good.

"I want a man like him," she had said once to Dr. Green, and then feared that Dr. Green would get all caught up in Freud, but surprisingly, she hadn't.

"I'd say that's a pretty good decision, from what you've told me of your parents' marriage. Do you think you could attract a man like him?" Dr. Green had asked her bluntly.

"Sure," Allegra said easily, but they both knew she didn't mean it.

Allegra promised to call her mother about dinner on Friday night as soon as she knew her plans, and after that she thought about calling Nicole, and then decided against it. Joanie probably wouldn't like it. So instead, eating a half-eaten yogurt from the fridge, Allegra called Carmen. She sounded completely hysterical, as she always did, whenever a fresh story hit the tabloids. But even she had to agree that this one was silly. They claimed that she had attended an orgy in Las Vegas with her plastic surgeon. Supposedly he had given her a whole new face, new nose, new chin, breast implants, and liposuction.

"How could I have done all that?" she asked, aghast, still surprisingly naive, and always shocked to realize to what extent people were willing to lie about her. Like all celebrities, people claimed they'd gone to school with her, were best friends with her, had taken trips with her, and of course the number of men claiming to have slept with her were legion. Recently, even two women had made that claim, and Carmen had been reduced to tears over that too. It just seemed incredibly unfair to her that people were so willing to make up stories about her.

"It's the price of success," Allegra always reminded her gently, finding it difficult to believe that she was only six years older than Carmen. The young star seemed so naive in so many ways, so unaware of the evil lurking everywhere, and surprised by the extent of the exploitation. She still wanted to believe that everyone was her friend, and no one wanted to hurt her. Except at two A.M., when she easily believed that half of Los Angeles was at her back door and about to break in and rape her. Allegra had hired a live-in housekeeper for her finally, and told Carmen to leave a light on outside her bedroom. She was afraid of the dark, and she was always scared to death of what she couldn't see just beyond her bedroom.

"Listen." Allegra reassured her again about the article in *Chatter.* "You're not old enough to have had all that work done."

"Do you suppose anyone else will figure that out? All I did was have a mole removed on my forehead," she said miserably, blowing her nose again, thinking of all the things her grandmother had said when she called from Portland. She said that Carmen had shamed them all, and that God would never forgive her.

"Of course they'll figure it out. Did you read the next page?"

"No, why?" Carmen asked, stretching her perfect figure out on the couch, as she held the phone and talked to Allegra.

"On the next page it probably says that a woman gave birth to identical quintuplets on Mars. And two pages after that a woman gave birth to a monkey on a UFO. If they believe that crap, then who cares if they say you had a face-lift at twenty-three? To hell with them, Carmen. You've got to toughen up a little bit, or they'll drive you crazy."

"They are," she said forlornly. They talked for an hour, and finally Allegra hung up and went to take a shower, and by the time she got out and was drying her hair, Brandon pulled into the driveway.

She was at the door in a terry-cloth robe as he came up the walk, her hair was hanging down her back, wet, and her face was scrubbed clean of makeup. In some ways she was even more beautiful than when she was all done up, and he liked it when she looked natural and clean and sexy.

"Wow!" he said, and then kissed her hello, as he followed her inside and she locked the door behind them. It was ten o'clock at night, and he looked exhausted as he dropped his briefcase in the front hall and put his arms around her. "This was definitely worth working late for," he said, kissing her, and slipping a hand inside the terry-cloth robe. She was naked beneath it.

"Are you hungry?" she asked him between kisses.

"Starved," he answered, referring to her, not dinner.

"What would you like?" she asked, laughing at him, as she entwined her legs around his playfully, and took off his jacket.

"Breast, I think . . . or maybe leg. . . ." he said hoarsely, and then kissed her again, and a minute later they were sitting on her bed, as he unbuttoned his shirt and looked at her with eyes filled with desire. He looked tired, after his long day, but his spirits didn't seem to be dampened. He didn't even want to talk to her, he just wanted to devour her body.

She helped him take off his shirt, and he slipped out of his pants, and a few minutes later they were both naked, lying on her bed, and making love in the soft lights she had left on. He was totally enraptured with her, and an hour later they both lay spent and pleased, and as she started to drift off to sleep, she felt him get up, and it woke her.

"Where are you going?" she asked, rolling over and opening an eye to look at him in all his long, tall, blond splendor. They were well matched, and their looks were so similar that sometimes people thought they were brother and sister.

"It's late," he said apologetically, slowly gathering up his clothes from the floor of her bedroom.

"Are you going home?" She looked surprised, as she sat up and stared at him. He seemed embarrassed when she asked him the question. They hadn't even talked to each other. All they'd done was make love, and fall asleep. And she didn't want him to leave her.

"I thought . . . I have to go in really early tomorrow, and I didn't want to wake you." He looked awkward, but anxious to leave. He did that often.

"What difference does it make if you have to get up early? So do I." She seemed hurt by his defection. "You have clean shirts here. I have to be up early too. It's nice when we sleep together." It was nice, and she knew he liked it, but she knew that he also liked going home to his own apartment. He liked his own space, his own things; he had told her several times over the past two years that he liked waking up in his own bed, and yet they seldom made love at his place. He always seemed to come here, to her house, but at least half the time he liked going back to his own apartment. In an odd way, it sometimes made her feel used, and discarded, and it was a particularly lonely feeling after he was gone and she was alone in her own house. For some odd reason, she had told her therapist, it made her feel abandoned. But she didn't like being put in the position of begging him, and she didn't want to push him now if he didn't want to stay. She was just very disappointed. "I'd like it if you stayed, Brandon," she said quietly, but she didn't say anything more as he finally went to shower, and then came back to bed. To Brandon it seemed easier to stay the night than argue.

And as they lay together that night, Allegra smiled at him. There may have been some things to work out in their relationship, like his divorce and his preference for sleeping alone, but there was no doubt in her mind that she loved him.

"Thanks for staying here," she said softly, as she lay in his arms, and he gently touched her cheek, and then kissed her. And a moment later, he was snoring.

CHAPTER 2

Allegra got up the next morning before the alarm went off at six-fifteen. That was the time Brandon had set it for. He got up and went to brush his teeth and shave, while she walked out to the kitchen naked, to make coffee.

He was at the breakfast table, fully dressed, by six forty-five, and she put two blueberry muffins in front of him, and a steaming cup of coffee.

"Great service at this restaurant," he said, looking pleased. "And I love what the servers wear," he said, admiring her body as she sat down across the table from him, still naked.

"You look pretty good too," she said, admiring his dark gray suit. He bought everything he wore at Brooks Brothers, and every now and then she tried wandering him through Armani on Rodeo Drive, hoping to jazz him up a little. But that wasn't Brandon's look at all. He was pure Wall Street. "I'd say you look pretty damn great for this hour of the morning." She grinned through a yawn, and poured herself a cup of coffee. She didn't have to be at her office till nine-thirty. "What are we doing tonight, by the way?" she asked. She'd been invited to a premiere, and she wasn't sure if he could go, with his trial to prepare. She doubted it, and she didn't really want to go either.

"I've got to work. No more playtime. I told the other guys I'd stick around tonight till midnight," he said, looking mildly panicked at all the work they had to do. Preparing for trial was always like that, which was why she was glad her firm had a litigation team, and she never had to do the actual trial work. She just had to collaborate with them, and give them information. In many ways, what she did was simpler. It was creative in its own way, but it didn't make the brutal demands on her that federal defense work did on Brandon.

"Do you want to come here when you're through?" she asked, trying not to sound like a supplicant. She liked having him come home to her, and he didn't always want to. And she didn't want him to feel pressured.

"I'd love to," he said regretfully. "But I really can't. I'll be bushed when I'm through. I've got to go home sometime."

"My parents invited us to dinner on Friday," she said, extending the invitation to him. She knew that, in the end, her mother would have invited him anyway, just to please her daughter, whether or not they liked him.

"I'm going to see the girls on Friday night," he said, matter-of-factly, finishing one of the muffins. "I told you."

"I didn't think you were serious," she said, looking surprised. "What about the Golden Globes?" Her eyes were filled with her expectations. "They're important." They were important to her, but not to Brandon.

"So are Stephanie and Nicky. I have to see them before the trial," he said firmly.

"Brandon, I told you about the Golden Globes months ago. That's a big deal to me, and to my parents. And Carmen is nominated too. I can't just forget all that and go to San Francisco," she said, trying to sound calmer than she felt. It was only seven o'clock in the morning.

"I understand that you can't go. I don't expect you to," he said perfectly calmly.

"But I expect you to go with me," she said, an edge developing in her voice, despite her best efforts. "I want you to be there."

"That's not a reasonable expectation, Allegra. I told you, I can't. I told you why. I don't see any point in belaboring it. Why do that?"

"Because it means a lot to me." She took a breath, trying not to get angry at him. There had to be a way to solve the problem to everyone's satisfaction. "Look, why don't you stay and go to the awards with me, and we'll fly to San Francisco for the day on Sunday? How's that for a compromise?" She looked totally victorious, thrilled that there had been a rational solution, but he was shaking his head and taking a last sip of coffee before he bolted.

"That won't work, Allie, sorry. I need more than a day with them. I can't do that."

"Why?" She knew she was starting to whine, and she reminded herself to stop it.

"Because they need more time, and frankly because I need some time to talk to Joanie about the condo at Squaw. She thinks she wants to sell it."

"That's ridiculous," Allegra said, losing it finally. "You can do that on the phone. For chrissake, Brandon, you've done nothing but talk to her about the condo or the house or the carpet or the car or the dog for the last two goddamn years. This award ceremony is important to us." She was including her family, and he was noticeably unmoved. To him, this was about his family, which consisted of his ex-wife and two daughters. "I'm not giving you up to Joanie," she said bluntly.

"You're not." He smiled as he stood up, unwilling to be swayed by her, and perfectly willing to show it. "But how about to Stephanie and Nicky?"

"They'd understand if you explained it to them."

"I doubt it. And anyway, that's not an option." He stood looking at her, and she stared at him, unable to believe that he was going to let her down and go to San Francisco.

"When are you coming back?" she asked, aching inside, and wishing she weren't. She was feeling abandoned again, and something in her gut was terrified, and she knew she shouldn't give in to it. He was going to San Francisco to see his kids, and if he was disappointing her it wasn't intentional. It just happened. And yet, why did she feel so terrible about his decision?

She couldn't quite seem to grasp the answer, or even decide if she should be really furious, or just sad that he wasn't going to the Golden Globes with her. Was it really such a big deal? Did she have a right to make those demands on him? And why, when it came to her needs, were his reactions always so confusing? Was it, as Dr. Green said, because she didn't want to admit to herself what he was doing? Was he rejecting her, or just doing what he had to? And why could she never bring herself to answer those questions?

"I'm coming back when I always do, on the last plane on Sunday night. I'll be back at ten-fifteen. I could be here by eleven," he said to pacify her, and then she realized with an ache in her heart that she wouldn't be there.

"I just remembered, I'm leaving for New York Sunday afternoon. I'll be there all next week, till Friday."

"Then you couldn't have come to San Francisco anyway," he said matter-of-factly.

"I could leave from there, if you want. If we fly up on Sunday."

"That's ridiculous," he said, dismissing her plan as he picked up his briefcase. "You have your work to do, Allie, I have mine, and sometimes we just have to be grown-ups about it." He smiled at her almost wistfully as they each realized they wouldn't see one another again for ten days, until the following weekend.

"Do you want to come by tonight and stay here, since I won't see you for such a long time?" She really wanted him to do that, but as usual, he stuck to his original plan. It was rare for Brandon to make changes.

"I really can't. By the time we're through, I'll be too beat to see straight. I wouldn't be much fun for you, and there's no point in just coming here to sack out, is there?" But that was where they differed.

"Sure there is. You don't have to entertain me," she said as she stood on tiptoe, put her arms around his neck, and kissed him.

"I'll see you next week, kiddo," he said coolly, after he kissed her. "I'll call you tonight, and tomorrow I'll give you a call before I leave for San Francisco."

"Do you want to have dinner at Mom's on Friday before you go?" she asked, hating herself for begging. It was exactly what she knew she shouldn't do, except she just couldn't stop herself. She wanted to be with him.

"I'd probably miss my plane like I did last time, and then the kids would be upset."

"The kids?" she asked, raising an eyebrow, and silently telling herself to stop before she blew it. "Or Joanie?"

"Come on, Allie, be a good girl. You know I can't help it. I've got a trial, you've got a trip to New York, I've got two kids in San Francisco. We've both got our obligations. Why don't we just do what we have to do, and then get together afterward and enjoy it?" He made it all sound so sensible, and yet some part of her didn't buy it—the part that was always disappointed when he didn't show up, like for the awards, or when he went home after they made love, to sleep alone at his place. At least he had spent the night with her the night before, and she reminded herself that she should be grateful for that, and stop nagging him about the weekend.

"I love you," she said, as he kissed her in the doorway, and she stood back a little bit so no one could see her naked.

"Me too," he smiled at her. "Have fun in New York. And don't forget to take your long johns. It said in the *Times* today it's snowing."

"Great." She looked forlorn as she watched him go, then waved as he got into his car. She closed the front door, and then watched him from her bedroom window as he backed down her driveway. She felt sick as she watched him drive away. Something felt wrong and she wasn't sure what it was, the fact that he wouldn't change his plans, or was going to see Joanie again, with the girls, or just the simple reality that she had to go to the Golden Globes alone now, and explain it to her parents. Or maybe just knowing that she wouldn't see him again for ten days.

All of it made her feel miserable as she walked into her bathroom and turned on the shower.

She stood there for a long time, with the water running on her face, as she thought of him and wondered if he'd ever change. Or would he always want to sleep alone, decide it was too much trouble to come by after work, and be married to Joanie forever? As her tears mingled with the hot water, and she told herself how foolish she was to be upset, somehow she couldn't find the answers.

She was exhausted when she finally turned the shower off half an hour later. He was probably at his office by then, and it seemed so odd to her to think that he was still in town, that he would be for two days and she wouldn't see him. And yet, when she tried to explain feelings like that to him, about needing him, or just wanting to be with him, he didn't seem to get it.

"Why do you think that is?" Dr. Green always asked her.

"How do I know?" Allegra had snapped at her on more than one occasion.

"Do you think it could be due to a lack of commitment on his part?" Dr. Green usually persisted. "Or maybe that he doesn't care as much for you as you do for him? Or maybe he's just unable to make the kind of commitment you want," she suggested pointedly, following a familiar theme that always unnerved Allegra. Why was she always suggesting that the men in Allegra's life gave her far too little? Why was it a recurring theme, and why did she keep trying to say that it was a pattern? It really annoyed her.

Allegra threw the rest of the blueberry muffins away. He had almost finished them, and she wasn't hungry anyway. She made herself a fresh cup of coffee, and then went to dress. She was ready to leave for work by eight-thirty, and she had some time to spare before she braved the freeway traffic. She glanced at her watch, and knew that her mother would have left for the studio at four A.M., but she left a message on her machine, confirming that she would join them for dinner on Friday night, and she'd be alone. She was sure that when she got there, it would cause comment, particularly if she told them where he was. But at least in the meantime, she didn't have to hear it.

And then, dialing from memory, she called a Beverly Hills number that half the women in America would have given their right arm for. They had been friends since they were fourteen, boyfriend and girlfriend for a brief six months in their sophomore year in high school, and best friends ever since then. He answered, as he always did, unless he was "occupied" or out, on the second ring, and she smiled at the familiar voice, that to all ears but her own sounded intolerably sexy.

"Hi, Alan, it's only me. Don't get too excited." She always smiled when she talked to him, he was that kind of person.

"At this hour?" He sounded horrified to hear from her, except that she knew he usually got up fairly early. He had just finished a film in Bangkok and he'd been home for three weeks. She also knew that he had just finished a romance with British film star Fiona Harvey. She had heard it from his agent. "What did you do last night? Get arrested? Are you calling to get bailed out?"

"Precisely. Pick me up at the Beverly Hills police station in twenty minutes."

"Not on your life. All lawyers belong in jail. As far as I'm concerned, you can stay there." He was thirty years old, with the face and body of a Greek god, but he also happened to be intelligent, and a genuinely decent person. He was one of Allegra's closest friends and the only man she could think of to take to the awards with her. Thinking of Alan Carr as her fallback date somehow made her laugh. Most of the women in America would have died just to meet him.

"What are you doing Saturday?" she asked bluntly, swinging her foot like a kid, and trying not to think of Brandon, or let him upset her.

"None of your business, thank you very much," he said, pretending to sound outraged.

"Do you have a date?"

"Why? Are you going to fix me up with another one of your scary partners? I think the last one was bad enough, you witch!"

"Oh, come on, you shit. That wasn't a date and you know it. You needed an expert on Peruvian law, and that's what she does, so don't give me any garbage. In fact, I happen to know that she gave you about three thousand dollars' worth of legal advice for free that night, so stop bitching."

"Who's bitching?" He sounded demure and pretended to be shocked by her language.

"You are, and you didn't answer my question."

"I have a date with a fourteen-year-old girl who will probably wind me up in jail. Why?"

"I need a favor." She could tell him anything without artifice or embarrassment; she loved him like a brother.

"Yeah. So what else is new? You always need a favor. Who wants my autograph this time?"

"No one. Absolutely not a soul. I need your body."

"Now, there's an intriguing offer." More than once in the past fourteen years, since their last attempt at romance, he had told himself that he should reach out to her again, but she was so like a sister to him that he could never quite bring himself to do it. Yet, she was beautiful, intelligent, and he knew and liked her better than any other woman on the planet. But maybe that was the problem. "What exactly do you have in mind for this beaten up, scarred old body?"

"Nothing pleasant, I swear." And then she laughed. "Actually, it won't be too bad. It should be fun. I need a date for the Golden Globes. Mom and Dad are both nominees, and so is Carmen Connors, one of my clients. And I've got two other clients who're contenders. I have to go, and I really don't want to go alone." She was honest with him, she always was, and he loved that.

"What happened to what's his name?" Alan knew perfectly well what his name was, and he had also told Allegra several times that he didn't like him. He thought Brandon was cold and pompous. And she hadn't talked to him for weeks after the first time he said it. Since then she had gotten used to it, because Alan never missed an opportunity to tell her what he thought, but this time he spared her.

"He has to go to San Francisco."

"How nice of him, Al. What great timing. Great guy. To see his wife?"

"No, you asshole, to see his kids. He's starting a trial on Monday."

"I'm not sure I understand the connection," he said coolly.

"He won't be able to see the kids for a couple of weeks, so he wants to go up and see them."

"Have they canceled all the flights from San Francisco to L.A.? Why can't the little darlings come here to see their Daddy?"

"Their mom won't let them."

"Well, that leaves you up shit creek, doesn't it?"

"Yeah, it does, which is why I called you. Can you make it?" she asked hopefully. It really would be fun to go with him. It was always fun being with Alan. It was like being kids again, and they usually told a lot of jokes, laughed a lot, and got pretty rowdy.

"It's a sacrifice, but I guess if I really have to, I could change some plans. . . ." He said with a sigh, and she laughed.

"You bullshitter, I'll bet you don't have a thing to do."

"I do too. Actually, I was going bowling."

"You?" She laughed even harder. "You wouldn't last five minutes before you'd be mobbed. There's no way you can go bowling."

"I'll take you sometime and prove it."

"That's a deal. I'd love it," she beamed. As usual, he'd bailed her out. She didn't have to go to the awards alone. Alan Carr was one friend she could always count on.

"What time shall I pick you up, Cinderella?" He sounded pleased with the arrangement. He always enjoyed being with her.

"It starts pretty early. Six o'clock?"

"I'll be there."

"Thanks, Alan," she said, and meant it. "I really appreciate it."

"Don't be so goddamn grateful, for chrissake. You deserve someone better than me—you deserve that jerk to take you, if that's what you want. So don't thank me. Just think how lucky I am. That's what you want to think. What you need is some attitude. How the hell did you ever get so humble? You're too smart to be like that. I'd love to teach that guy a thing or two. He doesn't know how lucky he is. San Francisco, my ass . . ." Alan was muttering and Allegra was laughing, but she felt a thousand times better.

"I've got to go to work. See you Saturday. And do me a favor, try to stay sober, will ya?"

"Don't be such a nag. No wonder you can't get a date." They teased each other. He drank a fair amount, but he rarely got drunk, and never misbehaved. The two just liked to play. But she felt human again as she drove to work. Alan had really lifted her spirits.

All day she felt better about things than she had early that morning. She met with some of the promoters for Bram's tour, worked out some security details for Carmen, met with another client about her children's trusts, and by the end of the afternoon she was surprised to realize that she had forgotten all about Brandon. It still bothered her that he wasn't going to the Golden Globes with her, but at least she didn't feel as devastated about it as she had that morning. And as she thought about it, she realized now, she'd been foolish. He had a right to see his kids. And maybe he was right. Maybe they both had to think of their careers, do what they had to do and then get together for whatever time was left over. It wasn't a very romantic way to live, but maybe for the moment it was all they had room for. Maybe that wasn't so bad after all, and maybe, as he suggested from time to time, she was just too demanding.

"Is that what you think?" Dr. Green asked her that afternoon when they met for their weekly appointment.

"I don't know what I think," Allegra admitted. "I know what

I think I want, but then when I talk to Brandon, I feel as though I'm being unreasonable and I'm asking too much of him. I'm not sure which is right, or if I just scare him."

"That's an interesting possibility," Dr. Green said coolly. "Why do you think you scare him?"

"Because he's not ready for as much as I want from a relationship, or as much as I want to give it."

"You think you're ready for more? Why?" Dr. Green asked her with interest.

"I think I'd really like to live with him, and I think he's scared to death to."

"What makes you say that?" Dr. Green was beginning to think Allegra was making headway.

"I think he's scared, because he wants to go home to his own apartment at night. He really doesn't want to spend the night at my place if he can help it."

"Does he want you to go with him? Is it territorial?"

"No." Allegra shook her head slowly. "He says he needs his own space. Once he told me that when we wake up together in the morning, it makes him feel married. And that wasn't a good experience for him, so he doesn't want it again."

"He has to work that out, or else be alone for the rest of his life. It's his choice to make. But his choices will affect your life with him, Allegra."

"I know that. But I don't want to rush him."

"Two years is not a rush," Dr. Green said, looking disapproving. "It's time for him to make some changes. Unless you're happy with the status quo," she said, always giving Allegra options. "If this is what you want, then we have no complaints, do we? Is it?"

"I don't know; I don't think so," Allegra said, looking nervous. "I'd like more. I don't like it when he withdraws to his own world. Or even when he goes to San Francisco without me." And then she admitted something that made her feel stupid. "I worry about his ex-wife sometimes, that she'll get him back. She's still very dependent on him. I think that's all part of what makes him shy away from commitment."

"Well, he'd better get his act together one of these days, don't you think so, Allegra?"

"I guess so," she said cautiously. "But I don't think it would be right to give him ultimatums."

"Why not?" Dr. Green asked bravely.

"He wouldn't like it."

"And?" She pushed harder, just as she wanted Allegra to push Brandon.

"He might end the relationship if I push him too hard."

"And what would that do?" Dr. Green asked her.

"I don't know," Allegra said, looking frightened. She was a strong woman, and yet she never was strong enough with Brandon, just as she hadn't been with the two men before him. She was afraid to be, which was why she still saw Dr. Green after nearly four years now.

"If the relationship ended, it might free you up to meet someone who would be more willing to make a commitment. Would that be so terrible?"

"Probably not." Allegra smiled anxiously. "But pretty scary."

"Sure. But you'd get over it. Sitting here waiting forever for Brandon to unlock the pearly gates may do you a lot more harm than a little fear over meeting someone more open to loving you, Allegra. It's something to think about, isn't it?" she asked, boring into Allegra's eyes with her own, and then, with her usual warm smile, the session was over.

In some ways, it was like going to a Gypsy fortune-teller. As she left Allegra tried to run through in her mind everything she'd said, and there were always things she remembered, and others that she tried desperately to recall but had forgotten. But on the whole, the sessions did her good, and they had done a lot of work together over the years about her penchant for finding men who were unable, or unwilling, to love her. It was an old, old pattern in her life, and one she didn't like to think about, or even talk about. She hoped that, after all this time, she was improving.

She went back to her office after that, tied up some loose ends, and her last meeting of the day was with Malachi O'Donovan, a new client. He was a friend of Bram Morrison's, her vastly successful rock star client, and this one was less so, but also very important. He was from Liverpool originally, but had long since become a citizen by marrying an American woman. His wife's name was Rainbow, and they had two children, named Swallow and Bird. Allegra was used to it. Very little that was done or said in the rock world surprised her.

O'Donovan had a checkered history of arrests and drugs, a couple of assaults, and some messy lawsuits. He had spent a little time in jail over the years, and a lot of time with lawyers, and he seemed very intrigued with Allegra. He responded to her sexually at first, but when she ignored it, and purposefully stuck to business with him, eventually he settled down, and they had a very interesting conversation. And she thought she could help him with some of his legal problems, most of which were stemming from a world tour he was trying to organize, but he was drowning in red tape and legal issues.

"We'll see what we can do, Mal. I'll be in touch, after I get some of your files from your current attorney."

"Don't bother with my last lawyer," he told her with a shrug as he left. "He's an asshole," he said in a rich brogue.

"We need his records anyway." She smiled at him warmly. "I'll call you as soon as I know something."

He liked her very much. Morrison hadn't steered him wrong. She was smart, and got straight to the point with no bullshit. He liked that. "You call me anytime you like, luv," he said softly as Rainbow went ahead to the elevator, and Allegra pretended not to hear him, and went back to close up her office.

In the end, she went home late herself that night. She read some files, and checked over some more of Bram's contracts. And Carmen had just had a very interesting offer to do a film that could be very important for her. It was challenging work, and Allegra loved it.

She was in good spirits when she got home, and it was only then that she realized she hadn't heard from Brandon all day, and she wondered if he had been irritated with her pressing him about the Golden Globe Awards that morning.

She called him at the office around nine o'clock, and he sounded pleased to hear from her. He told her he'd been working nonstop for the past thirteen hours, and he'd been just about to call her.

"Did you eat?" she asked solicitously, sorry that she'd gotten angry at him. And then she remembered what Dr. Green had said to her. She had a right to expect more than he was willing, or perhaps even able, to give her.

"They bring us sandwiches every few hours. Half the time, we forget to eat them."

"You should go home and get some sleep at a decent hour," she reminded him, wishing he would come to her house. But this time she didn't ask him, and he didn't suggest it. And then he felt the pull to go back to work and his colleagues.

"I'll call you tomorrow before I leave for San Francisco."

"I'll be at my parents'. I'm going to go straight from the office."

"Maybe I won't call then," he said simply, and she wanted to scream. Why did he shy away from everything she cared about, especially her family? It was all about his phobia about commitment. "I'll call you after I get there. I'll call you at your house."

"Whatever you like," she said calmly, glad that she had had the opportunity to review it with Jane Green. It always made it seem so much simpler and clearer, and less dramatic. It was so simple really. He wasn't able to reach out to her and love her openly and freely. But would he ever? She wanted to marry him, if he could ever get himself divorced and relaxed enough to let himself really love her. She thought he did, in his own way, but it was also obvious that he was severely hampered by his memories of what had happened to him with Joanie.

"Did you work things out for the Golden Globes?" he asked her suddenly, and she was surprised he'd brought it up at all, it was such a sore subject.

"Yes, it's fine," she said, dismissing it, not wanting to admit to him that she was still upset about it. "I'm going with Alan."

"Carr?" He sounded shocked. He had expected her to go alone, with her parents.

"I thought you'd just go with your brother and your parents, or something like that."

She smiled at his naïveté. The Golden Globe Awards was one of the most sophisticated events of the year, it was not the kind of place she would have wanted to go with her twenty-year-old brother. "I'm a little old for that, you know. Alan's fine about it though. He'll make me laugh all night and say rude things about all the big stars, but they all know him and love him."

"I didn't expect you to fill my shoes quite so handsomely," he said, sounding both peeved and jealous, and she laughed. Maybe it was good for him.

"I'd rather be with you than Alan any day," she said honestly.

"Just remember that," he smiled. "That's one hell of a compliment, Allie. I've never thought of myself in the same league with Alan Carr."

"Well, don't let it go to your head," she teased, and they talked for a few minutes and then hung up, but he never suggested spending the night with her, and she felt depressed again as she lay in bed and thought about it. She was twenty-nine years old, with a boyfriend who preferred sleeping alone in his own bed to being with her, at least some of the time, if not most, and who had ditched her for an event that was important to her, in order to be with his ex-wife and two daughters. No matter how you turned it around, or dressed it up, it still hurt her feelings. And it left her feeling lonely. He was oddly withdrawn in his own way, and no matter what her needs, he always did what he wanted.

"You deserve better than that." She heard Dr. Green's voice ringing in her ears that night as she fell asleep, and she couldn't remember if she'd actually said those words or if that was the gist of what she'd intended. But as she drifted off to sleep, Allegra could see the therapist's intense brown eyes staring at her, and reinforcing the message. I deserve better than that, she whispered to herself . . . better than that . . . but what did that mean? And then, suddenly, all she could see was Alan . . . laughing . . . but was he laughing at her? Or at Brandon?

CHAPTER 3

The Steinberg home in Bel Air was one of the prettiest in the area, and it was large and comfortable, but it was by no means palatial. Blaire had decorated it herself years before when they moved in just after Scott was born, and she was good about re-covering things and redoing rooms to keep them fresh and neat and current. The children teased her about their home being a constant work in progress.

But she liked keeping it looking new, and she used a lot of bright, cheerful colors. The feeling throughout was one of casual elegance and warmth. It was a place people loved to visit. The view from the patio and the living room was spectacular. And for months now, she'd been talking about replacing the kitchen walls with glass. But she'd been so busy with the show that she hadn't had time to do it.

Allegra went to the house straight from work, and as always when she arrived, she felt surrounded by the warmth and generosity of her family and the house she'd grown up in. Her room was still as it had been when she left for college eleven years before. The wallpaper and the curtains and bedspread had been redone once while she was in law school. It was a soft peach watered silk, and once in a while she still spent a night there, or a weekend. Coming home and being with them was always fun and relaxing. Her room was on the same floor as her parents' suite,

37

which consisted of their bedroom, two handsome dressing rooms, and two offices they each used when they had to work at home, which was often. There were two guest rooms on that floor too. And upstairs, Sam and Scott had their own suite of rooms, and a large sitting room between them. They shared a huge TV, a small movie screen, a pool table, and a fantastic sound system their father had given them for Christmas. It was every teenager's dream just being there, and there were always at least half a dozen of Sam's friends hanging around, talking about school, and plans for college, and their boyfriends.

Sam was in the kitchen when Allegra came in, and it was hard not to notice how beautiful she had become in the past year. Suddenly, at seventeen and a half, she had grown into looks that had been striking before, but were now even more so. She had star quality, her father's associates said, and her mother always growled when they said it. Sam's first priority had always been school. Blaire didn't mind her having a small modeling career, but she wasn't very enthused at the idea of her youngest child becoming an actress. It was a rough career, and seeing what she did all around her every day, she was beginning to think she'd prefer it if Samantha stayed out of the business. But there wasn't much they could say to her. She had been exposed to it all her life, and for the moment, an acting career seemed to be all that Sam wanted. She had applied to UCLA, Northwestern, Yale, and NYU for what they had to offer in drama, and given her top grades, she had a good shot at all of them. But unlike Allegra a decade before, she didn't want to go East. She wanted to stay in L.A., and maybe even live at home. She wanted to go to UCLA, and she had already been accepted, through early admission.

She was eating an apple, when Allegra walked in on Friday night after the office, and her long blond hair hung down her back like a sheet of pale yellow-gold. Her eyes were huge and green like her sister's.

"Hi, kiddo. How's life?" Allegra looked happy to see her as she walked over, gave her a kiss, and put an arm around her shoulders.

"Not bad. I did some modeling this week. For an English photographer. He was cool. I like the foreign ones, they're nice to me. I modeled for a French one in November. He was on his way to Tokyo. This job was a layout for the L.A. *Times*. And I saw the rough cut of Dad's new movie." Like all teenagers, she spoke in non sequiturs, but Allegra understood her.

"How was Dad's movie?" Allegra asked, helping herself to some carrot sticks, and giving Ellie a warm hug of greeting. She had been their cook for twenty years, and she shooed them both out of the kitchen.

"It was okay. It was hard to tell. They still had some of the scenes put in the wrong places. It looked pretty cool though." And so did Sam. Allegra smiled to herself as the younger girl bounded upstairs. She was all legs and arms and hair; she was like a wild, beautiful young colt bounding over everything. She seemed so young, and yet so grown-up suddenly. It was hard to believe how fast it had gone, but she was almost a woman. When Allegra had left home for Yale eleven years before, Sam had only been six years old, and in some ways that was how they all still thought of her, as the baby.

"Is that you?" her mother called down the stairs, peeking over the banister, looking barely older than her daughters. The soft red hair was swept up on her head, and framed her face softly, with two pens stuck in it, and a pencil. She was wearing jeans and a black turtleneck, and high-top black Converse sneakers that she had bought for Sam, but Sam wouldn't wear them. Blaire looked like a kid, until you looked closer and saw how lovely she was, and how gently touched by age, and she had the same lanky figure as her daughters. "How are you, darling?" she asked, kissing Allegra and then hurrying off to answer the phone. It was Simon. He was late. He had a problem at the office, but he'd be home in time for dinner.

It was their closeness to each other which had saved them from the stresses of Hollywood over the years, that and the fact that she and Simon had a wonderful marriage. She seldom admitted it, but Blaire's life had been a shambles when she met him.

She was in dark despair, and it seemed as though after they were married, everything changed for the better. Her career had taken off from there, their babies had come quickly and easily and been warmly welcomed. They loved their home, and their kids, their careers, and each other. There was absolutely nothing more that either of them would have added, except maybe more children. She'd been thirty-seven when Sam was born, and at the time that had almost seemed too old to her, so she stopped. And now she regretted not having had at least one more, but the three children they had gave them enormous joy, in spite of the occasional squabble with Samantha. Blaire knew she was a little spoiled, but she was a good girl. She did well at school, never really did anything wrong, and if she argued with her mother from time to time, it seemed appropriate to her age and her culture.

When Blaire hung up the phone, she went upstairs and saw Allegra staring out the window of her bedroom, and wandered in to see her.

"You can always come home whenever you want, you know," she said softly, watching her oldest child looking surprisingly wistful. She wanted to ask her if something was wrong, but she didn't quite dare. Blaire was always worried that Allegra didn't get enough emotional support from Brandon. He was so independent about everything, and he seemed so unaware of Allegra's needs and feelings. Blaire had done her best to like him in the past two years, but she just didn't.

"Thanks, Mom." Allegra smiled at her, and then lay spread-eagled on the big four-poster. Sometimes it felt great just being there, even if she only came home for a couple of hours, and sometimes she also resented the hold they still had on her. She was still so close to them, at times it worried her. She loved them so much, she had never cut ties that other women her age had long since severed. But why should she? Brandon complained that she was too close to them. He claimed that it was unhealthy, and not normal. But she got along so well with them, and they were so supportive of her. What was she supposed to do? Stop seeing them because she was turning thirty?

"Where's Brandon?" her mother asked, trying to sound casual. She had gotten Allegra's message that she was coming to dinner alone, and she had to admit, she was relieved, but of course she didn't say so. "Working late?"

"He had to go to San Francisco to see the girls," Allegra said, sounding as casual as her mother. But they both knew it was all a ruse to give the impression that they were neither concerned nor bothered.

"He'll be back tomorrow though, I'm sure." Blaire smiled, irritated on Allegra's behalf that he never seemed to be there for her. But she was startled by her daughter's answer.

"Actually, no. He needed the weekend with them. He's starting a trial on Monday, and he wasn't sure when he'd get back to see them."

"He's not coming to the awards?" Blaire looked stunned. Did this mean anything? Was this one of the early signs of a breakup? She tried to look merely surprised and not hopeful.

"No, it's no big deal." Allegra lied, not wanting to admit to her how upset she had been. It made her feel so vulnerable to admit to her mother when she had problems with Brandon. It made her feel so inadequate when she had trouble with him. Her mother never did with her father. Her parents' relationship had always been perfect. "I'm going with Alan."

"That's nice of him," Blaire said, looking tight-lipped, and sitting down in a comfortable chair near the four-poster. Allegra was watching her. She knew there would be more, and the inevitable questions. Why wasn't he divorced? Why did he go to San Francisco to see his ex-wife all the time? Did she feel that the relationship was going anywhere? Did she realize that on her next birthday she was turning thirty? "Doesn't it bother you when he's not here for things that are important to you?" Her mother's clear, blue-eyed gaze cut straight to her soul, and Allegra tried not to let it.

"Sometimes, but as he says, we're both grown-ups with big jobs, and a lot of obligations. Sometimes we just can't be there for each other, and we have to understand it. There's no point making a fuss over it, Mom. He's got two kids in another city, and he needs to see them."

"His timing just seems very poor. Doesn't it to you?" Allegra wanted to scream, listening to her. And the last thing she wanted to do tonight was defend Brandon. She was upset about it herself, and she didn't want to justify his behavior to her mother. But as the two women exchanged a glance, a tall, dark-haired young man appeared in the doorway.

"Who are you two tearing apart now? Brandon, I assume, or is there someone new on the horizon?" Her brother, Scott, had just arrived from the airport, and Allegra sat up on her bed with a delighted grin as he took two long strides, sat down next to her, and hugged her.

"My God, you've grown again," she said with a groan, as her mother watched them with a warm smile. He looked just like his father. He was six five, and, fortunately, seemed to have stopped growing. He was playing basketball at Stanford. "How big are your feet now?" Allegra teased. Hers were small for her height, but Sam wore a size nine, and Scott was wearing a size thirteen the last time she asked him.

"Still a size thirteen, thanks a lot." He walked over and hugged his mother then, and sat down on the floor to chat with them both. "Where's Dad?"

"On his way home from the office, I hope. He called a little while ago. Sam's upstairs. And dinner's in ten minutes."

"I'm starving." He looked great, and it was obvious, from the way she looked, how proud his mother was of him. They all were. He was going to be a terrific doctor. "So what's the inside scoop?" he asked, turning to Blaire. "Are you going to win, as usual, or are you going to disgrace us for once?"

"Disgrace you, I'm sure." She laughed, trying not to think of the Golden Globes. Even after all these years of writing and producing hit shows, award ceremonies always made her nervous. "I think Dad's the one who's going to make us proud this year," she said cryptically, but she wouldn't say more, and then five minutes later, he pulled into the driveway. They all hurried downstairs, and Blaire called upstairs to Sam to get off the phone and come to dinner.

It was a lively meal, and the two men tried to engage in serious conversation over the female hubbub of gossip and news and talk about the awards, and Sam's barrage of questions about Carmen, what she was like, what she wore, who she was going out with. And in the midst of it all, Blaire sat back with a small smile and watched them, her three children, and the husband she had loved for all these years. Not unlike Scott, he was still tall and dark and handsome. He was six four, and there was just a small smudge of gray hair now at his temples, and small crinkles around his eyes, but even those small traces of time only served to make him more attractive. He was a fabulous-looking man, and just watching him still made Blaire tingle. But there was a small ache to it now sometimes, when she let herself worry about the fact that she was changing. He never seemed to change, he only seemed to get better as he got older. But she felt different now; she worried more than she had before, about him, about the kids, about her career. She worried about becoming obsolete, about her ratings having dropped just a bit in the last year, and about Samantha leaving for college. What if she went East after all, or decided to live in the dorms if she went to UCLA? What would she do when they were truly all gone? What if they didn't need her anymore . . . or she lost the show? What would happen to her when it was all over? What if things should ever change with Simon? But she knew that was foolish.

She tried to talk to Simon about it sometimes. Suddenly she had so many fears, about herself, her life, her body. It had just been in the past year or two, and she knew her looks had changed, no matter how many people told her they hadn't. She was getting older and it was painful sometimes realizing that she seemed to have altered more than Simon. It seemed amazing to her that it had all gone so fast, and she had reached fifty-four so quickly. And soon she would be fifty-five . . . and then sixty. . . . It made her want to shout "Oh, my God," and "Stop the clock . . . wait . . . I need more time." It seemed odd to her that Simon didn't understand that. Maybe because men had more time, their hormones didn't suddenly start changing at fifty, their looks altered more subtly, and they always had the option of a wife half their age, and half a dozen more children. Even if they didn't want them, which Simon always said when Blaire reminded him that he could still have children and she couldn't, even if he had no interest in them at all, he had the option, and that made things different between them. But when she tried to say all those things to him, he just told her she was overworked and she was being silly. "For God's sake, Blaire, the last thing I want is more children. I love the ones we have, but if Sam doesn't grow up soon and get her own apartment one of these days to break the sound barrier in, I may go crazy." He said that, but Blaire knew he didn't want her to move out either. She was their baby. She wondered, though, why it was all so much easier for him, why he got less upset about things, why he didn't worry as much about Scott's grades, or the fact that Allegra was still with Brandon, after two years, and he was still married to another woman.

But none of that came up at the dinner table. They talked about other things. Simon and Scott talked about basketball, and Stanford, and a possible trip to China. And then they all talked about the Golden Globes, and Scott teased Sam about the last boy he'd seen her go out with. He said the kid was a real nerd, and Samantha defended him hotly, although she insisted she really didn't like him. And Blaire announced that their ratings had just gone up again, after a brief dip the month before, and she was planning to redo the garden and the kitchen next summer.

"Is that supposed to be news?" Simon teased, as a warm look passed between them. "When haven't you been ripping something out and putting something else in? And anyway, I like the garden the way it is. Why change it?"

"I found a fabulous English gardener, and he says he can change everything in two months. The kitchen is another story," she grinned. "I hope you all like Jack in the Box, we'll be eating all our meals there from May till September." There was a communal groan, and Simon looked at his only son with a meaningful expression.

"I think that's just about the right length of time for our trip to China."

"You're not going anywhere." She looked at him pointedly. "We're shooting all summer this year, and I'm not going to be left alone again." Every year the two men took a trip together, usually to someplace where Blaire couldn't reach them if she tried, like Samoa, or Botswana. "You can go to Acapulco for the weekend." Scott laughed at them, and the teasing and the arguments and the exchanges went on until after nine o'clock, when Allegra finally stood up and said she had to get home. She still had some work to do that evening.

"You work too hard," her mother chided her, and Allegra smiled in answer.

"And you don't?" Her mother worked harder than anyone she knew. And Allegra respected her a great deal for it. "I'll see you tomorrow night, at the awards," she said, as they all left the table.

"Do you want to come with us?" her mother asked, and she shook her head.

"Alan's always late, and he's got ten million friends wherever we go. He'll probably want to go somewhere afterward. We'd better meet you there, or we'll drive you crazy."

"You're going with Alan and not Brandon?" Samantha asked her with a look of amazement, and her older sister nodded.

"How come?"

"He had to go to San Francisco to see his kids," Allegra said matter-of-factly. She felt as though she had already explained it four thousand times, and she was getting tired of it.

"Are you sure he's not sleeping with his ex-wife?" Sam asked her bluntly, and for a minute she knocked the wind out of Allegra. Allegra was quick to respond once she caught her breath again, and she was furious at her younger sister for the question.

"That's a really bitchy thing to say, and totally unnecessary. You ought to watch your mouth, Sam," Allegra said hotly.

"Well, don't wet your pants over it," Sam said, looking all cat as the two sisters hissed at each other. "Maybe I'm right, maybe that's why you got so pissed off when I said it."

"Knock it off," Scott said to Sam, seeing how upset Allegra was. "His sex life is none of our business."

"Thanks," Allegra whispered to him later, as she kissed him good night, but she wondered herself why Sam's comment had upset her so much. Was that really what she thought? Was that what she was afraid of? Of course not. Joanie was dependent and whiny and overweight, and Brandon even said to her all the time how unattractive his ex-wife had gotten. That wasn't the point. It was just that it hurt so much to have to defend him. It was obvious that her whole family thought he should be there, and so did she. And secretly, she was furious that he wasn't.

She thought about it again all the way home that night, and by the time she got home she was angry at him all over again. She sat and stewed about it for a while, pretending to pore over her work, and then finally she decided to call him. She knew the number of the hotel where he stayed by heart, and she dialed it with trembling fingers. Maybe she could convince him to come back after all, but then she'd have to explain to Alan that he couldn't take her, and that could have been awkward, even though they were good enough friends that she could say anything to him, and if he was mad about it, he'd tell her.

They rang Brandon's room for her, and she waited interminably. It was after ten o'clock, but he didn't answer. She asked them to try again, just in case they'd gotten the wrong room, but he was clearly not in. He was probably still at the house, talking to Joanie about the divorce. After the girls went to bed, Brandon said, they argued for hours sometimes. But as she thought of it, Sam's words about his sleeping with Joanie popped into her head. And Allegra was furious all over again, at him for being there, and at her sister for having said it. She didn't need to spend her life worrying about him or feeling insecure because of something a teenager said. She had enough going on in her life without this bullshit. And almost as soon as she hung up, the telephone rang, and she smiled to herself. She was hysterical about nothing. It was probably Brandon, and he'd just gotten back to the hotel. But it wasn't. It was Carmen, and she was crying.

"What's up?"

"I just got a death threat." She was sobbing, and she said she wanted to move back to Oregon. But hers wasn't a career that would easily disappear. She had movie contracts now, and the entire world wanted a piece of Carmen Connors.

Allegra frowned as she listened. "How did you get it? Try to calm down and tell me."

"It came in the mail. I forgot to open my mail today, and I just got home from dinner, so I opened it, and there it was. It says"—she dissolved in floods of tears again—"it says that I'm a bitch and I don't deserve to live another hour. This guy says he knows I'm cheating on him and I'm a whore, and he's going to get me."

Oh, God, Allegra thought to herself. Those were the ones you had to worry about. The ones who imagined they had a relationship, or a right, and had somehow been wronged. They were the real ones, but she didn't want to frighten Carmen any further. "This doesn't sound like anyone you know, does it? Anyone you went out with, and who might be angry you don't want to go out with him again?" It was at least worth the question, although she knew how circumspect Carmen was. Despite the tabloid stories, Carmen lived like the Virgin Mary.

"I haven't had a date in eight months," she said unhappily, "and the last two guys I went out with have both gotten married."

"That's what I figured. Okay, let's calm down. Turn on the alarm," she said calmly, as though talking to a child.

"I did."

"Good. Call the security guard at the gate and tell him about the letter. I'll call the police and the FBI, and we'll meet with them tomorrow. There's not much point doing anything tonight, but I'll let them know. LAPD can put passing calls past your house every half hour. Why don't you take one of the dogs into the house with you tonight, just so you feel better?"

"I can't. . . . I'm scared of them," Carmen said nervously, and Allegra laughed, which relieved the tension.

"That's my point. They'd scare anyone. At least keep them loose on the property. You know, I think it's all probably bullshit anyway, but it doesn't do any harm to be careful."

"Why do they do things like this?" Carmen wailed. She had had threats before, and they terrified her, but no one had ever actually tried to harm her. It was just talk, and every celebrity Allegra knew of had had threats at some point or other. It just went with the territory, but it was never pleasant. Her own parents had had them too, and there had been a kidnapping threat against Sam when she was eleven. Her mother had hired a bodyguard for her for six months, and he drove everyone nuts, watching TV night and day, and spilling coffee all over the carpets. But if she had to, Allegra would hire one for Carmen. In fact, she wanted to hire one for her for the Golden Globes. There were two she particularly liked, and used fairly often, and one of them was a woman.

"They're just stupid, Carmen. They want attention, and they think that if they try to get close enough to you, they'll get a little piece of the limelight. It's a sick way to do it, but try not to let it upset you too much. I'm going to try to get you a couple of people for tomorrow night, a woman and a man, it'll just look like you're with another couple," Allegra said reassuringly. She had handled a lot of these situations for other clients, and she was very soothing.

"Maybe I just won't go," Carmen said nervously. "What if somebody shoots me at the awards?" She started to cry again and whimper about going back to Portland.

"No one is going to shoot you at the awards ceremony. Come on, you can come with us. Who's your date?"

"Some guy named Michael Guiness. The studio paired me off with him. I've never even met him." She sounded disgusted, but Allegra was quick to encourage her.

"I have. He's okay." He was gay, and very presentable, and one of their up-and-coming young actors, and they probably thought that being with Carmen Connors would be good for his image. The fact that he was gay was a fairly well kept secret. "I'll take care of everything. You just relax and try to get some sleep." She knew that Carmen sat up all night sometimes, watching old movies on TV, because she was scared, or lonely.

"Who are you going with?" Carmen asked casually, assuming it was Brandon. She had met him once or twice, and she thought he was respectable, but boring. She was surprised at Allegra's answer.

"I'm going with an old buddy from school, Alan Carr," Allegra said offhandedly. She was making notes to herself about calling the police and the FBI in the morning.

"Oh, my God!" Carmen said, sounding dumbstruck. "*The* Alan Carr? Are you kidding? You went to school with *him*?"

"The one and only," Allegra said, amused at her reaction. It happened often.

"I've seen all his movies."

"So have I, and believe me, some of them are rotten." Some of them were great though, and she knew it. "I keep telling him he needs a new agent, but Alan is very stubborn."

"Oh, my God, he's gorgeous."

"Better than that, he's a nice guy. You'll like him." She wondered if Alan would like Carmen. Maybe they'd hit it off at the awards, which would be kind of fun for all of them. "We'll go out for a drink or something afterward, and we'll drive you and Michael to the awards if you like."

"I'd love that." She was sounding a whole lot happier by the time they hung up, and Allegra sat and stared out the window for a while, thinking about how odd life was. The biggest sex symbol in America hadn't had a date in eight months, and was getting death threats from lunatics who thought they owned her. There was something very wrong with that, to say the least. And here Carmen was impressed that Allegra knew Alan Carr. It really was all a little topsy-turvy.

When she finished talking to Carmen, she looked at her watch. They had talked for more than an hour. It was close to midnight, and Allegra was almost afraid to call Brandon again by then, but she decided to anyway. He had probably returned her call when she was on the phone with Carmen. But when she dialed the hotel again, he was still out, and she left him another message, this time asking him to call her.

She went to bed at one o'clock, and she still hadn't heard from Brandon, but she didn't want to try again. She was beginning to feel foolish, and she did everything she could to put Sam's words out of her mind. She didn't know what Brandon was doing, though she was certain he was not sleeping with Joanie. But she couldn't imagine what he was doing at that hour in San Francisco. It was a sleepy little town, and from what she'd seen of it, they rolled up the sidewalks at nine or ten o'clock. He certainly wasn't in a nightclub. He was probably just arguing with her about the house or the condo near Tahoe. Sam had had no right to say things like that about him. She was still furious when she thought about it. Why was everyone always so disagreeable about him? And why did she always have to stick up for him and answer people's questions about his behavior?

The phone never rang and she finally drifted off to sleep about two o'clock in the morning. But it did ring at four, and she leapt to her feet with her heart pounding, thinking it was him. But it was Carmen. She had heard a noise, and she was terrified. She was whispering into the phone, and she was so scared she hardly made sense. It took nearly an hour to calm her down again, and Allegra wondered if she should just go over there. But Carmen insisted she was okay by then. It was five A.M., and she was embarrassed to have called, but Allegra reassured her that it wasn't a problem.

"Get some sleep or you'll look like hell tonight at the awards, and you're probably going to win, so you'd better look good. Now go back to bed," Allegra said, sounding like a big sister.

"Okay." Carmen laughed, feeling like a little kid. And five minutes after she turned off the light, Allegra was asleep. She was exhausted. She didn't stir until eight o'clock in the morning, when Brandon called and woke her.

"Were you up?" Brandon asked, as she tried to sound as though she'd been awake, and then groaned when she saw the clock. She'd had less than five hours sleep all night, and she felt it.

"Several times, actually," she said, regaining her composure. "Carmen had a little problem."

"Oh, for chrissake, I don't know why you put up with that nonsense. You ought to get an answering service, or just turn your phone off." It wasn't the way she was made, or the nature of her business, but he had never understood that.

"It's all right. I'm used to it. She had a death threat," and as she glanced at the clock again at eight oh five, she remembered that she had to call the police and the FBI to report it. She was going to have a busy morning. "Where were you last night?" Allegra tried to keep a tone of accusation out of her voice, and not to remember Sam's words of warning as she asked him.

"Out with some friends. What was the big deal? How come you called me twice?"

"Nothing," she said, feeling immediately defensive. "I just wanted to check in and say hi. I thought you were seeing the kids last night." If he wasn't, why did he have to leave for San Francisco on Friday?"

"I was, but the flight got in late, and Joanie said they'd had a long day, so I called a couple of guys I used to work with. We hit the bars and just got to talking." Sometimes she forgot that he used to live there. "I thought maybe something was wrong when I got in and saw you'd called, but I figured you'd be asleep by then. I guess I could just act like your clients and call anytime, day or night." He strongly disapproved of the calls she got late at night, but most of her clients only did that when they felt they really had to.

"It sounds like you're having a good time," she said, trying not to sound as angry or disappointed as she was.

"It's okay. Sometimes it's fun being back here. Last night was a kick with the guys. I haven't done the bar scene here in ages." It didn't appeal to her, but it was probably amusing for him to catch up with his friends. He worked so hard, he didn't do things like that very often. "I'm picking the girls up at nine. I promised them we'd go to Sausalito and maybe Stinson for the day. It's too bad you couldn't be here," he said, sounding warmer again.

"I'm going to have to see the police for Carmen this morning, and probably the FBI, since the letter came in the mail, and then I've got the awards tonight."

"That ought to be entertaining," he said, sounding completely disengaged, as though it had never been part of the plan for him to be there. "How was dinner last night?"

"Okay. The usual. The Steinbergs at their best and worst. Scott came home, so that was nice. Sam is getting a little big for her britches, these days. I guess it's the age, but I can't say I'm crazy about it."

"That's because your mother lets her do anything she wants. If you ask me, that's the surest way to wind up with a spoiled brat, and she's getting a little old for that. I'm surprised your father doesn't put his foot down." She thought that Brandon was being a little harsh, and although she didn't completely disagree with him, she was nonetheless surprised that he was so willing to criticize her siblings. She was always especially careful not to say anything less than flattering about his children.

"My father worships her. And she's been doing more modeling lately too. That probably gives her a fat head, and makes her think she can say anything she wants." She was still thinking about Sam's comments the night before, and now she was doubly annoyed at Sam for making her worry for nothing. It was interesting, though, that she had actually gotten to her, but Allegra knew it was only because she was so unhappy about his going to San Francisco for the weekend.

"She'll get into trouble with her modeling one of these days. One of the photographers will come on to her, or they'll offer her drugs. I think that whole scene is unhealthy for her. I'm surprised your parents are willing to let her do it." To Brandon, it was all about the evils of show business, in all its forms and variations. It was something he emphatically disapproved of. And he frequently said that he would never let his girls model, or act, or do anything that involved putting them in the public eye. He always made it clear to Allegra that he thought their business was seamy and very unappealing, in spite of the fact that her parents had done extremely well at it, and she obviously enjoyed it.

"You could be right," she said diplomatically, wondering if they were just too different, or if it was because he was away, and she felt as though he had let her down. Sometimes it was hard to know, even after two years, if this was the right choice for her. Most of the time, she thought he was right for her, and then occasionally, like now, she felt as though they were strangers.

"I'd better go pick up the girls," he said, and then pacified her with, "I'll call you tonight."

"I'll be at the Golden Globes," she reminded him gently.

"That's right. I forgot," he said, and the way he said it made her want to hit him. "I'll call you tomorrow morning."

"Thanks." And then, hating herself for it, she added, "I'm sorry you won't be there."

"You'll have fun anyway. I guess Alan Carr is a better date for that kind of thing than I am. At least he knows who he's talking to. I don't. Just make sure he behaves, and tell him you're my girl, Allie. No funny stuff," he said, and she smiled, faintly mollified again. He meant well, and he loved her, he just didn't get how important the awards ceremonies were to her. They were her life, they were important to her family, and to her business.

"I'll miss you. And just for the record, I'd rather be going with you than Alan."

"I'll try to make it next year, baby, I promise." He even sounded as though he meant it.

"All right," she said, wishing he were there in bed with her. At least that was one area where she never felt the differences, but only the similarities, between them. Sexually, they got on extremely well. And eventually, the rest would probably smooth out too. Divorces were never easy. "Have a nice time with the girls, sweetheart. And tell them I miss them."

"I will. Talk to you tomorrow. I'll look for you on the news tonight." But she laughed at him. She'd be the last person he'd see. She wasn't a nominee, or a presenter, she was just one of the insignificant masses as far as the news cameras were concerned, unless they caught a glimpse of her as one of her parents won, or maybe Carmen. But they narrowed in pretty tight for the shots of the winners. The only thing that might attract attention to her was being Alan Carr's date, but as a relative unknown, she doubted if even that would get her on camera. She seriously doubted that Brandon would see her.

They hung up after that, and she felt better after talking to him. Sometimes he just didn't understand her milieu, and he'd been slow at sorting his life out, but he was a great guy, and she was always having to explain to everyone that she really loved him. It was a shame they didn't see his virtues as clearly as she did.

She got up and put a pot of coffee on, and then she called the police, the FBI, the security firm that covered Carmen's house, and eventually she met with all of them at Carmen's, and Allegra was satisfied that everything possible was being done to protect her. She had contacted both of her favorite bodyguards, Bill Frank and Gayle Watels, who had retired from the LAPD SWAT team, and fortunately both of them were free and had agreed to work with Carmen for a while. They were going to the awards ceremony with her that night, and Carmen was relieved to know she'd be so well protected. Allegra had sent Gayle to Fred Hayman for a dress, which was no easy task, since it had to conceal her holster, and all of her weapons. But the ladies at Fred Hayman were used to unusual assignments.

Allegra managed to get home at four-fifteen, while the hairdresser and makeup artist worked with Carmen, and she barely had time to shower and do her own hair, and slip into the long, slinky black dress she had bought to wear for the occasion. It was quiet and discreet, but beautifully cut and very striking. It had been designed by Ferre, and had a fabulous white organdy coat covering it, and she wore the pearl and diamond earrings her father had bought her for her twenty-fifth birthday. Her long, silky blond hair was piled high on her head, in gently cascading rolls and curls, and she looked sexy and sensuous when Alan Carr arrived, looking breathtaking in a new Armani tuxedo. He was wearing a white silk shirt with a narrow collar and no tie, and his dark hair was slicked back. He looked even better than he had in his last half dozen pictures.

"Wow!" he said, before she could say the same. She had a slit in her dress all the way up one leg that revealed a pair of black lacy stockings, and she was wearing high-heeled black satin sandals. "Am I supposed to behave myself with you looking like that?" he asked, pretending to be incredulous, and she laughed as she kissed him. He could smell her perfume on her neck and in her hair, and as he had before, he asked himself why he had never tried to rekindle their old flame in recent years. He was beginning to think their time had come again, and to hell with Brandon Edwards.

"Thank you, sir. You look very handsome yourself," she said, admiring him with genuine affection. "You really do look good, you know."

"You're not supposed to look so surprised," he said, chuckling. "It's not polite."

"I just forget how good-looking you are sometimes. I kind of think of you the way I do Scott—you know, just a big kid, in ripped jeans and dirty sneakers."

"You're breaking my heart. Just shut up. I love the way you look," he said admiringly, his voice suddenly soft, his eyes filled with something she hadn't seen since they were fourteen, and she knew she wasn't ready to see again. She just pretended not to notice. "Shall we go?" he asked, as she picked up a small black evening bag with a pearl-and-rhinestone clasp. Everything about the way she looked was perfect. And they made a staggeringly handsome couple. She also knew that being with him meant that they would be constantly hounded by the press. They would want to know who she was, and whether or not to start a flood of new rumors about his love life.

"I told Carmen we'd pick her up," Allegra explained to him as they left and walked out to the waiting limo. It was a stretch, and she had no doubt they'd all fit. Alan leased it, with the driver, on a yearly basis. It was part of his current contract. "Is that all right?"

"I guess. I'm not nominated tonight, so I'm in no hurry to get there. Hell, maybe you and I should just take off and go somewhere else. You look too good to waste on all those clods, and all those assholes from the tabloids."

"Now, now, be a good boy," she scolded him, and he kissed her neck, but it was only playful.

"See how well behaved I am, never mess a girl's hair. I've been trained by experts." He looked extremely handsome as he handed her into the car, and she smiled as he slid in beside her.

"You know, half the women in America would give their right arms, and their left, to be sitting here next to you. I really am a lucky girl, aren't I?" She grinned and he laughed, and had the grace to look embarrassed.

"Don't be a jerk, Al. I'm a lucky guy. You really look great tonight."

"Wait till you meet Carmen. She's absolutely drop-dead gorgeous."

"She can't hold a candle to you, my friend," he said gallantly, but they both looked stunned when they reached her house and Carmen stepped into the driveway. She was flanked on either side by the bodyguards Allegra had hired for her. Bill looked like a wall in a tuxedo, and Gayle looked deceptively demure in a very good-looking bronze sequined dress that set off her coppery hair and her figure, and the matching jacket completely concealed both guns she was wearing, a Walther PPK .380 and a Derringer .38 Special. But it was Carmen who took their breath away and literally shocked Alan into silence. She was wearing a skintight red peau de soie dress with a high neck, long sleeves, and it showed off every inch of her flawless figure. Like Allegra's, it had a high slit, which showed off her legendary legs, and when she turned, there appeared to be almost no back to the dress, and you could see her creamy skin all the way to her shapely bottom. Her silvery-blond hair was pulled straight back into an elegant bun, and she not only looked incredibly sexy, but she also managed to look somewhat distinguished. She looked like a very sexy version of a very young Grace Kelly.

"Wow!" Allegra said for both of them. "You look fabulous."

"Do you like it?" Carmen looked like a kid as she grinned at them, and she was mortified when she blushed as Allegra introduced her to Alan. "I'm really honored to meet you," she said, almost choking on her words, and he shook her hand and assured her that he had always wanted to meet her too. He said that Allegra had said nothing but nice things about her, and Carmen smiled up at her attorney with gratitude and pleasure. "I guess she lied to you then. I'm a big pain in the neck sometimes," she grinned and they all laughed.

"It's the nature of the business," Alan excused her easily as the two bodyguards took the seats facing them, on either side of the television set and the bar. Allegra flicked on the TV as they drove away, so they could see who was arriving at the awards, and just before they arrived, she saw her parents. Her mother was wearing a dark green velvet dress and she looked very pretty as the Steinbergs smiled at the reporters. The announcer explained who they were to the viewers at home, just as the limousine stopped at Michael Guiness's apartment. He was waiting for them and he hurried out, greeted everyone, and jumped into the front seat next to the driver. He and Alan had worked on a picture once, and Allegra introduced him to Carmen and her bodyguards, as they took off toward the Hilton.

"I've never been to the Golden Globes before," Michael said, excited to be going with them. He was scarcely older than Carmen, but less sophisticated, and a lot less of a name than she was. In some ways, Allegra thought to herself, Carmen should have been Alan's date. But that would have been a story the tabloids would go wild with.

As they approached the Hilton, they got into the long line of limousines, waiting to disgorge their glittering passengers, like little bits of sparkling bait set out to excite the sharks patrolling the waters. Hundreds of reporters were lined up four or five deep, holding cameras, and extending microphones and tape recorders, trying to get just a moment, a glimpse, a word, with an important person. And inside, the crowds were even worse, there reporters and cameramen had been allowed to set up small areas in which to interview the nominees or any publicity hungry actor or actress who would give them a few minutes. And beyond them were lines of fans, banked against the walls, until the enormous lobby shrank to a tiny trail allowing people to trickle through to the grand ballroom. And once inside, there was every major and minor television and movie star anyone had ever seen, read or heard about. It was an extraordinary group, and even among the fans outside, there was an atmosphere of wild anticipation. As each limousine drew up, and a new face appeared, fans screamed their names or cheered, and dozens of reporters lunged forward in the light of a hundred flashing cameras.

Just watching it seemed to terrify Carmen Connors. She had been to the Golden Globes the year before, but this year, as one of the nominees, she knew that the press would be even more anxious to devour her. And having had a death threat only the night before, she was even more unnerved by the attention and the crowds and the cameras.

"Are you okay?" Allegra asked her, looking motherly.

"I'm fine," she said in barely more than a whisper.

"Let Bill and me get out first," Gayle explained, "then Michael, and then you. We'll be between you and the cameras at first," she said calmly, exuding a sense of protection just in the way she said it.

"We'll bring up the rear," Allegra reassured her, but she also knew that the attention on Alan would be extreme. It might deflect some of the attention from Carmen, but it would attract more reporters to them too. There was simply no way of avoiding the press here. There were hundreds of people waiting for them, possibly as many as a thousand. "We're right here, Carmen. You just have to get inside the hall. After that you'll be fine." There were plenty of other stars there to distract them, Allegra reminded her gently.

"You'll get used to it, kid," Alan said, gently touching Carmen's arm. There was a sweetness to her that he liked, and a vulnerability he hadn't seen in years, but that had great appeal to him. Most of the actresses he knew were pretty hardened.

"I don't think I'll ever get used to it," Carmen said softly, looking up at him with big gentle blue eyes, and he almost wanted to put his arms around her, except that he knew he'd have shocked her.

"You'll be okay," Alan said calmly. "Nothing's going to happen to you. I get those threats all the time. They're just nuts. They never follow through." He said it with complete confidence, which was not exactly what the FBI had said that afternoon. They said most of the threats that were acted on were usually preceded by some kind of explanation, like the one she'd gotten in the mail: the belief that she was cheating on this man, and that she owed something to him, although she was sure that she didn't even know him. They agreed with Alan that most threats were simply a weak cry from confused, ineffective people, but there was always the rare one who did what he promised to, and caused a real disaster. The police and the FBI had both recommended that she be careful for a while, and try to stay away from advertised or expected appearances, or highly public places. Tonight's appearance was exactly what she shouldn't do, but on the other hand, going to the Golden Globe Awards was part of her business, and she knew that. She was trying to make the best of it, but Allegra could see that she was scared stiff, as Carmen reached unconsciously for Alan's hand and squeezed it, although she scarcely knew him. "I'm right here," he said quietly, holding her arm, and helping her out to Bill and Gayle, her bodyguards, and Michael, waiting for her on the sidewalk. Alan never took his eyes off her, nor did Allegra. The effect was almost instantaneous as a hundred reporters lunged toward her and the crowd began screaming her name at the top of their voices. Allegra had never seen anything like it. It was almost like a wave that seized them, as they looked at her, and she and Alan both found themselves wondering when the last time was that Hollywood had produced a star with as much charisma as Carmen.

"Poor kid," he said, feeling sorry for her. He knew what it was like. But somehow, he had never felt quite so overwhelmed as he could sense she did. He had been a little older than she was when his first major success hit, and as a man, they never pushed him quite as far or took quite as much advantage. "Come on," he said, grabbing Allegra, but keeping his eye on Carmen, trying to dodge and weave and smile as she was oppressed by fans, reporters, and cameras. There were hundreds of them now, and even the line of limousines was blocked. Nobody could move until the mass of humanity settling around Carmen could be disbanded. "Let's give her a hand," Alan said, and shoved his way through the crowd, where the bodyguards were struggling, the police had started to move in, and Michael Guiness was lost in the crowds and looking completely helpless. But within seconds Alan was at her side, with Allegra hanging on to him, and he put a firm arm around Carmen's shoulders. "Hi, guys," he said knowingly, as though offering himself up just to give her a breather. And the moment they recognized him, the crowd went wild, screaming his name as well as Carmen's. "Sure do. . . . Sure am. . . . We've got a winner here. . . . That's right. . . . Thanks so much . . . happy to be here . . . Miss Connors is going to be one of our winners tonight. . . ." He exchanged a constant banter with them, as he set his football shoulders into the crowd and continued to move forward. And seeing what he had done, Gayle and Bill were able to move ahead of them. Gayle came down on several arches with stiletto heels while feigning total innocence, and Bill applied elbows to ribs as they cleared a path for her to enter the building. It was slow going, but they were finally able to move, and Alan kept up the momentum, holding to both Allegra and Carmen, and in a moment they were inside, and there were fresh screams from the fans, and a new onslaught from the media as television cameras were pushed into their faces. For a moment, Carmen started to turn aside, but Alan held on to her tightly and kept talking to her, keeping her calm and urging her forward.

"You're okay," he kept repeating to her. "You're fine. . . . Come on, now, smile for the cameras. The whole world is watching you tonight." She looked as though she were about to cry, and his grip on her only got firmer and tighter, and then with a last burst of energy, they exploded into the ballroom, free of the hangers-on at last. One of the ruffles on Allegra's coat had been slightly torn, and the slit in Carmen's dress had gotten noticeably higher. One fan had actually grabbed her leg, and another one had tried to take one of her earrings. It was a total free-for-all, and Carmen's eyes were filled with tears as they reached the ballroom. "Don't you dare," Alan said quietly to her. "If you let them see how terrified you are, they'll be worse every time they see you. You have to look as though this doesn't bother you at all. Pretend you love it."

"I hate it," she said as two little tears spilled onto her cheeks, and he handed her his hankie.

"I mean it, you have to be very strong when you face them. I learned that five years ago. If not, they'll tear your heart out, after they rip your clothes off."

Allegra was nodding at her, grateful that Alan had joined them. Maybe it had all worked out for the best. Brandon would have been no help at all—if anything he'd have been irritated by the press—and Michael still hadn't made it into the ballroom. "He's right, you know. You've got to look like you can handle this with your eyes closed."

"What if I can't?" she said, still looking visibly shaken as she glanced gratefully up at Alan. She was still embarrassed to look at him. He was so handsome, and so famous. The truth was she was just as famous as he was, but in her heart of hearts, she didn't know that. It was part of what made her so appealing.

"If you can't do this," Alan said quietly, "then you don't belong here."

"Maybe I don't," she said sadly, handing him back his handkerchief. She had only dabbed at her eyes, and there was the faintest trace of mascara on it.

"America says you do belong here. Are you saying they're liars?" he asked her pointedly, as a whole flock of people suddenly appeared who knew him.

He introduced them to everyone. Allegra knew most of them, and Bill and Gayle had moved a few feet away, knowing that the danger had diminished. Alan and Carmen were with their own kind now, other stars, and producers and directors. And a few minutes later, Allegra's parents joined them. Blaire kissed Alan and told him how happy she was to see him again, and how much she had liked his last movie, and Simon shook his head, silently wishing, as he always did, that Allegra would fall in love with him.

Alan was the kind of son-in-law every man dreamed of. He was handsome and intelligent, easygoing, and athletic. Simon and Alan had played golf and tennis several times, and while he and Allegra were in high school, Alan had literally lived in their kitchen. But he had been pretty busy in recent years, and Simon wasn't sure now if Alan was escorting Allegra or Carmen Connors to the Golden Globes. He seemed to be equally attentive to both of them, and Michael had finally arrived but found a clique of his friends, and he was standing a few feet away talking animatedly to them.

"We haven't seen you in a long time," Simon complained to Alan in good-natured fashion. "Don't be such a stranger."

"I was in Australia for six months last year, making a picture in Kenya for eight months before that. And I just got back from Thailand. They keep me on the road most of the time in this insane business. Next month I'm off to Switzerland. It's kind of fun sometimes, you know what it's like." He looked knowingly at Simon. He had never worked for him, but like everyone else in Hollywood, he had always been extremely fond of Simon Steinberg. He was smart, he was fair, he was always a gentleman, and both in his dealings and his word, unfailingly honest. In many ways, he was a lot like Allegra, and those were the same qualities

Alan loved about her. That, and the fact that she had great legs, and a figure that still made him want to think of her as something other than a sister. But he was extremely confused as he looked at her. At the beginning of the evening, he had started having romantic notions about her again, but the moment Carmen had appeared, he felt as though someone had thrown all his insides out the window. He didn't know if he was right side up or upside down, or what he was feeling for her. But all he knew was that he wanted to pick Carmen up in his arms, and run straight through the crowd with her until he reached a place where they could be alone for a long, long time, and he could get to know her. Despite all the feelings he'd had for Allegra for over fifteen years, he had never felt that way about her. Since she'd first stepped into the limousine, he couldn't take his eyes off Carmen Connors.

Allegra had noticed it too, and it made her smile at him. She knew that he'd been hit hard, and fast, and she wasn't even sure she minded.

"I told you you'd like her," she said in a wheedling tone as they made their way to their table, and a dozen photographers snapped their picture. Carmen and Michael were just behind them, with Bill and Gayle bringing up the rear. Carmen was well sandwiched between them all, but the press was also being kept busy by other major stars, though none as devastatingly beautiful as she was.

"Why is it that you remind me of Sam when you talk to me like that?" he asked, sounding faintly annoyed, and not wanting to admit to her how taken he was with Carmen.

"Are you calling me a brat, or just telling me I sound like I'm seventeen?" she teased as another photographer, this one from *Paris Match*, took their picture.

"I'm telling you that you're a pain in the ass, but I love you anyway," he grinned with the look that a million women would have died for.

"You really are cute, you know," she said, wanting to give him a shove, but not daring to get out of hand there. "I think

Carmen thinks so too, to tell you the truth," she said, sounding like an omniscient older sister.

"Maybe you should just stay out of this," he warned her, suddenly wanting to kiss her neck again, and feeling completely schizophrenic. It was ridiculous, he had known her and loved her, mostly as a brother, for fifteen years, and now suddenly he was having sexual feelings about her again, and at the same time he was wildly attracted to her incredibly beautiful blond-bombshell client. None of this was supposed to be happening, and he turned and ordered a Scotch on the rocks from a passing waiter. He needed a drink to clear his head, or maybe just to numb it. "I don't want you saying anything to her," he warned Allegra as they found their table. It was a table for ten. She and Alan were sitting there, as were Carmen and Michael; a producer friend of her father's she had known for years, and his wife, who had been a very famous actress in the forties; a couple Allegra had never heard of before, which was rare; and Warren Beatty and Annette Bening. "I mean that, Allegra," Alan said again. "I don't want you mixing in, and trying to start something here."

"Who said I was going to mix in?" she said with the innocence of an angel as Carmen joined them. She was looking a little more at ease, and she looked up at Alan with huge blue eyes and a big grin as he sat down beside her. They talked for a few minutes, and then Allegra slipped away to see some friends. Several of the senior partners from the law firm were there, and almost all of their most important clients. Her parents had a table filled with their closest friends, most of them directors and producers, and the star of her father's latest picture. It was old home week for all of them, and Allegra was totally at ease as she floated through the crowd saying hello to people she knew well, and laughing here and there with an old friend, most of them either movie stars, writers, producers, or directors. There were also studio and network people heavily in evidence. It was an incredibly important evening.

"You're looking great," Jack Nicholson commented as she skipped past, and she thanked him. He was one of her father's oldest friends, and she and Streisand exchanged a nod. She wasn't sure if Streisand knew who she was, but she certainly knew Allegra's mother, Blaire Scott. And Allegra was particularly pleased to stop and chat with Sherry Lansing. It was also somewhat reassuring to note that a lot of men were looking at her with open admiration. In some ways, Brandon was so restrained that it was rare to get this kind of reinforcement from him. Even among the stars, Allegra could hold her own. And in a way, that always surprised her.

"What are you doing?" Alan asked her when she got back. "Cruising? Not when you're my date. That guy you go out with is really giving you bad habits." He pretended to be mad at her, but she knew he wasn't.

"Oh, shut up and behave yourself," she said with a grin as she sat down, and a few minutes later they were served dinner. As soon as coffee was served, the lights went down, and they were on the air with the music, the show, the televised Golden Globe awards in all its glory. As it began, their hearts all began to beat a little faster. They skipped back and forth for a while between movies and TV, and began with some of the lesser awards, but even at the beginning of the evening a number of people she knew were honored.

People were quick to powder their noses and put on lipstick during the commercial breaks, and with each award the cameras would zoom in on the nominees, and make everyone even more nervous. Then, finally, it was her mother's turn. She had won the award for best comedy series for so many years that Allegra never doubted for a minute that she would win it this year. She and Alan exchanged a look of certainty, and she was sorry she wasn't closer to her parents' table so she could squeeze her mother's hand in anticipation. It seemed hard to believe that her mother would be really worried after all these years, but she said she always was, and as Allegra saw her mother's face on the monitor, she realized that she was as terrified as all the other nominees. She looked panicked, and then they called out the names, one by one. The music, and then the endless silence, as everyone waited. And then her name . . . except that this year, for the first time after seven successive years of victory, it was not her mother's name they called out, but someone else's. Allegra was stunned, as she was sure her mother was. She just couldn't believe it. She looked at Alan and her eyes filled with tears, thinking of her, and the pain and disappointment she knew she must feel at that moment. They showed her mother's image on the monitor again, right after the winner's, and as the new winner made her way to the podium, Blaire was gracious and smiling, but Allegra could see that she was devastated. It was a reflection of what the audience had told them with their ratings.

"I can't believe it," she whispered to Alan, feeling crushed, and wishing she could offer her mother some comfort. But they couldn't move around the room with the cameras rolling.

"I can't believe it either," he whispered back. "It's still one of the best shows on TV. I watch it whenever I'm home," and she knew he meant it.

But seven years of awards out of nine was a long time. It was time for someone else now. And that was exactly what Blaire Scott was afraid of. As she sat in her seat, she felt a stone sink from her heart to her stomach, and as she looked at Simon, he nodded and patted her hand, but she wasn't sure he really understood what she was feeling. He had won so many times, but his victories were always individual events. He didn't have a recurring show like hers, which had to maintain its standard of excellence time after time, week after week, season after season. In some ways, what she did was much harder. Then she reminded herself that Simon was also nominated, and she tried to remind herself not to be so selfish. But it was difficult anyway. She felt as though she was losing in a number of ways, even if no one else understood that.

"I hope my mom is okay," Allegra said, worrying about her as the awards went on, and Alan shared her hope with her. She wished it were over now, but there were so many awards left to be given. It started to feel like it was taking forever. And then it was Carmen's turn. The names for the best film actress award were read, and the cameras zoomed in on each of them, and under the table Carmen was squeezing Alan's hand, and he was holding tightly to it, and hoping she'd win it. And then suddenly the explosion of her name, the cameras, the flashes, the applause as she stood up and looked down at him, and he beamed up at her as though he had lived his entire life for this moment. And at that very instant, Allegra knew, looking at them, that something had happened that night which neither of them really understood yet or were aware of. She didn't know how long it would take for them, but she sensed that something magical had occurred between them.

Alan was standing up, waiting for her, when Carmen returned, breathless and overwhelmed, laughing and crying and clutching her award, and he put his arms around her and kissed her, just as one of the photographers snapped their picture. Allegra was quick to tug at his sleeve, and he quickly sat down next to her.

"You'd better watch out," she warned, and he knew she was right, but for a moment he just couldn't help it. Carmen was so excited, she could hardly sit there quietly, and Allegra was so happy and proud of her, it almost took away some of the disappointment of her mother not winning. In some ways, Carmen was like her kid sister. She had groomed her and helped her, and overseen her career for the past three years, almost since she'd joined the firm, and now Carmen had come up winners. And what's more, she deserved it.

There was another hour of awards after that, when people started wishing that they could go home, and everyone began to feel that they were spending the week there. And then, at last, the final awards. Best actor in a film, the counterpart to Carmen's award, which went to another of Allegra's firm's clients. Best film, best director, and finally best producer of a feature film. Best producer went to her father this year, as it had twice before at the Golden Globes. And he looked immensely pleased as he went to the podium and picked up his award, and thanked all the appropriate people, and his wife, Blaire, whom he said would always be number one to him. There were tears in her eyes as she smiled up at him, and he kissed her when he got back to the table.

And then, at the very last, there was the humanitarian award, which they did not give every year, but only when it was truly deserved by an outstanding human being in show business. They showed film clips from various films, and listed countless achievements across forty years, and by then everyone had figured out who it was, except for the recipient himself, who looked completely dazed as they called his name, and this time Blaire stood up to salute him, and cried as she kissed him and he walked to the podium. It was Simon Steinberg, her father.

"My God . . . I—I don't know what to say to all of you," he said, looking deeply moved. "For once, I'm completely speechless. If I have won this, and I certainly don't deserve it, it's because of all of you, and your kindness to me over the years, your decency, your hard work, the goals you've helped me achieve, and the extraordinary moments we've shared. I salute all of you," he said to the audience, with tears in his eyes, as Allegra felt hers roll down her cheeks and Alan put an arm around her shoulders. "I thank you for all that you've meant to me, and done for me, and given me. You are the great human beings here, along with my wife, Blaire, my daughter Allegra, my two children at home, Scott and Sam, and all of you whom I've worked with, and I remain your humble servant." And with that he left the podium, and the entire audience in the grand ballroom of the Hilton Hotel gave him a standing ovation. He was truly the great man they said he was, and Allegra stood there and cried tears of pride and joy for her father.

It had been, in many ways, a wonderful evening, and as they all gathered up their things, Allegra told Alan that she wanted to go and see her mother. He told her he'd wait for her at the table with Carmen, and she found her mother in the midst of a group of friends and colleagues a few minutes later.

Allegra gave her a big hug, and told her she loved her. "Are you okay?" she asked in a whisper, and her mother nodded. Her eyes were still damp from the tears she had shed for Simon. It had been an important night for him, and she was happy for him, and proud enough of him to forget her own disappointment.

"We'll just have to try harder next year," Blaire said, apparently undaunted, but Allegra saw something in her eyes that she didn't like, and as she left her and approached where her father stood, she noticed her mother glance nervously in his direction. He was speaking to Elizabeth Coleson, a director she knew he had worked with. She was English and very unusual, in that she was very young, and had already been made a "Dame" in England in recognition of her enormous talent. They were deep in conversation, and her father was laughing, and there was something infinitesimally intimate about the way they stood. It was nothing Allegra could put a finger on, but it was just a feeling she got as she watched them. And then, before she could pursue the thought at all, her father turned away from Elizabeth and saw her. He beckoned to her immediately, and introduced her as the only respectably employed person in their family, and Elizabeth Coleson laughed a deep, husky laugh as she shook Allegra's hand and told her how pleased she was to meet her. She was only five years older than Allegra, and she had the sexual quality that some English women had, seeming very alluring while remaining enticingly aloof, and making no visible effort to be sexy, but achieving it totally because they didn't pursue it. Looking at her, Allegra thought she exuded sex and talent. There was an I-just-got-out-of-bed quality about her that made you wonder if she was wearing anything at all under her rather plain, somewhat out-of-date navy blue evening gown. It was obvious even to Allegra that her father liked her.

They chatted for a few minutes, and she told her father how proud she was of him. He gave her a big hug and a kiss, but when she left them, Allegra still had a faintly uneasy feeling about Elizabeth Coleson. She went back to her own table then, and the next time she looked over at them, she could see that her mother had joined them. And Allegra sensed easily that it had been a difficult evening for her mother, though she would never have admitted it to anyone, even to her older daughter. She was desperately worried about her show anyway. After nine years, it was hard enough to keep it interesting and keep it going. They had lost some important advertisers recently, as a result of the ratings dip. And not winning an award could make the ratings drop even further.

But Allegra could see yet another kind of worry in her mother's eyes tonight, and she wondered if it had anything at all to do with Elizabeth Coleson, or if she was imagining it, and Blaire was just dismayed that her show hadn't won the award after all. It was hard to tell with her mother. Blaire Scott was a pro, and a consummate good sport. On the way out, at least a dozen reporters asked her how she felt about not winning. She expressed her excitement for the writer/producer who had won the award, and her admiration for that show, and as usual, she was completely gracious. She said how much her husband's awards meant to her, and what an exceptional human being he was, and that maybe it was time for some of the younger, and very talented, people to be recognized.

On their way out, Carmen was set upon by reporters again, even more so than on the way in, and the fans went wild when they saw her. They threw flowers at her, and reached for her, and a teddy bear almost hit her in the head as a woman threw it at her, screaming her name. But fortunately, Alan caught it.

"Just like football," he grinned at Allegra. Much to his own surprise, he had actually enjoyed the evening. And he suggested to Allegra that they go to a fifties-style restaurant he knew for a hamburger, and they take Carmen and Michael with them.

It took them half an hour to get back into the car again, and by the time they did, they all felt as though they had been pawed and mauled and dragged around by ten thousand hands and twice as many reporters.

"God, I think I want to be a bagger at Safeway when I grow up," Michael said from the front seat with an exhausted groan, and they all laughed. But when Alan suggested a hamburger to him he said he was wiped out, and was working on a film, and had an early studio call the next morning. He said that if they didn't mind, he wanted to go home, and Carmen said that was fine. She was happy to go out with Allegra and Alan.

They dropped him off first and then went to Ed Debevic's on La Cienega, and Carmen said she was only sorry she couldn't change into a T-shirt and blue jeans.

"So am I," Alan said wickedly as the two women laughed. "Actually, I'll bet you look incredible in jeans. How about coming to Malibu with me tomorrow so I can decide what I like you in better, red evening dress or blue jeans? You know, kind of like the Miss America Pageant . . . hell, you could win the Miss Congeniality Award . . . or the bathing suit competition. . . ." Carmen was laughing at him, and Allegra grinned as they slipped into a booth, and a few of the regulars watched them, as Carmen's two bodyguards slipped into their own booth. It was after midnight.

Alan ordered a double cheeseburger and a chocolate malt, which reminded Allegra of their youth, and she ordered a cup of coffee and a side of onion rings, which was all she wanted. And they all smiled at the waitress, done up in fifties housewife garb. She looked just like Ethel on *I Love Lucy*.

"What about you, Miss Best Actress of the Year?" Alan asked Carmen, and she giggled. He had a nice quality with her, part big brother and part romantic hero, and Allegra had to admit as she looked at him that he was everything most women wanted. She had just known him for too long to ever take him seriously, or be turned on by him. And all she wanted now anyway was Brandon.

"I'll have apple pie à la mode and a strawberry milkshake," Carmen said, feeling wicked.

"Now that we've all won our awards, to hell with calories, give me greasy food before I die," he said, and then gave Carmen a squeeze and a look of admiration. "You were great tonight, by the way. You handled it a hell of a lot better than I could have at your age. All that star stuff is pretty goddamn scary." Only another person who lived with the same pressures and pains really understood it, although Allegra did because she lived so close to it.

"Every time they come at me, photographers or fans, I just want to run back to Oregon," Carmen said with a sigh.

"Tell me about it." Allegra rolled her eyes, and then looked at her more seriously. "Alan's right, you were terrific. I was very proud of you."

"Me too," Alan said softly. "For a minute there, I was afraid they'd trample you on the way in. The press and the media sure get out of hand, don't they?" But the bodyguards Allegra had hired had done a good job, she thought, as she glanced over at them at their separate table.

"The press scares me to death," Carmen confessed, not that anyone was surprised to hear it. And then Alan asked Allegra how her mom had been when she went over to see her.

"Upset, I think, not that she'd ever admit it. She's too proud to ever let anyone know she was hurting. And she probably had mixed emotions. I know she was happy for my dad. But she's been pretty worried about her show and this won't help it. When I went over to talk to her, she was telling my father how great he is, and he looked very excited. I think the humanitarian award really meant a lot to him. More so even than the one for his picture."

"He really deserves it," Alan said, and Carmen looked longingly at Allegra.

"I sure would like to be in one of his pictures."

"I'll say something to him," she said. He was probably interested in her too. She was a big name at the box office, and she had a rapidly growing talent. But Allegra didn't say anything to either of them about Elizabeth Coleson. It was the first time she had ever seen her father look quite that way at anyone other than her mother, but it was probably just professional admiration, and the look she had seen in her mother's eyes was probably just raw emotion after a very exciting night, full of roller-coaster rides of pride and disappointment.

They left Ed Debevic's at two o'clock, after talking about what it had been like to go to Beverly Hills High School, and what Carmen's childhood had been like in Portland. Hers sounded a lot more normal to them than theirs had been, and it made it even harder for her to adjust to the insanity of her life now with tabloids and paparazzi, and awards, and death threats.

"Just an ordinary life we all lead," Alan said with a look of amusement as they got back into the limousine, and he pulled Carmen onto his lap, and she made no attempt to escape him.

"Would you two like me to take a cab?" Allegra teased. It had become even more obvious in the last two hours that they were both extremely attracted to each other.

"How about the trunk?" Alan asked, and Allegra got into the car and gave him a shove, as Carmen laughed at both of them. In some ways, she envied them their long-standing friendship. She had no friends like that in Hollywood, no friends there at all in fact, except for Allegra. The only people she knew were the people she had worked with, and she never saw them after she finished a picture. They just moved on, and so did she, and one of the things she disliked most about her life in L.A. was how lonely she was, and how seldom she went out, except for evenings like this one, with a studio-appointed date, who was as bored as she was. And she said as much to both of them on the way home, as Alan looked at her in amazement.

"You know, half the guys in America would probably give their lives for a date with you. And nobody in the country would believe that you sit home and watch TV every night," he said, but he believed her. His own romantic life was less exciting than most people thought it was, except for the occasional sensational brief affair, which always wound up in the tabloids. "Well, we'll have to see about that," Alan said matter-of-factly. She had already agreed to go to his house in Malibu with him the next day, and now he was talking to her about going bowling.

Allegra asked to be dropped off first, and she kissed them both good night, and congratulated Carmen again, and then she let herself into the house, and was surprised to realize how tired she was as she slipped off her high-heeled sandals. It had been an exhausting evening.

Alan and Carmen seemed to be well on their way to a new romance. She was happy for them, and it made her think of

Brandon again, as she walked into her kitchen and listened to the messages on her machine. He wasn't supposed to call, but there was always the chance that he had anyway, or had called just to tell her he loved her.

Three of her friends and one of her associates had left messages for her, none of them urgent or even important. And then, finally, there was a message from Brandon. He had just called to say that he'd had a great time with the girls, and would talk to her on Sunday. He never mentioned the awards, hadn't watched them on television, didn't know or say anything about Carmen or her father. And it suddenly made her feel lonely again, listening to him. It was as though he was never really a part of her life, except when he chose to be, and even then only to the extent that he dared enter into it, which was never very far, or very deep. He was always a tourist. And no matter how much she felt for him, or how long their relationship went on, there was always a carefully maintained distance between them.

She flipped off the machine, and walked slowly into her bedroom, taking the pins out of her hair. It cascaded down her back, and she wasn't sure why, but there were tears in her eyes as she unzipped her dress and dropped it over the back of a chair. She was twenty-nine years old, and she wasn't even sure that any man had ever really loved her. It was an odd feeling of solitude as she stood naked in front of the mirrors in her dressing room, wondering if Brandon loved her, if he was even capable of pushing beyond the boundaries he set for himself, and being there for her, just the way she instinctively sensed that Alan wanted to be there for Carmen. It was as simple as that, Alan and Carmen had known each other for one night, and he was reaching out to her, without fear or even hesitation. And here was Brandon, after two years, like a man on a ledge, afraid to take the leap, unable to retreat, and not even willing to hold a hand out to her for comfort. She was alone. It was one of those shocking realizations that make you tremble with the terror of it in the dark of night, until you almost screamed. She was entirely alone. And wherever he was at that precise moment, so was Brandon.

CHAPTER 4

The first call Allegra got on Sunday morning was from Brandon. He was going out to play tennis with the girls, and he wanted to be sure he caught Allegra before she left. He knew she was leaving for New York sometime that afternoon, and he didn't want to miss her.

"How did all your little chickens do?" he asked with interest, but it seemed odd to her that he hadn't bothered to watch the news. He could have at least done that, for her parents' sake, if not for Carmen's. But she didn't say anything to reproach him; she was just glad he had called her.

"Carmen won best actress in a film, and my father won for best producer of a feature film. And they gave him a special humanitarian award too, which is a really big deal. It was terrific. My mom, unfortunately"—she sighed as she said it, remembering the look of worry and defeat in her mother's eyes—"didn't win anything, and I think it upset her pretty badly."

"You've got to be a good sport in that business, if nothing else," he said glibly, and Allegra was suddenly angry at him. The fact that he hadn't been at the ceremony was bad enough, but she didn't like him being insensitive about her mother.

"It's a little more complicated than that. It has to do with the life of a show, whether or not you win an award. She's been

75

fighting for the show's survival for the last year, and this could lose them important sponsors."

"That's too bad," he said, but he didn't sound particularly sympathetic. "Tell your dad I said congratulations."

"I will," she said, and then he went on to tell her about the day he had spent with his daughters. And the way he changed the subject started to bother her. Seeing the way Alan had treated Carmen the night before, and even the way he had treated her, had reminded her of how sensitive some men were, how solicitous and protective. Not all men were as backed-off, or as purposefully independent as Brandon. He was totally self-sufficient, and he expected her to be equally so. He didn't want her making any demands on him. They were like two parallel ships floating side by side, but with considerable distance between them, in one ocean. But the loneliness she'd felt the night before engulfed her again as she listened to him. More and more lately, she was feeling anxious about their relationship, and abandoned whenever he wasn't there for her. She had always wanted a relationship like the one her parents shared, but she was beginning to wonder if she was even suited to it, or if she was just continuing to pick men who were unwilling to commit, as Dr. Green had suggested.

"What time are you leaving for New York?" he asked conversationally. She was going to meet a very important bestselling author. His agent had asked her to represent him for a film deal, and she had set up a number of other meetings in New York as well. She was going to have a very busy week, and expected to be involved in some serious negotiations.

"I'm taking a four o'clock flight," she said, sounding sad, but he didn't seem to notice. She still had to pack, and she wanted to drop by and see her mother, if she had time, or at least call just to make sure she was all right after the night before. And she thought she should check on Carmen. "I'll be at the Regency in New York."

"I'll call you."

"Good luck with your trial."

"I wish I could get him to make a deal, it would go a lot

better for him with the prosecutor if he would. But he's very stubborn," he said about his client.

"Maybe he will at the eleventh hour," Allegra said hopefully.

"I doubt it, and I've done all the groundwork by now." As usual, he was wrapped up in his own world, his own life, and Allegra felt as though she had to fight for his attention. "I'll see you next weekend," he said, sounding regretful suddenly. "I'm going to miss you." He sounded surprised, and she smiled at the phone. Those were the little hooks that kept her attached to him, ever hopeful. He was capable of loving her, he just didn't have much time, and he was so traumatized by his ex-wife. That was always the excuse. Trauma caused by Joanie. Allegra had explained it to everyone a thousand times. And there were instances when it was so obvious to her, and equally obvious to her that he loved her.

"I miss you now," she said, her feelings raw, and there was a long beat of silence.

"I couldn't help it, Allie. I had to come here this weekend."

"I know. But I missed you last night. That was important to me."

"I told you. I'll be there next year." He said it as though he meant it, and she smiled finally.

"I'll hold you to that." But where would they be next year? Would he be divorced? Would they be married by then? Would he have overcome his fear of commitment? They were questions that still had no answers.

"I'll call you tomorrow night," he promised again, and just before they hung up, he reached out and touched her heart. "I love you, Al," he said softly.

"I love you too," she said, squeezing her eyes shut. He *was* there for her, he just had his own fears and obligations to contend with. She understood that. "Take care of yourself this week."

"I will. You too," he said, sounding as though he was really going to miss her. It made her smile wistfully as she hung up. What they had wasn't easily acquired, but they were getting there, despite what other people thought. She just had to be patient. He was worth it.

She called her parents after that, congratulated her father again, and extended Brandon's congratulations. And then she asked to talk to her mom, and she could still hear the edge of sadness in her voice when she answered.

"Are you okay?" Allegra asked sympathetically, and Blaire smiled, touched that she had called her.

"Oh, no, I'm going to slash my wrists this afternoon, or maybe I'll just stick my head in the oven."

"You'd better hurry up," Allegra said with a grin, pleased to hear her joking about it, "before they rip out the kitchen. Seriously, Mom, you deserved that award again this year, and you know it."

"Maybe not, dear. Maybe it's time to give someone else a turn. We had an awful lot of trouble with the show this fall." One of the stars had quit, tired of it after nine years, and several of the others had asked for enormous raises when they renewed their contracts. Some of the other writers had left too, and as usual, all of the burden of the changes had wound up on Blaire's shoulders. "Maybe I'm just over the hill," she added, sounding humorous, but something about the way she said it worried Allegra. It was what she had seen in her mother's eyes the night before too, and it scared her. She wondered if her father was aware of it, and if it concerned him.

"Don't be ridiculous, Mom. You've got another thirty or forty years of hits ahead of you," she said optimistically.

"Oh, God forbid." Blaire groaned, just thinking of it. And then she laughed and sounded like her old self again. "I think I'll shoot for another twenty and then hang it up for good."

"I'll settle for that," Allegra said, feeling better about her again, and about Brandon. She was in a much better mood than she had been the day before, and she almost wished she didn't have to leave and go to New York without seeing him. She would have loved to have spent a night with him before leaving.

She told her mother about the trip to New York, and that

she'd be back at the end of the week. She always let them know where she was going.

"We'll see you when you get back," her mother said, and thanked her for calling. And after that, Allegra called Carmen. She was not yet hysterical, but she was panicking fairly quickly. The press had laid siege to her front gate, and she said there were hordes of them, waiting to pounce on her if she moved a foot out of her house. After winning her award the night before, she was a hot item. The guards Allegra had hired were there, but Carmen was afraid the press would storm the house if she opened the gate to go out. She was a prisoner in her own home, she hadn't been able to go anywhere since that morning.

"Isn't there a back gate for deliveries?" Allegra asked, and Carmen said there was, but there were photographers waiting there too, with television cameras from several of the networks.

"Is Alan coming by?" Allegra asked her pensively, trying to figure a way out for her without a major confrontation with the media.

"We talked about going to Malibu last night, but he hasn't called, and I didn't want to bother him," Carmen said, sounding hesitant, but Allegra had an idea, and she was sure Alan wouldn't mind helping Carmen.

"Do you have any wigs that don't look like you?"

"A funny black one I wore for Halloween last year."

"Good. Hang on to it, you may need it. I'll call Alan."

And together they worked out a plan. He was going to come to the main gate, in an old truck he had and rarely drove, so no one would recognize it unless they ran the plates, and by that time they'd be gone. And Allegra suggested he wear a wig too. He had lots of them. She told him to drive to the back of the house and act like he was picking up the maid, and then just drive off again, and hopefully no one would figure out who he was, or that Carmen had left with him.

"I can let her use the house in Malibu for a few days if she wants, till things settle down again," he offered helpfully, and Allegra thought Carmen might like that.

He said he'd pick her up at one o'clock, and Allegra called to tell her, and all of a sudden Carmen was shy and embarrassed about Alan picking her up. She said she didn't want to take advantage of Alan's kindness.

"Go ahead, take advantage of him," Allegra teased. "He'd love it."

He showed up on schedule at one, they reported to her afterward, wearing a blond wig that made him look like a hippie, and the Chevy truck was so old and dilapidated that no one paid any attention to it at all when he picked up the little Mexican maid with the short black hair, wearing a tank top and bell-bottom blue jeans. She was carrying two paper shopping bags for her days off, and they went back out the gate without anyone giving them a second glance or taking a single picture. It was the perfect escape, and they called Allegra from a gas station ten minutes later.

"Well done," she congratulated them. "Now have fun, you two. And don't get into too much trouble while I'm gone." She reminded Carmen that she'd be at the Regency in New York, and back in L.A. the following weekend, and before they hung up, she thanked Alan for taking care of Carmen.

"It's not exactly a sacrifice," he said honestly to his old friend. "I'd be lying to you if I said it was," he said gently. He was surprised by how much he liked her. He had no idea where it would go between them, but he loved the idea of taking care of her in Allegra's absence. They hadn't even brought her body-guards. It was going to be just the two of them, at his beach house.

"You won't get crazy, will you? While I'm gone, I mean. She's a nice girl. . . . She's very religious, and she's a good kid. . . . She's not like the rest of the girls we know." Allegra was groping for the right words, suddenly afraid that he was going to have a wild affair with her and drop her.

"I understand that, Al. You don't need to spell it out for me. I know. I get it. I'll behave. I swear . . . more or less, anyway." He was looking at Carmen longingly as she wandered around in

her jeans and tank top just outside the phone booth. "Look, Allie
. . . she's different, I know. . . . I've never met anyone like her
. . . except maybe you, and that was a long time ago. She's kind
of the way we were when we were young, honest, sincere, un-
spoiled, before we all got cynical and grown-up, and somewhat
fucked-up by the people who didn't live up to our expectations.
I'm not going to hurt her, Al. I promise you that. I think . . .
never mind. . . . Just go to New York and mind your own business. And one of these days, when you get back, we'll have a talk
about our lives, like the old days."

"You got it. Take good care of her." It was like entrusting
him with her younger sister, but she knew what a good man he
was, and something in his voice and what he had said to her told
her that he cared about her.

"I love you, Allie. I wish *you'd* get someone who'd be good to
you one of these days, instead of that jerk with the permanent ex-
wife and the lifelong divorce. That's not going anywhere, Al, and
you know it."

"Go screw yourself," she said pleasantly, and he laughed.

"Okay. I get it. So go to New York and get laid, at least, it
might do you good."

"You're disgusting." She was laughing at him, and a minute
later they hung up, and he and Carmen took off their wigs and
drove to Malibu. And when they got there, his house was quiet
and sunny and peaceful, and completely deserted. She thought it
was the prettiest place she'd ever seen, and he was happy to be
there with her, and suddenly wished they could stay forever.

Allegra was on the way to the airport by then. She had called
Bram Morrison before she left, and left him the name of her hotel
in New York. He liked knowing where she was all the time. It was
one of his quirks. The others could all reach her, if they had to,
through the office.

She boarded the plane shortly after three o'clock, in business
class, and she sat next to an attorney she knew from a rival law
firm. Sometimes it was easy to let oneself believe that the world
was full of lawyers. It certainly seemed to be, and it was odd to

think, as she flew East, that at that moment Brandon was flying back to L.A. For the moment, at least, they certainly seemed to be going in different directions.

She read her papers for the movie deal the next day, made some notes, and even had time to read some journals. By the time they got to New York, it was just after midnight. She picked her bag off the carousel, and went outside to hail a cab, and she was surprised to find it was freezing cold. By one o'clock in the morning she was in her room at the hotel, and she was wide awake and wished she could call someone. It was only ten o'clock in L.A., but she knew Brandon wouldn't be home until eleven. So she took a shower, put on her nightgown, turned on the TV, and slipped between immaculate, crisp sheets. It was total luxury, and there was something fun and very grown-up about being in a fancy hotel in New York on business.

She wished she knew someone to call, or had friends to see. All she had planned to do in New York that week was meet the author she was seeing the next day, and then several other attorneys and agents. It was going to be a busy week, but she had nothing to do at night, except sit in the hotel and watch TV, or read her legal papers. And lying there, in the enormous bed, she felt like a kid, with a mischievous grin, eating the chocolates they had left at her bedside.

"What are you laughing at?" she asked the face she saw in the mirror when she went to brush her teeth. "Who told you you were grown-up enough to stay in a place like this, and meet with one of the most important authors in the world? What if they figure out who you are, and you're really just a dumb kid?" The idea that she had made it this far, and had so much responsibility, suddenly seemed funny to her, and she laughed again as she finished brushing her teeth, and went back to the enormous, luxurious bed, and ate the rest of the truffles.

CHAPTER 5

The alarm went off at eight o'clock the next day. It was barely light on a snowy January day in New York, and it was still five o'clock in the morning in California. Allegra turned over with a groan, and forgot where she was for a minute or two, and then she remembered the author she had to meet that morning. He was a much older man, and he was leery about anything to do with the movies. But his agent thought it would be a boost to his career at this point, since he was inevitably slowing down. And she had come to New York to help convince the author to let her pursue the deal, at the request of the agent. The agent himself was as illustrious as the people he represented, and having him ask her to come to New York to work on the deal was a feather in Allegra's cap. It was an important step toward her becoming a full partner in her law firm. But as she rolled over in bed, the prospect of meeting with either of them had very little appeal, no matter who they were or how important. It was a cold, snowy day, and she would have been happy to stay in bed all morning.

As she lay arguing with herself about getting up, her breakfast came, and with it *The New York Times* and *The Wall Street Journal*. And by the time she was drinking coffee, and eating oatmeal and croissants with jam, and glancing at the newspapers, the prospect of a day in New York seemed almost exciting. The literary agency where she was going was on Madison Avenue, and the law firm where she had meetings later that afternoon was on Wall Street. And somewhere between the two were a thousand stores, at least as many art galleries, and a plethora of fascinating people. Sometimes just being in New York was a heady experience. There were so many people doing so many interesting things, a myriad of cultural events, opera, concerts, exhibitions of all kinds, theater. It made even Los Angeles seem provincial.

She wore a black suit and a heavy coat and boots to the meeting she had at ten o'clock that morning. She arrived by cab, holding on to her handbag and her briefcase, and by the time she got inside, she was sorry she hadn't worn a hat. Her face was tingling from the cold, and her ears were frozen.

The elevator stopped at the top floor, which the agency occupied in its entirety, and on the walls were an impressive collection of Chagall, Dufy, and Picasso, some pastels, one small oil, and a series of drawings. The agency was clearly doing well. And in the center of the room was a small Rodin sculpture.

Allegra was quickly ushered in to see the head of the agency, a small, round man with the faintest of German accents. His name was Andreas Weissman.

"Miss Steinberg?" He extended a hand, looking her over with interest. Her fine, blond, Anglo-Saxon looks couldn't help but catch his attention. He thought her very beautiful, and he was intrigued by her throughout their meeting, before the arrival of the author. And then finally, an hour later, he arrived, a man of perhaps some eighty years, but as sharp as anyone half his age. Jason Haverton was quick and witty and very shrewd, and Allegra suspected from looking at him that he had once been very good-looking, and even at his age he was still very attractive. They talked about the film industry generally for about an hour, and Jason Haverton very calmly asked her if by any chance she was related to Simon Steinberg. And when she admitted that she was, Haverton told her how much he admired his movies.

The two men invited her to lunch then at La Grenouille, and it was only when the main course came that they finally got down to business. Jason Haverton admitted to her that he had done everything possible to avoid this deal, and he had no interest whatsoever in having one of his books made into a movie. He thought it was prostitution at his age, but on the other hand he wrote less often than he had in the past, his readers were no longer young, and his agent felt strongly that selling a book for film was an ideal way to expand his audience again and appeal to younger readers.

"I'm afraid I agree with him," Allegra said, smiling first at Haverton, then at Weissman. "It doesn't have to be a bad experience for you," she went on, outlining several possible avenues to minimize the stress for him and make the deal more appealing. He liked what she had to say, and he was impressed with her. She was a smart girl, and a good lawyer. And by the time the chocolate soufflé came they were fast friends, and he told her he wished he'd met her fifty years earlier. He'd had four wives, but he claimed to no longer have the energy to acquire a fifth one.

"They're so much work," he said with a twinkle in his eye that made Allegra laugh, and she could easily see why he had been so successful with women. He was intelligent and amusing, and incredibly charming. Even at his advanced age, there was something totally appealing about him. He had lived in Paris in his youth, and his first wife had been French, the next two had been British apparently, and the last one American. And she, too, had been a famous author. She had passed away a decade before, and although he had been involved with several women since, none of them had succeeded in luring him to the altar. "They take so much energy, my dear. Like fine racehorses, they're far too delicate, but so lovely to watch, and unbearably expensive. But they certainly do give one a great deal of pleasure." He smiled at her, and she could feel herself melt as she looked at him. He made her want to put her arms around him and hug him. But she suspected easily that if she had, he would have pounced on her with glee, like a cat on a mouse who had been overcome with trusting emotions for the feline. Jason Haverton was clearly no pussycat. He was still very much a lion, even at eighty. And a very attractive one. It amused Weissman to watch him pursue her. They were old and dear friends, and he couldn't disagree with Jason's opinion of her. She was an extraordinary girl, and he wouldn't have been at all surprised to hear that Jason had at least tried to woo her. But she seemed too smart for him, and although she wore no ring on her left hand, she managed to convey, from small things she said, the impression that she was taken.

"Have you always lived in L.A.?" Jason asked as they sipped their demitasse and played with the last of their soufflés. It would surprise him if she had, there was something far more sophisticated about her, which suggested Europe to him, or the East of the United States at the very least. But she did, in fact, surprise him.

"I've lived in L.A. all my life, except when I went to Yale."

"Then you must have remarkable parents," he complimented her and them, and she smiled. He already knew who her father was and he thought, looking at her, that, spiritually in any case, Allegra was very much like him. Sensitive and sincere, direct and spare with words, but not with feelings.

"My mother is a writer too," she explained. "She wrote fiction when she was very young, but she's been writing for television for years. She has a very successful show. But I think she always secretly regrets that she never went on to write a novel."

"They must be very talented," he said, far more interested in her than them, but still greatly intrigued by this beautiful young woman.

"They are talented," she smiled. "And so are you," she said, cautiously turning the conversation back to him, which pleased him most. Weissman watched her handle Haverton with both admiration and fascination. She was both wise and artful. And he said as much to her when the elderly author was finally picked up by his driver and taken home. He left, waving fondly at Allegra as though they were old friends, having agreed to most of the deal she had proposed to him. And the agent and attorney went back to Weissman's office in his limousine to discuss the fine points of the contract.

"You're very good with him," he said, intrigued by her, and

amused too. She was very young, but she was quick, and she had a natural instinct for people.

"That's what I do for a living," she said without artifice. "Handle people like him. Actors are like children most of the time."

"So are authors." Andreas smiled at her; he liked her.

They spent the next two hours working out the deal, and what they both thought Jason Haverton should get. After they worked it out, Allegra said she'd call the movie company, and let him know their reaction. Hopefully they could finish the deal that week, possibly before she left New York on Friday. In the meantime, she had several other meetings scheduled on other matters, but she would be in touch with Andreas as soon as she heard something from California about Jason's movie.

"How long will you be here?" he asked her again.

"Till Friday, unless I get everything done before that. But I think it might be a good idea for me to be here while we work this out. I'm sure we're going to be getting some answers on this deal by Wednesday, at the latest."

He nodded agreement with her, and then jotted down an address for her on a piece of paper from an Hermès scratch pad. Everything around him was of the finest quality. He was a man who liked the best of everything, even clients.

"My wife and I are having a little party tonight. One of my clients has an important new book, we think it could win a literary prize. But in any case, it's a good excuse for a small reception. I doubt if Jason will be there, but several of our clients will, and you might enjoy it." He handed the paper to her with an address on Fifth Avenue, and his home phone number, and he told her to come anytime between six and nine o'clock that evening. They would love to have her.

"That's very kind of you," she said. She'd enjoyed the time she spent with him that afternoon, and she liked the way he did business. He was sharp and precise, and beyond the polish and the European charm was a brilliant businessman who knew exactly what he was doing and stood for no nonsense. And Allegra liked that about him. She had always heard good things about him, and she had always had successful dealings with his clients.

"Try and come, you might get a taste of New York literary life, which could amuse you."

She thanked him again, and left his office a few minutes later. It had been a surprisingly pleasant afternoon. When she got out on the street, the snow had already turned to slush, and she slid slowly to the curb and hailed a cab to take her back to her hotel to make the calls she had to make to California.

It was five o'clock by the time she'd made all her calls from her hotel room, to begin the negotiations for Haverton's film deal. And an hour later, after she'd made some notes, she still hadn't decided whether to order room service or go to the party at the Weissmans'. It was freezing cold outside and she had brought nothing to wear except business suits and two wool dresses, and the idea of going out in the cold again was extremely unappealing. But on the other hand, meeting some of the local literary types seemed almost worth going out into the cold for. She thought about it for another half hour, as she watched the news, and then she got up hurriedly and went to the closet. She had decided to go to the Weissmans' party. She put on her only black wool dress. It had a high neck and long sleeves, and it was very flattering as it hugged her figure. She put on high heels and brushed her hair, and appraised what she saw in the mirror. Compared to the New York sophisticates, she was afraid she'd look like a bumpkin. The only jewelry she had brought with her was a gold bracelet her mother had given her, and a pair of plain gold earrings. She swept her hair back into a neat French twist, and put on some lipstick, before putting on her heavy coat again. It was an old one she had worn while she was in law school, whenever she went to the theater, but at least it was warm, even if it wasn't pretty.

She went down to the lobby and the doorman got her a cab, and by seven-thirty she was at Eighty-second Street and Fifth Avenue, right across from the Metropolitan Museum. It was a handsome old apartment building with a doorman and two elevator men, several big, dark red velvet couches, and a Persian-looking rug that kept her high heels from echoing on the marble floor of the lobby. The doorman told her that Weissman was on fourteen, and half a dozen people stepped out of the elevator as she got in it. They all looked like they had just come from the Weissmans' party, and she wondered if she was too late. But Andreas had said up to nine o'clock, and as soon as she got upstairs, she followed the noise. It was still very loud, so at least she knew the party was still going. She rang the bell, and a butler answered. At first glance, she could see that there were well over a hundred people there, and she could hear a piano playing somewhere in the distance.

She stepped inside and gave up her coat, as she looked around at the hallway of the elegant duplex. But it was the people who caught her eye. They looked totally New York in cocktail dresses and dark gray suits, a few tweeds, and everyone seemed to have excited eyes and looked alive, and as though they had a thousand stories to tell about a million places they'd been to. This was definitely not laid-back California. And for once there were no famous faces she recognized. She knew that the faces she was looking at were probably just as well-known, but in a different world from Hollywood, and they were intriguing to her because she didn't know them. She realized that she probably knew most of their names, and then as she looked around she saw Tom Wolfe and Norman Mailer, Barbara Walters and Dan Rather and Joan Lunden, and an array of illustrious figures sprinkled in among publishers and editors, professors, and writers. And there was a small group who someone said were curators from the Metropolitan Museum. The head of Christie's was there, and a handful of important artists. It was the kind of gathering that never happened in L.A., because there wasn't the available variety of important eclectic figures. In Los Angeles it was all people involved in "the industry," as it was called, as though they made automobiles instead of movies. But in New York it was everything from theatrical designers, to actors from off-off-Broadway, to the heads of department stores, and important jewelers, mixed in with editors and writers and playwrights. It was a fascinating mix, and Allegra watched them all as she took a glass of champagne from a passing tray and was relieved to see Andreas Weissman in the distance. She made her way toward him in the library as he stood in front of the view of Central Park, talking to his arch competitor in the literary world, Morton Janklow. They were talking about a mutual friend, who had been one of Weissman's clients, and had recently died. It was a great loss to the literary community, they agreed, just as Andreas spotted Allegra, and came to greet her. In her black dress, and her upswept hair, she looked more serious than she had that afternoon. She looked incredibly beautiful and young, as Andreas Weissman watched her. She had a lovely, graceful way as she moved slowly toward him, holding her glass of champagne. Everything about the way she moved was elegant and fluid, it made him think of the ballet, and Degas paintings. Jason Haverton was right, Andreas Weissman thought with a private smile. He had called late that afternoon to say again that she was not only a good lawyer, but he thought she was exquisite. He had loved having lunch with her, and told Andreas that if it had been only a few years before, things might have been different. He said it in a wistful way that made his agent smile, even now, as he extended a hand toward Allegra. She seemed to inspire fire in men's hearts, even in the depths of winter.

"I'm so glad you could come, Allegra." He carefully put an arm around her shoulders and guided her across the room to where another knot of guests stood. There were more faces she recognized, an important gallery owner she'd read about, a famous model, and a young artist. It was an incredibly mixed group, and exactly what she loved about New York. It was why people in New York never wanted to leave and come West. New York was much too exciting. Andreas introduced her around the room and explained to everyone that she was an entertainment lawyer from L.A., and everyone seemed happy to meet her.

Andreas disappeared then, and left her with her new friends. An older woman challenged her, and said she moved like a dancer. Allegra admitted to having done eight years of ballet as a child, and someone else asked if she was an actress. Two very handsome young men said they worked with Lehman Brothers on Wall Street. Several more worked at a law firm where she'd interviewed while she was at Yale. And her head was spinning by the time she made her way upstairs to the upper floor to see the spectacular view of the park, and meet more guests, and then came back to the lower floor again at nine o'clock. The party was still going strong, and a fresh group that looked like businessmen had just arrived, accompanied by an equal number of well-dressed women. Some of them had on fur hats, and all of them had perfectly done hair. It was a different look from L.A., with its face-lifts and its youthful look and its blond hair; this was a darker look, a more interesting one, with less artifice and less makeup, but with expensive clothes, a smattering of jewels, and serious, intense faces. There were a handful of face-lifts too, and bodies so thin they looked like pencils, but for the most part these were people accomplishing things, and affecting the world just because they'd been there. Allegra was fascinated by them, and the things they were saying. They talked about interesting things, and they were in fact interesting people.

"It's quite something, isn't it?" a voice said just behind her, and she turned to see a man watching her, just as she had been scrutinizing the others around the room. He was long and lean, with dark hair, and the aristocratic look of a true New Yorker. And he was wearing the right uniform, a white shirt, dark suit, and conservative Hermès tie in two shades of navy, but something about him didn't match the way he looked. She wasn't sure if it was his tan, the spark in his eye, or the broad smile. In some ways, he looked more California than New York, and yet he didn't fit that description either. She couldn't figure him out, but as he sized her up, he was mystified by her as well. She seemed to fit in, yet there was something about her that made him think she didn't belong here. He liked coming to the Weissmans'—he always met the most fascinating people, from ballet dancers to literary agents to venture capitalists to conductors. It was fun just mingling with them, and trying to guess why they had come and who they were.

He was doing that now, and getting nowhere. Allegra could have been anything from decorator to doctor. She was trying to guess what he did too, and she was debating between stockbroker and banker. And as she looked at him pensively, he smiled broadly.

"I was just trying to figure out what you do, who you are, and where you come from," he confessed. "I love playing that game here, and I always manage to guess wrong. You're probably a dancer, judging by the way you move and stand, but I guessed copywriter at Doyle Dane. How bad am I?"

"Pretty bad," she laughed, amused by his game, as he was pushed a little closer to her by the crowd. He looked as though he had a good sense of humor, and he seemed totally relaxed with her as he looked her straight in the eye. "Maybe you're not too far off. I am in business, and I do a lot of writing. I'm an attorney," she said, returning his gaze, and he seemed surprised.

"What kind of firm?" He pressed on, enjoying their guessing game. He loved figuring out what people did, and in New York, there was such a rich assortment of jobs and people. There was never a simple answer to any question, least of all to what one did. He guessed silently again, and figured corporate law. "I guess corporate, or probably something very serious like antitrust law. Am I right?" It seemed incongruous to him because she was very feminine and very pretty, and he liked the combination of a beautiful woman involved in serious business.

She laughed in answer, and he loved watching her. She had a gorgeous smile, incredible hair, and there was an immediate warmth about her. He could tell she liked people, and there was something very intriguing about her eyes. They said a lot to him about who she was and what she thought about. She was a woman of principle, he could tell, and firm beliefs, and probably strong opinions. But she obviously had a sense of humor too. She laughed a lot, and there was something very gentle and feminine about the way she moved her hands. And her mouth looked delicious.

"What makes you think I'm such a serious lawyer?" she asked, laughing again. They didn't even know each other's names, but that seemed relatively unimportant. She liked talking to him, and playing his game about what she did, and who she was. "Do I look that intense?" she asked, curious as to how he would answer, and he considered her for a moment, tilting his head as he looked her over, and then he shook his head. And she couldn't help noticing that he had a great smile. He was very handsome.

"I was wrong." He corrected himself thoughtfully. "You're a serious person, but you're not in a serious branch of law. How's that for an odd combination? Maybe you only represent prizefighters or skiers. Am I right?" He was teasing her and she laughed.

"Why did you decide that I'm not in corporate or anti-trust?"

"You're not boring. You're serious and conscientious, but there's a lot of laughter in your eyes. Antitrust guys never laugh. So, was I right? Are you in sports law? . . . Oh, Jesus, don't tell me it's P.I. or malpractice. I'd hate to think of you doing work like that." He winced as he set his empty glass down, and she grinned at him. It had been fun for a while, and she felt surprisingly at ease with him as she looked him in the eye.

"I'm in entertainment law, in Los Angeles. I came here to talk to Mr. Weissman about one of his clients, and see some of our other contacts here. I represent people in show business generally, writers, producers, directors, actors."

"Interesting, very interesting," he said, looking her over again, as though trying to decide if the information all fit together. "And you're from L.A.?" He looked as though he was surprised when she said she was.

"All my life, except for seven years at Yale."

"I went to a rival school," he said, and she held up a hand.

"Wait. It's my turn now. This one's easy. You went to Harvard. You're from the East, probably from New York, or"—she squinted as she looked at him—"maybe Connecticut or Boston. And you went to boarding school . . . let's see, Exeter, or St. Paul's." He was laughing at the profile she was describing, ultra-conservative, ultrapredictable, totally upper-crust New York. He wasn't sure if the dark suit had done it, or the Hermès tie, or maybe a recent haircut.

"You're close. I am from New York. I went to Andover. And I did go to Harvard. I taught at Stanford for a year, and now I'm—" She interrupted him and held up her hand again, as she looked him over. He didn't look like a professor, unless he taught in the business school, but he seemed too young and good-looking for that. If she'd been in L.A., she would have thought he was an actor, but he also looked too intelligent and not self-centered enough to be an actor.

"It's my turn again," she reminded him. "You've already told me too much. You probably teach literature at Columbia. But to be honest, I thought you were a banker when we first met." He looked very Wall Street, and very respectable, except for the mischief in his eyes.

"It's the suit." He smiled, looking a little like her brother. He was almost as tall, and in an odd way, he reminded her of her father too. There was something familiar about his smile. "I bought the suit to please my mother. She said I needed something respectable to wear if I was going to come back to New York."

"Have you been away?" she asked. He still hadn't told her if he was a banker or a professor, and they were both enjoying the sparring, as the crowd finally began to thin out. There had been almost two hundred people milling around the Weissmans' elegant apartment, and it seemed almost empty now with roughly half that.

"I've been away for six months, working somewhere else," he gave her a clue. "I hate to tell you where." He was highly amused by the things they had said about each other, and she was still trying to figure where he had been, and what he'd been doing.

"You've been teaching in Europe?" He shook his head. "Teaching anywhere?" She was looking puzzled now. Maybe the suit had misled her. When she looked at his eyes, she could see that he had imagination, and he obviously liked assembling facts.

"No teaching in a long time. But you're not far off. Shall I tell you?"

"I guess so. I give up. It's all your mother's fault. I think the suit confused me," she said lightheartedly, and they both laughed.

"I can see why. It confuses me too. When I looked in the mirror tonight, I had no idea who I was. Actually, I'm a writer—you know, torn running shoes, English carpet slippers, old bathrobes, faded jeans, and Harvard sweatshirts with holes everywhere."

"I figured you were that type." He looked great in the suit though, and she suspected that there was more in his wardrobe than torn sweatshirts. He was a terrific-looking guy, and she guessed him to be about thirty-five. He was actually thirty-four, and had sold his first book to the movies the year before. His second book had just come out, and was getting splendid reviews, and selling very well, actually much to his surprise. It was very literary, but it had been something he felt he had to write. Andreas Weissman had been trying to convince him that his real talent lay in commercial fiction, and he was about to begin writing his third book, and trying to broaden his horizons.

"So where have you been for six months? Writing on a beach in the Bahamas somewhere?" It seemed very romantic to her, and all he could do was laugh at the suggestion.

"A beach, but not the Bahamas. I've been living in Los Angeles for six months, in Malibu, adapting my first book for a movie. I was crazy enough to agree to write the screenplay and coproduce it, something I probably wouldn't do again, though I'm sure no one will ever ask me. A friend of mine from Harvard is producing it with me, and directing."

"Did you just move back?" It seemed so odd that he should be here, and they should meet, after he'd been in L.A. for six months. It was strange that among all the people there that night they had singled each other out. Both of them freshly arrived from California, drawn to each other like magnets.

"I'm here for a week," he explained, "to see my agent. I have an idea for a third book, and if I ever finish this damn screenplay

I'm working on, I'm going to lock myself up for a year and write it. I've already had an offer to do a screenplay on the second one, but I'm not even sure I want to do it. I'm not sure if I'm cut out for Hollywood, or the film business. I've been trying to decide if I just want to come back to New York and stick to writing books from now on, and forget the movies. I haven't made up my mind yet. For the moment, my life is a little schizophrenic."

"There's no reason why you can't do both. You don't even have to write the screenplays yourself if you don't want to. Sell the books, and let someone else do that, it would give you more time to write your novel." She felt as though she were advising one of her clients, and he smiled at the serious look in her eyes.

"And if they butcher the book?" he asked, looking worried, and as she saw the expression in his eyes, she had to laugh.

"Spoken just like a writer. The agonies of giving your baby up to strangers. I can't guarantee you it's without problems, but sometimes it's less stressful than writing the screenplay yourself, not to mention coproducing."

"I can believe that. Walking on nails is less stressful. The people out there drive me crazy. They have no regard whatsoever for the writing. All they care about are the cast, and maybe the director. The script means absolutely nothing to them. As far as they're concerned, it's just words. They cheat, they lie, they tell you anything that suits them just to get what they want. I think I'm getting used to it now, God forbid. But at first they really drove me nuts."

"It sounds like you need a good attorney in L.A., or maybe a local agent to give you a hand. You should have Andreas refer you to someone at CAA," she said practically, as he smiled and held out a hand to her.

"Maybe I should call you," he said, finding the idea very appealing. "I haven't even introduced myself. Here I am, complaining at you, I'm really sorry. I'm Jeff Hamilton." She met his eyes and smiled, as they stood very close to each other in the thinning crowd at the Weissmans' party. She recognized his name as soon as he said it.

"I read your first book. I liked it very much." It had been quite serious, and at times very funny. But it had made an impression on her, and she'd remembered it, which said something. "I'm Allegra Steinberg," she supplied.

"No relation to the producer, I assume," he said casually, still amused by the game they'd been playing, and the fact that they both lived in L.A. But she corrected him quickly. She was proud of her family, although she never rested on their laurels.

"Simon Steinberg is my father," she said calmly.

"He passed on my first book, but I liked him a lot. He spent a whole afternoon in his office telling me what was wrong with it as a screenplay. And the funny thing was that I realized he was right. Eventually I made a lot of the changes he suggested. I've always wanted to call and thank him, but somehow I never got the chance."

"He's very smart about a lot of things," she smiled. "He's given me some pretty good advice over the years."

"I can imagine that." He could imagine a lot of things, but one of them was seeing her again after that night. She was starting to look around by then; she realized that another several dozen guests had left while she and Jeff were talking. "I guess I'd better go," she said regretfully. It was long after nine o'clock, which was supposed to be the end of the party.

"Where are you staying?" he asked, anxious not to let her slip away. There was something very unusual about her, and he had to resist an urge to reach out and touch her.

"I'm at the Regency. What about you?"

"I'm spoiled. I'm staying at my mother's apartment here in town. She's away on a cruise until February. It's quiet, but very convenient. It's just a few blocks from here." He followed her casually to the foyer, along with half a dozen other guests. She claimed her heavy coat again, and he took his off a rack, with a long wool scarf. "Can I give you a lift somewhere?" he asked hopefully, after they thanked Mrs. Weissman for the party. Andreas was upstairs, deep in conversation with two young authors, looking as though he didn't want to be disturbed, so they left him, and went back downstairs.

"I'm just going back to the hotel," she said as they got in the elevator and started down. "I'll take a cab." They crossed the lobby side by side, feeling comfortable together. He held the door for her, followed her out, and then gently took her arm. It was snowing again outside and the ground was very slippery.

"Would you like to go for a drink someplace? A hamburger maybe? It's early, and I'd love to talk to you for a while. I hate meeting someone like this, getting all excited about them, and then suddenly they're gone. It seems so futile somehow. All that energy and excitement for nothing." He looked at her hopefully, and he seemed very young. But there was something about her that fascinated him. He had no idea what it was, but she felt drawn to him as well. They both lived in Los Angeles; they were in related fields; they seemed to have a lot in common. But whatever it was, he didn't want to leave her yet, and she had no desire to go back to the hotel. It would have seemed so lonely after talking to him. And now they stood outside, watching the snow, her hand tucked in his arm.

"I've got some contracts with me I ought to read," she said unenthusiastically. They had faxed her a whole bunch of them that afternoon for Malachi O'Donovan's next tour. But she could always do them later. This seemed so much more important. It was as though she and Jeff Hamilton still had things to find out about each other, a story to tell, a mission to accomplish. "Actually, I'd love something to eat. The hamburger you mentioned sounds fine."

He looked pleased, and hailed a cab. They got one instantly, and he gave the driver the address of Elaine's. While he had been living in New York and writing his first book, he had often gone there. And whenever he was back now, he liked to stop by, in memory of old times.

"I was afraid you wouldn't want to go out," he admitted to her, looking handsome and boyish, his eyes bright, and with snowflakes in his hair. Going out with her meant a lot to him. He wanted to know more about her, her job, her life, the father he had met months before. He wondered why their paths had never crossed in L.A. It was as though they had had to come here to meet each other, and he was very glad they had, like two planets, finally colliding.

"I don't go out very often," she explained when he said as much to her. "I work all the time. My clients expect a lot from me." Too much, according to Brandon, who hated the extent of the service she gave them. But it was part of her, part of who she was, and she liked it.

"I never go anywhere," he mused as they headed east in the cab. "Most of the time, I write at night. I like living in Malibu. Sometimes I walk on the beach late at night. It clears the head. Where do you live?" He was curious about her, and he hoped to see more of her, even before they left New York.

"I live in Beverly Hills. I have a funny little house I bought when I came back from Yale. It's small, but it's perfect for me. It's got a great view, and a Japanese garden that's mostly rocks, so I can't kill anything. And when I have to, I just lock the door and leave." She smiled at him. "Like now."

"Do you travel much?" he asked, and she shook her head.

"I try to be there as much as I can for my clients. Except when I need to be with them somewhere else. Two of my current clients are musicians. Sometimes I meet them on their concert tours here and there for a day or two. But mostly I'm in L.A." She had already promised Bram Morrison that she would try to fly in to see him on his tour. And if Mal O'Donovan wanted her to, she'd do it for him as well. They were both long, arduous tours, and she'd be traveling halfway around the world to hold their hands from Bangkok to the Philippines to Paris.

"Would I know any of them?" he asked, intrigued again. She spoke of them as though they were sacred people she had vowed to protect from harm, and in some ways, she had.

"Some."

"Are you allowed to say who they are?" he asked, as he paid the fare and they walked into Elaine's. It was crowded and loud, but the maître d' recognized him immediately and signaled that they'd have a table for him in a few minutes. "So who are these clients you're so devoted to?" The way he said it made her feel as though he understood how she felt about them. And that didn't surprise him about her. It was a far cry from Brandon taking her to task for every spare moment she gave her clients.

"You probably know most of them, and quite a few of them are pretty open about who their lawyers are. I can tell you those. Bram Morrison, and Malachi O'Donovan is a client now. Carmen Connors, Alan Carr off and on. To name a few." She was proud of them, like a mother hen, and as Jeff watched her, he understood something about her, and about how loyal and protective she was, and he admired that part too.

"Are you saying that they are represented by your firm, or those are personally some of your clients?" The names seemed too important for someone as young as she was. She looked about twenty-five. But she laughed at his question, and he realized that he loved it when she laughed.

"No, those are my clients, specifically," she explained. "There are others too, of course, but I'm not free to disclose those names. I think Bram would tell anyone who his doctor was, and Mal is pretty free about it as well. And Carmen tells the newspapers who represents her all the time." She looked very matter-of-fact as she mentioned their names. They were the people who filled her life.

"My God, that's quite a group, Allegra. You should be very proud of yourself," he said admiringly. "How long have you been with the firm?" Maybe she was a lot older than she looked, he mused, but she laughed, reading his mind.

"Four years. I'm twenty-nine. Thirty pretty soon, much too soon for me," she complained, and he smiled at her.

"I'm thirty-four, and you make me feel like I've been asleep for the last ten years. That's quite a load you're juggling, and they can't be easy people to represent."

"Some of them are," she said, always anxious to be fair. "And don't be ridiculous, you've written two books and you're about to start a third, and you're writing a screenplay, and coproducing a movie. What have I done? Nothing but represent a bunch of talented people, people like you. I write their contracts, I negotiate for them, I do their trusts and wills. I protect them whenever I get the chance. I suppose that's creative in a way, but let's be honest here, nothing like what you do. So don't feel sorry for yourself," she chided him. The truth was they were both accomplished people and they both loved what they did.

"Maybe I need your services," he said thoughtfully, thinking of his last conversation with Andreas Weissman only that morning. "If I'm going to sell another book to Hollywood, I should have an entertainment lawyer look at the contracts, at least."

"What did you do last time?" she inquired, curious about what Weissman did for him.

"Andreas handled it all from here. It was pretty straightforward, and I can't say I got screwed. The deal was for me to get a fixed amount to write the screenplay, and I'll get a percentage of the gross, if the movie makes it. Since I'm producing it with a friend, I didn't want to get too aggressive. I did it more for the experience than the money. I seem to make that mistake a lot," he grinned, but he didn't look as though he was starving. The suit he was wearing was expensive. "If I do this again," he went on, "I want to get more out of it economically, and give up a lot less of my life to do it."

"I'd be happy to look at the contracts for you anytime." She smiled, and he looked as though he liked that idea. A lot, actually.

"I'd like that very much." Jeff smiled at her, wondering why Andreas had never mentioned her, or offered to introduce them. In fact, it had never occurred to Andreas that his protégé, his young star writer, would take a shine to the beautiful blond attorney from L.A.

They sat at a back table at Elaine's and talked for hours, about Harvard and Yale, and his two years at Oxford. He had hated it at first, and eventually came to love it. His father had died while he was there, and he had started writing seriously after that. He talked about his mother's disappointment in him for not becoming an attorney like his father, or better yet, a doctor like her own.

He described her as very strong, and very much a Puritan and a Yankee. She had definite ideas about work ethics and responsibility. And she still felt that writing wasn't a serious job for a man.

"My mother's a writer," Allegra explained, talking about her parents again, surprised at how much she suddenly wanted to share with Jeff. There was so much to talk about, so much she wanted to tell him. It was as though she had waited all her life for him to be her friend. He was so totally in tune with what she felt and what she thought. He was so understanding. Neither of them could believe it was one o'clock in the morning the next time they looked up. "I love the way the law works," she'd been saying to him, "the sheer logic of it, and the satisfaction of solving problems. It drives me to distraction sometimes"—she smiled across the table at him, unaware that they were holding hands—"but it's really what I love most." There was fire in her eyes as she said it, and he loved looking at her. He couldn't remember feeling that way about anyone on the first date in his entire lifetime.

"What else do you love, Allegra?" he asked gently. "Dogs? Kids? The usual?"

"All of that, I guess. My family. They mean everything to me." He was an only child and he envied the stories she told about Sam and Scott and her parents. He envied her in many ways. His own family life had dissipated after his father died, and his mother was not a warm person. But it was easy to see that Simon Steinberg was a warm, loving man. "You'll have to come and meet them sometime," Allegra said kindly. "And Alan, he's my oldest friend. Alan Carr." She wanted to introduce him to everyone, like a little kid with a new best friend.

"Oh, no." Like everyone, he reacted immediately to the name. It was impossible not to. "He's your *oldest* friend? I don't believe you," he teased.

"He was my high school sweetheart, sophomore year. We've been best friends ever since." It was odd how easily Jeff seemed to fit into all of it—he liked hearing about her work, her family, her friends. It was all so unlike her exchanges with Brandon, and yet she knew that comparing Brandon to a stranger wasn't fair. She knew nothing of Jeff's quirks, his foibles and failures. And yet she was so comfortable with him. It was very odd. And he loved her directness and total lack of pretension. She was the kind of woman he had always admired, and he hadn't met anyone like her in a long time. But as he looked at her, as the evening drew to a close, Jeff knew there was an important question he hadn't asked her. At first, he had told himself he didn't want to know, but he realized now that he should ask her.

"Is there a man in your life, Allegra? A serious one, I mean. Other than Alan Carr." He smiled, trembling slightly in anticipation of her answer.

She hesitated for a long time, not completely sure what to say. He had a right to know. Or did he? They had spent a lot of hours talking to each other. They were obviously powerfully attracted, but there was no denying that Brandon was an important factor in her life, and she knew she ought to tell Jeff about him.

"There is," she said sadly, looking into Jeff's eyes.

"I was afraid of that. I'm not really surprised, only regretful." He didn't look as though he were about to run out the door into the night. "Are you happy with him?" That was an important question. If she was, he was out. He was willing to fight for what he wanted, but he wasn't stupid or crazy, or anxious to get hurt.

"Sometimes I am," she said fairly.

"And when you're not happy with him, why is that?" he asked her very gently, anxious to know if there was still a chance for him. If not, it hadn't been time wasted. He would always be glad they had met. He had thoroughly enjoyed her.

"He's had a difficult time," Allegra explained, always anxious to make excuses for him, and surprised at how often she had to. "He's going through some rough times. He's getting divorced. Or actually," she went on, as Jeff watched her. And there was something about the way she looked and what she said that didn't match up for him. "Actually, he's separated. He hasn't filed yet." She didn't know why she told Jeff that, but it was part of the story, and at the way she said it, he looked up at her with a question.

"How long has it been?" It was as though he knew this was the key to the story; she had thrown it to him, and he had picked it up and now he was examining it carefully.

"It's been two years," she said quietly.

"Does that bother you?"

"Sometimes. Though not as much as it seems to bother everyone else. They've been arguing over property for two years. Actually, what bothers me is that there are still some things in the relationship that need to be worked out."

"Like what?"

"He still needs to keep his distance," she said honestly. "He's afraid to make a commitment, which is probably why he hasn't filed for divorce. If you get too close to him, in small, subtle ways, he backs off. He says he was traumatized by being forced into marriage the first time, and I understand that, but somehow I don't understand why, after all this time, I should still pay for it. It's not my fault."

"I lived with a woman like that once," Jeff said quietly, remembering a writer in Vermont who had made him desperately unhappy. "I've never been so lonely in my life."

"I know," Allegra said softly, not wanting to betray Brandon to Jeff. She loved him. She wanted to marry him. And it didn't seem fair to talk about him to someone else. And yet, she knew she had to. She needed to tell Jeff what her relationship with Brandon was all about. She felt as though she owed it to him, even though she had only met him that night.

"Does he have kids?"

"Two. Two girls. He's very close to them, and they're adorable. Nine and eleven. He spends a lot of time with them in San Francisco."

"And you go too?"

"When I can. I work a lot of weekends, depending on what's happening with my clients, who's having death threats, doing a film, making a new deal, going on tour." They kept her busy, but he was sure that Brandon's frequent absences contributed to her loneliness too.

"You don't mind him going alone?"

"I can't help it if I can't go. He has a right to see his children." She sounded defensive, but he was more intrigued by what he was hearing. He suspected she wasn't happy with this man, but she wouldn't even admit it to herself yet.

"You're not worried about his hanging on to his wife for that long?" he asked her openly, and she frowned.

"You sound just like my sister."

"What does your family think?"

"They're not crazy about him," she answered with a sigh, and he was beginning to like what he was hearing. She may have been in love with him at one point, but it was by no means a done deal. Not with a girl like this one. She deserved so much more than this, and her family's approval counted for a lot with her. It was easy for anyone to see that. "I don't think they understand," Allegra complained. "After everything he went through, Brandon has a problem with commitment. That doesn't mean he doesn't care. It just means he can't give what everyone else expects him to."

"What about you? What do you expect?" he asked her gently.

"What my parents have," she said, without thinking. "That kind of warmth and love for each other and their kids."

"Do you think he'll give you that?" Jeff asked, taking her hand in his again, and she didn't take it away. He reminded her of a number of people she loved, her father, Scott, even Alan. But not Brandon. Brandon was cool, and removed, and afraid to be forced to give. Jeff seemed willing to give openly. He didn't seem to hold back. He wasn't afraid of her, or of what she might feel, or even of what he might feel if he got to know her. He seemed so willing to stand next to her, to be intimate, she could hear the words ring in her head as she thought of Dr. Green, and she smiled at Jeff for no reason. But he repeated his question. "Do you think Brandon will give you what you want, Allegra?" That was important for him to know.

"I don't know," she said honestly. "I think he'll try." Or would he? How hard had he really tried so far?

"How long are you willing to give it?" he asked, and she was startled by his question. Dr. Green had asked her that as well, and she'd never been able to answer.

But she wanted Jeff to know how she felt. She didn't want to mislead him. "I love him, Jeff. It may not be perfect, but I accept him the way he is. I've waited for two years, and I can wait longer if I have to."

"You may have to wait a long time," he said thoughtfully as they left the restaurant. It was easy to see that the relationship was troubled, but equally so to see that Allegra wasn't ready to let go yet. But Jeff was a patient man and he wondered if their paths had crossed for a reason. And as they waited for a cab in the snow, he put an arm around her and held her close.

"What about you?" she asked, as they waited in the cold, side by side, stamping their feet in the snow. "Who is there in your life?"

"My cleaning lady, Guadaloupe, my dentist in Santa Monica, and my typist, Rosie," he said, and she smiled.

"They sound like a good group." She looked up at him, amused at the descriptions. "And that's it? No gorgeous young starlet, hanging from your every word, watching you type by candlelight, and waiting for you to finish work?"

"Not lately." He smiled again. There had been serious women in his life, and two he'd lived with. But no one in a long time. The only hurdle they had to overcome was Brandon, and Jeff wasn't quite sure how to do that.

A cab came by finally and they got in, relieved that it was cozy and warm. He gave the driver the address of the Regency, and as they took off, he pulled her closer, and neither of them spoke as they rode along and watched the snow swirl around them.

The ride to the hotel was too brief, and they were both sorry when they reached it. But it was so late by then that even the bar was closed. It was just after two o'clock, and she didn't want to invite him to her room, and give him the wrong impression, so they said good-bye downstairs in the lobby.

"I had a great time, Jeff," she said wistfully. "Thank you for a wonderful evening."

"I had a good time too. For the first time in my life, I really feel as though I owe something to Andreas Weissman." They both laughed when he walked her to the elevator. "How does the rest of your week look?" he asked hopefully, and she shook her head with a look of disappointment.

"Pretty busy." For the next four days she had lunches and meetings. She had to work on Bram's concert tour and see Jason Haverton again. The only free time she had was in the evening, but at night she'd been planning to work.

"How about tomorrow night?" he asked hopefully, and she hesitated. She really shouldn't.

"I've got meetings at a law firm on Wall Street till five, and a drink with an attorney here after that. I don't think I'll even be free till seven," she said regretfully. She wanted to see him again, but she wasn't sure if she should because of Brandon either. But on the other hand, she told herself, there was no reason why they couldn't be friends.

"Why don't I call you? See how tired you are. Maybe we could just eat something here, or go for a walk. I'd really like to see you," he said, looking at her, and she felt his meaning somewhere deep in her soul. He was asking, and he was definite, but he wasn't pushing.

"You don't think it would be confusing, Jeff?" she asked softly. She didn't want to be unfair to anyone, not to him, or Brandon, or herself.

"It doesn't have to be, as long as we know where things stand," he said honestly. "I won't press you. But I'd still like to see you again."

"So would I," she nodded, and then the elevator came and they said good night.

"I'll call you tomorrow at seven," he reminded her with a wave as the doors closed, and as she rode upstairs, all she could think about was Jeff. She wondered if she had been unfaithful to Brandon, just being with him, and talking about the things they had. She wouldn't have liked it if Brandon went out to dinner with another woman, and yet there had been something so seemingly predestined about this night. It was as though she had been meant to meet him, as though she needed him in her life, and they were meant to be friends. He understood so much of what she was saying, everything in fact, and she sensed what he thought too, almost before he said it.

She let herself into her room, still feeling faintly guilty, and there was a message from Brandon under the door, which seemed like a reminder of real life. She thought about calling him, and hesitated because of the hour, but it was only eleven-fifteen in San Francisco, and then, finally, she took off her coat, sat down, and dialed him. He answered on the second ring. He was working on his material for the trial the next day, and he sounded surprised that she was calling so late. But he seemed glad to hear her.

"Where were you tonight?" He sounded more curious than angry.

"I was at the home of Haverton's agent. It broke up very late. In New York these literary types go all night." It was a lie, but she didn't want to tell him she'd gone to Elaine's, and have to explain to him who Jeff was. She'd been honest with Jeff, and told him that she was seriously involved. That was all that was important, and all that she owed Brandon. Nothing had happened. She didn't have to tell him about Jeff.

"Are you having a good time?" he inquired with a yawn. He had been working for hours on the trial.

"How's it going?"

"Very slowly. We're just starting to pick the jury. I wish the guy would just plead so we could all go home." He hadn't liked this case right from the beginning.

"How long do you think it'll take if he doesn't?"

"A couple of weeks, max. That's long enough." They were

covering a vast amount of material and Brandon was using three assistants. It was white-collar crime at its most complicated.

"I'll be home before you finish, at least."

"I'll probably have to work this weekend," he said, matter-of-factly, but she had expected that. She'd have to go into the office Saturday anyway to catch up, and maybe she could talk him into relaxing a little on Sunday.

"Don't worry about it. I'll be home Friday night." She was booked on a six o'clock flight, and she'd be home by ten California time. Maybe she'd even go to his place and surprise him.

"I'll catch up with you sometime over the weekend," he said coolly, and it reminded her of her conversation with Jeff as they left Elaine's. She hated it when Brandon made a point of keeping her at a distance. "I'll call you tomorrow night," he said mechanically. "Will you be in this time?"

"I have a business dinner actually," she lied for the second time. "Why don't I call you when I get back? I don't think it'll be late." She couldn't stay out till two every night, or she'd be too exhausted to work, and she was sure that Jeff understood that. Tonight had been a rare thing, one of those unusual meetings of the soul where two people discover that they have a million feelings and ideas in common. But it couldn't go on night after night.

"Don't work too hard," Brandon said briefly, and hung up, telling her he had to go back to work on his trial. There had been no "I love you. . . . I miss you." No promise to meet her at the airport or at home when she got back. It reminded her all over again of how tenuous their situation was, and yet, in spite of that, she always hung on, because she loved him. What was she waiting for? she asked herself. What did she think was going to change? As Jeff had said, she might have to wait for a long, long time. Maybe forever.

She walked slowly into the bedroom, thinking of Brandon, and the good times they'd had. There had been a lot of them in two years, but what she didn't let herself think about were the disappointments, like tonight. There had been plenty of those, moments when he couldn't be there for her, in soul or body.

Moments when he didn't say the words she needed to hear, or when he didn't come to the events that mattered to her, like the Golden Globes. She wondered if she was thinking of them now because she was angry, or because she had met Jeff and she wanted him to be right for her, and Brandon wrong. Did she want him to be everything Brandon wasn't? Was he a fantasy, and was she only imagining their similarities? She stood there, with none of the answers, thinking of both of them, as she looked out the window.

CHAPTER 6

On Tuesday, when Allegra got up when the alarm rang at eight o'clock, New York was covered with a blanket of snow. It looked like mounds of whipped cream sitting on Park Avenue, and there were already children leaping and sliding, and throwing snowballs at each other as they walked to school. From her vantage point far above, it looked like fun, and she wished she could be there with them.

She spent the day in meetings, and just to be sure she was all right, she called Carmen Connors.

The housekeeper was out, the answering machine was on, and Allegra could only assume that she was either shopping or out of town. She left a message for her, hoping that everything was fine, and called Alice to make sure there had been no messages from her, no further threats, or problems.

"Not a sound since you left." In fact, all of her clients had been quiet. Mal O'Donovan had left a message that he was drying out again, and Alan had left a message for her to call him when she got back to town, but not before. And other than that, everything was in order. "How's New York?" Alice asked.

"Very white," Allegra responded.

"Not for long." It would all be black, and slush by the next morning, but it was pretty in the meantime.

Allegra had lunch with an attorney she'd been correspond-

ing with for a year, at the World Trade Center, and she spent the
rest of the afternoon with Bram's promoters, and two more lawyers. After that, she hurried back to the hotel for a meeting with
another lawyer. It was about a licensing agreement for Carmen.
Someone wanted to do a perfume and use her name, but Allegra
was not enthused about it. The product was not high-end, and
Carmen had no intention of sitting around department stores,
selling perfume. The more Allegra heard about it, the less she
liked it. And at six-thirty, she was back in her room, exhausted. It
was snowing again, and traffic had been a nightmare all day. It
had taken her an hour to get back from Wall Street for her
meeting at the hotel. And the prospect of going anywhere in the
mess outside sounded dreadful. Cabs were honking, cars were
sliding, and pedestrians were wading through snow and slush, and
now the snow was starting again. The only place it might have
been pretty was Central Park, but on the streets of New York it
was a nightmare.

She went through her messages and made notes. Carmen
had not returned her call, but Alice had checked with the police
and the FBI and security, and there had been no further threats or
problems. Everything was in control. There was a message from
Bram wanting to know her impression of the promoters she'd
seen, and she had been pleased with them, and there were several
faxes from the office, none of them important. The phone rang as
she was sifting through her messages, and she picked it up without thinking.

"Steinberg," she said distractedly, and then realized what
she'd done, but the response at the other end was instant.

"Hamilton. How was your day? Sounds busy."

"Busy enough. I spent most of it battling traffic."

"Are you still working?" He hadn't wanted to bother her,
but he wanted to hear the sound of her voice, even if she was
busy. He had waited all day to hear it, and she was smiling,
listening to him. He had a deep, smooth voice that sounded incredibly sexy as she sat in her hotel room.

"Not really. I was just going through my messages and faxes. It all looks pretty tame actually. How was your day?"

"Pretty good. Weissman did a good job negotiating the new contract."

"For the movie, or the book? I'm confused, you've got too many projects."

"Look who's talking." He laughed. "Book number three. I'll let you negotiate the movie. Actually, I talked to him about that. He thought it was an excellent idea. He said he never suggested it before because he figured I'd be out of the movie business in no time. He thought I'd hate it, and he wasn't wrong, but it looks like I might try it again, once at least. He says you're a terrific lawyer, but I shouldn't bother you unless I mean it. He says you're very busy, and you have a lot of *very* important clients." They both laughed at Andreas' warning.

"I'm impressed." She laughed, amused by what he'd said about her clients.

"So am I, Miss Steinberg. Now how about some dinner? Do you still have the strength to eat, after making all those important deals today?"

"I didn't make a single important deal, I'll have you know. I talked to attorneys and music promoters all afternoon, and this evening I turned down a perfume for Carmen."

"At least it's fun. How were the music guys? Pretty sleazy?"

"Probably, but they were smart actually. I liked them. They have an incredible tour planned for Bram. If he's up to it physically, I think he should do it." He liked hearing about what she did. He liked her voice, her ideas, her interests. He had thought about her all day, he couldn't stop thinking about her in fact, and he liked everything about her. It was crazy. He scarcely knew her and suddenly she was all he could think about. And she had to admit that all through her meetings that afternoon, the thought of Jeff had made her smile, and she was constantly distracted.

"You're bad for my business life, Mr. Hamilton. These people in New York are going to think I'm a drug casualty from the

West Coast. I kept forgetting what they were saying, and thinking of things you said last night. This is no way to do business."

"No, but it's kind of a good feeling, isn't it?" he said honestly, and they both smiled. He wanted to ask her if she'd heard from Brandon, but he didn't. Instead he asked her if she'd brought warm clothes with her, some slacks, and a wool hat, and mittens.

"Why?" She couldn't imagine why he was asking, unless he was just concerned that she was warm enough, but he seemed to have something else in mind. He'd been planning it all afternoon, and he just hoped she had the right clothes with her. "I've got wool slacks, I wore them today, and a wool hat I brought, but it's pretty ugly."

"No mittens?" he asked solicitously.

"Not in about twenty years." She had even forgotten to bring gloves, and her hands had been frozen all day as a result every time she left a building.

"I'll bring you a pair of my mother's. Are you up for something a little offbeat, or do you want to do something fancy?" He was assuming she was still willing to have dinner with him, and she was. She'd been looking forward to it all day, and she'd been telling herself it was all right, and there was no harm in it, in spite of Brandon.

"We don't need to do anything fancy," she said quietly. She had enough fancy doings in her life, when she went out with her clients or to award ceremonies or Hollywood dinners. She liked simple evenings. "What did you have in mind?" she asked, both excited and suspicious.

"You'll see. Dress warm, wear slacks and boots and your ugly warm hat, and I'll meet you in the lobby in half an hour."

"Is this ominous? Should I be worried? Are you spiriting me away to Connecticut or Vermont or something outrageous?" She felt like a kid going on senior sneak, or with a bunch of friends from college.

"No, but actually, I'd love to spirit you away somewhere. I

didn't realize that was an option." He chuckled, intrigued by the suggestion.

"It isn't. I've got work to do here tomorrow."

"I figured that. Not to worry, nothing ominous. Just a little simple fun, New York style. See you in half an hour." He hurried her off the phone, and she finished reading her messages, and even thought about calling Brandon, to get it over with, but she doubted he'd be home yet, or even back in his office. It was only four-thirty in California. And she felt mean thinking that calling him was something that had to be "gotten over with," like taking medicine. It was odd suddenly feeling this way, but she felt faintly guilty about Jeff, although they certainly hadn't done anything to feel guilty about, and she was sure they wouldn't.

She was in the lobby right on time, in her slacks and her warm coat, and her old red ski hat. And she saw as she looked through the revolving door that it was still snowing. People were walking into the lobby and stamping their feet to get the snow off them, dusting their hair and brushing off their hats, as they stood laughing at each other, with snowflakes on their lashes. It was fun watching them, and as she looked outside, she saw a hansom carriage pull up, an enclosed old-fashioned one, like an old English carriage. It had windows and a roof, and the driver wore a top hat, and it looked wonderfully cozy. It stopped in front of the hotel, and the driver got down, as the doorman helped him hold the horses, and someone got out, and hurried inside. And as soon as he came through the revolving door, she saw that it was Jeff, wearing a ski hat much like her own and a heavy parka.

"Your chariot awaits," he said, beaming at her, his eyes bright, his cheeks red from the cold, as he tucked her hand into his arm and handed her a pair of white angora mittens. "Put them on, it's freezing outside."

"You're incredible," she said, looking up at him in amazement. He'd brought the hansom carriage for her, and he helped her into it, and closed the door, and then settled a heavy fur blanket around her. The driver already had his instructions. "I can't believe this." She was beaming at him, and very touched.

She felt like a kid on her first date, as she sat next to him, snuggled under the fur blanket as he put an arm around her.

"I took your suggestion, we're going to Vermont. We should be there by next Tuesday. I hope that doesn't screw up any of your appointments," he said delightedly.

"Not at all." Sitting there next to him, she felt as though she would have done anything he wanted.

They headed slowly toward the park, and she put on the white angora mittens while he helped her. They were cozy and warm, and his mother's hands were about the same size as her own. She looked up at him then, and their eyes met. He was a nice man, and he had really spoiled her.

"This is wonderful, Jeff. Thank you."

"Don't be silly," he said, embarrassed. "I thought we should do something a little special, since it was snowing."

They provided even more confusion to the already strangled traffic, and then finally reached the park, at Central Park South, and then headed north for a few blocks, until they reached Wollman skating rink, and the carriage stopped, as she looked out into the darkness.

"Where are we?" she asked, faintly nervous. But it was so cold and blustery that even the muggers couldn't have been around. The door opened and the driver helped them out, as Jeff looked at her with pleasure.

"Can you skate?"

"More or less. I haven't since Yale, and I'm no Peggy Fleming."

"Want to give it a try?" She laughed at the thought, but it sounded like so much fun, she couldn't resist, and nodded.

"I'd love it."

They hurried toward the rink arm in arm, and the carriage waited for them. Jeff had paid for it till midnight. He rented skates for both of them, and he helped her lace hers up, and then gave her a hand as she slid onto the ice tenuously, but she got her footing fairly quickly. And Jeff was a beautiful skater, he had been on the hockey team at Harvard. He took a quick turn just to warm up, and then came back to her, and stayed with her, and halfway into the session, she was skating pretty smoothly. It was still snowing and there was hardly anyone on the ice. They ate hot dogs to give them energy, and had three rounds of hot chocolate. She had a great time, and they were laughing and teasing like old friends by the end of the session. For her, it was a lot like being with Alan, only just a little better.

"I can't remember when I've had so much fun," she told him when they finally sat down for a rest because her ankles were getting tired.

"I go in L.A. once in a while, but the rinks in California are pretty crummy. I went skiing in Tahoe last year, and the rink is even pretty small there. It's definitely not a western sport. It's too bad. I still enjoy it."

"So do I." She looked up at him happily. He looked like what her sister Sam would have called a "hunk" as he stood there, tall and virile and athletic, and his eyes always seemed to be laughing. "I'd forgotten how much fun this is," she said happily, thanking him again, and a few minutes later he bought her a pretzel and a cup of hot coffee. It wasn't really that cold, the wind had died down, but the snow was still fairly heavy.

"The city is going to be crippled tomorrow if this keeps up. Maybe all your appointments will get canceled," he said hopefully, and she laughed, thinking of it. She was meeting with Jason Haverton again, and she told Jeff about him.

"I really like him. He must have been a terror in his youth, but he's a nice man, so interesting and literate, and he's as sharp as ever." She really admired him, and had enjoyed their meeting. "It's funny, things seem so much more civilized here than in California. There really is a literary world, full of ladies and gentlemen, and erudite people who behave properly and observe the traditions. But there, everyone is still a little rough around the edges. I forget it sometimes, but then you come back here and are reminded again. In California, a man like Jason Haverton couldn't exist, he'd be buffeted by the newspapers, and the tabloids would make insinuations that he was having an affair with a geriatric nurse, and he'd be getting death threats."

"Actually, you know, Allegra, for an old guy, it might put a little excitement in his life. He might like that."

"I'm serious," she said. They were skating again, and he was holding her tightly, under the pretext of keeping her from falling. She didn't object, she liked it. "It's a different world, Jeff."

"I know it is," he said more seriously. "It must be rough on some of your clients to live so publicly with fear of death threats and constant harassment of them and their families."

"It'll happen to you one day, it happens to everyone who makes some money and has celebrity status. It's almost automatic. You make money, you get well-known, and someone wants to kill you. It's sick. Like the Wild West. Bang, it's all over. And the tabloids aren't much fun either. They invent any lie they think will sell papers for them, and they don't give a damn who they hurt in the process."

"You must deal with that crap all the time with the kind of clients you have. Can you do anything about it to protect them?"

"Pathetically little. I learned from my parents years ago that you have to keep a low profile, lead a clean life, and learn to ignore it. But they go after you anyway. They used to try to take pictures of us when we were kids, but my father was a real lion about that. He never let them. And he got restraining orders when he had to, to protect us. But things are a lot looser now. They have to try and kill you twice before you can get any protection. We actually had a scare on Carmen right before I left, but I talked to the police and the FBI today, and everything seems to have settled down. It scares her to death, poor thing. She calls me at four o'clock in the morning sometimes just because she heard a noise and she's frightened."

"You must get a lot of sleep," he said, teasing her, and she laughed. She didn't mention that Brandon hated it and complained constantly about the intrusions from her clients. It seemed unfair to complain about him to Jeff, and she didn't want to encourage Jeff unfairly, by sounding too unhappy with Brandon. They were still very much together. And by the following week, Jeff would be back in L.A., and she wouldn't be able to see him for evenings like this. Maybe they could have lunch sometime. She had already given it a lot of thought. She could introduce him to Alan, or even her parents. She knew Blaire would love him, and Simon had already met him. It was very strange thinking about him, as if she were taking him home to meet her parents.

"What were you thinking just then?" Jeff asked as he watched her face. She had such expressive eyes, and she'd been frowning. And she hesitated before she answered.

"I was thinking that I'd like to introduce you to my family, and it seemed strange somehow. I was trying to justify it to myself."

"Do you have to, Allegra?" he said gently.

"I don't know," she answered. "Do I?" He didn't answer her. They were standing at the far end of the skating rink, leaning against the railing for a few minutes. And as he stood there, looking down at her, with the snow falling on both of them, he simply moved closer to her and kissed her. She was so startled, she didn't move away, she just held on to him so she wouldn't fall, and then she kissed him back, as he pressed closer and closer against her. And when they finally stopped, they were both breathless.

"Oh . . . Jeff . . ." she said softly, stunned by what they'd done. She felt like a kid again, and at the same time, very much a woman.

"Allegra," he whispered her name, and pulled her into his arms again, and she didn't fight him. And then, finally, they stopped kissing and skated again, and neither of them said a word for a few minutes. "I'm not sure if I'm supposed to apologize for that," he said seriously, looking at her as they skated, "but I don't really want to."

"You don't have to," she said quietly. "I kissed you too."

And then he looked at her squarely. "Do you feel guilty about Brandon?" He wanted to know what she felt. He was falling in love with her, he was completely taken with her, her ideas, her principles, her dreams, not to mention her beauty. He wanted to be with her and hold her and kiss her, and make love to her, and to hell with Brandon.

"I don't know," she answered his question as honestly as she could. "I'm not sure what I feel. I know I'm supposed to feel guilty about him. I want to marry him. I have for two years. But he's so rigid, Jeff. He refuses to give anything more than what he wants, and everything he does is measured and limited, and restricted."

"Why do you want to marry someone like that, for heaven's sake?" Jeff asked her, sounding irritated as they stopped skating again. The session was almost over, and the already sparse crowd was thinning.

"I don't know why," she said plaintively, tired of explaining it to everyone, and trying to justify it, even to herself. "Maybe because I've been there for this long, or because I think he needs me. I think I'd be good for him. He needs to learn to give, to loosen up, to not be so afraid to love and commit. . . ." Her eyes filled with tears as she looked at Jeff, it all sounded so stupid now, in the face of Jeff's generosity of spirit.

"And if he doesn't learn to do those things, what'll you have? What kind of marriage would that be? Probably the same kind he had with his ex-wife, lousy. Maybe he'd always resent you for trying to force him to give something that's not in him. It sounds like that's what bothered him about the first one, and yet he hasn't even divorced her. How long is that going to go on? Two more years? Five? Ten? Why are you doing this to yourself? It's like you're punishing yourself. You deserve so much more than that, don't you see that?" It was what her own mother had said, but Jeff's voice was clearer.

"And what if you turn out to be just like him?" she said sadly, voicing her worst fear, her greatest terror. In the end, they all turned out to be like Brandon, but that was how she chose them.

"Do I remind you of him now?" he asked, and she laughed through her tears.

"No, you remind me of my father." Simon Steinberg.

"I take that as a real compliment," Jeff said sincerely.

"It is, and I mean it. You remind me a little bit of my brother, and Alan too," she said, smiling wistfully at him, thinking of all the good men in her life, and not the ones frozen in their inability to give, like Brandon, and the men who had come before him.

"Have you ever tried talking to someone about this?" he asked naively, and she laughed.

"Ah, yes, the great western sport of therapy. And for how many years can you play it? I've been doing it for four. I see my therapist on Thursdays," she said matter-of-factly.

"And what does he or she say . . . or would you rather not discuss it?" he asked hesitantly. He was puzzled by why she was hanging on to someone who was obviously giving her so little. Even she seemed to see it, although Jeff noticed that she defended him a lot, and she seemed used to doing it, so others must have told her the same thing before him.

"No, I'm used to discussing it," she said openly as they skated around the rink again. "She says it's an old problem, and it is. I pick men who are constitutionally unable to love me, or anyone. But I think Brandon is better than the earlier models." Jeff didn't know what they'd been like, but he wasn't impressed by what he'd heard of Brandon. "At least he's trying."

"How can you tell?" Jeff said almost meanly. "What is it that he does for you?"

"He loves me," she said stubbornly. "He may be uptight and repressed, but behind all that, I think he'd be there for me if I needed him." She always told herself that, but he'd never had to prove it.

"Are you sure of that, Allegra?" Jeff asked her pointedly. "Think about it. When was the last time he was there for you? I hardly know you, and I already think he's going to let you down badly one of these days. He can't even divorce his ex-wife. What's he saving her for?" But she looked so unhappy when he asked her that, that Jeff decided to drop it. "I'm sorry," he said apologetically. "I'm probably just jealous. I have no right to say those things. It just seems so unfair. It's so hard to meet anyone you really care about, and suddenly there you are, with Brandon standing next to you, like a trail of tin cans on a cat's tail. I guess I'd like to get rid of him and simplify the situation." She laughed at the analogy, and she understood the implications.

"I understand," she said, and he had hit some nerves in her, but she didn't admit it to him. She'd been with Brandon for two years, and she wasn't about to break up with him because he didn't go to the Golden Globes, or because he didn't tell her he loved her on the phone, or because he liked to go back to his own apartment after he made love to her, or because she had met a handsome, appealing writer in New York. You didn't throw your whole life out the window because someone took you skating. But there was also no denying how much Jeff appealed to her. He had knocked her right off her feet, and she knew it. But that had nothing to do with Brandon.

They skated arm in arm until the end of the session, then returned their skates, and she was still quiet when they got back in the carriage. Jeff was sorry he had blown off steam, and he invited her up to his mother's apartment for a drink, but she thought she should go back to the hotel. It was already late and she had to get up early in the morning.

"I promise I'll behave. I shouldn't have said all those things about him, Allegra. I'm sorry."

"I'm flattered." She smiled at him. "And I'd love to have a rain check for the drink. I've got to get up early tomorrow morning." And with that, she settled back against the seat, in his arms, and he sat there thinking that he'd like to be getting up with her in the morning. But he didn't say anything as they rolled along, listening to the sound of the horse's feet and watching it snow out the window.

"It's pretty, isn't it?" he said gently, and she nodded, and smiled up at him.

"I loved the skating. Thank you, Jeff." It had been so much more fun than a fancy French dinner. She loved every moment she spent with him, even when he hassled her about Brandon. And no matter how much it irritated her, she understood perfectly why he did it. Brandon certainly left himself wide open to criticism, but she wasn't thinking about Brandon now. She was thinking about Jeff as they rolled through the park toward the Plaza.

"You're a pretty good skater," he praised her, and she laughed easily. "But you're a truly great kisser." She giggled in answer.

"So are you, and a good sport." They started chatting again then, and by the time they left the park, they were laughing and talking and at ease with each other. When they reached her hotel, the driver helped them down, Jeff paid and tipped the driver handsomely, and then the horse and buggy left them. "I feel like Cinderella," she said, as she watched them go in the snow, down Park Avenue, and handed him the angora mittens, as he chuckled.

"Now what? We both turn into pumpkins?" he asked, amused, and happier than he'd been in ages. He thought Allegra was terrific.

"It was so much fun. I loved it." It had been perfect with the snow, and the skating. And as she looked up at him, and thought of kissing him, she felt a twinge of desire for him deep in the pit of her stomach. He walked her inside, and waited for the elevator with her, and then he surprised her by stepping into it with her. Much to her own astonishment, she didn't object, and they stood side by side, very quietly, and got out on the fourteenth floor. He followed her to her room and she took the key out of her pocket. She didn't invite him in, she just stood there looking at him, feeling wistful. She wished that things were different than they were, that Brandon hadn't been in her life for two years, but he had, and there was no point changing that now for a romantic night in the snow, with a stranger.

"I'll leave you here," he said quietly, looking as troubled as she was. He didn't want to bang his head against a brick wall either. But he couldn't seem to let her go, nor believe that she wanted what she had, or didn't have, with Brandon.

He was about to say good night to her, and he had no intention of pressing her any further, when she took a single step toward him, and he couldn't help himself. He pulled her into his arms, and kissed her, holding her so tight she almost couldn't breathe, but she loved it. She felt safe and protected and desired, and there was no question of how badly he wanted her, and she knew that if she ever spent the night with him, he would never want to leave before morning.

She kissed him again and again, wanting him as badly as he wanted her, and then she pulled away and shook her head sadly. "I can't do this, Jeff." There were tears in her eyes when she looked at him, and he nodded.

"I know that. I wouldn't even want you to right now. You'd hate me afterward. Why don't we just let it be like this for a while? Kind of an old-fashioned romance, some hugging and kissing, and just being there, or maybe just friends, if that's what you want. I'll do whatever you want," he said gently. "I'm not going anywhere, don't feel pressured."

"I don't know what I feel," she said honestly. "I'm so con-fused." She raised her eyes to his, and she looked truly tormented. "I want you. . . . I want him. . . . I want him to be what he never has been, but I think he could be . . . and why do I care? Why am I doing that? . . . and I don't understand what I'm doing here. I feel like I'm falling in love with you. Is this real? Just a New York fling? I don't know what the hell's going on," she said, stumbling over her own words, as he smiled lovingly at her, and then kissed her again, and she didn't stop him. She loved kissing him, loved being in his arms, loved being with him, sitting in hansom cabs, and skating. "What happens when we go back?" she asked, as they both leaned against the wall outside her room. She didn't dare take him inside, she was sure they'd end up in bed in the first five minutes. And that wouldn't be fair to anyone, though it was very appealing. Or could he live up to what her life was really like? That was an interesting question. "This is all very romantic. But what would happen when I have to go to Safeway and buy groceries, when Carmen calls me at four A.M. because the dog turned over a garbage can, or Mal O'Donovan gets arrested for being drunk and disorderly in Reno, and I have to get out of bed and go bail him out?"

"I'd go with you. That's what it's all about. I don't find any of that so shocking, or such an imposition. It sounds like fun to me. It would give me some great ideas for my new ventures in commercial fiction."

"Be serious. It's like having half a dozen unruly teenaged children."

"I think I could survive it. Do I look that delicate to you? I've always been pretty flexible. This would be good training for when we have kids, who do all those same things, or hopefully not, if you bring them up right."

"What are you saying to me?" She looked totally confused, and somewhat miserable. But these were nice miseries to have, and she knew that.

"That I want to be with you, that I want to spend time with you, and see what happens. The same thing is happening to me that's happening to you. I'm falling in love with you, and I don't know why, but I don't want to lose it either, or give it all back to a guy who I think doesn't appreciate you, or deserve you." He gently pushed a lock of her silky hair away with his fingers, and looked into the eyes he had known only for two days, but which trusted him so much already. "What I don't want to do is make you unhappy, or pull you apart. Don't do anything right now. It'll all work itself out. We'll see what happens when we go back to L.A.," he said reasonably, and she nodded, and then she looked up at him with terror.

"What if I decide we can't see each other there?" she asked. It wasn't going to work if they hung around kissing each other all the time. Brandon certainly wasn't going to like that.

"I hope you don't decide that," he said calmly.

"I don't know what to do," she said, feeling like a child, and he smiled at her, took her key from her hands, and opened the door for her.

"I've got some ideas, but I don't think any of them are appropriate given the situation." He kissed her on the lips again, gave her a small shove inside, and handed her the key, without ever leaving the hallway. "What about tomorrow?"

"I'm meeting with Haverton and the promoters again, and I've got a couple of other meetings uptown." And then she remembered a dinner meeting she'd made with an attorney who couldn't see her any other time. It was going to be a long day, and she wasn't going to have much time to see him. "I don't think I'll be through till nine, maybe later."

"I'll call you then." He leaned toward her and kissed her again, and she felt peaceful as she closed the door to her room, and he went back downstairs to the lobby.

She thought about calling Brandon then, and this time she knew she couldn't. It would have been too dishonest calling him, pretending that she was sitting in her room, thinking of him. She knew she had to stop seeing Jeff, or at least kissing him, but the thought of giving it all up was far too painful. Maybe she could just treat it as a small, unimportant interlude, a few kisses, and then everything would be back to normal once they went back to California. She was still telling herself that an hour later when Jeff called. She jumped when she heard the phone, and she almost didn't answer it. She was sure it was Brandon. He hadn't called that day, and there had been no messages from home. And when she picked up the phone, she felt instantly guilty.

"Hello?" She felt like a criminal as she held the phone, and at the other end Jeff laughed.

"Oh, God, don't ever try to play poker. You sound awful."

"That's how I feel. Jeff, I feel so guilty."

"I thought you would. Look, you haven't done anything. The damage can be repaired. You haven't broken his trust, and if you really feel better that way, we can take a breather." He offered it to her, but it cost him dearly to make the sacrifice. As often as she'd let him, he wanted to see her.

"I think we should, take a breather, I mean," she said unhappily. "I just can't do this."

"You're an honest woman. It's a damn shame," he teased, but he didn't want to tear her apart. The thought of not seeing her again, though, almost killed him.

"I can't see you tomorrow night," she said, suddenly firm, as he felt a vise squeeze his heart.

"I understand. Call, if you change your mind." She had all his numbers. "Will you be all right?" He barely knew her, but he worried about her.

"I'm fine. I just need to get my equilibrium again. The last two days have been completely crazy."

"And very nice," he added, longing for her lips again, and afraid he'd never have them. He had called to say good night, and instead he'd given her the opportunity to run away, which was not what he had intended.

"The last two days were wonderful," she said, thinking of the skating, the hansom cab, and kissing him in the snow. He had completely bowled her over. And now she had to concentrate on real life, and going back to Brandon. "I'll call you," she said, choking on her own words, thinking of Jeff again, and not Brandon. "Good night, Jeff."

"Good night." He never told her why he'd called. He had called just to tell her that he loved her.

CHAPTER 7

Wednesday seemed endless to Allegra as she made her rounds. She had some appointments, uptown and down, a late lunch, and finally a last-minute dinner with a tax lawyer who did work for one of her clients. It was a long day, and as she walked down Madison Avenue from the restaurant, to get some air, she thought of Jeff for the thousandth time since that morning.

She had held firm, and it had almost killed her, but she hadn't called him. She couldn't, their feelings were too raw, the power of what they felt too strong. It was too dangerous to play with the fire that drove them.

And as she walked along, she looked casually into a bookstore, and there he was. His face on the back of his book stared at her from the window. She stopped, and looked deep into the eyes that said so much, and in spite of herself, she walked inside and bought one.

Back in her room, she set it on the table next to her, and looked at him, and then finally she put it in her briefcase. There was no message from him, nor anyone else. A stack of faxes had come in, and she had had long conferences on the phone with Bram Morrison and Malachi O'Donovan that morning. Carmen had left a cryptic message with Alice that she was okay, and everyone else seemed to be holding their own. Only Bram had a problem—there had been an odd threat against one of his children. It had come by phone, and the Spanish housekeeper had scarcely understood what the man said, but it didn't sound good. Bram had called the police himself, and had put bodyguards on both his children. It was just as she had explained to Jeff, the problems were limitless, contracts, threats, decisions, tours, licensing, exploitation of all kinds, and the endless contracts.

But she found no solace in her work tonight. All she could think about was Jeff, and then, finally, at ten o'clock, he called her.

"How was your day?" He tried to sound nonthreatening, but he was so nervous, his palms were wet. Just hearing her voice and knowing he couldn't see her made him unhappy.

"Fine." She told him about Bram, both the tour and the threat, and Jeff thought that the threat against Bram's kids was disgusting.

"Those people are sick. They should all go to jail. How was the rest of your day?" he asked, and she looked mournfully across the room at her briefcase.

"I bought your book."

"You did?" He sounded pleased. It cheered him up to think she'd actually thought about him. "What made you buy it?"

"I wanted to have your picture." She sounded like a little kid, and he laughed, and wished he could put his arms around her.

"I could come by and show you the real thing," he said hopefully, and this time she laughed.

"I don't think we should."

"How's Brandon?" he finally asked after a pause. He hated the sound of the guy's name by now, but he was curious if she'd called him.

"I called a little while ago. He was out. I'm sure he's all wrapped up in his trial."

"What about us, Allegra?" Jeff asked softly. He hadn't been able to concentrate on anything, think of anything, make sense at all since that morning.

"I guess we're on hold, until we learn to control ourselves," she said, and he chuckled.

"I'll buy you a little stun gun and you can zap me every time I get near you. You'd have to use it a lot though."

"I'm as bad as you are," she said, still sounding guilty.

"Don't be so hard on yourself, for heaven's sake. You're only human. And you did all the right things. You stopped me. You sent me away. You told me you wouldn't see me again." He counted her virtues, hating every one of them, but respecting her for her courage and ethics. She was determined to be faithful.

"Yeah, I did all that," she said, correcting him, "*after* I kissed you, repeatedly, I might add."

"Listen, counselor, kissing is not a crime in this country. Take it easy. This is not Victorian England. You did all the right stuff, you should be pleased with yourself," he reminded her, still wishing she were less faithful to Brandon.

"I'm not pleased. I'm miserable and I miss you," she confessed, and they both laughed.

"I'm glad to hear it," he said, beaming. "How does tomorrow look, or does that make any difference?"

"Pretty busy, and no, it doesn't."

"I figured that," he said, sounding depressed. "When are you going back?"

"Friday."

"So am I. Can we at least fly back together? I promise not to do anything outrageous on the airplane." She laughed at the idea, but then that didn't seem smart to her. Why torture themselves? They obviously couldn't keep their hands off each other.

"I don't think so, Jeff. Maybe lunch in L.A. sometime."

"Come on," he complained, "that's bullshit. We deserve better than that. Can't we be friends, at least? This doesn't make sense. You're not a nun, you're a woman. And you're not even married to the guy." And his guess was she never would be. But by the time she figured that out and got free again, God only knew what he'd be doing, or where he'd be living. Timing was important in life, and he had no intention of waiting to see her again until she gave up Brandon. At the rate she was going it could take years. "Allegra, just see me once, before you go back. Please. I need to see you."

"You don't need to, you want to," she argued.

"I'll make a real nuisance of myself if you don't. I'll come to the hotel and lie on the floor in the lobby. I'll bring the hansom cab back and bring the horse through the revolving door." He always made her laugh, and he made her happy. "What are you doing to us, you silly girl? What's this all about?"

"Keeping my word. Living up to a commitment."

"That guy doesn't know the meaning of it, and you know it. He doesn't deserve this. And neither do I. At least let me take you to the airport."

"I'll call you in L.A.," she said firmly.

"And say what? That you won't see me because of Brandon?"

"You said you wouldn't push me," she reminded him, feeling frazzled.

"I lied," he responded calmly.

"You're impossible."

"Go read my book, or look at the picture. I'll call you tomorrow night."

"I'll be out." She had to try to discourage him, but she really didn't want to.

"Then I'll call you later."

"Why are you doing this?"

"Because I love you." There was a long silence at her end, and Jeff waited and closed his eyes, knowing he shouldn't have said it. "All right, I don't love you. That's insane. I like you very much, and I want to get to know you." There was a small, silvery laugh at her end. "You know, Allegra Steinberg, you're driving me insane. And how are you going to represent me if you won't see me?"

"You don't have a deal right now anyway," she reminded him, and he sounded outraged.

"Then get me one. What kind of a lawyer are you?"

"A crazy one, thanks to my newest client."

"Go away, go back to him," he played with her, "I don't want to see you anyway. And besides, you're a lousy skater."

"Yes, I am," she agreed with him, laughing again, but they both treasured memories from the night before when they'd gone skating. And as she thought of it, she found it hard to believe that it had been only a day since she'd seen him. It seemed like an eternity. How was she going to survive in L.A. if she didn't see him?

"You're a lovely skater," he said warmly. "You're a lot of wonderful things. And I suppose one of those virtues is faithful. I just hope I'm lucky enough to get someone like you one day. The women in my life always seem to take the broad interpretation of fidelity to include at least half a dozen people, or most of the adult male inhabitants of a small city. Anyway, I'll call you tomorrow night, Miss Steinberg," he persisted politely.

"Good night, Mr. Hamilton," she said primly. "Have a lovely day tomorrow. I'll speak to you in the evening." She couldn't tell him not to call; she liked talking to him too much, and it gave them both something to look forward to, which was fortunate because the next day proved to be dreadful.

It poured with rain, cabs were impossible to find, the subway broke down when she finally tried that, and all of her appointments either ran overtime or were canceled. And she felt like a drowned rat by the time she got back to the hotel at six o'clock to change. That morning, she had been invited to the Weissmans' for dinner at seven-thirty. And just to keep her mind off Jeff, and so she wouldn't sit in her room and think of him, she had accepted. He had sent her long-stemmed red roses that morning. They had made her smile, but he hadn't broken her resolve. After two years, she owed more than that to Brandon. And she knew he was faithful to her. Despite his many failings, wandering wasn't among them. She had been surprised at herself with Jeff. Nothing like that had ever happened to her before, being seized in the grip of an irresistible attraction.

She was going back to L.A. the next day, but she hadn't

spoken to Brandon since Monday. She'd called and left messages several times, but he was always out, or in court, or at meetings. It was unnerving not talking to him, but she decided that it was probably her punishment for almost having been unfaithful. She had been bad enough, kissing Jeff repeatedly, and she knew that if she'd seen Jeff again, she wouldn't have been able to resist him. She was sad but relieved to know that she would be out that night if he called her.

She wore a red wool dress and her hair down, with her winter raincoat. And she tried Brandon one more time before she left, and was told again that he was in a meeting, and she left a message that she'd called, and hurried downstairs to have the doorman find her a taxi.

It took the doorman half an hour to find a cab, and she was late when she arrived, but so were most of the guests, for the same reason. The Weissmans were expecting fourteen for dinner. Andreas had already told her that Jason Haverton would be there, and two or three of his other writers.

Allegra was introduced to a very attractive young woman as she came through the door. She was a very controversial feminist writer, another of Andreas' clients. A well-known newscaster was there, a correspondent for *The New York Times*, the director of CNN and his wife, and an actress Allegra's mother knew who was appearing on Broadway. Allegra made a point of saying hello to her before she sat down. The woman was very respected, and very grand, and she had made a sweeping entrance into the room, which had been observed by all. It was the perfect New York gathering for a rainy evening.

They were all there save one, and the doorbell rang one last time. She looked up as he entered the room, and she realized that she should have known. It was so obvious. Neither of them had guessed, and Jeff looked even more surprised than she did.

"Destiny," he said, looking at her with a small, wicked smile, and she laughed, relieved, and far more pleased than she wanted to admit, and unable to fight it any longer. She held out her hand to him, as though they'd just met. "No, Allegra."

"Did you know?" he asked in an undervoice, as he sat down next to her, his hair still damp from the rain, and he looked incredibly handsome.

"Of course not," she said, her eyes alive with all the feelings she had been fighting. It was all he could do not to kiss her in front of the Weissmans.

"Tell the truth." He was teasing her now, and enjoying it. "Did you arrange it? You don't have to be embarrassed to tell me." She gave him an evil look, and he laughed as he leaned over and kissed her on the cheek, and then went to get himself a Scotch and water. He was back instantly, and sat in quiet conversation with her for a little while, and then Jason Haverton joined them. He was pleased with the deal they'd arranged, and his qualms about having a movie made from one of his books had been dissipated for the most part by Allegra.

"She's quite something," the older man said to Jeff admiringly, when she went to say something to Andreas. "She's good at what she does, and good-looking too." He sang her praises as he sipped a gin and tonic.

"I just hired her," Jeff confirmed, amused by the conversation.

"She'll do well for you," the older man reassured him.

"I hope so," Jeff said, as she rejoined them.

It was an interesting evening for all of them, and it seemed the perfect way to end her stay in New York. And as they put on their coats to leave, Jeff left with her. She had given up keeping him at bay, it was so natural just being with him. And he looked so happy as he left with her. He seemed very proud, and very protective.

"Do you want to go somewhere for a drink?" he asked harmlessly. "That is, if you trust me." His eyes were gentle and loving.

"You were never the problem," she smiled up at him in the elevator as they left. "I was."

"I think we both were. Do you want to come to my mother's place for a while? It's three blocks from here. I promise to behave myself. And if I start to get out of control, you can leave whenever you want to."

"You sound positively dangerous." Allegra laughed at all of his precautions. "We ought to be able to manage that, don't you think?" But in truth, neither of them were sure, as she shared his umbrella and they walked the three blocks down Fifth Avenue to his mother's apartment.

The wind was fierce, and she was almost blown against him, as they walked into his building. It was a co-op building much like the one where the Weissmans lived. There was one apartment on each floor, and in each case, the elevator stopped at a private, individual lobby. The building was small, and the apartments were not large here, but they were well laid out, the views were excellent, and it was a very handsome building.

The elevator lobby on his mother's floor was all done in black and white marble, with an antique table and chair she had bought at auction at Christie's. And inside the apartment were a large collection of English antiques. The fabrics were delicate yellow brocades, and gray silks, and a few subtle chintzes. It was well-done, but somehow the atmosphere was austere. It was only in a small study with a leather couch that she and Jeff felt they could sit and chat comfortably. It was the only room he really liked, and Allegra picked up a photograph of his mother and studied it with interest. She was tall and thin, and she looked a great deal like him. But the eyes were sad, and the lips were thin, and it was hard to imagine her smiling. She didn't look like much fun; it was hard to compare her to Jeff. His whole face was touched by laughter and good humor.

"She looks very serious," Allegra said politely, so different from her own family where everyone smiled and laughed and cried and talked, and her own mother was so pretty.

"She is serious. I don't think she's ever really been happy since she lost my father," he explained to Allegra.

"Oh, dear, how sad." But she looked to Allegra as though she had been that way for a lifetime.

"Dad was the one with the sense of humor."

"Mine too," she said, and then remembered that Jeff knew that.

She sat on the couch next to him, with a glass of wine, and stretched out her legs as he lit a fire. It had been a long week, and she was tired, but it had had its high points too, among them the carriage ride and the skating, and even the dinner tonight. They'd been dinner partners and it had really been fun sitting next to him. With him on her right side, and Jason Haverton on her left, they had kept up a lively conversation.

"I had fun tonight," she said, watching him light the fire, and enjoying just being there with him. "Did you?"

He turned and looked at her with a slow smile. "Obviously, I had a great time. You know, it's funny, I wondered if you'd be there, but I didn't even dare ask you. I was afraid you wouldn't go if you knew I was coming. Would you have gone anyway?"

She shrugged, and then nodded. "Probably. I didn't even let myself hope you'd be there. It kind of took things out of our hands, didn't it?" It had been such a relief to suddenly see him there, it had made her heart leap the moment she saw him. No matter how unreasonable she told herself this was, it was becoming impossible to control her feelings. And yet, there was always Brandon, lurking near them, in the shadows.

"What now?" Jeff asked, as he sat down on the couch next to her with a glass of wine, and an arm around her shoulders. They were incredibly comfortable together, as they had been since the moment they met. And now it felt perfect sitting side by side on the couch in his mother's apartment.

"We go home and see what happens, I guess," she said honestly. "I suppose I ought to say something to Brandon." There was no avoiding it now. In some ways, she felt she owed it to him to tell him what had happened. Seeing Jeff again had made her realize she couldn't remain completely silent.

"You're going to tell him about us?" Jeff looked shocked.

"Maybe." She hadn't thought it out yet. "Maybe all I need to say is that it worries me that I can be so attracted to someone else. It certainly says something about what's missing with Brandon."

"Frankly, I think you ought to keep it to yourself. See how you feel about him, what you want, and what you're not getting, then draw your own conclusions." It seemed like a lot to worry about, and they were both tired of thinking about it. Instead, their conversation turned to other things; his new book, his next movie contract. He had picked up some suggestions that night from Jason, all of which had been instigated by Allegra.

Jeff was excited about starting a new book, and less so about finishing his screenplay. He was planning to settle down in Malibu and get to work as soon as he got back. He had no plans at all for the weekend.

"What about you?" he asked her with interest, as the fire crackled and they both got sleepy. It was warm and cozy in the little room, and Jeff smiled at how pleasant it was to see her there. His mother's apartment always seemed so stern to him. It was lovely to see Allegra tucked into the couch now beside him.

"I've got to get organized for next week." She had to negotiate Carmen's new movie, and she wanted to talk Alan into a new deal. There were a lot of large and small projects she had to attend to. She couldn't even imagine what had been dumped on her desk while she was gone. "I guess I'll work Saturday, maybe have dinner with my parents that night, and then see Brandon on Sunday."

"That's it?" He looked surprised. "Won't he join you at your parents' on Saturday night?" He looked shocked when she shook her head. "Will he pick you up at the airport?"

"He can't, he's in trial. He says he needs to work till at least Sunday. And he doesn't want me to distract him."

He raised an eyebrow then, and took another sip of wine. "I'd love for you to distract me, Allegra." He smiled. "Call me if you get lonely." But he said nothing else, and after that, neither of them mentioned Brandon.

They sat there together on the couch for a long time, and they behaved surprisingly well, until he went out to get some ice in the kitchen. She followed him there, and everything was immaculate and pristine. His mother was meticulous, and her housekeeper had been cleaning up behind Jeff all week. But when he put the ice down on the sink and looked at her, he couldn't stop himself, he took one long stride toward her and held her. He felt her trembling in his arms, her legs against his, and his whole body seemed to melt against her. "Oh, God, Allegra . . . I don't know how you do this to me. . . ." There had been countless women in his life, but none who did to him what she did. Perhaps it was knowing that he couldn't have her yet, perhaps never would —there was something unbearably bittersweet about the longing they felt for each other. Her lips found his, and a moment later she was leaning against the wall, and he was holding her as he pressed hard against her. But she didn't object. She wanted him. But he was forbidden fruit. She knew she couldn't have him.

"I think we should stop," she said distractedly, sounding hoarse as he ground slowly against her and she matched his movements. Her face was warm, and her neck, and he had his hands cupped around her breasts as he kissed her.

"I'm not sure I can stand this . . ." he said, groaning, as he tried to make himself stop, but for just a moment more, he couldn't. And then, finally, slowly, painfully, he brought himself back to his senses. It was an excruciating effort, but he did it for her, because he believed that this was what she wanted. But their lips still met, and her hand drifted slowly down his leg, and was sweet torture.

"I'm sorry," she said hoarsely.

"So am I," he said, wanting to take her there on the kitchen floor, on the couch, the table, anywhere, in the silence of his mother's apartment. "I'm not sure how many times I can do this again."

"Maybe we won't have to," she said sadly. "I'll meet you at Spago for lunch in L.A. We won't be able to do anything there but talk."

"How disappointing. I kind of like this," he teased her, touched her breast tantalizingly again, and then kissed her.

"We're torturing each other," she said unhappily. Somehow, it all seemed so stupid, and she couldn't help wondering if Brandon would have been as honorable about his obligations to her in a similar situation.

"It's kind of fun," Jeff said with a lopsided grin, trying to make the best of it, "in a perverted way. I wouldn't want to do a lot of this though," he said, looking her square in the eye, and she wondered if it was a warning.

He showed her his room, a somber, masculine room, with striped green curtains and lots of dark English antiques, and they managed to stay out of bed, which seemed miraculous to both of them, and they laughed about it as he showed her the rest of the apartment. And he took her back to the hotel a little while after midnight. He rode upstairs with her, and this time he came in. There was a little sitting area, and he sat on the couch and she showed him his book. She had stood it up again so she could look at his picture.

"We're both crazy, you know. I'm chasing after you like a kid, and you're looking at my picture." It had been a strange week for both of them, and in an odd way it was like they had been on a cruise. They were far from their everyday lives and their daily obligations. It remained to be seen what would happen once they got home. Right now, it was hard to imagine.

Jeff stayed for a little while. But they'd had all they wanted to drink, said everything they could, there was nothing to do now except say good-bye, for a while at least, or never say it again. That point had come to them very quickly. It had happened to them faster than most, but the time had come to do or die, to let go and flee, or seize the moment. And yet, whatever path they chose, they knew it would be painful.

It took every effort he could make to finally stand up, and he stood for a long time, looking down at her, and then he held her. He wanted to stay with her, and take care of her, and be there for her, but he knew he couldn't.

"Promise you'll call me if you need anything. You don't have to do anything for me, you don't have to end it with him if that's not what you want to do, just call me if you need me."

"I will. You too," she said sadly. It felt like good-bye, and neither of them was sure what this would be yet, perhaps nothing at all except a memory of a few snowy days in New York, and a ride in a hansom carriage at midnight.

"I'll call you when I get my first death threat," he grinned. "Take care of yourself," he warned. She walked him to the door, and then he held her again, and closed his eyes as he felt her hair on his cheek and smelled her perfume. "Oh, God, I'm going to miss you."

"Me too." She wasn't even sure what she was doing. Nothing made sense anymore. She was trying to do the right thing, and instead, everything she did seemed so stupid.

"I'll call, just to see how you're doing." He was going to give her a few days to settle in, and then call her in the office.

And then suddenly there were no words, they just held each other and kissed, and finally he left, and when he did, she sat down on the bed and cried, she already missed him. The phone rang shortly after that, but she didn't pick it up. She was too afraid it would be Brandon.

CHAPTER 8

The next day was a mad rush for her. She had two last appointments downtown, and she was on a six o'clock plane, which meant she had to leave the city by four, possibly even earlier if the weather was bad, and because of the Friday traffic. She called Andreas Weissman to say good-bye, and thank him for all his help that week, and both of his extremely hospitable invitations. He assured her that it had been a pleasure to have her, promised to call if he came to L.A., and thanked her for her work with Jason.

She packed in a huge hurry at three o'clock, after a late lunch, and then in a rush of guilt and panic, she decided to call Brandon. She hadn't talked to him in days, and she was beginning to feel awkward about it. But at least, as a rule, he was never jealous, and he hadn't seemed worried about what she was doing in New York. He knew she was working. And she had been. But there had been Jeff. And she was still wondering if her life would ever go back to normal. Jeff had called her that morning when she got up, and just hearing him had brought tears to her eyes. He had just wanted to tell her he was thinking about her, and he didn't say it, but she could tell he was in bed, and thinking about it had haunted her all morning.

When she called Brandon's office, his machine was on, and she pressed the appropriate button to summon up his assistant.

Allegra asked if he was in court, and was surprised to hear from his assistant that he wasn't.

"Isn't he in trial?" Was something wrong?

"They pleaded it out this morning."

"How great for him. Is he pleased?"

"Very much so," his assistant, whom Allegra didn't like, said dryly.

"Tell him I'll see him tonight then. If he wants to meet me, I'm coming in on United 412. We land at nine-fifteen. I'll be home by ten o'clock if he can't make it."

"He can't. He's catching a four o'clock to San Francisco."

"He is. Why?"

"To see his family, I assume," she said nastily, and for a moment Allegra thought about it. He had gone the previous weekend, and he knew she was coming home that night. But not having spoken to him in two days, she didn't know if one of the girls had a problem.

"Just tell him I called," Allegra said curtly. "I'll be home by ten. He can call me."

"Yes, ma'am," she said with obvious sarcasm. Allegra had complained to Brandon about her before, but he said she was a great secretary and he liked her.

Allegra thought about it for a minute after she hung up the phone. He had finished the trial. He was free for the weekend. He was going to San Francisco. He had told her that he couldn't see her till Sunday anyway, so maybe he thought she had made other plans, or maybe he was going to ask her to fly up as soon as she got home, probably on Saturday. But what was the point of that? That would just be exhausting. And as she thought about it, she had a great idea. She called the airlines, and asked if they had a seat on a flight to San Francisco. She knew where he stayed, she could meet him there. What a great idea . . . she could surprise him!

They had a flight at five fifty-three, just seven minutes before she had been scheduled to take off for L.A. She knew she could make it. They had a seat in first class for her, the only seat left on the plane, and she grabbed it. It was worth it just to see him. She really needed to see him now, after all the insanity she'd gone through with Jeff for the past four days. Maybe it had all been a romantic illusion. Brandon represented solidity to her, and time, and history. They had been together for two years. She had seen him through his entire separation. She loved his kids, and they loved her. She and Brandon had a life together. What she and Jeff had was a flash of something magical. It happened sometimes, but you couldn't build a life on it, she told herself firmly as she called the porter for her bags.

She hadn't called Jeff to say good-bye. She knew he had left on an earlier flight, and enough had been said between them. It was time to let go now, and see what was there if they ever met again. But she was not going to jeopardize her future with Brandon, and she was glad that things with Jeff had gone no further. It would have been wrong of her, and she felt guilty enough about it now. But she had decided not to say anything to Brandon. It would only hurt him. She smiled to herself then, thinking how pleased he would be to see her, and how happy she would be to see him. She thought about leaving a message at the office for him, to tell him that she had changed her plans, and then she decided that it would be more fun to surprise him.

She checked out of the hotel, and got into the waiting limousine. The ride to the airport was New York rush hour traffic at its worst, and she barely made it. She had to change her ticket, and check her bag through, and she boarded the plane with one minute to spare before they closed the doors. Every seat was full, and most of the flight attendants looked as though they were in bad humor. It was the end of the week, everyone was tired, the plane was too full. They were half an hour late taking off because of bad weather, and it was stuffy and hot in the plane, and the movie broke in coach, which made everyone crabby.

She took Jeff's book out during the flight, and turned it over several times to look at him. There was something so haunting about his eyes, so familiar about his lips, he looked as though he were going to say something to her, or move. He was leaning up against a brick building. It was a great photograph, and she finally put the book away in her briefcase.

When they finally arrived in San Francisco, they had to wait on the runway for forty-five minutes for a gate. It was eleven o'clock local time, two hours later than they were supposed to arrive, and everyone looked frazzled and exhausted. It was a typical modern-day flight, the food had been bad, the flight uncomfortable, there were endless delays, and the people leaving the flight all looked disgruntled. Welcome to New Age travel.

She walked to the carousel, and despite the aggravations of the trip, there was something fun about being there unexpectedly. It was like sharing a giant secret. She wasn't going home to a dirty house and unread mail. She didn't have to unpack, or take her clothes to the cleaners. She couldn't go into the office on Saturday. It was like a little extra gift. A weekend with Brandon in San Francisco, and right now it was just what they needed, more than he knew, or would ever need to know. But Allegra was thrilled that she'd done this.

As she picked up her bag, she thought briefly of Jeff again. He would be in L.A. by then, in his house in Malibu, and she couldn't help wondering what he was feeling. He said he would call in a few days. But she wasn't even sure she should take the call now. They both needed to get over the insanity that had struck them, and seeing each other would only make it harder. Now that she'd left New York, she was determined to strengthen her resolve and try to forget everything that had happened.

Allegra hailed a cab outside the terminal, and asked him to take her to the Fairmont. It was a grand, old hotel, and Brandon always liked to stay there. He thought it was an adventure for the girls, and it was close to everything they needed. She had tried talking him into a smaller hotel in Pacific Heights, but old habits were hard to break and he always insisted that his daughters loved it.

At that hour of night, it took them twenty minutes to drive into town, and Allegra felt as though she were moving underwater as the porter picked up her suitcase.

"Checking in, ma'am?" he asked pleasantly, and Allegra mustered a wintry smile and told him she was meeting her husband.

She realized that he was probably asleep by then, but the surprise of seeing her there would be worth it. She was going to pick up a key, let herself into the room, take off her clothes, and slip into bed beside him. She would have loved to take a shower, but she didn't think it was fair to make all that noise when he was asleep; she'd have to settle for a shower in the morning.

It was eleven-thirty when she reached the desk, and people were coming and going in the lobby. There were assorted restaurants where people from all over town came for special dining. The Tonga Room for Oriental and Polynesian food, the Venetian Room for name bands and well-known entertainers, Mason's for something more intimate. But all Allegra wanted was the key to the room where Brandon was staying.

"Edwards, please," she said, looking vague, and pushing the hair out of her eyes. She felt a mess as she stood there holding her heavy New York coat, and wearing the raincoat. She had a tote bag in one hand, and her briefcase in the other, and next to her, her suitcase.

"First name?" the woman in charge asked her, without expression.

"Brandon."

"Have you already checked in to the hotel?"

"I'm sure he has. He arrived earlier this evening. I just flew in from New York to meet him."

"And you are?" She stared blankly at Allegra.

"Mrs. Edwards." She felt perfectly comfortable with the lie. She always stayed at the Fairmont as Mrs. Edwards. It was simpler.

"Thank you, Mrs. Edwards, five-fourteen." She handed her a key, and signaled to the porter. He picked up the suitcase, and walked her to the elevator, offering to take the smaller bags from her, and she gladly gave them up. She felt as though she were about to fall over. It was two-thirty in the morning Eastern time, and she'd been going nonstop since seven-thirty. And in the end, her trip East had been fraught with emotion. She pushed that from her mind now, and rode upstairs, trying to suppress a small smile as she thought of Brandon's surprise when he saw her. Maybe he wouldn't even wake up and see her there, next to him, until morning. She wondered if he already had the girls with him, or if they were joining him in the morning. She suspected they might already be there, which was probably why he had come up so early.

The porter turned the key in the door for her, and she told him to set the bags down just inside the door and leave them there, as she tipped him and put a finger to her lips, for fear that Brandon was sleeping. He'd had a hard week with the trial, and he was probably exhausted. She tipped the porter handsomely, and turned on one small light in the living room of the suite, and closed the door behind her. Brandon was such a good customer that they almost always gave him a two-bedroom suite for the price of two king-size rooms, and she made her way through the living room of the suite now in the dim light, careful not to wake anyone up. There was no sound in the room beyond, and she was sure he was asleep. His briefcase stood near the desk, his jacket was hung over the back of a chair, there were several books and newspapers, *The Wall Street Journal, The New York Times*, a Law Review, and there was a pair of his shoes, the loafers he often wore to work, under the chair where he'd hung the jacket. He was fairly neat at home, but in hotels he was never as careful.

She set down all her bags, and with a small smile, she tiptoed into the darkness of the bedroom. She just wanted to see him, and then she'd get undressed, and get into bed beside him. The room was dark as she went in, but as her eyes adjusted to the darkness, she saw that there was no one in the bed. The covers were turned back, and there were chocolates on the pillows. Brandon wasn't there. She wondered if he was with the girls, or still with Joanie talking about business again, or maybe he'd gone to a movie. He liked going to movies so he could unwind, particularly after a hard week, like the trial. But she was a little disappointed not to

see him. She realized quickly though that this would give her time
to shower and wash her hair, and she'd have time to relax before
he got home, and they could go to bed together, possibly with a
more interesting outcome. She had to force Jeff from her head
again as she thought of it, and it was ridiculous but she felt unfaithful to him too now. It was a totally schizophrenic situation.
But she would not allow herself to think of him, as she flicked on
the light so she could get ready.

She took off her suit jacket, and went to hang it up in the
closet, and as soon as she got there she realized why Brandon
wasn't in bed. They'd given her the key to the wrong room.
There were someone else's clothes there. There were half a dozen
women's dresses hanging there, two of them fairly dressy, and a
pair of jeans, and some shoes. And as she realized it, Allegra
backed out of the closet quickly. She hurried back to the living
room, to pick up her things before the people returned and were
outraged by her intrusion. But as she reached the living room, she
saw his jacket again, and the familiar shoes, and she went and
looked at them again. She was sure of it. They were Brandon's.
And the briefcase was his too. She'd have known it anywhere, and
it bore his initials. It was Brandon's room . . . but there were
women's things in the closet. She went back and looked again,
wondering if they were her things and he had brought them in
case she'd join him, but that was ridiculous. These were the
clothes of a woman who was at least four or five inches shorter.
Allegra fingered the dresses, as though trying to understand why
they were there. She was so tired, her mind refused to absorb
what she was seeing.

She walked into the bathroom then. There was makeup, and
gold slippers with little white feathers on them, and an almost
transparent white lace nightgown. And as Allegra stared at it, the
full impact of what she was seeing finally hit her. He had come to
San Francisco with another woman. These weren't her things,
they didn't belong to his daughters, who were clearly not there.
And she realized he didn't even have a two-bedroom suite this
time, as usual, to accommodate the girls. And the clothes she had

seen were far too small to be Joanie's. These were clearly someone else's. But whose? That remained an unanswered question.
As she looked around, she saw feminine articles of clothing everywhere, panty hose on the bed, a bra over the back of a chair,
panties next to the sink. Allegra wanted to scream as she looked at
all of it. What had he been doing? What had he done? And for
how long? How many times had he fooled her? How many times
had he come to San Francisco with someone else, while telling
her that he wanted to be alone with his children? She had never
suspected it, not even for a minute. She had always trusted him.
And he had cheated and lied. And there had been plenty of opportunity for him to do it in Los Angeles too. Jeff's face loomed into
her head as she thought of all of it. She had been consumed with
guilt over a few kisses, and left a man who claimed to be seriously
interested in her, all because she felt such an obligation, and a
bond, to Brandon. And all the while he was a cheat and a liar. Hot
tears stung her eyes as she continued to look around. But there
was no more to see, and she knew she didn't want to be there
when they returned from dinner.

Her face blazed as she thought of all the times he had been
so aloof, and needed "space," and had to be "alone," and could
never make a commitment to her. No wonder. He was a complete
bastard.

Juggling all her bags awkwardly, she hurried from the room,
and rushed to the elevator, praying that they wouldn't come out
of it just as she was leaving. But the elevator was empty when she
got in, and she went all the way downstairs to the California
Street entrance, and hurried outside to look for a cab, knowing
full well it might take a while for her to find one. Taxis in San
Francisco were not as easy to find as they were in New York, and
most of them would be waiting at the hotel's main entrance. But
that was the last place she wanted to be now. She didn't want to
run into Brandon as they came back from wherever they'd been.
And she stood on California Street, holding her bags, as the cable
cars lumbered by laden with tourists. She looked up at them with
eyes filled with tears and anger.

It was beyond incredible what he'd done to her. He'd been cheating on her, and God only knew for how long. The master of noncommitment had been spreading himself around.

She finally saw a cab, and dropped her briefcase to hail it, and the driver got out to help her organize her bags.

"Thanks very much," she said distractedly, and got into the taxi.

"Where to?"

"The airport," she said as her voice shook, and she covered her face with her hands.

"You all right, miss?" He was a nice old guy, and he felt sorry for her. She looked like a little kid running away from home.

"I'm fine," she said, her face awash with tears, as they drove back the way she had come less than an hour before, and as she looked down, she saw that she still had the room key in her hand. She dropped it on the seat next to her, and stared out the window, wondering for how long her life with him had been a lie. She tried to think back to all the times he had said he had to come and see the children, and the other times when he had said he needed to be alone and have some space. Looking back on it, she wondered if he had always cheated on her right from the beginning, if this was just a very old game with him, and part of his lifestyle.

They got back to the airport again in twenty minutes, and the driver helped her out of the cab. "Where are you going tonight?" he asked her gently. He was an old man with a paunch and a bushy mustache. But she was such a pretty girl, and she had cried all the way to the airport. He felt sorry for her, and he wanted to help her.

"Back to L.A.," she said, fighting to regain her composure, but it seemed hopeless as she reached into her bag for a tissue and blew her nose. "I'm sorry. . . . I'm really fine," she said apologetically.

"Honey, you don't look it. But everything's gonna be okay. You just go on home. Whatever he done, he'll be sorry in the morning," he said, assuming she'd had trouble with a man. But Brandon would never be as sorry as she was that night.

She thanked him and walked into the terminal, only to be told that she had missed the last flight. The last flight for L.A. left at nine o'clock. It was after midnight, and all she could do now was sit in the airport and wait for the first flight the next morning. There wasn't even anyone there to check her bags for her. They suggested she go to the airport hotel, but she didn't even want to do that. She didn't want to go anywhere. She just wanted to sit there. She had a lot to think about, and for a fraction of a second, she thought of calling Jeff. But that didn't seem right either, whining to him after all she'd put him through in New York. She had made him sweat for every one of her kisses, while Brandon was probably getting laid all week. She couldn't help wondering who the girl at the Fairmont had been, but she had been too taken aback to try to look for identification, or her name anywhere. It had been such a cozy scene, with her underwear and her see-through nightgown. Allegra still couldn't believe what she'd seen. She had felt like an intruder, and she was only grateful they hadn't walked in on her. That would have been the last straw. Or worse yet, if she had walked in on them while they were in bed. Just thinking about it made her shudder.

She rented a locker and put her bags in it, so she could get a cup of coffee and not have to drag them around with her. She started to feel calmer after a while, and for a little while she got really angry, but most of the time she felt just plain sad. She thought about calling her mother and telling her, but her mother disliked Brandon so much, she didn't want to give her the satisfaction of telling her he'd been cheating on her all along. Or had he been? There was no way to know now. And she doubted that he'd be honest with her. For the moment, he didn't even know he'd been caught red-handed.

She drank five big cups of black coffee, and stayed up all night, reading magazines, thinking about him, and wandering around. She thought about writing him a letter, and telling him everything she felt, but that didn't seem strong enough. She didn't know what to do. She could have gone back to the Fairmont, or called him to see what he'd say. She could have done a lot of things, but most of all, she just wanted to go home and think about it.

She sat and watched the sun come up, and she started to cry again as she thought of him. And she felt like a madwoman when she got on the first plane at six o'clock. There were a handful of what looked like businessmen, and a couple of families, but it was Saturday and there was hardly anyone on the flight at all.

The stewardess poured her another cup of coffee and gave her a breakfast roll, which she never touched. She felt completely wrung out. She'd been traveling for almost twenty hours by then, and she looked every bit of it when she finally got off the flight. It was seven ten, and once again she got a cab from the airport. This was the third airport she'd seen in less than two days. She lay her head back against the seat, as the taxi drove her home, and at eight o'clock she walked through her front door. She'd been gone for nearly seven days, and she'd half fallen in love with a man three thousand miles away, and found the man she had been devoted to for two years cheating on her. It had been a rough week, particularly since the night before in San Francisco.

She set her briefcase down, and stood looking around. There was a stack of mail on her desk the cleaning lady had left for her, and her answering machine was almost full when she turned it on. There were the usual messages from the dry cleaner about a jacket they couldn't repair, the laundry about the pillowcases they'd lost, a health club that wanted her to enroll, the garage where she bought tires for her car. Her mother had called the night before to see if she wanted to have dinner with them on Sunday night, and Carmen had called to say she was staying at a friend's. She had left a number that Allegra knew she'd heard before, but she didn't quite remember it, and it went by too fast anyway. And then at the very end, Brandon had called. He said he was going to San Francisco to see the girls, they had pled at the trial and ended it early, and the girls really wanted him to come up. He was sure she was tired after a week in New York, and had a lot of catching up to do. And he would see her on Sunday night when he got back. She wondered if he would bother to call her again, or if he thought that covered it. And she wondered too if he thought she might call him.

She had no intention of calling him, or anyone else at the moment. She wanted to be alone, to lick her wounds, and decide what had to be done. She wasn't sure yet how she was going to tell him. But it was pretty straightforward, there was no mystery to what he'd done, and she couldn't imagine continuing the relationship beyond that.

She unpacked and put her clothes away. She made herself some toast, and a cup of tea. She took a shower and washed her hair, and tried to achieve some kind of normalcy, but all the while there was a constant, almost physical ache in her heart. It felt like something she was carrying deep inside her, as though something had broken inside as she looked at Brandon's girlfriend's bra and her see-through nightgown.

She called her parents at ten o'clock that morning, but she was relieved when they weren't there. Sam said they were playing tennis at the club. Allegra told her only that she was fine, and had just gotten back from New York that morning, but she had too much to do to come to dinner on Sunday night.

"Tell Mom for me, will you, Sam?"

"Sure," she said offhandedly, and Allegra immediately worried that her mother wouldn't get the message. Samantha did that sometimes if she had more important things on her mind, like a party, or a boy, or a shopping spree with a girlfriend. "Don't forget, will you, please? I don't want her to think I didn't call her back."

"Well, listen to Miss Important. Your messages aren't such a big deal, you know, Allie."

"Maybe they are to Mom."

"Relax, I'll give it to her. How was New York, by the way? Did you buy anything?" Yes, a book by a man I met and went ice-skating with. . . .

"I didn't have time to do any shopping."

"Bummer. That's no fun."

"It wasn't really a fun trip. I was working." But there had been more than work involved. "How's Mom?"

"Fine. Why?" Sam sounded surprised that Allegra had asked her. It never occurred to her that something might be wrong. At seventeen her entire world was bordered by her own interests, and currently her parents were low on her scores.

"Is she okay after not getting the award?"

"Sure." Sam shrugged. "She never said anything. I don't really think she cares," which only proved to Allegra how little Samantha knew their mother. Blaire was a perfectionist, and a high achiever, who worried about every little detail. Allegra was sure that she had agonized about not winning the award, but she was too proud to say it, and, of course, seventeen-year-old Sam was completely unaware of their mother's feelings. This was her senior year, and all she could think about was modeling and shopping, and her excitement over going to college.

"Tell her I'll call her when I have time, and send my love to Mom and Dad."

"Gaaad . . . anything else you want me to write down?"

"Knock it off."

"You're in a crabby mood."

"I was at the airport all night." Not to mention what had happened with Brandon. And she was in no mood to take any guff from a seventeen-year-old girl.

"Sorreee . . ."

"Good-bye, Sam." She'd had enough by then, and after she hung up, she thought about it for a while, and decided to call Alan. But he was out and there was no answer there.

She would have liked to talk to him about what had happened. He didn't like Brandon particularly, but he was always fair. And eventually, she wanted to talk to him about Jeff too, and see if he thought she was completely insane for the way she was feeling about a relative stranger.

By noon she was so worn out, she couldn't even think straight, and she finally gave up and lay down on her bed. No one called her, the doorbell never rang. Brandon never even called to see if she'd gotten home from New York all right, and she woke up six hours later. It was dark outside again, and she felt as though she had a ten-thousand-pound weight on her chest and a bowling ball in her stomach. She lay on her bed for a long time, looking at the ceiling, thinking about him, and as she remembered what had happened, tears slid slowly from the corners of her eyes and down her face. The night before had been miserable for her, and she couldn't even think of what to do now. She didn't want to go on, or start again, or trust anyone ever again. Jeff was probably just another one of them. That was all she picked, men who avoided her and hurt her, men who couldn't give and eventually ran away. The only man in her life who had never hurt her, or run away from her, was Simon Steinberg. He was the only man she could trust, or even dared to love. And she knew to her core that he would never betray her.

And now she would have to confront Brandon. It was all so tiring, she couldn't bear to think about it. She didn't want to see his face or his eyes when he lied to her. She would have hated him for it.

She didn't even bother to eat that night, she just lay there, alternately crying and sleeping. She did a lot of both, and when she woke again the next day, on Sunday morning, she finally got up. She felt as though her whole body had been beaten, she ached from head to foot, and she wasn't even sure why. Her outsides hurt almost as much as her insides, and she still had the same dull ache in her heart. She didn't want to talk to anyone, and when Carmen called, Allegra didn't even pick it up. She was giggling and laughing, so Allegra knew she was all right. Allegra didn't pick up a single call until Brandon finally called at four o'clock on Sunday.

She picked up the phone as soon as she heard him. She wanted to get it over with, and he had said he might come to see her that night when he returned from San Francisco.

"Hello, Brandon," she said calmly. Her hand was shaking

terribly, but there was nothing even remotely suspicious in her voice as she answered.

"Hi, babe, how are you? How was the flight from New York?"

"Fine, thanks." She was cool, but not vicious, and he just thought she was distracted by her work. He was that way sometimes too, and to him it seemed normal.

"I called Friday afternoon, but I guess you hadn't gotten in," he said in a relaxed voice.

"I got the message. Where are you?" She was getting tenser.

"I'm still in San Francisco," he explained easily. "I had a great weekend with the girls. Now that the case is settled, I feel as though I have a huge weight off my back. It's terrific." And apparently, so was his weekend.

"I'm glad to hear it. When are you coming back to L.A.?"

"I thought I'd take the six o'clock. I could come by around eight."

"That would be fine," she said, feeling like a robot, and he finally picked it up as he listened.

"Is something wrong?" He didn't sound concerned, only surprised. She was usually so cheerful. "Are you still tired after the trip?"

"Yes, I am." More than she had ever been in her life. "I'll see you at eight then."

"Great." He hesitated for an instant, as though sensing that more was needed than usual, and for once he was willing to give it. He was very artful at covering his tracks. "Allegra . . . I really missed you."

"So did I," she said, her eyes filling with tears again. "So did I. I'll see you later," she said, covering it again.

"Do you want to go out to dinner?" She was surprised he had the energy after his weekend with Miss Peekaboo Nightgown, or maybe she was already an old flame and didn't require quite as much zeal as it had appeared to Allegra.

"Actually, I'd rather stay here." What she had to say to him she couldn't say in a restaurant, or any public place. The next four hours seemed endless to her. She needed to get it off her chest as soon as possible, for her own sake.

She went for a long walk that afternoon, and called her parents. She told her mother she had to go into the office and work late that night.

"On Sunday? That's ridiculous," Blaire said, worried about her. She worked much too hard, and she sounded exhausted.

"I've been gone for a week, Mom. I'll come by sometime this week."

"Take care of yourself," Blaire said, and for once she didn't ask about Brandon. Allegra was grateful for that.

She ate a yogurt for dinner, tried to watch the news on TV, but found she didn't know what she was seeing, and eventually she just lay down and waited on the couch. She heard him in the driveway at eight-fifteen, and when she heard his key in the door, she sat up. She had given him the key over a year before, and he looked happy and relaxed as he smiled at her and came to give her a hug where she was sitting. But she avoided him completely, and surprised him by standing up to greet him. She took a step backward from him, looking him over. She was searching his eyes, but there were no answers there to any of her questions.

He looked shocked. She was usually so affectionate and so friendly, it startled him when she avoided him, and for a long moment, she didn't speak at all, as they stared at each other in silence. "Is something wrong?" he asked her finally.

"I think so. Don't you, Brandon?" It was all she said, and she could see a muscle in his neck become tense immediately as he became wary.

"What's that supposed to mean?"

"Maybe you should tell me. I have the feeling suddenly that some things have been going on that I knew nothing about, Brandon. Things that maybe you should have mentioned."

"Like what?" He stood looking at her, beginning to get angry, but she knew it was a defense. He'd been caught, and he sensed it even before she told him. "I don't know what you're talking about." He walked across the room, and watching him, she sat down again.

"Yes, you do. You know exactly what I mean, you're just not sure how much I know, and neither am I. I guess that's what I want to know now. How often, and for how long? How many women have you been screwing? Have you been cheating on me for the whole two years, or did it start recently? When did it start, Brandon? All of a sudden I remember all the times you went to San Francisco, all the times you told me you wanted to be alone with the girls, or you and Joanie had to talk. That doesn't even take into account the time you went to Chicago, and the deal you were supposedly making in Detroit. So what was it?" She looked at him coolly. All the pain she'd felt for two days was suddenly ice cold. "Where do we start?"

"I have absolutely no idea what you're talking about," he said, trying to make her sound and feel foolish. But he looked pale as he sat down. And she saw that his hands were shaking when he lit a cigarette.

"This must make you very nervous. It would me, if I were in your shoes," she said, watching him. "The thing is, I just don't see the point. Why bother? We're not even married, why cheat on me? Why not just call it a day before it gets to that point?"

"What point?" he said, trying to look confused. He would have liked to imply that she was crazy, but he didn't quite dare. He could see easily that she was seething.

"The point you were at this weekend, at the Fairmont. Surely, I don't have to spell it out." Her long blond hair hung over her shoulders, and she had no idea how lovely she looked in her blue jeans and an old navy blue sweatshirt.

"What is all that supposed to mean?" He was playing it to the end, and she looked at him with utter contempt.

"All right, if you want things made a little clearer—though if I were in your shoes, I don't think I'd do that. I called your office on Friday, and your secretary told me the case was over and you were going to San Francisco to see the girls. So, fool that I am, I decided to surprise you, and I changed my ticket from New

York." His face was getting whiter and whiter as she spoke, but he continued to look calm and smoke his cigarette, as his eyes narrowed.

"I flew to San Francisco," she went on. "The flight was delayed, but I'll spare you all that. I got to the Fairmont about eleven-thirty Friday night, and I thought I'd surprise you and just slip into bed. They gave me the room key when I said I was Mrs. Edwards."

He looked annoyed as he stubbed out his cigarette. "They really shouldn't do that."

"I guess not," she said sadly. It wasn't a pretty story, and telling it to him brought it all back. "Anyway, I let myself into the room, and I guess, all things considered, I got lucky. You and your friend were out. At first I thought I had the wrong room, but then I recognized your briefcase and your jacket. What I didn't recognize though, was everything else. It wasn't mine, it wasn't Nicky's or Stephanie's, it wasn't Joanie's. So whose was it, Brandon? Should I bother to ask, or do we just call it quits and forget it?" She sat staring at him and he looked at her in total silence, searching for words with which to answer. For a long moment, he found none.

"You had no business being there, Allegra," he said at last, which truly startled her. She couldn't believe that.

"Why not?"

"You weren't invited. Considering that, maybe you got what you deserved. I don't just show up when you go away on business. We don't belong to each other; we're not married. We have a right to our own lives."

"Really?" She looked at him, truly amazed at what he was saying to her. "I thought we were more or less, what do they call it these days—steadies? Or is that passé? We're not live ins, so what are we? I thought we were both monogamous, but apparently not."

"I don't owe you any explanations. I'm not married to you," he said as he stood up.

"No, you're not," she said, watching him. "You're married to someone else."

"That's what bothers you, isn't it? The fact that I maintained my own independence. I'm not owned by you, or anyone else. You don't own me, Allegra. You never will, not you, or your family, or anyone. I do exactly what I want."

She had never understood the depths of his resentment; she had no idea that that was how he felt. "I never wanted to own you. I just wanted to love you, and maybe eventually be your wife."

"I'm not interested in that. If I were, I'd have gotten divorced. But I never have. Couldn't you figure that out?" She not only felt hurt, she felt stupid. The message had been clear, just as Dr. Green had said, and she had ignored it. She hadn't wanted to hear it, just as she didn't want to hear it now. But they were both angry, and it was all finally getting said. And it was very painful.

"You took advantage of me," she accused him from across the room. "You lied to me, you cheated! You had no right to do that. I was decent to you, Brandon, that's not fair!"

"Fair is a lot of bullshit, who do you know that's fair in this world? Don't give me that crap. You have to look out for yourself, Allegra."

"By screwing another woman when you tell me you're with your children? What kind of shit is that?"

"It's my life, it's my business, they're my kids. All you ever wanted was to horn in on everything, and be a part of it. I never wanted that, and you knew it."

"No, I didn't," she said plaintively. "I never understood that. And maybe you should have explained it, before it came to this, and we both wasted two years of our lives."

"I didn't waste anything," he said smugly. "I did exactly what I wanted."

"Get out of my house," she said as she looked at him, and she truly meant it. "You're a miserable human being, you're a liar and a cheat, and I've been carrying your emotional deadweight for the last two years. You don't give anything to anybody, not to me, or your friends, or the people you meet, or even those you pretend to care about. You don't even give anything to your kids. You're so worried that someone's going to get under your skin, or make you feel something, or ask for a commitment. You're a pathetic excuse for a human being. Now get out of my house."

He hesitated for just an instant, glancing toward her bedroom, and she stood up and walked to the front door and held it open for him. "You heard me. Get out. I mean it."

"I believe some of my clothes are still in your bedroom, Allegra."

"I'll mail them to you. Good-bye." She stood there and waited and, looking as though he would have liked to strangle her, he brushed past her, without a kiss or an apology, a last look back, a twinge of regret, or even a good-bye. He was completely heartless, and the things he had said to her had cut right through her heart. She had heard all of them, about how he had never been faithful to her, and he had always done what he wanted. He had been selfish and cold, and all the warmth and patience in the world wouldn't have drawn him out. And the worst thing she had heard were the words he hadn't said, the fact that he hadn't loved her. But everything else he had said added up to that. Dr. Green had been right. And Allegra stood there wondering how she could have been so stupid.

She sat down and thought about it for a long time after he left, and then finally she started to cry. He was what she had said to him, a miserable, selfish human being, but she had still been telling herself for two years that they loved each other, and it hurt terribly to have been so wrong about him. She didn't even dare call Dr. Green for comfort. She didn't want to hear how she had made the same mistake again, nor hear her mother say that it was a blessing he was gone. She knew now that she was better off without him, but it still hurt terribly to realize that she had been so ill-used and so misled by him. He hadn't given a damn about her, and he had pretty much admitted it, as he sat there, smoking on her couch and destroying what was left of her feelings. She wanted to tell someone that she didn't believe it, that it was unfair, that he was a sonofabitch, but there was no one to tell. She was all alone. It was the way she had been when she met him, rejected, alone, jilted by her last lover. She thought she had learned since then, but apparently not. That was the worst part. There was no hiding from the truth now.

She lay on her bed for a long time after he left, thinking about him, telling herself that she was better off, and remembering how she had felt in his room at the Fairmont. But still, as she looked at a photograph of them in Santa Barbara the year before, when things had been going so well, and she thought she was so in love with him, she felt a sense of loss beyond measure.

She wondered if he would call her again, if he would ever tell her how sorry he was, how unfair he'd been. But she had already been there twice before, and no one ever did that. They just disappeared after breaking your heart, and moved on to do it to someone else. She had just watched two years of her life walk out the door with Brandon Edwards.

And it took all the strength she had later that night to get up and turn the lights off. As she did, she stood looking at the view, and thinking about him. She knew she could have called Jeff, and told him she was free, but she didn't want to do that. She needed time to mourn Brandon. However inadequate he may have been, or disliked by her family, she had still loved him.

CHAPTER 9

When Allegra went to work on Monday after her trip to New York, she looked as though she'd been through the wringer. She seemed tired and pale, and Alice commented that she looked tired and thinner.

"What happened to you?" she asked discreetly, and Allegra shrugged. It was still very painful. She kept thinking of what a fool she had been, and how long he must have been cheating on her. She felt like a total moron. As she worked throughout the day, she began to realize that her pride was hurt, but she wasn't so sure how devastated she was, or even how much she had loved him. That was the odd thing about it. She was sad, but she wasn't all that sorry it was over. In a way, it was a relief that it had ended. For the last week in New York, she'd been questioning her relationship with him, and she had started to see the things that other people talked about, the distance, the aloofness, the lack of intimacy, the fact that he was never there for her, which was no longer a surprise, if he had ten other girlfriends, or even one. She would never know now how many there were, or how serious they may have been. But knowing there had been any at all not only made her feel angry, but foolish.

But by midday, she was so busy with the work that had piled up on her desk that she was no longer thinking about Brandon. Bram loved the tour she and the promoters had organized. And

Malachi had called from rehab, and said he wanted money, and at his wife's request she had refused him.

"Sorry, Mal. Ask me again in thirty days after you detox, and we'll talk about it."

"Who the hell are you working for?" he asked in a fury, and she smiled, scribbling notes for her next meeting.

"I'm working for you. You need to do this." She told him about his tour too, and it distracted him for a little while before he went for his massage and biofeedback. "I wish I had time for things like that," she told Alice, gulping a yogurt and a cup of coffee as she went over a contract for a movie deal that had just come in for Carmen. It was fabulous, and she was going to be thrilled with it. It was a film for a very major star, and after it, she would be one for a lifetime. But when Allegra dialed Carmen's number she got the answering machine. "Where the hell is she?" Allegra muttered. She had tried all the numbers she had for her but nothing answered. Allegra tried to remember other names Carmen had given her, of friends, or of her grandmother in Portland. She had never disappeared that way before, and usually she called Allegra half a dozen times a day, with the most minute problems. This was extremely unusual behavior for Carmen Connors. It seemed as though absolutely no one could find her.

There had only been one story about her in *Chatter* after the Golden Globes, with a picture of Allegra on Alan's arm as they got out of the car, and Carmen just behind them. The story suggested that Allegra was only a beard for them, and that there was a big romance brewing between Alan Carr and Carmen Connors. The funny thing was that, for once, they were ahead of the story.

Reading it made Allegra think of a message she'd gotten on her home machine while she was in New York, with a phone number that had sounded familiar. She dug through her briefcase for her appointment book. She had written the number, along with several others, on a piece of paper, and stuck it in there. She flipped through it for a few minutes, and finally she found it. She had missed it entirely, and as she looked at it, she recognized the number. It was Alan's number in Malibu. Carmen was staying there, and Allegra remembered he had offered her the house, and Allegra smiled to herself as she dialed the number, and Alan answered.

She had called him herself at his house in Beverly Hills over the weekend and he hadn't been there. She hadn't even thought of calling him in Malibu because he so seldom went there. And she had been incredibly stupid not to figure out that he was probably still there with Carmen.

"Hi, there," she said innocently, as though she were just calling him for no particular reason.

"Don't give me that," he said, laughing at her. He knew her too well. "The answer is, it's none of your business."

"What's the question?" she asked, laughing at him. He sounded happy and even silly, and she could hear someone talking and giggling in the background, and she was sure it was Carmen.

"The question is where have I been all week. And the answer is 'none of your business.' "

"Let me guess. In Malibu, with a certain Golden Globe winner this year. Am I getting warm?"

"You're positively boiling. She called and left you my number anyway, so you're not that great a detective. You had a clue."

"Yeah, and I was too dumb to figure it out. I thought the number sounded familiar, but I didn't get it till just now. So how's life on the beach?" It was good hearing his voice again. She had wanted to tell him about Brandon, but she didn't feel like talking about it now, and definitely not in front of Carmen. She didn't like sharing her personal problems with her clients. Alan was different. They'd been bosom buddies since they were children.

"Life is pretty good." He was beaming. "Pretty damn good." As he said it, he leaned over and kissed Carmen.

"Aren't you supposed to be working?" Allegra had lost track of him. His agent at CAA had done his last contract.

"Not for another month or two. I'm still waiting for final word on this picture."

"Well, I've got a great one for Carmen, maybe she'll beat

you to it." Although she wouldn't start rehearsing till June, if she took it.

"Where's it shooting?" He tried to sound nonchalant about it, but Allegra knew he had a vested interest.

"Right here in L.A., unlike yours," she added. His movies always seemed to be shot in god-awful, remote places. His next one was going to be shooting in Switzerland, but he'd recently been offered another one for Mexico, Chile, and Alaska. It was a great adventure film, but it was going to be a lot of work, and very rugged. His last one had been shot in the jungles of Thailand, and two of the stuntmen had been killed. Maybe now, with Carmen around, she'd at least get him to stop doing his own stunt work. "Does Carmen know where you're going on the next one?"

"I already told her. She said she'll come with me." At least Switzerland was civilized, unlike most of the countries he worked in.

"Maybe you'll finish in time to watch her do this one." It was really going to be a great movie, and Allegra was excited for her, which was why she had called her. "Can I talk to her?"

"That's it? Fifteen years of friendship, a date for the Golden Globes, and now you're through with me like an old hankie."

"Not exactly," she laughed at him, feeling better than she had all day. She still felt an odd combination of sad and stupid over Brandon, but there was something about having dealt with it and confronted him that made her feel stronger. She was tempted to tell Alan, but she wasn't ready to do it. It would take time to admit to the world that he'd made a fool of her and she'd found him out. But at least she'd ended it. That was something.

"How was New York? Make any great deals there?"

"Some. It was fun. There was lots of snow." And skating. And kissing.

"Snow's not much fun in New York." He couldn't understand why she sounded so cheerful about it.

"Actually, I went skating."

"You did? Uh-oh, there must be something going on. Did

you have an affair with that old author you said you were going to see? What's his name? Dickens? Tolstoy?"

"Jason Haverton. He was terrific. And no, I did not have an affair with him, you irreverent idiot, though I liked him a lot, and he probably would have been willing."

"Old guys will do anything for sex, Al. You should know that by now."

"Are you doing research firsthand these days? Is that it?"

"Nasty, nasty. It's not nice to be rude to your high school sweetheart."

"You're no one's sweetheart anymore, you know, except maybe Carmen's." Not to mention several million women around the world. But they were such old friends, it was easy for her to ignore it. "Are you ever going to let me talk to her, or do I have to put up with this bullshit all afternoon?" She was laughing at him; he was impossible, but she loved him.

"I'll ask her if she wants to speak to you. And by the way, when are we going to see you?" He made it sound as though they were married, and Allegra thought it was sweet as she listened.

"Maybe this weekend, if I don't have anything else to do," which she now knew she didn't.

"I said see 'you,' that was singular, not plural, as in including the dead one."

"Don't be rude about Brandon," she said, more out of habit than feeling. She would have liked to be very rude about him, but she wasn't ready to tell Alan.

"I'm never rude about the dead. Try to get rid of him before we go out to dinner. Or maybe we'll stay here. I'll let you talk to the boss about it," he said, handing Carmen the phone as he kissed her. And at Allegra's end, there was a long silence as she waited.

"Hi," Carmen said finally, sounding bouncy and happy. She had had a great nine days in total seclusion with Alan. Several people in the colony had recognized her as she walked down the beach, but no one had bothered her. There were people there who were even more famous than she was. They were used to seeing celebrities on the beach then. They saw Nicholson and Streisand and Nick Nolte almost every day, and Cher, and Tom Cruise and Nicole Kidman. Carmen Connors was among her own kind in Malibu with Alan, and the security was terrific. "I missed you," Carmen said, but she'd been busy.

"I missed you too. New York was crazy, but I loved it. Guess what I've got for you though?" Allegra was so excited she felt like a kid as she dangled it in front of Carmen.

"I don't know. The perfume? Did you talk to them in New York?"

"I did. It sounds awful. You'd hate it, and you'd have to spend months in department stores selling it. Forget it. Noooo . . ." she said tantalizingly. "How about a big, new, juicy movie, with a part that will win you the Academy Award or I'll eat my briefcase."

"Wow! Who's in it?"

"You are." And she named five other stars, who took Carmen's breath away. "And how about three million dollars for starring in it, for the winner of this year's Golden Globe Award? How does that sound?"

"I'm dying!" Carmen screamed, and ran to tell Alan, and then she came back again to talk to Allegra. "I can't believe it."

"You deserve it," Allegra reassured her, wondering why it was that she thought everyone in her life deserved something wonderful, from relationships to movies, and she never seemed to feel that she deserved as much herself. It was an interesting question. "I'd like you to come in and talk to the producers about it," Allegra told her gently.

"Sure. When?"

"You tell me what's good for you, and I'll set it up." She glanced at her calendar. "How about Thursday?"

"Wow! Can Alan come?"

"If he'd like to."

At Carmen's end, Alan was nodding. "He said he would . . . and Allie," she hesitated, but it was important to her now, "maybe next time, Alan and I could do a picture together." Oh,

God, thought Allegra. It was going to be one of those deals. They weren't always easy. And America's females, not to mention females the world over, weren't going to love having it rubbed in their faces that their favorite sex symbol was as good as married, and to a girl who looked like Carmen.

"We'll talk about it. Those things aren't quite so simple, but it can be done. Eventually. If you're both serious about it." What she didn't want was to set something up for a cool seven or eight million dollars for both of them, or maybe ten total since it was Alan, and then have them break up, and either refuse to make the picture, or worse, kill it. Those headaches she didn't need. "Let's wait awhile."

"I know. You think we'll break up," Carmen said wisely. "We won't. I'm sure of that. He's the most incredible man I've ever known," she said, lowering her voice conspiratorially to Allie. "I can't live without him."

"How are the threats these days? Quiet again?"

"Completely." But she also hadn't gone anywhere, and after she won the Golden Globe, surprisingly, even the tabloids had left her alone. "I feel so safe here," Carmen explained to her, and Allegra smiled. Who wouldn't, with Alan? Her sister Sam was right, he was a hunk, and such a nice one.

"I'm happy for you two," Allegra said sincerely.

"Thanks, Allie. It's all thanks to you. Will you come to dinner and celebrate with us this weekend?"

"I'd love to."

"Come on Saturday. On Sunday, Alan likes to go bowling."

"Why don't I come on Sunday then? I'd love to beat him."

"Then we'll go bowling on Saturday if you want. But come to dinner then."

"Who's cooking?" she teased, and Carmen giggled.

"We both are. He's teaching me. And Allie . . ." She laughed excitedly again. Her life was just beginning. "Thanks for the movie."

"Thank the producers, don't thank me. They called me. I really think you'll like it."

"I love it."

"See you Saturday. Unless we meet with the producers first. Call me if you need anything in the meantime." But Alan seemed to be taking care of everything these days. She had only called once all week, and even then left a very ordinary message. Things were settling down, which was just as well. Allegra needed a little time to herself, to lick her wounds and figure out what had really happened.

And by the end of the week, all she had done was work, and see her clients. Carmen and Alan had come in on Thursday, and the deal for her new movie was as good as signed. And that afternoon, she went to Dr. Green, and braced herself for a beating. But she was pleasantly surprised. Dr. Green was proud of the way she had handled things, and her only reproach was that Allegra hadn't called her.

"Why didn't you call and talk to me over the weekend? It must have been very difficult for you, after you went to San Francisco, and before you saw Brandon on Sunday."

"It was, but there was nothing much to say. Mostly, I just felt terrible that he had probably been doing it all along and I was too stupid to figure it out. I kept thinking he needed time and space and love, and the truth was, he didn't give a damn about me."

"He probably did care about you," Dr. Green corrected her. She had gone too far the other way now, in her anger at having been betrayed, and having found him with another woman. "He cared about you, to the best of his limited abilities. That's not saying much, Allegra, but it's something."

"But why was I so stupid? How could I have been such a fool for two years?"

"Because you wanted to be. You needed companionship and protection. The only unfortunate thing is that he was a very unwilling companion to you, and you were the one protecting him. It was a very unsatisfactory arrangement. But what about now? How do you feel about all this?"

"Angry, stupid, resentful, furious, independent, whole, free, sorry, not sorry at all, scared that the next one won't be any different. Maybe they're all the same, or at least the ones I find are. I think that's what scares me the most, the idea that it could happen again, and again, and again . . . that I'm just going to keep finding lemons forever."

"You don't have to, you know, and I think you learned something this time." The therapist sounded more confident than Allegra felt, which surprised her.

"What makes you think that?"

"Because as soon as you realized what was happening, you confronted it, you brought it to a head, and you let it end there—whether he ended it or you did. You did, actually, you exposed him, and he disappeared, like a little worm down a hole. But at least you didn't pretend to yourself that he was still there for you when he wasn't. That's a big step, Allegra."

"Maybe," she said halfheartedly. "But now what?"

"You tell me. What do you want? Whatever it is, you have the power to get it if you want. It's up to you, you know. You can find someone wonderful, if you want that."

"I think I met someone wonderful in New York," she said cautiously, "but I'm not sure." She was suspicious of him now that she was back. She was suspicious of everyone, and her memories of him couldn't be as fantastic as she remembered. He had to be just like the others, if she'd picked him.

"Long-distance relationships are another way of avoiding intimacy," Dr. Green reminded her, and this time Allegra smiled at her.

"He was there on business too, although he's originally a New Yorker. But he lives here now." An eyebrow immediately shot up, and Dr. Green nodded.

"How interesting. Tell me about him." Allegra told her all she knew, and all she'd seen of him. And just telling her about the carriage ride and the skating made it sound unreal, even to her own ears, but as she talked about him, she really missed him. She had promised herself not to call him for a while, and she hadn't. She wanted time for the dust to settle after Brandon.

"Why? Maybe he'll think you're not interested in him," Dr. Green said encouragingly. "He sounds very nice and very normal. Why not call him?"

"I'm not ready yet." Allegra balked at the idea, and nothing Dr. Green said that afternoon convinced her. "I need time after Brandon."

"No, you don't," Dr. Green called her bluff. "You've been making excuses for him for two years with everyone you know, and you've just spent a week kissing some man in New York every chance you got. I don't even think you're that sad over Brandon."

Allegra smiled. The doctor had her number. "Maybe I'm just hiding for a while."

"Why?"

"Scared, I guess." Allegra confessed to her. "Jeff seems so terrific, I don't want to be disappointed. What if he isn't? It would kill me."

"No, it wouldn't. What if he's human? How would that be? Too disappointing? Do you like him better as a fantasy, or a counterpoint to Brandon?" Allegra hoped not.

"I don't know what I feel for him, except that when I was with him, I would have followed him to the ends of the earth. I trusted him completely. And now that I'm home, I think that scares me."

"That's understandable, but you could at least see him."

"He hasn't called me. Maybe he has someone else."

"Or maybe he's busy, or writing, or he's afraid to intrude since you made such a fuss about your relationship with Brandon. Maybe you owe it to him to at least tell him it's over. That might be something." But Allegra was playing a waiting game, and she wanted to see if he called her.

And as it turned out, he did, on Friday. He called late in the afternoon, and he sounded tentative when he asked for her, as though he wasn't sure he should be calling her in the office. Alice told her he was on, and Allegra took a deep breath and picked up the phone, but her hand was shaking. She felt as though the rest of her life had just begun the moment she heard him.

"Allegra?"

"Hi, Jeff. How are you?"

"Better now. I know I said I wouldn't call for a while, but you've been driving me up the wall. I figured I had to, and then I'd leave you alone again for a while. I really miss you." They were the words she had sweated two years for with Brandon, and with Jeff it was all so easy. He sounded wonderful, and she felt guilty for not calling him, as Dr. Green had suggested.

"I miss you too," she said softly.

"How are all your kids now that you're back? Everyone behaving? Or are you fighting off death threats and crazies and paparazzi at four in the morning?"

"It's been a quiet week, actually." Except in her own life, but she didn't say that. "What about you? How's the screenplay coming?"

"Miserably. I haven't felt like working since I've been back. I think you distracted me severely." There was a moment's pause, and then he asked her something he'd wondered since he left New York. "How was your weekend?"

"It was interesting," she said coolly. "We'll have to talk about it sometime." But she didn't want to discuss it in the office.

"That sounds like a date in the very distant future," he said sadly. He had waited all week to call her, and she sounded so good to him now. He was dying to see her.

"I don't think it is," she said quietly. She tried to force herself to be brave and remember Dr. Green's words. "What are you doing this weekend?" She held her breath and waited. Oh, God, don't let him be like the others. . . .

"Is that an invitation?" He sounded stunned. What had she done with Brandon? But he was afraid to ask her and spoil the moment.

"It could be. I'm having dinner with friends in Malibu tomorrow night. Do you want to come? Very informal, in blue jeans and old sweatshirts. We may even go bowling."

"I'd love it." He sounded thrilled. He couldn't believe she had asked him. "Can I ask who the friends are, just out of curiosity, so I don't make a fool of myself when we get there?" He knew the kind of people she hung out with, and he was right.

"Alan Carr and Carmen Connors, but you can't tell anyone you saw them together. They're hiding out in Malibu, to get away from the tabloids."

"I'll be sure to keep it a secret," he said, laughing. There was no one in the world who would ask him. "That sounds like quite an evening."

"It won't be," she said happily. "They're both lousy cooks, but good people. With any luck, they'll buy take-out pasta. I'll suggest it. Carmen hasn't learned to cook yet, and Alan's teaching her. It could be pretty awful." She laughed, happy just talking to him, and they chatted for a while about what the week had been like without each other.

"Were things all right for you when you got back?" he asked her obliquely, and she said they were. But she knew what he was asking her. He wanted to know about Brandon, but it seemed so awkward to tell him on the phone. She really didn't want to. It would be easier to tell him on Saturday, before they went to Alan's.

They talked for a few more minutes, and then they hung up, and she thought about him constantly for the rest of the evening. She had planned to go to her parents' for dinner that night, until she found out they were going out, and she went home and made scrambled eggs for herself, and thought about Jeff, and Brandon. She didn't want to make the same mistake again. She didn't want to believe that someone was what they weren't.

And she was very quiet when Jeff arrived at her house on Saturday, looking immaculate in faded, pressed blue jeans, a crisp white shirt, and a blazer. He still looked very Eastern, and she loved it. He looked like a Ralph Lauren ad. And she was wearing white jeans and a white shirt, and a red sweater over her shoulders.

She felt shy with him at first, and he looked around, admiring her house. It was like starting all over again, until he pulled her slowly into his arms and kissed her.

"That's better," he said softly. "I've waited a long time for this," he whispered.

"Nine days," she whispered back, and he shook his head in answer.

"Thirty-four years. I've waited a long time for you, Miss Allegra Steinberg."

"What took you so long?" she asked as he folded her into his arms, and they sat on the couch together, admiring the view. She was totally at ease with him again, as though she'd never left him.

"I don't want to be rude," he finally said cautiously, as she went to get him a Diet Coke in the kitchen, and he followed her, and looked around, admiring what she had done. But there was no sign of Brandon. "Where is he?"

"Who?" She looked puzzled as she poured his drink. They were meeting Alan and Carmen in Malibu, not at her house.

"Brandon. My rival." He was curious as to what had happened and why she was available on a Saturday night. She had offered no explanation whatsoever on the phone. Maybe he was in San Francisco. "Is he away?"

"Permanently." She smiled mischievously at him, looking like a naughty kid who's done something she shouldn't. "He's gone. I guess I forgot to tell you." He stood staring at her, and then set his drink down on the granite counter.

"Wait a minute. He's gone . . . out of the picture . . . adios . . . and you didn't tell me? I don't believe it. You little shit!" He grabbed her again, and squeezed her tight in his arms. "How dare you do that to me! I've been trying to figure it out since yesterday when I called you, and you asked me to dinner. Why didn't you call me? I thought that was our deal, you'd call me if anything happened."

"A lot did happen when I got back, but I needed some time to sort it out in my own mind, before I called you." He understood that, but he had agonized over her all week. He would have loved to have known that she had broken up with Brandon. And now he had a thousand questions he wanted to ask her.

"What dastardly deed do I have to thank him for, if I ever see him?"

"Apparently quite a few I didn't know about. But the real topper was when I flew to San Francisco and showed up at the Fairmont last Friday night. That was a good one. He had a woman with him, staying in his room. And suddenly I realized that he's been doing it all along, and he pretty much confirmed that."

"Nice guy. Great principles. I like that in a man. Good moral fiber." He was joking with her, but he was seething inside at what she'd been through. How humiliating, and how cruel. But in an awful way, he was glad it had happened, and so quickly. It was kismet.

"The trouble is," she commented, "I like all those nice things too, principles, ethics, fidelity, all that boring stuff that's out of fashion these days. And I seem to like to delude myself about people I convince myself have them. Unfortunately, I'm wrong usually. I seem to miss the call most of the time. In fact, so far, when it comes to picking losers, I've been batting a thousand."

"Maybe things have finally changed for you," he said, pulling her close to him again, as he stood behind her, and felt her willowy warmth against him. "Maybe your eyesight has gotten better."

"Has it?" She asked him cautiously, wanting answers from him, and reassurance.

"What do you think?"

"I'm asking you. I don't think I could go through that again. This is the third one for me. Three strikes, I'm out."

"No, Allegra," he said, turning her around to face him so he could look at her. "You're just beginning. You're only a baby. That was all practice stuff. Now we go for the brass ring. And you're gonna get it this time . . . you deserve it. . . ." Her eyes filled with tears as she looked at him, and this time when he kissed her, she kissed him back, with all her heart, and the faith that she had given so foolishly before. But he was right. This one was the biggie. He was the genuine article, and he wasn't going to fool her. To her very core, she knew it.

They sat together for a while, and she showed him around. She had the odd feeling that he would be spending a lot of time there, and she was showing him his new home. It was a funny feeling.

"I love it," he said, admiring what she'd done, and the easy warmth of the place. She loved it too, and she was happy he did.

And a little while later, they left for Malibu. It took them forty-five minutes to get to Alan's. She told Jeff about him all the way there, and the pranks they'd committed together over the years, but even knowing all of that, Jeff was still startled into silence when he met them. Carmen was so incredibly beautiful, even in a T-shirt and blue jeans. She had the same breathy, sensual quality Monroe had had, but she was so much more beautiful, so much more breathtaking, that Jeff hadn't been adequately prepared to meet her. And meeting Alan was just like looking straight at a movie screen, except that he was alive and looking at you, and laughing with those perfect teeth, and incredible blue eyes, and finely chiseled features. He reminded Jeff a lot of Gable. They were quite a combination. He could just imagine it once the press got a hold of them, never mind the tabloids.

Their hosts ushered them inside, and Alan had made tamales and guacamole for them, and he served Jeff a tequila. But as hospitable as he was, there was a puzzled expression as he looked at Allegra's date for the evening, and then finally when he got her alone, he challenged her and she laughed mischievously at him.

"What the hell is going on, you little holdout? Who is he? Where's the creep?" Alan never spoke of Brandon in pleasant or even civil terms, because he'd never liked him. But this time Allegra didn't say anything in his defense. She was just grinning at Alan. "I like this one. What did you do with the other one? Kill him?"

"Just about. He's been cheating on me for two years or thereabouts," she summed it up for him in a nutshell. "I walked in on him with one of his sweeties, at the Fairmont last weekend.

Actually, they were out of the room, but her bra and panties weren't, or her see-through nightgown."

"Why didn't you tell me, you turkey?" He looked hurt that she hadn't called him.

"I needed time to get used to it. I don't know." She looked serious for a minute. "I called you once, and you weren't home. And I felt like such a horse's ass, I didn't feel like telling anyone about Brandon. I've been licking my wounds all week."

"Count your blessings," Alan said seriously, pouring her a soda. She didn't want tequila. "That guy would have made you miserable for the rest of your life. Trust me. I know it."

She knew he was right now, and as they talked about it, Carmen and Jeff came in to join them.

"What are you two up to?" Jeff asked, putting an arm around her she smiled coyly. "What's the drill here? Do I trust you with this man? Tell me the truth now so I know what I'm up against. I'm afraid I can't compete with him. Is he a threat?"

Alan laughed and was quick to reassure him. "Not for the last fifteen years, I'm afraid. She was cute as hell at fourteen, but all I ever got out of her were a bunch of sloppy kisses. I hope you've at least gotten better at that," Alan told her rudely, and she shoved him.

"Thanks for nothing. You used to give me beard burn, and get me in trouble with my mother all the time, you creep."

"You know, he still does that." Carmen looked at her sympathetically, and Allegra laughed. It was fun being together, the four of them, and Allegra had never seen either of them as happy.

Alan made tacos and tostadas for dinner, and Carmen made Spanish rice and a huge salad. And there was ice cream and hot fudge sauce for dessert, and they toasted marshmallows in the fireplace, like kids. Then they went for a walk on the beach, and laughed and talked, and played tag as they ran in and out of the ocean as the waves lapped gently against the sand in the bright moonlight. It was a lovely evening.

When they went back inside finally, Carmen grinned at Allegra, and then at Alan. She looked up at him with her huge blue eyes, and whispered something. She was asking if she could tell them, and he hesitated, looking at his old friend, and at Jeff, wondering if the one would disapprove and the other could be trusted. But he decided he could handle either of them, and Carmen could barely keep herself from exploding with excitement.

"We're getting married in Vegas on Valentine's Day," she announced, and Allegra pretended to faint and fall backward.

"Cupid's dream, and a lawyer's nightmare." Her eyes met Alan's immediately, wondering if this was really what he wanted. But it seemed to be; he looked sure of her and of himself, and she had never seen him as happy. He was thirty years old and he ought to know by then what suited him and what didn't. "The papers are going to kill you. I hope to hell you use another name, and you go incognito. Wear wigs, paint your faces, do anything. This is going to be the news of the century. Princess Di and Prince Charles were nothing to this, kids. Please God, be careful."

"We will be," Alan assured her, and then he had an idea. "Will you be our maid of honor, our witness, whatever?" And then he looked at Jeff expansively. "You can come too, if you can put up with her by then. We'd love to have you," Alan said generously and Jeff was touched when he said it. They were warm, genuine people, and he had had a great evening. It wasn't pretentious, or intellectual, or like any of the supposed salons in New York, but it was much more down to earth, and he enjoyed it. It was why he had come to California originally, but these people were special. He liked them both, and he hadn't been able to take his eyes off Allegra all evening. He still couldn't believe his good fortune that she'd broken up with Brandon so quickly.

And since the wedding was only two weeks away, they all talked about it for the next hour. Alan wanted to take Carmen fishing in New Zealand for their honeymoon. He had made a picture there and he really liked it. And she wanted to go to Paris, because she'd never been there.

"I'll take you to New Zealand, Jeff," Alan said expansively, lighting a cigar. "The girls can stay home and go shopping."

But even as they joked about it, Allegra urged them to be careful. The press were going to make their lives miserable once they figured it out. It was vital that no one suspect anything for as long as possible. "How are you going to get to Vegas?"

"I thought we'd just drive," Alan said practically.

"Why don't I rent you a bus? Bram uses a great one. I'll see if I can get it, as a gift from me." It would cost her about five thousand dollars to send them to Vegas in it, but it was fabulous, and well worth it. It was like driving in a yacht, or a private airplane. And if she rented it in her name, no one would be the wiser.

"That sounds like fun," Carmen admitted, and Alan indulged her, and thanked Allegra.

Jeff and Allegra helped them clean up, and they put the dishes in the dishwasher for the maid to deal with in the morning, and Jeff and Allegra left at eleven. The moon was still bright, and he asked her if she'd like to see his house on the way home. It was only a few blocks away. She was hesitant at first, and then she nodded. It was all so new to her still, and in some ways she felt shyer with him now than she had in New York. Everything had been so rushed there. They had to take what they could, while they had it. It was a little bit like a shipboard romance, and now suddenly this was real life, and she knew they both meant it. It was more than a little scary. And she still couldn't believe Carmen and Alan were getting married.

"I introduced them to each other two weeks ago," she said to Jeff incredulously, as they stopped near a small, well-tended beach house.

"That's Hollywood," he laughed and yet, the funny thing was, they seemed perfectly suited to each other. Getting married a month after they met was a risky thing to do, and yet he had a feeling that it was going to work, and so did Allegra.

"They're both great people. I just wish they'd move a little more slowly." It didn't surprise her of Carmen, but it did of Alan. He was usually so cautious. But maybe he sensed too that this was right for him, and he knew it. "Will you really come to the wedding?" she asked Jeff, as she followed him to the door of his house. He unlocked it, and turned to look at her, wondering if he should carry her over the threshold. He wanted to, but he was afraid to scare her by the seriousness of the gesture, especially with the other two getting married after a four-week courtship.

"I will if you'd like me to. I've never been to Las Vegas."

"Wait till you see it!" she laughed. "It makes L.A. look like Boston."

"I can't wait," he said with a laugh, thinking about it. There were a lot of things he couldn't wait for, a lot of things he wanted to do with her, and show her. This was just the beginning.

He showed her around his house. It was small and neat, and surprisingly orderly for a writer. There were sisal rugs on the floor, and comfortable couches covered in denim. He had only rented it, but like him, it looked very Eastern. It reminded Allegra of Cape Cod, or summer houses in New England. It was perfect for him, it looked like a good place to write, and a cozy place to tuck oneself in with a book on a gray day. There was a fireplace, and several large leather easy chairs. And in the bedroom beyond, there was a large four-poster bed made of logs, and it looked very Western.

There was a huge bathroom with a marble tub and a Jacuzzi, and a big country kitchen with a table for twelve. And other than that, he had an office, and a small guest room. It was really perfect.

"How did you ever find it?" She was impressed. Finding a house in Malibu was like finding gold in your breakfast cereal, and just about as likely.

"It actually belongs to a friend, who went back East last summer. He was happy to rent it to me, and I was happy to get it. He moved back to Boston, and I think he'll want to sell it eventually. I thought I might buy it. Right now, I just rent it." She looked around with a smile; she liked it, and it suited him. And interestingly, it was very different from Alan's, which was much more L.A., and somewhat Southwestern.

They went for a walk on the beach, but eventually the

breeze drove them back in, and then they sat on the couch for a little while, cuddling and talking. It was one o'clock when she thought of going back to the city. She hated to make him drive all the way in, but they had gone to Alan's in his car, and she had no other way to get back to Beverly Hills.

"That was stupid of me," she apologized. "I should have met you here. I feel awful making you drive back."

"I don't mind it. That's what California is all about. Driving." He was easy and good-natured, unlike Brandon, who had always been angry about something. It was so pleasant being with Jeff. It was as though they had been together for years. Like Carmen and Alan, they felt completely at ease with each other.

They kissed again. But this time, it seemed to be with more fervor. And she responded to it. It was so nice being alone with him, having time, and not having to go anywhere, or even think about anyone but each other. It was a real luxury just to be together.

"I'll never go if I don't get up soon," Allegra said softly, as he kissed her again.

"That's what I'm hoping," he whispered.

"So am I." She laughed. "But I think I should go," she said softly.

"Why?" Jeff asked her, as he lay down next to her on the couch, and she had no objections. They lay there together for a while, watching the fire in the fireplace that he had lit when they'd come in. It was a cozy place to be, with the ocean lapping at the sand outside, and the moon high overhead. But all Allegra could think about was Jeff as he held her. "Would you think I was crazy if I told you that I loved you?" he asked, as he looked at her next to him, but it all seemed so natural between them, as though this had been meant to be. It was what she had felt about him from the moment she met him at the Weissmans'.

"No, I wouldn't. Does that seem odd to you? I feel as though I've always known you, like Alan."

"I wish I had known you then. I'll bet you were cute at

fourteen," he said, looking at her, imagining her with freckles and pigtails and braces.

"Yeah, me and my sloppy kisses. We had fun then, every-thing was so simple."

"It's simple now," Jeff said easily. "It's only complicated when it's wrong, and this isn't. This is completely right, and you know it."

"Is it?" she asked, looking up at him, and with that he rolled closer to her and kissed her even harder. "I get so scared some-times," she confessed in the dimly lit room with the fire going near them.

"Of what?"

"Of doing the wrong things, or being with the wrong per-son. I don't want to screw my life up, like . . . like people who marry the wrong man and regret it for the rest of their lives or almost kill themselves trying to change it. I never want to have to do that."

"Then you won't," he said matter-of-factly. "You haven't yet, why should you start now?"

"I've been too scared to do the wrong thing, or the right one." And as he listened to her, he knew what was right for them, and what they both needed. It was time, there was no point tor-turing themselves any further. And very gently he picked her up, in her white jeans and her red sweater, and carried her into his bedroom. He laid her down gently on the big four-poster bed made of logs, and hung with denim. It was a comfortable place to be, she knew she was safe with him, and she made no move to leave or move away from him. She just lay there and looked at him, with her big green eyes, and then she responded instantly when he kissed her. And bit by bit, he stripped her clothes away, and looked at every inch of her and held her and kissed her. His tongue and his hands and his eyes feasted on her, and she on him, and they lay together and made love for hours, and she slept like a baby in his arms when the sun came up in the morning.

He got up and cooked breakfast for her, and brought it back to bed on a tray, and then he woke her gently with kisses all up and down her back, as she stirred and looked at him with a long, slow smile of pleasure. It had been a night she would never forget. He had been right. It was their time now.

She had breakfast with him, and they talked for a long time. And then they got up, and shared a long, lazy bath in the Jacuzzi, and then she walked on the beach with him. And in the distance, they could see Carmen and Alan. But before they were seen, Jeff and Allegra went back to his house and made love again. They spent a lazy Sunday afternoon in each other's arms.

And in Alan's house, Carmen was insistent.

"I know I saw Allegra this morning, walking with Jeff."

"They went back last night," Alan corrected her, already sounding like a husband. "Allie wouldn't do that. Not yet. She takes her time about things. And I think she's still scared after Brandon."

"I'm telling you, I saw them." She was sure of it, and when Jeff drove Allegra past their house late that afternoon, on their way back to town, Alan and Carmen were outside in the garden, and Alan looked surprised when he saw them.

"See!" Carmen said, as the pair in the car waved to them and sped past on the way back to the city.

"Well, I'll be damned," Alan said, watching them. He wished them well. Jeff seemed like a good man. And Allegra deserved the best life had to offer, as far as Alan was concerned. He loved her like a sister.

"Maybe we'll make it a double ceremony in Vegas," Carmen said, and she laughed as they went back inside again. But that, Alan wisely doubted.

CHAPTER 10

Allegra's workload was enormous at the beginning of February. She had Bram's concert tour to set up, Carmen's new movie deal, several other movie offers to negotiate for a variety of clients, and an assortment of smaller, more mundane projects to take care of for the firm. But she seemed to be smiling all the time, and Alice thought she had never seen her as happy.

Jeff dropped in to see her sometimes when he took a break, or had an appointment nearby, and whenever possible, he'd take her out to lunch. Sometimes they even disappeared mysteriously to her house in Beverly Hills at lunch time. And when she'd return to the office afterward, she had to force herself to look serious and concentrate on working. All she could think about was Jeff. She had never been this happy. They seemed to be perfectly suited to each other, they liked the same things, the same books, shared many of the same ideas and interests. He was always kind and flexible, and he had a wonderful sense of humor.

And after their first week of bliss, most of which they spent in Malibu at his cozy house, Allegra suggested he come to dinner at her parents'. She still hadn't told them about breaking up with Brandon.

"Are you sure?" He looked somewhat cautious. Jeff was crazy about her, but he didn't want to push things. He knew how close she was to her family, and he was afraid that his appearance with her might be viewed as an intrusion.

"Don't be silly, my mom loves us to bring friends." She always had, from the time they were kids, until they were adults. They liked having their children's friends around and always made them feel welcome.

"They're awfully busy people." He felt hesitant and a little nervous about getting their approval. Meeting parents had never been one of his favorite pastimes, and at his age, it made him feel a little foolish.

"And I know they'd love to meet you," she said warmly, and eventually, she talked him into coming to dinner on Friday night, despite all his apprehensions.

He was wearing a blazer and slacks when he picked her up, and he looked very much the way he had when she'd met him in New York. Conservative and respectable, and very handsome. And she smiled at him as they drove to Bel Air. He actually looked nervous.

"Is this because of who my father is?" she teased, "or just because they're my parents?" It was kind of like being sixteen again and it actually amused her. She knew they were going to love Jeff, even more so since they'd hated Brandon. Her father had been indifferent to him but her mother had really disliked him. She had seen right through him.

Jeff smiled at her as they drove through Bel Air. "I keep remembering how I felt when I sent my first book to him. What if he thinks that's why I'm back?" Jeff looked like a kid as she laughed at him, and gave him directions.

"I think he'll be able to figure it out. If not, my mother will explain it to him. She's pretty savvy."

It was an apt description of her, and Blaire was poring over the plans for the new kitchen when they arrived. They were spread all over the living room floor, and she was on her hands and knees, explaining them to Simon.

Blaire looked up, with a pencil in her hair, and smiled

warmly at her older daughter. And then she looked surprised when she noticed her escort, but she made no comment.

"Hi, darling, I'm showing Dad what the new kitchen will look like," she said, smiling up at Allegra, and then she stood up as Allegra introduced Jeff. She had said she was bringing someone to dinner with her, and Blaire had just assumed it was Brandon. Blaire carefully hid her surprise, but she was obviously curious about Allegra's companion and dying to ask her about him.

Simon stood up and kissed his daughter with a woebegone grin. "She's showing me what the hole in our backyard will look like for six months, and the empty room at the back of the house where we used to have breakfast. It's going to be a disaster here this summer." And then he introduced himself to Jeff with a casual look of interest. He liked the fact that Jeff had a warm smile and a powerful handshake.

"We met a year ago," Jeff explained. "You were kind enough to see me about a screenplay I wanted to write from a book I'd written, *Birds of Summer*. I'm sure you see so many you can't remember," he said, looking unassuming and pleasant.

"Actually, I do remember." Simon nodded his head pensively and smiled. "Your ideas for the screenplay were very good, but the outline needed more work, as I recall. What book doesn't?"

"I've been working on it ever since," Jeff said ruefully, and then shook Allegra's mother's hand politely. He had been carefully brought up, and it showed as Allegra watched him.

Sam joined them after that, and they sat and talked for a while before going in to dinner, about Jeff's career, their new kitchen, and Hollywood vs. New York. Jeff had to admit that he missed the New York life, but there were a lot of things about living in California that he found very appealing. Allegra most of all. He had originally planned to stay for a year, and go back to New York to write his next book. He had even thought of moving to New England or Cape Cod. But before he went anywhere he had to make his movie in May and probably wouldn't be finished till September. But Allegra looked faintly concerned as he explained his plans. She'd had no idea until then that he might be leaving to move back East again and she looked crestfallen as she listened.

"That's not good news," Allegra said softly as they went in to dinner. It upset her to think of his leaving now, so soon after they'd met, and everything was going so smoothly.

"I can be talked out of it," he whispered, and his lips brushed her neck reassuringly.

"I hope so," she answered.

And all through dinner Allegra was amused to see her mother watching them. She wanted to know who he was, and where he'd been, where Brandon was, and what this man meant to Allegra. But as long as Jeff was there, there was no way Blaire could ask her. The group was very congenial, and Allegra noticed Sam looking Jeff over as well, and afterward when they went back to the living room, her mother finally cornered her and asked some questions.

"Is there something different in your life, Allegra?" she asked, when Jeff went outside for a brief walk with Simon to talk about the movie business. They were talking about unions, and production values, and problems, and Blaire smiled into her daughter's eyes. She wanted to know the whole story. She had obviously missed several chapters.

"What do you mean, Mom?" Allegra played her along and the two women laughed, as Sam rolled her eyes. It was easy to figure out he was crazy about Allegra.

"I never thought we'd see the end of Brandon," her mother said. "Is he in San Francisco this weekend, or does this mean what I think it does?" She didn't dare be too hopeful.

"Possibly." Allegra looked like a blonde Mona Lisa. She wasn't giving anything up yet. It was too soon to issue statements. She had just wanted them to meet him.

"You could have said something," Blaire chided her, as Sam lay down on the couch. She was exhausted, and she thought her sister's love life was boring, although she liked Jeff a lot better than Brandon.

"He's a lot cuter than Brandon," Sam pronounced with polite interest. "So what happened, Allie? Did Brandon dump you?"

"That's no way to ask." Blaire frowned, and then turned back to Allegra. "What did happen, dear?" She couldn't resist the urge to ask the question. She hoped it was nothing too unpleasant. She was just pleased that he was gone, or seemed to be. She had never thought he had really cared about Allegra. He had always seemed so indifferent to her, and so aloof, even disapproving, and the fact that he never got divorced had really disturbed them.

"I guess it was just time," she said cryptically.

"How long's it been?" Sam asked, curious. She sensed that there was more than Allegra was telling.

"A few weeks. I met Jeff in New York." She decided to throw them a bone and her mother looked pleased. She liked him, and so did Simon.

"He's very good-looking," Blaire said easily, and a few minutes later, he and Simon came back in, and they were still deep in conversation about Jeff's movie.

"I'd like to see your new book sometime," Simon said seriously. "Actually, I'll buy it. It just came out, didn't it?"

"It's been out for a while. I just finished a brief publicity tour. I don't see how you have time to read, with everything you do," he said, impressed by their conversation.

"I manage." Simon looked at his wife then, and Allegra saw an odd little look pass between them. It wasn't animosity, or anger certainly, it was just the faintest of chill breezes between them. She'd never seen anything like that before, and she wondered if something had bothered either of them early on, like maybe the kitchen. He hated the inconvenience, and her mother loved remodeling, so that occasionally provided some domestic friction.

Allegra didn't say anything, but when she went out to the kitchen with her mother afterward, she glanced at her carefully, and there didn't seem to be anything seriously amiss. But she had looked tired lately. She was worried about the show, and she was always much too busy.

"Is Daddy okay?" Allegra asked calmly, not wanting to pry. All couples had arguments sometimes, and perhaps they'd had one earlier that evening.

"Of course, dear, why?"

"I don't know . . . he just seemed a little cool tonight. Maybe it was my imagination."

"Probably," Blaire said, unconcerned. "He's furious about the garden. He likes it the way it is, and he just can't believe that what I'm doing will improve it." It was an old battle with them, and it made Allegra smile. She had thought it was something like that. It was never anything more serious with them. They had a terrific marriage. "I like your friend, by the way. He's so intelligent and pleasant and easygoing. Nice-looking too." She smiled, pouring herself a glass of water. "I'm awfully glad," she said, and Allegra laughed, she knew what her mother meant. She was relieved to see the last of Brandon.

"I thought you would be," Allegra said to her. It was a little bit sad that everyone was so pleased that she had broken up with him. It seemed odd to her that everyone had seen all that she hadn't. "This has been sort of a whirlwind with Jeff for the past few weeks. We met in New York at the home of an agent I was meeting with, and we've been together almost constantly ever since." She looked at her mother shyly then, and it touched Blaire to see it, "He's so good to me. . . . I've never known anyone like him . . . except Daddy."

"Oh, my," Blaire said, staring at her. "This *is* serious. Women only compare their fathers to the men they marry."

"Hardly, Mom," Allegra said, blushing in embarrassment. "We've known each other for three weeks."

"You'd be surprised how fast things happen when the right man comes along." Hearing her say it reminded her of Carmen and Alan, and she was tempted to tell her mother about them, but she knew she shouldn't.

They went back to the living room to join the men, and by

then Sam had gone to call her friends. Jeff and Allegra stayed till eleven o'clock, and they chatted and laughed, and had a very pleasant time with her parents.

And as soon as they left, Blaire grinned broadly at her husband.

"Now, come on, Blaire . . . never mind . . . don't get all worked up. She hardly knows him." He was chuckling, and could see in his wife's eyes all her excitement about Allegra's new romance.

"That's what she said, but you're both missing the point. The guy is absolutely wild about her."

"I'm sure he is, but give him a chance before you put a noose around his neck." He had meant it jokingly, but the moment he had said it, he knew he shouldn't. "I didn't mean it like that," he said, trying to correct it, but it was too late. She had turned away with a small shrug. She had gotten the full gist of his meaning. He never used to make comments like that. Nor had she. But lately, she noticed that they both did. He insisted it didn't mean anything, but she knew better. There was no serious unraveling yet, but there were suddenly the slightest of frayed edges around the borders of their marriage. She thought she knew why, but she wasn't sure of it. And when she looked up at him, something distant and cold struck at her heart. It was nothing you could really define, but it was there, like a poltergeist, drifting through rooms, and wafting icy fingers along her spine as she watched him.

"Are you coming upstairs?" she asked quietly, the kitchen plans rolled up under her arm.

"Eventually," he said, and then as he saw her face, he corrected himself. "I'll be up in a minute."

She nodded and went upstairs, feeling sad about them again. There had been no major rift, no terrible tear, but lately there had been this awkward cooling between them. She wondered sometimes if it was just a stage they were passing through, a little bump in the road, or a signal that there was something really wrong. But she wasn't sure yet.

* * *

"So how do you like my parents?" Allegra asked undiplomatically as they drove home. They were staying at her place tonight, because it was closer.

"I think they're great," he said with unabashed admiration. They were unassuming; they were warm, and charming, and involved, and a delight to be with. He told her all about his conversation on the patio with Simon. "He says he wants to read my book, but I think he's just being polite. It's nice of him to offer."

"He loves doing stuff like that. He's always encouraging my friends with their films, and their plays, and their new businesses. He thinks it's exciting, and it keeps him young." At sixty, he looked more than ten years younger. And then as she thought of her mother, she frowned slightly. "Actually, it's my mom I'm worried about."

"Why?" Jeff looked surprised. She was beautiful and youthful, talented and successful, hardly someone one worried about, and she was in excellent health. He couldn't imagine why Allegra would worry about her. "She looks fine."

"I know, but I'm not sure she is. I think losing the Golden Globe award hit her hard this year. She's had a lot of aggravation with the show. And I don't know what it is," she tried to put her finger on her concern, but couldn't, "it's just a feeling I have. She seems sad all the time, I mean underneath all the smiles and the good sportsmanship. Something's bothering her."

"Have you asked her?" It seemed an easy solution to him, but Allegra shook her head.

"I honestly don't think she'd tell me. I asked if there was some kind of a problem with Dad, because he looked kind of serious tonight, but she says he's mad about the garden."

"That's probably all it is," he reassured her. "They must work awfully hard, and that has to take a toll. They're amazing people." He was the most important producer in Hollywood, and she had one of the most successful TV shows. It was quite a standard to maintain, and not surprising that none of their children had chosen to compete with them. "I liked Sam, by the way." She was spectacular-looking, and so young in her views that it was actually refreshing.

"So do I, sometimes." Allegra grinned. "She's kind of a brat though, lately. It's not good for her to be alone with them all the time. They really spoil her. It was better for her when Scott and I were home, but that's been a while. Daddy is the original push-over when it comes to Sam, and she knows it. Mom holds a harder line, but Sam sails right on by and does what she wants. I never would have dared to do that."

"I think it's always like that with the youngest kids. They get a real break after the older ones pay their dues. But she doesn't look too indulged to me. She was actually very polite."

"That's just 'cause she thinks you're cute." Allegra grinned again.

"And if she didn't?"

"She'd ignore you."

"Then I'm flattered that she didn't."

They had reached Allegra's house by then, and they went straight to bed. They were both tired, but she loved lying there next to him, holding each other. Their caresses rarely stayed chaste, and in a short time they were overcome by passion. They were happy times, and in the morning, Allegra loved waking up next to him. Sometimes he was already up, making her a pot of fresh coffee. It seemed the perfect life to both of them. And on Saturday morning, Alan called and invited them to dinner.

"What a life," Jeff commented as she served him hot break-fast rolls and sweet butter, standing naked in her kitchen wearing a white lace apron. "Now, there's a picture for the tabloids," he said, pretending to snap one, while she took a sexy pose, and he pulled her down on his lap, and that had immediate results, which eventually drew them back to the bedroom.

It was noon before they got up again, and Allegra tried to decide what to make for lunch, while Jeff commented that all they did anymore was eat and make love.

"Are you complaining?" she asked with interest, biting into an apple.

"God, no. I love it."

"So do I." And then she remembered Alan's invitation. "What do you want to do about dinner tonight? Do you want to go?" She didn't want to push him. She was sure he had his own friends, but he had actually hit it off beautifully with Alan and Carmen, which delighted Allegra.

"Actually, I'd like to go," he said, sharing the apple with her. It was a big, juicy one, and after he took a bite of it and swallowed, he kissed her. Their lips tasted like apple, and their kisses almost took them back to the bedroom.

"We're never going to get anything done if we keep this up," she said, and then laughed at her pun, while he kissed her neck and held her. "Never mind, I'll call Alan."

They agreed to go to Alan's house in Malibu, and they said that maybe after that they'd go bowling. When they arrived at seven o'clock, Carmen was cooking pasta this time, and Alan was making the sauce, pretending to sing Italian opera. They all laughed, and Jeff put on some music.

It was a beautiful, balmy night, and they almost decided to eat outside, but in the end they didn't. Instead, they sat around the kitchen table, and all complained about having eaten too much. Alan's sauce on the fettuccine had been delicious.

"I'm going to have to start starving again pretty soon," he said with a groan. "We start rehearsals the end of March here, and then we start shooting in mid-April. We're going to Switzer-land, to play in the Alps, like little mountain goats." It was an-other wild adventure movie, with a meaty part for him. And they were paying him an absolute fortune.

"Isn't that going to be dangerous?" Carmen asked, looking worried.

"Not unless I slip," he said, teasing her, but she didn't look amused, and then Allegra heard her say that she wanted to go with him. It was going to be difficult if she insisted on following him to the set; women who did usually became a major nuisance. And Alan was too independent to put up with it, and most of his locations were far too rugged for Carmen.

"You're going to be shooting in June anyway," Allegra said, trying to distract her. "You won't have time to go with him."

"I could stay for six weeks till we start rehearsals."

"I'd love that," Alan said, encouraging her, and Allegra was almost sure he'd be sorry for it. But the conversation moved on to other things, and after dessert, banana splits this time, perfect to kill everyone's diets, Alan suggested that they go into town and go bowling. He loved hanging out in bars, playing Ping-Pong or shooting pool, just being one of the folks. And bowling was one of his favorite pastimes. Eventually he convinced them all to go, and they were all laughing and talking as they drove into Santa Monica in his Lamborghini. It was actually an armored car, built as a tank, especially for an important Arab. There had been only a dozen or so made, and he had found a bright, shiny red one in San Francisco. The inside was all burl wood and glove leather. It drove like a Ferrari, and could supposedly ride over a sand dune at a hundred and eighty miles an hour. It was one of Alan's favorite toys, and he loved it. It was a lot more conspicuous than his old Chevy truck, but it was a lot more comfortable too, and had an elaborate stereo system. And every time someone looked at it, they honked in admiration.

"Where did you get this thing?" Jeff asked. He had never seen another car like it.

"Up north. It was built for a Prince in Kuwait, and he never picked it up. It's completely bulletproof, and the sides are totally armored." It was a wonderful machine and Alan really enjoyed it, more for its speed and flash than for its protection.

They parked it outside the Hangtown Bowl, and went inside to rent shoes and reserve a lane. And they were surprised to see that the whole bowling alley was unbelievably crowded. They were told there would be a wait, but they decided to have a beer and be good sports about it, and twenty minutes later they had their lane, and they got down to it in earnest.

Alan was pretty good, and Carmen was lousy but she always had a good time, Allegra could hold her own, and Jeff was a good match for Alan. They were well suited to play the game, and none of them took it quite as seriously as Alan. He loved to win, and always nagged Carmen to pay attention.

"I am, baby, I am," she said, and as she said it, Allegra noticed that people were watching. They hadn't been aware of it, but people had slowly gathered around, and it was obvious that they had not only recognized Alan, but Carmen.

"Hi," Carmen said to one of them, completely unaware of what she looked like. She had on skintight white jeans, and a tight white T-shirt that probably showed off too much of her figure. The ugly turquoise and brown bowling shoes completed it incongruously, but in spite of the shoes, she looked like a beauty queen, and several of the men looked as though they'd had too much beer and would have loved to grab her.

Alan was quietly aware of it, and maneuvered her between himself and Jeff, but they were watching him too, and out of the corner of his eye, he saw a hoodlum with slicked-back hair start talking to Allegra.

She was completely cool, and made very little of it. He asked about the car outside, and she said they had rented it for the evening. There were specialty dealerships in L.A. where you could rent hot rods or Rolls-Royces or antique Bentleys. You could rent almost anything, and it was perfectly conceivable that the Lamborghini outside had been rented.

"She thinks she's pretty slick, don't she?" another guy asked Allegra as he eyed Carmen, who was trying to ignore him and concentrate on her game. "We know who she is. What does she think, she's just slumming for tonight? That's pretty crappy." Allegra didn't say much and moved away, but she didn't want to piss them off further. Both of them were drunk, and they were beginning to catch the attention of the others in the bowling alley. Then all of a sudden a woman asked for an autograph, and then a few more, and suddenly there were dozens of people pressing Carmen against a table. And before Alan could turn around, some guy had grabbed him and thrown a punch, but he was too drunk to connect, and by using a neat karate move he had learned from the stuntmen on his last set, Alan sidestepped him completely.

But Allegra knew all too well what the rest of this "movie" looked like. She'd been around it for too long not to know when they were in trouble. And with a single stride away from Jeff, she walked to a pay phone and dialed 911. No one even noticed her as she told the officer at the other end who she was, where they were, who her companions were, and what had happened.

"It's about to turn into a bar fight," she said calmly, "and Miss Connors could get hurt. There's a mob here of about a hundred guys about to grab her."

"We'll be right there," he said, giving rapid orders to someone on a radio. "Stay on the line, Miss Steinberg. How's Mr. Carr?"

"Holding his own for the moment." She kept an eye on them from where she stood. No one else had thrown a punch after the first one, but there was a seething mob closing in on them, of people who wanted to be with them, touch them, strip them, press them, be them. And as she kept an eye on what was happening, Jeff saw what she was doing. He tried moving closer to her, but she could see that he was afraid to leave Carmen, there were too many men pressing her, touching her, and someone was trying to rip a sleeve off her T-shirt.

But as Allegra watched, three policemen strode purposefully through the bar and into the bowling alley. They could see what was going on, and they were wielding billy clubs and not willing to take any nonsense. One went straight to Carmen, and another spoke to Alan Carr, and within minutes they were keeping the crowd at bay, but people were still ripping at Carmen's hair, trying to grab her clothes, pulling her toward them. It almost became a tug-of-war between the thugs and the policemen. It took two of them to free her from what felt like human quicksand, and as they did, a woman screamed and threw herself into Alan's arms, begging him to kiss her. She was young and drunk and overweight, and this was her life's dream, being this close to Alan Carr, just as tearing Carmen's clothes off seemed to be every man's dream in the bar. It took all three of the policemen to get Carmen, Alan, and Jeff free and clear, and they moved together to leave the bar. Allegra tried to join them, but just as she reached them, one of the billy clubs shoved Allegra back, and the crowd closed again between them. Jeff was beckoning frantically, but she couldn't get through, and he was trying to fight his way back to her with no success, and no cooperation whatsoever from the throng of fans who had become crazed with lust and excitement.

"Allegra!" Jeff was shouting at her. She could see him, but she couldn't hear him. "She's with us!" he shouted at one of the policemen for help, and together they forced their way back, and put their arms around her, pushing her toward the door, again just behind Carmen and Alan. And outside, there was yet another patrolman. Alan's hands were shaking as he opened the car, and the four cops surrounded them as they got in, and then they locked the doors, and the officers waved at them to go as quickly as they could. It was all over, and they'd barely had time to thank them.

In the rearview mirror as they pulled away, Alan could see it becoming an angry mob, cheated of the objects of their affection.

"God, does that happen to you guys all the time?" Jeff said, trying to straighten his shirt and jacket. They all looked as though they'd been shipwrecked. All of their clothes had been torn, their hair was tangled, Alan's hat had been ripped off and stolen along with his dark glasses, and Jeff had actually lost one of his loafers. "How do you stand it?"

Carmen was crying a little bit, and Allegra was consoling her. It was the nature of the beast that loved them. It half hated them too. It owned them, and devoured them, and eventually, if they weren't careful, it destroyed them.

"It's scary stuff," Allegra said gently. It always unnerved her, and Carmen hated it. It terrified her.

"They're like animals. Did you see those guys?" she said, with tears running down her face as she looked at Alan. "They would have raped me. One of them kept grabbing my boobs, and I swear someone kept trying to slip a hand into my pants. They're disgusting." She looked like a total innocent as she complained about the invasion. They had been a hungry, lusting, angry mob. Angry that they didn't completely own them. They wanted to take those people home, to be part of them, to touch their bodies and their lives, to be them. "I'm not going bowling ever again," Carmen said, looking like a kid. "I hate that shit."

"So do I," Alan admitted. "Who doesn't?" But he liked to go bowling. It was why so many stars had bowling alleys in their own homes, and sports arenas, and skating rinks and movie theaters, because they couldn't go anywhere, they couldn't go out with their kids, they couldn't do any of the things normal people took for granted.

"You should see what Bram Morrison goes through at his concerts," Allegra said consolingly. Jeff was still in total admiration of her having had the presence of mind to call 911. But she had seen a lot of that and she knew what she was doing. She sensed almost instantly when it was going wrong, and it usually did, especially when it involved a woman. She had warned Carmen of all of that, told her what to do, had hired someone to teach her to defend herself, but it was still terrifying when you had to face it.

"Thanks for calling the cops, Al," Alan said, sounding faintly depressed. There was always something degrading about being mauled like that, even if the reasons for it were originally well-intentioned. But as they went home that night, Allegra could tell that it had made a big impression on Jeff, and in the end, it had put a damper on the evening. Alan dropped them off at Jeff's house a few minutes later, and told them he was sorry the night had been such a bomb. But Jeff and Allegra said they understood, and were sorry too, and thanked Alan and Carmen for dinner.

"I don't know how those poor people live like that. Can they ever go out? Normally, I mean," Jeff asked, after Alan had driven off with Carmen.

"They go to premieres, but they have to be careful there too. At big, publicized events, they run a tremendous risk of serious attacks, the kind of things that people don't always survive. You can really get hurt in mobs like that. And the rest of the time, if you try to get too normal, it turns out like tonight, unless you go someplace like Spago. That's different," she smiled. It was her favorite restaurant and always full of stars. No one would have dared bother them there; they just admired them from a distance.

But at a place like the bowling alley there were no boundaries. And sometimes it got rough. But Allegra handled it remarkably. She had seen it for years, when she was with her parents. They had never had that kind of fame, because they were on the other side of the camera, but the people they knew, their stars, always went through what Jeff had witnessed tonight, and so did her clients.

"It scared the hell out of me losing you in that crowd," he said as they walked into his bedroom and took their clothes off. There was something seamy just about having their clothes half torn off. And then Jeff laughed, looking at his own stocking foot. "Poor jerks, they probably think my shoe is Alan's."

"You can buy it back at auction one day," she joked with him. It had worried her too. Crowds like that were always scary, because you couldn't predict how out of hand things would get before you escaped them.

"I just can't believe it. I feel like a real star now. And frankly, Scarlett, you can have it," Jeff said, lying on his bed with abandon.

"Not I," she said. "That's why I'm an attorney and not an actress. You couldn't sell me that crap for anything. I couldn't stand it for a minute."

"But you sure handled it well," he praised her. "You were the only one who thought of calling the police. I was just standing there with my mouth open wondering how we were going to get out of there without having them kill us."

"The secret is in calling fast. The minute I saw it, I knew."

But as she got into bed, and they lay holding each other tight, still rattled by their experience at the bowling alley, Jeff couldn't help wondering what they were going to do at the wedding.

"They ought to get married on a deserted island some-where, if tonight is any indication of what can happen."

"They're actually worse at weddings. That's where fans are about the worst. It drives them into a frenzy. Celebrity weddings are a nightmare, almost as bad as concerts." She laughed, but they both knew it wasn't funny. "But try telling Carmen that. She refuses to believe me, and Alan says she ought to do it whatever way she wants. I've been talking to security experts about it ever since they told us they were getting married."

"What do they say?"

"You'll see," she smiled, looking like Mata Hari. "But it'll be tight. I can promise you that. As tight as it can be in Vegas."

"Why is it," he asked, pulling her even closer under the covers, "that I'm beginning to dread it?"

"Because you're smart. And if they were . . . they'd elope to somewhere where no one would ever suspect it . . . some one-horse town in the middle of South Dakota. The trouble is, that's not much fun. But neither is being mauled by strangers."

"Next time, I'll wear shoes with laces," he said, wiser after his experience. But even after that, he wasn't prepared for the Alan Carr–Carmen Connors wedding.

CHAPTER 11

The bus Allegra had hired picked Alan and Carmen up at Jeff's house in Malibu. They both wore wigs, blue jeans, and old sweatshirts. Carmen wore a brown wig and a scarf, and Alan wore a black one. They wore sunglasses, chewed gum, and had Southern accents. Jeff and Allegra got on with them, also wearing wigs, and polyester leisure clothes. They were a lot more dressed up than the other two, and most of what Allegra wore was dusted with rhinestones.

"I didn't know this was a dress affair," Jeff said as he donned his costume with amusement. But one thing was sure, no one would recognize Alan or Carmen.

They sat in a large, paneled room in the back of the bus, telling stories, and eating ice cream, and laughing at how they looked whenever they saw themselves in the mirror. They made occasional forays into the kitchen, for cheese or fruit or sandwiches, and both ladies occasionally used the pink marble bathroom, but not the bathtub. It was the kind of bus frequently used by movie stars or rock stars. This one happened to be immaculately kept and was privately owned, and Allegra used it often. She had rented it as a dressing room for one of her clients once, and for driving trips. It was one of the better kept, more luxurious ones, although it didn't compare with Eddie Murphy's double-decker bus, filled with antiques and precious objects. But this one was comfortable enough, and the foursome were "in hog heaven," as they said loudly from time to time, all the way to Vegas.

Once in Las Vegas, they went straight to the hotel. They were staying at the MGM Grand, and six bodyguards waited in the lobby for their arrival. As soon as the bodyguards spotted them, they became part of the faceless crowd around them. There were two women and four men, and they didn't even acknowledge them as they moved into suites on either side of Alan and Carmen's.

Jeff and Allegra were across the hall, and she had been keeping an eye out for tabloids, but she hadn't seen even one photographer as they entered. There had been some talk for a while, about Alan and Carmen having an affair, but it had only been a month, and no one suspected they were going to get married.

They changed wigs at the hotel, and everyone became redheads, except Alan, who became a bad peroxide blond, and he loved it.

"My God." Allegra grinned at him and he laughed uproariously. "You look awful."

"I kind of like it," he said, pretending to give her the eye and a little pat on her bottom, and then he switched back to his black one again, and imitated Elvis.

"It's a good thing you already have a career," Allegra said, looking disgusted. "I don't think I could get you a job anywhere if you didn't."

"Ya never know, kiddo. Ya never know."

Carmen disappeared into the back bedroom then, with the long plastic garment bag she'd been carrying. And half an hour later she emerged in a short white satin dress, and her hair in a smooth French twist underneath a short veil. Her makeup was flawless, as was her face, and her long, slender legs, exposed by the short skirt, were even better. It was quite a transformation from the polyester dress and the wig, and she looked really lovely. She was wearing white satin high heels, and her dress was low cut. She looked breathtaking, and Alan was really moved when he saw her. He was still wearing the polyester pants and the wig, and he went to put on a linen jacket, and "real" shoes. But he had decided to get married in the blond wig. That way, he said, they'd have blond children.

"You're crazy," Carmen said, kissing him.

Half an hour later the justice of the peace Allegra had arranged for appeared. She knew that if she'd asked the hotel to do it, it would have hit the tabloids. But it might anyway, if the justice of the peace recognized them, which he had to, looking at Carmen. And their names would inevitably be on their marriage certificate, but it would be too late to tip anyone off by then.

Allegra had decided to stay in her funny clothes too. She had actually brought a poodle skirt, and she slipped it on with the red wig, and she was wearing sandals. It was quite an outfit.

"I can't wait to see the wedding pictures," Jeff said, standing up for Alan. Allegra was touched that Alan had asked him.

"You don't look so hot either, you know," Alan said, cutting Jeff down to size. He had put on a Ralph Lauren blazer over a bowling shirt, and he wore the same blond wig as Alan.

The justice of the peace didn't know who they were, but he thought they were completely crazy. He ran the ceremony by them in less than three minutes, pronounced them man and wife, and signed the license without even glancing at the names. He had called Carmen "Carla" twice during the ceremony, and Alan "Adam." But as soon as it was over, Allegra poured champagne, they ordered caviar, and it was official that they were married.

"Carmen Carr." Allegra was the first to say it, and the second to kiss her, after Alan. "I like it."

"So do I," Carmen said, with tears in her eyes. She still wanted a church wedding in Oregon, but she knew what a circus that would have been, with paparazzi and helicopters, screaming fans and police lines. They just couldn't face it.

"Good luck," the justice of the peace said from the doorway. He handed Alan his marriage certificate, and then hurried off to perform dozens of other weddings. He had no idea who he had just joined in matrimony. As far as he was concerned, they were just Adam and Carla.

An hour later, they all went downstairs to play the slot machines and gamble. Allegra tapped discreetly on the bodyguards' doors as they went by, and they fell in behind them. It was a completely smooth operation, and there were no hitches at all until almost midnight, when someone recognized Carmen and asked for her autograph. Carmen was always gracious about it, and she had taken her veil off by then, but she was still wearing the short wedding dress she'd been married in. A few minutes later someone snapped her photograph, and Allegra knew the onslaught was coming.

"It's time to go, Cinderella," she said quietly. "Your chariot awaits." Two more bodyguards were guarding the bus, and no one had entered it since they left it, except the driver, and he knew nothing.

"It's too early," Carmen complained, but the casino was jammed with people, and the prospect of a stampede, or even a crush, didn't appeal to anyone. . . . *Look, everybody! It's Carmen Connors, she just got married. . . . And Alan Carr . . . snap . . . scream . . . shriek . . . grab . . .* Forget it.

"Come on, Mrs. Carr. Move your ass. This is my wedding night, and I'm not going to stand around here all night playing bingo." Alan kissed her firmly, and patted her bottom, and the entire group headed out to where the bus was waiting. As Carmen boarded the steps she looked back at Allegra and Jeff, and Allegra handed her a plastic bouquet of white flowers she'd had the bus driver hold for them, and Carmen threw it gracefully from the top step of the bus, and Allegra caught it. In spite of all the craziness and the funny outfits they had worn, she looked really lovely, and the assembled company smiled as they watched them. And the bus driver thought that in that outfit, she looked a little like Carmen Connors. If she hadn't had the accent, and she were a little taller, she might even look a lot like her, he said to Allegra.

"Yeah, maybe," she said, looking unconvinced. And then they closed the doors. The bus started up, and the bridal couple waved as Jeff and Allegra stayed behind with the bodyguards. It was over. They had done it. They were safe. And there had not been a single hitch or tabloid. Allegra had done an incredible job of setting it up for them, and Jeff was more impressed than ever.

"*You* are a genius," he complimented her, as they watched the bus drive into the distance. At four A.M. they'd be at Alan's house, and all they had to do was pick up their bags, change their clothes, and catch a nine o'clock flight to Tahiti. End of story.

"It was cute, wasn't it?" Allegra smiled up at him. She was happy it had gone so well. She hadn't wanted the tabloids spoiling it for them, or vicious paparazzi stalking them.

"They couldn't have had a real wedding, could they?" Jeff asked pensively. He couldn't see how they'd have pulled it off, without the costumes or the wigs, or the privacy of the suite, or the bodyguards, or even the rock-star bus. It had all been perfect.

"They could have," Allegra admitted, but she had discouraged it, particularly to Alan, and he had convinced Carmen. "But it would have been a nightmare. Helicopters everywhere, photographers, the media would have paid off every supplier they used. It's like a tug-of-war after a while, everything is a battle. She would have hated it." Jeff nodded. He didn't disagree with her anymore. The experience in the bowling alley had taught him a lot about the way they lived. In spite of the lives everyone envied and wanted for themselves, none of it was easy. "I thought it was more fun like this anyway," Allegra said, thinking how cute Carmen had looked in the short veil, and later tossing the plastic bouquet at Allegra.

"I'll have to save this." She waved the bouquet at Jeff as they walked back into the hotel. The bodyguards had already discreetly left them. They were no longer needed. And the law firm would be billed for their time. She had thanked them at the bus, and now they were gone. She was alone with Jeff and several thousand people in the lobby.

They went back up to their suite. They were staying for the night, and in the morning they were going back to L.A. in a limousine. By then, Alan and Carmen would be in the air and on their way to Tahiti. She and Alan had agreed how the announcement would be handled. Nothing would be said until after their honeymoon, so stringers around the world wouldn't find them. Probably someone in their hotel might tip the press off eventually, but Bora Bora was fairly remote, and Alan thought they'd be safe there. And after they got back, there would be a press conference with both of them, for five minutes, with photo opportunities, announcing their marriage. Just give the sharks a little bit, a finger or a toe, to keep them happy, Allegra had told them.

Allegra lay in his arms that night, cozy and happy, thinking of Carmen and Alan. He was one of her oldest friends, and it was funny to think of him being married.

"Happy Valentine's Day," Jeff said softly.

"Same to you," she said, turning her back to him, as he put his arms around her. And she never stirred again until morning. She dreamed of catching the bouquet, and she kept laughing because it was plastic. And when she caught it, Jeff drove away on a bus, and she had to run all night to catch him. In her dreams, as in her life, people were always running away from her. But not anymore, she reminded herself when she woke up, not now . . . and not Jeff . . . He was staying.

CHAPTER 12

Carmen and Alan came home from Bora Bora in mid-March and this time there was no avoiding the tabloids. The list of nominees for the Academy Awards had come out while they were gone, and they were both on it. The press were out in force when they got off the plane. Someone at the airlines had tipped them off, but the newlyweds were ready. They each had a deep tan, and they looked fabulous as the cameras flashed and they made their way slowly through the small crowd waiting for them at the airport.

Allegra had arranged for a car to pick them up, and they got to it as quickly as they could, after posing for a couple of pictures. They got right into the limousine, and two bodyguards waited for their luggage.

Allegra had also arranged for a bottle of champagne in the car for them, and when they got home to Alan's house in Beverly Hills, they found the house filled with flowers. But within days, the media had made their life there almost too complicated to put up with. Photographers clamored at the gates, as helicopters hovered overhead trying to catch glimpses of them in the garden or the pool, and researchers for the tabloids stole their garbage. It was unbearable, and they rapidly moved to Malibu, but it was worse there, and finally they hid out for a few days at Allegra's.

She moved in with Jeff for a few days, and the foursome

donned wigs and went to small, unknown restaurants in the valley.

"I can't believe this," Jeff said, appalled at the intrusions they had to live with. He was still working on the last polish of his screenplay. He and Allegra had had a nice, quiet month, with the exception of another threat against Bram Morrison, which had kept her busy. His family had gone to Palm Springs again, and he had borrowed a friend's home at an unknown location. He never went anywhere without bodyguards now, and a series of articles that said he was making a hundred million dollars from his concert tour only made it worse. Now everyone wanted a piece of the action, whatever they had to do to get it, even kidnapping or blackmail.

Alan and Carmen had been back for two weeks on April first, and Allegra and Carmen met for two hours that afternoon to go over the details of her new contract. She'd already signed it before she left on her honeymoon, but there were some fine points Allegra had wanted to go over with her, to determine just exactly what her expectations would be when she started the picture. They needed to talk about what kind of dressing room she would have, the schedules she would work, and iron out all the little details ahead of time, to avert any unnecessary crisis.

They had worked most of it out when Carmen looked at her attorney with a mischievous smile, and Allegra remembered that it was April Fools' Day. Growing up, she and Alan had made all kinds of mischief around that, and played awful pranks on each other. And her brother Scott loved torturing his entire family on April Fools' Day. She was surprised that he hadn't called her. Every year, he gave her some dreadful shock, either claiming to be in Mexico, in jail, married to a prostitute, or in San Francisco having a sex change. But she had given it back to him over the years. And as they looked at Carmen, she could suddenly see one coming.

"There's something I've been meaning to tell you," Carmen said with a huge grin, and Allegra laughed even before she heard it.

"Let me guess. You and Alan are getting divorced. Ha-ha, April Fools' Day."

Carmen laughed at what she said. Alan had pulled two of those on her that morning. He had claimed that an old boyfriend of hers was at the door, and then that his mother was moving in with them for the next six months. Both announcements had given Carmen quite a jolt first thing in the morning.

"No, nothing like that," she said, looking suddenly shy, but Allegra was still suspicious of what was coming. In her own way, she was too much like Alan. "We're having a baby," she said, beaming.

"You are? So soon?" She knew they wanted kids, but she thought they would wait at least a little while longer. She was due to start her movie in June. She was only shooting for three months, but now it wasn't going to be easy. "How pregnant are you?" Allegra asked, holding her breath, terrified that they would lose the picture.

"Only a month," Carmen said sheepishly. "Alan said it was too soon to say anything, but I wanted to tell you. And I thought maybe it would make a difference to the studio. I'll only be three months' pregnant when I start. But I'll be six months' when we finish. Do you think they'll break the contract?"

"I'm not sure," Allegra said honestly. "They may be able to shoot around it. You probably won't show till close to the end of the picture. Thank God, you don't have a longer shooting schedule." Some movies took eight or nine months to make, which in this case would have been a disaster. But Carmen was the main focus of the picture, though she wasn't in the entire movie. "Maybe they can move it up. They'll do something to work it out —I know how badly they want you. I'll call them this afternoon," Allegra said, and then smiled at her. "Congratulations . . . Alan must be going crazy." He loved kids. For him, it was what he had always wanted, a wife, a family, and a baby. "That's quite something. And it's not April Fool, I hope!" Allegra asked pointedly and Carmen laughed.

"I don't think so. That's not what the doctor said anyway. I went yesterday. We saw it on a sonogram. You could even see its little heart beating. It kind of looks like a jelly bean. I'm five weeks' pregnant." She giggled proudly.

"It's hard to believe," Allegra said, suddenly feeling very old. Carmen was only twenty-three years old, she had a career as a major movie star, and now she was married and having a baby. Allegra was almost thirty, and all she had was a career she loved, and a man she'd known for a little over two months, whom she loved certainly. But who knew where that would lead? It was still very new, and life was uncertain.

She sat at her desk, feeling wistful, and a little jealous after Carmen left, and then she felt stupid for feeling that way. They had a right to their happiness, and she still had things to work out in her own life. At least she wasn't with Brandon anymore, waiting for him to get up the guts to divorce Joanie. He had only called her once since he left. He wanted to know where his tennis racket was, and Nicky's bicycle. He had left both at her place. And he had come to pick them up the following weekend. Jeff had been there, and Brandon had eyed him curiously but he hadn't said much. He still looked very angry at Allegra, and he was cool when he thanked her, and left quickly. That was it. Two years and all that was left was a kid's bike and a tennis racket, and a lot of emptiness. But she had Jeff now, and the relationship was far more fulfilling. It was what she had always wanted with a man, understanding, companionship, emotional support—he was interested in her work, liked her friends, and he wasn't afraid of being close, or of loving her. Even after two months, they shared a bond she had never shared with anyone else, and certainly not Brandon.

She called Alan to congratulate him, and he sounded pleased but a little embarrassed. "I told her not to tell anyone yet. I think she got excited when she saw it on the sonogram yesterday. She wanted to run right out and buy a crib for it after we saw it."

"It's better that I know anyway. I need to tell the studio what's going on. It's better if they know ahead of time," she said matter-of-factly, tossing her long blond hair over her shoulder, and trying not to feel the emptiness and the envy she had felt when Carmen told her. She didn't know what was wrong with her. She wasn't usually this sentimental about babies. Maybe it was just because it was Alan.

"Do you think it'll be a problem with them?" Alan sounded worried. He didn't want to mess up her big movie deal, but it was too late now. The baby was due in December.

"I hope not. I'll let you know as soon as I call them. I think with this particular movie, they can pull it off. If they'd planned to have her in a bathing suit for three months, we'd be in big trouble. But the costumes call for a lot of coats and baggy clothes." It was supposed to take place in New York in the winter. There were a few location shots, and most of it was indoors. But even then she wasn't going to be wearing a lot of slinky costumes.

"She's really excited, Al," he said, sounding pleased, as though they were the first couple who'd ever done it.

"I know, it was sweet. It kind of made me feel old, to tell you the truth." And a little left out. She had known Alan a lot longer than Carmen.

"It'll happen to you one of these days," he reassured her.

"I hope not," she laughed and said without hesitating, "I'd rather wait till I get married, if I can help it."

"I think you ought to grab Jeff before he moves back East. He's a good one."

"Thanks, Dad," she said, amused at the advice. He was a good one, but it wasn't up to Alan to decide that.

"Anytime, and by the way, I saw Sam today, that's quite a sparkler she's wearing."

"What sparkler?" Allegra looked blank at her end.

"The ring. Her engagement ring. Why didn't you tell me? She looks mighty proud of it."

"Sam?" Allegra looked horrified. "She hasn't said a thing. She's *engaged*? Since when?"

"Since yesterday, she said," Alan said innocently, and then suddenly Allegra remembered.

"You shit. April fool, right?" she asked hopefully, but he was laughing at the other end. "I hate you."

"You believed me though. I should have kept you going a while longer. You're terrific."

"You're an asshole. And I hope you have quadruplets," she said vehemently. He got her every year, and she always believed him.

She called the studio after that and told them the news, and they weren't thrilled, but they were grateful for the early warning. They assured her that the contract would remain in place, which was good news, and they would have a meeting with the director as soon as possible to figure out how to shoot it and work around the "problem."

"We really appreciate it," Allegra said.

"Thanks for telling us early," the producer said. She was a woman whom Allegra liked very much and had worked with before, though not with Carmen.

"I'll reassure Carmen that everything is okay. I know she'll be pleased. She was very worried."

"Sometimes you just have to work around Mother Nature. I was working with Allyson Jarvis last month, and she'd forgotten to tell us that she was nursing. She must have worn a forty-eight double D, and I swear I thought we wouldn't even be able to get her chest into the picture." They both laughed, and Allegra called Carmen to reassure her that she hadn't lost the picture.

And by the end of the day, when she went home to Jeff, she wasn't sure why, but she was drooping. It hadn't been a bad day, and things had worked out for Carmen, despite her pregnancy, but nonetheless Allegra felt let down somehow, and she wondered if it was because of their baby. Maybe she was jealous of them, she suggested to herself as she drove home, but that seemed really stupid. It was just that their lives seemed so fulfilled, so complete, and hers always seemed like a work in progress. She was still seeing Dr. Green, who seemed very pleased with her. She was impressed by the relationship with Jeff. And Allegra reminded herself of how happy she was with him, as she

let herself into the house in Malibu. She had never had a relationship like this with anyone. She had never loved anyone as she did
him. He was really everything she'd ever wanted.

"Anyone home?" She shouted toward the back of the house
where his office was. And half a minute later he came out, with a
pencil behind his ear and a grin on his face. He'd missed her all
day, and had been working hard, and he was dying to see her.

He swept her into his arms, and kissed her long and hard,
and any mild dissatisfaction she might have felt with her life,
disappeared on the instant.

"Wow! What was that for? Either you had a great day at the
typewriter, or a really bad one."

"A little of both, as usual. I just missed you. How was your
day?"

"Pretty good." She grabbed an Evian out of the fridge, and
handed him a Coke, and told him about Alan and Carmen's baby.

"So soon? That was quick. It must have been fun in Bora
Bora. Maybe we should try it for our honeymoon."

"By the time I get married," she smiled at him, she was
feeling a lot better, and she knew he was just kidding about the
honeymoon, "I'll be so old I'll need a wheelchair, not a baby
carriage."

"What makes you say that?" He sounded interested, as they
both sat down on the stools at the counter in his kitchen.

"I'm almost thirty, and I've spent a long time building my
career, and I'm not there yet. I haven't made full partner yet, and
I have a lot of things to do. I don't know, I haven't thought about
marriage in a long time," she said honestly. She just rolled along
from day to day, and took things as they came. It seemed a more
realistic way to look at her life, than sitting around waiting for
Prince Charming and a white wedding.

"I'm kind of disappointed to hear you say that," Jeff said,
looking surprised, and somewhat mischievous. She figured she
was in for another April Fools' joke, like Alan's.

"Why? Were you planning to ask me today?" she asked with
a grin, turning it around on him. "Ha! April Fools' Day!"

But he just laughed when she said that. "Actually I was. I figured that April Fools' is a great day to get engaged. No one really knows if you're serious or not. I kind of like that."

"Very funny. Alan already beat you to it," she said, looking very relaxed as she sipped her Evian. It was always fun coming home to him. They had such a good time together.

"He asked you to marry him today? I think that's in really poor taste if his wife is pregnant."

"No, you goof." She laughed at him again. "He said Sam got engaged yesterday. I actually believed him. I should know him better than that after all these years. He does this to me every year. And I *always* believe him."

Jeff was smiling at her, as they sat in his comfortable kitchen at sunset. "Would you believe me if I asked you to marry me today?" he asked, leaning closer to her until they were almost kissing. And she laughed at him softly, thinking about what he had said.

"No, I wouldn't believe you." She played the game with him, and he kissed her and then shook his head.

"Then I guess I'll have to ask you again tomorrow," he said, pretending to look crushed, and she laughed again, and kissed him again, but something in his eyes suddenly made her tilt her head to one side and look at him strangely.

"You're not serious, are you? This is all a joke, right?"

"Actually, being married to me probably would be something of a joke . . . but, yeah, I mean it. What do you think? Too far-out, or would you like to give it a try for fifty or sixty years? I've got the time, if you'd like to try it." He was looking at her with such tenderness that it took her breath away as she realized he meant it.

"Oh, my God . . . oh, my *God!* . . ." She put her hands on her head and almost screamed as she looked into his eyes. "You mean it?"

"Of course I mean it. I've never proposed to anyone in my life. I just figured this might be a good day to do it. You'd always remember."

"You're crazy," she said, and threw her arms around his neck. It was incredible. She had known him for a little over two months, and yet it felt completely right to both of them. She had had other relationships for years, and they had hemmed and hawed, and kept her at arm's length, and avoided any real intimacy. And here she was with Jeff, and it was as natural as could be. It was amazing. "I love you so much," she said, with her arms around him and kissing him. She had never been this happy. And even Carmen's baby seemed unimportant now. This was so much better. Jeff wanted to be with her for the rest of her life. It was what she had always wanted. It was a dream come true, and it was all so easy. It wasn't "work," and it didn't have to be "ironed out," and they didn't have to "try" or "give it some thought." She didn't need therapy to figure out if she wanted him, and he didn't need ten years or two or four to figure out if he loved her. They loved each other, and it was right, and they were getting married.

"You haven't answered me, you know," he reminded her, and she gave another squeal of delight, and ran around the kitchen like a kid, and he laughed and watched her.

"Yes, I have. The answer is yes . . . yes . . . yes . . . yes . . . yes!" And then she ran over and kissed him.

"April fool! Just kidding," he said, but she laughed and didn't believe him.

"Don't even try to get out of this one." And as they were talking about it the phone rang, and it was her brother. "Hi, Scott," she said casually. "What's new? . . . Not much . . . oh, nothing . . . Jeff and I just got engaged . . . no, seriously. Not April fool, for real." She sounded so casual, he didn't believe her, and Jeff was laughing as he listened.

"You're a monster," he scolded her, knowing what she was doing.

"Honest. We were just sitting here and we decided to get married. . . . Yeah, sure," she said when he said he'd just gotten engaged too. Needless to say, he didn't believe her. "Really, it's not April fool, it's for real." But she sounded as though she were putting him on, and she was laughing.

"Well, be sure to invite me to the wedding," was his final sarcastic response. She had totally spoiled his annual call, by the pretense that she was getting married. And he had to get back to his classes at Stanford.

"He didn't believe a word of it, I'll bet," Jeff said and laughed.

"Nope. He's going to croak when he realizes I was telling him the truth, or have you changed your mind yet?" she asked, pretending to be worried, as he kissed her.

"Give me a day or two. I've never been engaged before. I'm kind of enjoying it for the moment."

"Yeah," she said, "me too." And then as they kissed, they forgot their engagement and thought only of each other. He stripped her slacks and silk shirt away, and she stripped away his shorts and T-shirt. His legs were long and brown. He lay on the beach sometimes in the middle of the day when he was thinking and needed a break from his screenplay. And she looked very white and thin and graceful as she lay in his arms. It was dark when they finally stopped making love on the living room carpet. And she laughed as she looked around them.

"Can we still do this when we're married?"

"I'm counting on it," he said, sounding very sexy. They stood up finally amidst the debris of their clothes, and went back to his bedroom. And it was late that night before they thought of dinner, or going anywhere, or even their engagement.

"I like being engaged," Allegra said, as she brought a bag of Oreo cookies back to bed, and he opened a bottle of champagne in honor of their engagement.

"Shouldn't we call anyone?" he asked. "Should I ask your father for your hand?" he asked formally, toasting her with the champagne a moment later.

"Eventually. Let's enjoy it first, before everyone goes crazy." And then she began to think of the logistics. "When do you want to get married?" she asked. This was really fun. She'd never been engaged before either.

"Isn't it kind of traditional in June? I like traditions. I'll still be shooting the movie then, but we can probably fit it in. As long as you don't mind waiting till September for the honeymoon. Would that be too terrible? I'd rather not wait that long to get married." Even two months seemed too long to him. He couldn't wait to be married to her. And the idea of marrying Jeff in two months didn't scare her at all. She loved it. They were almost living together now anyway. Why wait any longer? She had waited long enough with all the people who had never been there for her. She didn't need a waiting period with Jeff. She would have married him right then, if he'd asked her.

"We could go to Bora Bora for our honeymoon. Maybe we'll get as lucky as Alan and Carmen," he said, smiling.

"Do you want kids that soon?" she asked, looking surprised, but she didn't mind that either.

"If you do. I'm thirty-four, you're twenty-nine. I wouldn't want to wait a hell of a lot longer. Anytime you feel ready. It would be nice to have them while we're still relatively young, though you're younger than I am. But I think having my first kid at thirty-five would be terrific."

"Maybe we'd better get started right now then. Your birthday is in six months. It could take a while." She was teasing him, but she liked everything he had said. In fact, she loved it. "My parents invited us to dinner tomorrow night, by the way," she said. "Maybe we should tell them then. Or do you want to wait a while?"

"Why wait? I don't need a due diligence period in which to change my mind, counselor. As far as I'm concerned, it's a done deal, if that's all right with you?"

"Maybe we should try it out again," she teased, "to make sure everything works, kind of like a test drive." She leaned over and kissed him again, getting cookie crumbs all over their bed, but he didn't seem to mind it.

"I plan to test drive it a lot over the next several years," he said, kissing her again. And he set his champagne glass down on their bedside. And a moment later, they were making love again. By midnight, they were happy and exhausted. "I think you're going to wear me out long before the wedding," he complained. "Maybe we should reconsider."

"Don't you dare!" she warned. "You can't take it back now. It's one minute after midnight. It's not April Fools' anymore. You're stuck with me, Mr. Hamilton."

"Hallelujah!" he said, and kissed her.

"Do you want a big wedding or a small one?" she asked, lying in bed, smiling at him.

"I don't think we have time for anything very big, if we only have two months, don't you think?"

"I agree. Forty or fifty people in my mom's garden would be perfect. That's all I want. Maybe even smaller." She looked at him, embarrassed that she hadn't asked him. "Unless you want to invite a lot of friends. I didn't mean to just announce what we were doing."

"That's all right," he smiled at her. "The only one I really want is my mother. I have a few friends out here, but not many. And the rest of my friends are pretty spread out all over the East, and Europe. It's a lot to expect them to come all the way out to California. I think forty people sounds just fine. I'll have to call my mother and tell her. She goes to Europe in June every year, and she likes plenty of warning if she has to make changes."

"Will she be pleased?" Allegra asked seriously, a little bit worried. The photograph of the woman she had seen in the apartment in New York had terrified her. She had looked so austere, and so cold, so unlike Jeff or his late father.

"She'll be fine. She finally stopped asking me about four years ago if I was ever going to get married. I think she gave up when I turned thirty." That, and the fact that she had hated all his girlfriends for the past twenty years. But he was sure she was going to like Allegra. Who wouldn't?

"I can't wait to tell my mom." Allegra beamed. "She's going to be so happy. They really like you."

"I hope so." And then he turned to Allegra seriously, and kissed her very gently. "I'm going to take very, very good care of you, for the rest of my life. I promise."

"So am I. I promise, Jeff . . . I'll always be there for you."

And then as they lay side by side in bed, holding hands and talking about their plans, Jeff suddenly chuckled. "Why don't we go to Vegas on the bus—we could wear wigs again and you could toss a bouquet of white plastic orchids." His mother would have croaked. But it had actually been fun at Carmen and Alan's wedding.

"There's something to be said for that," Allegra said. "If my mom can jazz this wedding up, she will. Count on it. We may have to go to Vegas."

They both laughed, and they cuddled into their bed, like two kids, planning an enormous adventure.

And when Allegra left for work the next day, she was so excited she forgot her car keys, and had to come back sheepishly to get them. She collected another kiss instead, and Jeff almost had to force her out the door so she wouldn't be late for her first appointment.

"Go on . . . go!" he called after her. "Get lost! Go away!" He waved her away down the short driveway and she was still laughing as she turned up the road. She had never been so happy.

She smiled all the way through her morning, and looked like the proverbial cat that swallowed the canary. But she didn't want to tell anyone until she had dinner with her parents that night, and she and Jeff told them. It was particularly hard to look Alice in the eye, and not say anything to Carmen when she called her. Carmen was still in seventh heaven about the baby. But Allegra thought her own news was even more exciting.

She tried to get Jeff to come into town to have lunch with her, but he said he couldn't. He had too much work to do on his screenplay.

"But I can't have lunch with anyone else," she complained. "I'd never make it all the way through lunch without telling them. You have to come in and see me."

"Not if you want me to go out tonight, Mrs. Hamilton." She loved the sound of it and so did he, and they loved playing with the words. She had written *Allegra Hamilton* all over her notepad. She hadn't played games like that since she was fourteen or fifteen, and in love with Alan.

And in the end, she decided to walk down Rodeo Drive and do a little shopping to see if there were any pretty white dresses, or suits, that would be suitable for a wedding in her mother's garden. She went to Ferre and Dior and Valentino, and Fred Hayman and Chanel, just to glance through the racks and get an idea what they had in white that was pretty. But she didn't find anything. Valentino had a beautiful white linen suit, but it didn't seem dressy enough, and Ferre had a fabulous organdy blouse, but nothing to go with it. But she had fun anyway. She couldn't believe what she was doing. She was shopping for her wedding dress, barely two months after she had met him. She almost wanted to call Andreas Weissman in New York to thank him.

She was going to skip lunch, but then she decided to stop in at the Grill for a quick sandwich and a cup of coffee. She usually saw people she knew there, either attorneys from her own firm, or agents from ICM and CAA or William Morris. There was the usual smattering of actors too, and some of her friends. The food was good, the service was fast, and the location was perfect.

And as her eyes scanned the booths as she arrived, she suddenly realized that her father was in a back booth. He was laughing at something, and she couldn't see who was with him. There was a huge temptation to just go over and tell him she was engaged, but she knew her mother would never forgive her for telling him first. She had to wait until that evening, when she and Jeff went to dinner. But she could at least drop by to say hello to him, which she did. She put her blue blazer over a chair at her own table, and went over to see him. She was wearing a short beige skirt, a pale blue sweater, and beige Chanel flats with a matching Chanel backpack. She looked very sleek and very fashionable, and as usual more like a model than an attorney.

As soon as she reached the booth where Simon sat, he glanced up and saw her, and his eyes immediately filled with pleasure. And then Allegra saw who he was dining with. She looked familiar at first, and then Allegra realized it was the British director she had seen him talking to at the Golden Globe Awards, Dame Elizabeth Coleson. She was very tall, and very young, and quite beautiful. She had a wonderfully deep, sexy laugh, and she was barely older than Allegra.

"Well, hello there," her father greeted her. "This is a surprise." He stood up and kissed her and introduced her to Dame Elizabeth, who was completely without pretension. She was very talented and very down-to-earth and she seemed to be having a very good time with Simon. "This is my daughter, Allegra," he explained to Elizabeth with a smile, and he explained to Allegra that they were talking about a picture. "I've been trying to talk Elizabeth into working with me for months, and so far, I haven't succeeded," he complained, and he sat down again, as Allegra watched them. They seemed completely at ease, and as though they were old friends, and had spent a lot of time together. Her father asked her if she would like to join them, but she didn't want to interrupt his meeting.

"That's okay, Dad. I've got to get back to the office in a few minutes. I just stopped in to grab a sandwich."

"What were you doing around here?" he asked, and she grinned at him, dying to tell him, but she couldn't.

"I'll tell you tonight."

"That's a deal," he said. She shook hands with Elizabeth and left them, and went back to her own table. She ordered the Caesar salad, and a cappuccino, and fifteen minutes later she went back to her office. As she drove back, she found herself thinking of her father and Elizabeth Coleson. She didn't know why, but she had felt the same thing the last time she saw them together, that they knew each other very well and were completely at ease with each other. She wondered if her mother was friendly with Elizabeth as well, and reminded herself to ask her. And then her thoughts went back to her wedding. Her head was filled with it, and she called Jeff three times that afternoon just to giggle and talk about their secret. She could hardly contain herself a moment longer, and by the time they were driving through her parents' gate that night, she felt as though she were about to explode with excitement. She could hardly stand it.

"Take it easy. . . . Take it easy. . . ." Jeff said calmly. But he was nervous too. What if they objected, or thought it was too soon, or didn't like him. He had voiced his concerns to her before they left Malibu, and she had told him he was ridiculous, but he was still worried.

Her father greeted them at the front door, and explained that Blaire was on the phone in the kitchen. She was talking to the architect, and from what Allegra could hear in the distance, it was not a pleasant conversation. He had just explained to her that given the cabinetry she'd chosen, and the tiles, it would take at least seven months to finish the kitchen. And Blaire wasn't shrieking at him, but she was close to it.

"Maybe we'll just move to the Bel Air for six months," Simon said, not entirely in jest, as he offered Jeff a drink, and Jeff asked for a Scotch and water.

They chatted pleasantly for a few minutes, and Blaire finally joined them, looking ruffled and irritated and excited.

"Do you realize how absurd that is?" she huffed at her husband, declining a drink as she ranted. "Seven months! He must be crazy. Sorry, darling," she said to Allegra, and then kissed her and Jeff, trying to regain her composure. "I just can't believe that."

"Why don't we keep the kitchen we have," Simon suggested cautiously, but Blaire said it was out of date and completely out of the question. "I'm moving out," he said in an undertone, and his wife shot him a warning look, and they moved on to other subjects. But Allegra could hardly contain herself. And as they sat there, in the lull before dinner, Jeff set down his glass, and looked at both her parents.

"Allegra and I have something to tell . . . er . . . rather, ask you. . . . I—I know it hasn't been long since we've met, but . . ." He had never felt so awkward in his life, he felt like a kid again, and Blaire was staring at him in disbelief, while Simon smiled at him. He felt sorry for him.

"Are you asking me what I think you are?" Simon said, trying to lend him a hand, and Jeff shot him a grateful look.

"Yes, I am, sir." He felt like a five-year-old sitting there next to her, asking her parents for her hand. "We'd like to . . . we're going to . . ." he said, trying to sound like a grown-up again, "get married."

"Oh, darling." Her mother rushed to take Allegra in her arms, and there were tears in their eyes as they hugged each other, and then Allegra looked at her father. His eyes looked damp too, but he looked happy for them.

"Daddy?" She wanted his approval too, but she could see that she had it.

"I heartily approve." He shook Jeff's hand firmly, and both men looked pleased, as though closing an important deal, and it was—the rest of Jeff and Allegra's lifetime. "Well done."

"Thank you," Jeff said, looking enormously relieved. It had been much harder than he thought it would be, though they had made it very easy for him. But it was still one of those ghastly, never-to-be-forgotten moments.

And from then on, everyone talked at once, and they hardly noticed when dinner was called. They talked of nothing else all through dinner. Samantha was out with friends, and they talked only about the wedding.

"All right, all right," Blaire said after the first course. "Now let's get down to details. How many, when, where, what kind of dress, long veil or short . . . oh, my God!" Blaire said, dabbing at her eyes with her napkin. It was one of the happiest nights of their lives, and certainly Allegra's, who tried to answer all of her mother's questions.

"We want about forty or fifty people here, at the house, in the garden," Allegra said happily, "nothing too fancy, just very cozy. In June." She beamed at Jeff, and then back at her mother.

"You're kidding, darling, of course," her mother answered, smiling. Obviously. But Allegra looked at her innocently, not understanding the question.

"No, we talked about it last night, and that's what we want."

"Out of the question," Blaire said, sounding like the producer and not the mother. "Forget it. No contract."

"Mom, this isn't your show, it's my wedding," Allegra reminded her gently. "What do you mean, 'forget it'?"

"I mean that the garden is going to be completely torn out in the next two weeks. There won't be anything in the backyard except dirt and the swimming pool till the fall, so the garden is out. And you can't possibly be serious about having forty or fifty people. Do you realize how many people we know? Allegra, this is crazy. Think of your clients, and all your friends from school, not to mention friends of the family. And, of course, Jeff and his parents will want to invite people. Frankly, I don't see how we'll manage to get away with four or five hundred. Six is probably more like it. Which means we can't do it here. And you can't possibly mean June. You can't throw together a wedding like that in two months. Allegra, now, let's be serious, dear. Where and when are we going to do it?"

"Mother, I *am* serious," she said, starting to look stressed. "This is our wedding, not yours, and we don't want more than fifty people. That's the whole point; if you make it a mob scene, we *have* to invite everyone. With forty or fifty, we just have our closest friends and it'll mean more to us that way, and it doesn't take six months to plan a wedding for fifty people."

"Why bother?" Blaire asked, looking more upset than Simon had ever seen her. Blaire was overreacting to everything, first the architect and now her own daughter's wedding.

"Mother, please!" Allegra said, near tears herself. "Why don't you just let us organize it ourselves? You don't have to do it."

"That's ridiculous. And where will you hold the wedding? In your office?"

"Maybe. We could do it at Jeff's house in Malibu. That would be perfect."

"You're not a hippie. You're an attorney, with a lot of important clients, and our friends mean a lot to us, and to you." She

turned to Jeff then, appealing to him, "You have to rethink this."
He nodded and turned to Allegra.

"Why don't we talk about it tonight and see what we can do
differently," he said calmly, as Simon watched him.

"I don't want to do anything differently. We *did* talk about
it, and we want a small wedding in June, in the garden," Allegra
said hotly.

"There is no garden," her mother snapped at her. "And I'm
shooting in June. For God's sake, Allegra, how difficult do you
have to make it?"

"Never mind, Mother." She threw down her napkin and got
up from the table, looking at Jeff as tears swam in her eyes. "We'll
go to Las Vegas. I don't need this from you. All I want is a small
wedding. I've waited thirty years for this, and I want to do it the
way Jeff and I want it, not the way you want it, Mom. We're the
ones getting married."

Blaire looked flustered as she saw how upset Allegra was,
and Simon tried to calm them both down.

"Why don't we talk about this after dinner? There's no need
for anyone to get so excited," he said quietly, and both women
looked mollified as Allegra sat down again. But it was obvious that
this wasn't going to be so simple.

The rest of the dinner was somewhat tense, with both
women saying very little. By the time coffee was served in the
living room, they were all up in arms again, with Allegra wanting
forty friends, and Blaire thinking they should have five or six
hundred. She was suggesting their club or the Bel Air Hotel, and
Allegra felt having her wedding there was tacky. She wanted it at
the house, and Blaire said she couldn't manage a show and a
wedding all at the same time, and trying to do it by June was
ludicrous. For at least two hours there appeared to be no possible
compromise whatsoever. And then finally, both sides having worn
each other down, Allegra grudgingly agreed to a hundred and
fifty, while her mother pushed for two hundred, and she said that
if they'd wait till September, when she was on hiatus with the
show, and the backyard would be finished, she thought she could

manage it at the house. Allegra hesitated for a long time over that one, and she consulted in an undertone with Jeff. They really didn't want to wait five months to get married, but he pointed out that he'd be finishing his movie right around then and they could leave for their honeymoon immediately, instead of waiting three months after the wedding to take it. There was a certain benefit there, and although she hated to do it, Allegra conceded, at Jeff's urging.

"But that's it, Mom. Don't push me any further. A hundred and fifty people in the garden in September. Period. Not one more person. And I'm only doing this for you." It sounded like a game of Monopoly as the two men listened, and Simon looked at his wife hopefully.

"Does this mean I get to keep my kitchen? There's no way they can put the new one in by September, from what they were saying tonight."

"Oh, shut up," Blaire said to her husband, angry all over again. "Mind your own business." But she smiled sheepishly, and a few minutes later, they all seemed to be unwinding. It had been an exhausting evening.

"I had no idea weddings took so much out of you," Jeff said, accepting another Scotch, while Simon poured himself a brandy.

"Neither did I," Simon admitted. "Ours was pretty small. But I know Blaire has always wanted to go all out for her daughters."

"She can do it for Sam," Allegra added, still shaken by the battle with her mother. They were both tough and the compromise hadn't been easy. And more than anything, she hated waiting five whole months till the wedding.

"We'll manage," Jeff reassured her, kissing her, and then she went out to the kitchen to talk to her mother. When she got there, Blaire was in the kitchen, blowing her nose. She'd been crying.

"I'm sorry, Mom," Allegra said, contrite for any harsh words. "I just know what I want, but I didn't mean to upset you."

"I want it to be beautiful for you, I want it to be special."

"It will be." As long as Jeff was there, that was all that mattered. The whole idea seemed stupid to her now, and she was sorry they weren't eloping like Carmen. It would have been so much simpler. And she had a suspicion that it was all going to get worse before it got better.

"What about a dress?" her mother asked then, moving on to another topic. "I hope you'll let me help you choose one."

"I started looking today, at lunchtime." Allegra smiled at her and told her where she'd been, what she'd seen, and what she wanted. Her mother thought that short was a good idea, but she still thought she should go dressy, maybe with a big hat, or a small veil.

"I saw Dad while I was shopping. I had to bite my tongue not to tell him, but I wanted to tell him with you, and Jeff, so I didn't."

"What was he doing shopping on Rodeo Drive?" Particularly since she knew he didn't like to shop under any circumstances. She did all his shopping for him.

"He wasn't. He was at the Grill, having lunch with Elizabeth Coleson. They were talking about a picture. I think Daddy's probably trying to hire her for one of his movies," she said conversationally, and went on to discuss whether or not she wanted bridesmaids. She hadn't decided, but she noticed something strange in her mother's eyes, and when they went back to the living room, she saw Blaire glance at Simon. They all went on talking about the wedding until the young couple left at eleven. And just before they left, Blaire said something odd to her daughter, and Jeff overheard it.

"You'll have to call your father," she said quietly as they stood in the doorway, and Allegra looked at her uncomfortably, and nodded. A few minutes later, she and Jeff were in the car on the way back to Malibu, exhausted by their first dose of wedding arrangements. It had been quite an evening.

"What did your mother mean?" he asked casually, as they headed toward the freeway. Allegra had leaned her head back against the seat with her eyes closed.

"We should have gone to Vegas and called them afterward," Allegra said, sounding exhausted.

"What did she mean about 'telling your father'? What does that mean?" But Allegra didn't answer. She just sat there, with her eyes closed, pretending to be sleeping. But he glanced at her, and sensed the tension in her silence. He didn't understand it, and he gently touched her cheek with his fingers. "Hey, don't ignore me. What did she mean?" He had instinctively sensed something painful.

Allegra opened her eyes and looked at him. "I don't want to talk about it now. Tonight was bad enough."

They drove in silence for a while, but Jeff refused to be put off. Her reticence disturbed him. "Allegra, isn't Simon your father?" There was a long, long pause. She was looking for an escape, a way not to tell him. She hated talking about it, even with him. It was too painful. She shook her head sadly, but she still didn't look at Jeff. She just stared out the window.

"My mom married him when I was seven." For Allegra, it was a terrible confession, something she hated talking about or admitting.

"I had no idea," he said cautiously, not wanting to tread on old secrets, but he was marrying her and he wanted to help her if he could, if this was as painful as it appeared from her silence.

"My 'real' father is a doctor in Boston. I hate him and he hates me too," she said as she looked at Jeff finally. It was a difficult subject to pursue, and he decided not to for the moment. He just touched her cheek gently again, and at the next light he leaned over and kissed her.

"Whatever happened, I just want you to know that I'm there for you, and I love you. No one's ever going to hurt you again, Allegra." She had tears in her eyes when she kissed him and whispered "thank you," and they drove the rest of the way to Malibu in silence.

In Bel Air, the Steinbergs were in their bedroom by then, and Blaire was watching Simon take his tie off.

"I hear you had lunch with Elizabeth today," Blaire said coolly, pretending to rifle a magazine, and then she looked up at her husband again. "I thought that was all over."

"It never began," he said quietly, as he unbuttoned his shirt and walked into his bathroom. But he could sense her just behind him. She had followed him in, and her eyes bored into his when he turned around to face her. "I told you, it's strictly a working relationship." He said it very calmly, but her shoulders sagged as she watched him. She felt so old just looking at him. He was having lunch with women her daughter's age, and he still looked so handsome. And she felt so faded and barely a woman anymore. She was a has-been, even professionally. And now she was the Mother of the Bride. She felt ancient.

"What were you working on with her in Palm Springs?" Blaire asked quietly.

"Don't do this," he said, turning away. He refused to play the game with her again. They had done this too often already. "We were just talking. That's all. We're friends. Let it go, Blaire, for both our sakes. You owe me that much."

"I don't owe you anything," she said, with eyes full of tears as she left his bathroom, and then she turned to look at him again from the doorway. "Are you offering her a picture? That's what Allegra said."

"That's what I told her. We were just talking. That's all. She's going back to England."

"And you?" she asked sadly. "Are you shooting your next picture there?"

"We're shooting the next one in New Mexico," he said, and walked slowly out of his bathroom to put his arms around her. "I love you, Blaire. Please know that. . . . Please don't push this anymore. . . . You'll hurt both of us." But she wanted to hurt him, as much as he had hurt her when she found out he was having an affair with Elizabeth Coleson six months before. He had been perfectly discreet. No one else had ever known. But she had. She had found out by accident when someone saw them in Palm Springs, and reported it to her without realizing it. But she had understood instantly. A chill had run down her spine the minute she heard it. And he had denied it, of course, but when she saw them speak to each other for a few minutes at a party, she had been certain. They had the look of people who had told each other secrets in bed late at night, that private conspiracy that only happens in the bedroom. And when she'd pressed him about it again, he said nothing. And she knew then that she was right about her suspicions.

Allegra didn't know about it. No one did. Blaire had never told anyone. She just kept it inside, as her soul slowly wilted, as it had again tonight when Allegra had said she'd seen them.

"Why do you have to go to a restaurant with her? Why can't you just see her in your office?"

"Because if I did, you'd think I was sleeping with her. I thought it would be better to see her in public."

"It would be better not to see her at all," Blaire said quietly, her whole body seeming to sag as she sat on the bed, just as her soul did. "Maybe it doesn't matter anymore," she said softly, and went to her own dressing room, and he didn't follow. Things were so difficult now. They hadn't slept with each other in months. Without even discussing it, they stopped once she knew he had had an affair. She felt he didn't love her and didn't desire her and she was growing older.

He was reading when she got back to the bedroom in her nightgown, and he looked at her kindly. He knew how painful it had been for her. He had regretted it terribly, but it was one of those things that just happened. And there was no way to undo it. He knew now, much to his chagrin, that Blaire would never let him forget it. And perhaps he deserved that. He accepted his fate at her hands and always wished that there were some way to let her know how much he still loved her. But she never believed him. All she ever focused on, other than her show, was Elizabeth Coleson. He wondered if the wedding would change all that and lift her spirits. He hoped so.

"I'm happy for Allegra," he said quietly. "Jeff is a nice guy. I think he'll be good to her." Blaire shrugged. Simon had been good to her too, for more than twenty years, and now it was all changed. They had been so happy, they had been so close. They had considered themselves special, and among the lucky ones, untouched by the hand of fate. And then, finally, it had touched them. And now everything was different, and it would never be the same again. He knew that. Even if he had broken it off after Palm Springs. It was too late now.

Blaire got into bed, and picked up a book. It was Jeff's new one. She had bought it the week before, and now he was going to be her son-in-law, but she could hardly think of him now, all she could think of was Simon having lunch with Elizabeth Coleson again. She couldn't help wondering what else they'd been doing. Was a lunch out in the open simply a brazen, sophisticated cover? She turned to look at him then. He had fallen asleep with his glasses on, and his book in his hands. And she lay watching him, feeling the ache where her love for him had once been, and now it was all so painful. It had been that way for months. As she closed his book and put his glasses away, she wondered if he had fallen asleep like that when he was with Elizabeth Coleson.

She put her own book away, and turned off the light. She was getting used to the pain and the loneliness. She had learned to live with them, but she remembered too well what it had been like before, before things had changed between them. And as she lay there, remembering the past, she forced herself to think of Allegra's wedding. Perhaps they'd be luckier than she and Simon had been. Perhaps the hand of fate would never touch them. She wished that for them, as she silently prayed for her daughter.

CHAPTER 13

For an entire week after they got engaged, Allegra felt as though she'd been hit by a hurricane at the office. Practically everyone she represented had a problem of some kind, a new deal being made, or a licensing arrangement that someone had offered them and that needed to be investigated. It was as though someone pulled a rip cord somewhere and was trying to drown her.

And when Jeff called his own mother to tell her about their engagement, it only made things more complicated. Her only comment was that it seemed rather hasty, since she'd never even heard him mention her before, and she hoped he wouldn't regret it. She'd spoken to Allegra for a few minutes, and she told Jeff that she certainly hoped they would come to New York, at least for a few days, so she could meet her.

"We really ought to go before they start to shoot in May," he had said after they'd talked to her, but Allegra couldn't begin to see when they'd do it. She was still much too busy at the office. But she promised him that they'd manage it in the next few weeks, come hell or high water.

The one thing she didn't do that week, and again her claim was that she was just too busy to do anything, was call her father. Jeff avoided pressing her about it, but she had eventually volunteered that her parents had gotten divorced and there was a great deal of bitterness between them. She had only seen him a few times in the past twenty years, and it had never been pleasant. He seemed to hold her responsible for her mother's actions. "He always tells me how much like her I am, and how spoiled we are, and how he disapproves of our 'Hollywood lifestyle.' He acts like I'm a go-go dancer and not a lawyer."

"Maybe he doesn't know the difference." Jeff tried to inject a little humor into it, but it was very clear to him that Allegra was not receptive. His own mother was not overly fond of Hollywood, and everything she thought it represented. She was highly suspicious of what he did there. But the situation with Allegra's father sounded a great deal more serious. And he got the impression that there was more she wasn't saying. But Jeff decided sensibly that she would tell him when she was ready. He couldn't help wondering though if this was the reason for the difficult men she had previously gotten involved with. If her father had rejected her, perhaps she was looking for men who would do the same, in which case she was going to be seriously disappointed in Jeff. He had no desire to reject her.

On the contrary, he loved their quiet days, their afternoons in bed, their very rare lazy mornings. The weekend after they'd told her parents, they finally shared a quiet evening at home. And on Saturday, they even managed to go to a movie. They had gone to bed as soon as they got home—they could never resist making love—and they were drifting off to sleep in each other's arms when the phone rang.

Jeff was inclined to ignore it, but Allegra never could. She was always sure it would be some major crisis that she had to handle for one of her clients. And sometimes it was, admittedly, but more often than not it was a wrong number.

"Hello?" she said, sounding groggy, and for an instant there was silence. She was about to hang up, and then she heard a sob. "Hello?" she said again, frowning now as she waited. "Who is this?" There was another long beat, and then another sob, and then a strangled voice at the other end. "It's Carmen."

"Are you okay?" Had there been an accident? Was something seriously wrong? Was she hurt? Had Alan left her? What could possibly have happened? "Carmen, talk to me," she said, trying not to sound exasperated, as Jeff groaned on his side of the bed. Every time Carmen and Alan had a fight, Carmen called, hysterical, and Jeff did not find it amusing. He was extremely fond of them, but he didn't think it was Allegra's job to solve their minor marital problems. After all, everyone had them, and most people did not call their attorneys and expect them to solve them.

"He's leaving," Carmen finally managed to force out, and then she collapsed in fresh sobs, and Allegra could hear someone shouting in the background.

"What's going on?" Allegra said, trying to exude calm to her through the phone, but it wasn't working. "Is he leaving you?"

"Yes, he's leaving." She gulped, and then the phone was taken out of her hand and Alan came on, sounding angry and exhausted.

"I am *not* leaving her, for chrissake. I am going to Switzerland to make a movie, and I am not going to be killed, or have an affair," he repeated for the ten thousandth time that night. "I'm going to work, that's all. And when it's over, I'll come home. This is what I do for a living." With that, he handed the phone back to his hysterical wife, who was just crying harder.

"But I'm pregnant."

Allegra sighed. She got the picture now. Carmen didn't want him to leave to make the movie. But he had a contract, and a very handsome one at that. He had to. "Come on, Carmen, be fair. He's got to do this. You can fly over and visit him before you start work in June. Go now, for heaven's sake. You can stay over there for a month before rehearsals." The sniveling suddenly stopped and there was silence.

"I could, couldn't I? Oh, God, thank you, Allegra, I love you." Maybe she did. But Allegra wasn't sure that Alan would be just as thrilled. When she wanted to be, Carmen could be terribly clingy and distracting. "I'll call you tomorrow," Carmen said hastily, and literally hung up on her. Allegra shook her head, turned off the light, and went back to bed with Jeff, but he muttered into the pillow as she snuggled closer.

"You have to tell these people to stop calling you every five minutes like a ten-cent shrink. It's ridiculous. I don't know how you stand it." Allegra knew it really bothered him, but he was a pretty good sport about it. He knew her clients had done that for years. Carmen certainly, and Bram Morrison's wife, and even Bram when he felt he needed to, and Malachi every time he got stoned or drunk and thought he had a brainstorm, not to mention when he got into trouble. And even Alan. And the others too. That's what L.A. attorneys did, and if these people didn't call their attorneys, they called their agents.

"It goes with the territory, Jeff. It's hard to get them not to expect that."

"It's neurotic. What happened then? Did they have another fight? This is going to seem like a very long marriage, if we get a call at midnight every time they have an argument over who's taking out the garbage." In truth, their garbage had to be shredded and then locked up with a combination lock, so no one would steal it. "If you don't tell her, I will."

"She doesn't want Alan to go to Switzerland next week. She wants him to stay home with her and the baby."

"There is no baby yet," Jeff said, even more annoyed at her than he had been. "That's really stupid. She's ten minutes' pregnant and she expects him to stay home with her for nine months?"

"Only for seven and three quarters. She's already five weeks' pregnant." Jeff groaned again and Allegra laughed. It really was silly. But it was real to Carmen.

"Maybe you should go into antitrust work," he suggested, and then finally decided not to waste the opportunity, since they were both wide awake now. He rolled over toward Allegra and started making serious overtures to her. At least it put him back in good humor. And this time, when they fell asleep, there were no more interruptions.

The Oscars distracted all of them the week after that, and Carmen was busy making plans for their trip by then. They were leaving two days later. She and Alan were both nominated, though neither of them expected to win this year. But it was great for their careers to be nominated, though Carmen seemed completely disinterested in her career. The only thing she cared about at the moment was the baby, and, of course, Alan.

Allegra and Jeff saw her parents at the ceremonies, and Simon's picture won five awards including Best Picture, much to Allegra's delight. Her mother looked thrilled for him too, but Allegra kept noticing something taut about her whenever she saw her. She wasn't sure if it was the state of her show, or just a mood, or Allegra's own imagination, but it was something she felt more than saw, and she kept trying to put her finger on it when she talked to Jeff, but he swore he didn't see it.

"She just looks upset, or troubled, or sad or something," Allegra said with certainty.

"Maybe she doesn't feel well. She could be sick," he explained practically, and Allegra looked even more worried.

"I hope not."

As predicted, Alan and Carmen didn't win, but neither of them seemed to mind.

And Blaire was true to form when she asked Allegra after the ceremony if she had called her father about the wedding.

"No, Mom, I haven't," she said, with pursed lips. Allegra had worn a clinging silver dress that molded her body and she looked spectacular, and the last thing she wanted to hear about was her father, and whether or not she had called him.

"I have to know for the invitations," Blaire harped again, and Allegra rolled her eyes at her mother.

"Okay, okay, I'll call him." And then she thought better of it. "Why don't *you* call him and ask if he wants to be on the invitations? I don't want him on them anyway. Simon is my father. I don't need this guy, and all his miserable bullshit. Why don't we just *not* call him, and you two announce it? I don't even use the name anymore, so what's the difference?" People knew her only as Allegra Steinberg, although Simon had never been able to officially adopt her. Blaire had never wanted to broach the matter with Allegra's real father, Charles Stanton. Allegra Stanton had always had a nice ring to it, but not to Allegra. "And I'm not walking down the aisle with him, just so you know. I'm walking down it with Daddy." But before Blaire could comment, they got separated by the crowd, as well-wishers and the press pushed around them.

Later, when the crowd thinned, Allegra saw Dame Elizabeth Coleson come over to congratulate her father. They were chatting easily in the midst of a cluster of people, and Blaire had moved off slightly to talk to friends. But Allegra saw her glance over her shoulder at Simon and she looked tense. Allegra was beginning to wonder if Jeff was right and her mother didn't feel well.

They all went out to various parties afterward. Allegra and Jeff went to one that Sherry Lansing gave, upstairs at the Bistro right after the awards, and then to another at Spago after that, but none of them was as good as the one that Irving Lazar used to give in the old days. But they had fun anyway, and two days later Carmen and Alan left for Switzerland, with a mountain of suitcases and hanging bags and garment bags and boxes. It looked like a traveling circus leaving town, but in the midst of it all, Carmen looked ecstatic. She was going with him.

"Just don't forget to come back in time," Allegra reminded her after accompanying them to the airport. Alan was looking totally aggravated at the amount of stuff Carmen had brought, and the press had appeared, tipped off as usual, and was adding even more irritation to an already chaotic departure.

The VIP agents from the airline and Allegra finally got them on the plane, and she got Alan to sign a few last papers she'd brought in her briefcase, and she went back to town in peace in the limousine, and even had free time to call Jeff. It was heaven.

"How was it?" Jeff asked when she called him.

"Unbelievable, as usual."

"Were they wearing the polyester suits and the wigs? They should have."

"You're right, they should have," she laughed. "Alan was

carrying some kind of a bear that Carmen takes everywhere, and she was wearing a sable parka, and a stretch suit that would have knocked anyone's eyes out. I still wish we were getting married in Vegas the way they did."

"So do I. Speaking of which," he said cautiously, "I spoke to my mother today. She really wants us to come East to see her. I'd like to do it before I start the movie." That was in two weeks and she couldn't imagine it. She was handling all the last-minute details for Bram Morrison's tour. And just double-checking the security arrangements and their contracts and liabilities was overwhelming. She had also met Jeff's Harvard friend by then, Tony Jacobson, who was coproducing his film with him. And she knew Tony and Jeff both had a ton of work to do before starting to shoot. She couldn't imagine how either of them could go East, even to meet his mother.

"I don't see how, Jeff . . . but I'll try. I promise."

"I told her we'd come out the last weekend in April." He was holding his breath, praying she'd agree to do it. His mother was already upset that Jeff had proposed to Allegra before she had met her. "Can you do it?"

"I'll do it, I'll do it." It was two days before the first concert of Bram's tour, a local one fortunately, but it was still going to be a major effort.

"We'll just go over the weekend, overnight if you'd prefer." He was willing to do anything to accommodate her, but it meant a lot to him, and she couldn't deny him that. He'd done nothing but help her and be understanding since the day they met. She owed him this much. "If you want, we could stop and see your father in Boston on the way back," Jeff suggested, trying to be equitable, but there was an immediate silence.

"Charles Stanton is not my father." He was still dying to know why not, and she still hadn't told him. But her comment gave him the opportunity to ask her that night, while they were both cooking dinner. They had it down to a science now. He did the meat, and she did all the trimmings. She was good at vegetables and salads and all the tasty, decorative little goodies, and he loved doing steaks, and chops, and chicken. But when he asked her again, as usual, there was a long silence.

"Maybe I should stop asking you?" he suggested. She'd been avoiding the questions for two weeks, ever since he'd first heard about him. "But I'd kind of like to know why it was so traumatic. Maybe we do need to get this over with. What does your therapist think? Have you asked her?" he asked fairly, and Allegra nodded.

"She said to tell you." There was another long silence as she put his rice and broccoli on his plate, and Jeff added a slice of broiled fish to it. It made a very appealing dinner. She had also made garlic bread, and a small salad.

"Voilà!" he said with a flourish as they sat down, and Allegra smiled a wintry smile at him. She was thinking of Charles Stanton. And it was as though Jeff had read her mind. "Why do you hate him so much, Allie?" he asked quietly. "What did he do to you, or your mom?" Jeff guessed it must have been pretty awful. But she shrugged as she started to pick at her dinner.

"He really didn't do anything . . . then. . . . It's more what he didn't do after. . . . I had a brother named Patrick . . . Paddy." She smiled, looking up at Jeff. "He was my hero. He was five years older than I was. He did everything for me . . . I was his little princess. Most brothers beat their sisters up. . . . Paddy never did. He fixed my dolls when they broke, he put my mittens on, he tied my shoelaces, till . . ." Her eyes filled with tears; they always did when she talked about Paddy. She still had a picture of him. She kept it in a locked drawer in her office. She couldn't bear putting it on the desk. It still hurt too much almost twenty-five years later. "He died when I was five," she said in a strangled voice. "He had a rare form of leukemia, which they couldn't cure in those days. And they're not always lucky with it now either. He knew he was going to die. He used to tell me that he was going to go up to heaven and wait for me." Her eyes filled with tears again and Jeff stopped eating and reached out a hand to touch her.

"I'm sorry." He felt a lump in his throat as he said it.

She nodded, but went on now that she had started. Maybe Dr. Green was right. It was better to tell him and have it done with. "I used to beg him not to leave me. But he said he had to. He was so sick at the end. I still remember it. You're not supposed to remember things about when you were five, not much anyway. I remember everything about Paddy. I remember the day he died." She choked on the words but went on anyway, and Jeff handed her a paper napkin. She smiled at him through her tears, and wished he could have met her brother. She wished he were still alive. She had wished that often.

"I think my dad went kind of crazy when he died. He had tried treating him at the end, apparently. I didn't know that, but Mom told me later. But he couldn't do anything. No one could. But that was my father's specialty and it drove him crazy that he couldn't help him. He never thought much of me, maybe because I was so young, or a girl, or . . . I don't know . . . I don't remember much about him, just Paddy. My father was never really there, he was always working. And then my brother died and he fell apart, and he took it out on my mother. He shouted at her all the time, he blamed her for everything. And somehow, like all kids, I thought it was my fault. I thought I had done something terrible to make Paddy die and my father hate us. All I remembered was his screaming.

"It went on like that for about a year. I think he was drinking a lot. My parents fought all the time, their whole marriage fell apart. I used to hide in the closet and cry at night, so I wouldn't hear them fighting."

"It sounds awful," Jeff said sympathetically.

"It was. Eventually, he started hitting her. I was always afraid he would hit me, and I always felt guilty for not stopping it, but there was nothing I could do. And I kept thinking that if Paddy hadn't died, none of that would have happened, but maybe it would have. He started blaming my mom for everything, he even said it was her fault Paddy had died, and she said she was going to leave him. He told her that if she did, he'd turn his back on us and we'd starve in the street without him. My mom had no family, and I guess she didn't have any money saved up. A long time later, she told me she had a plan, and she started sending short stories to magazines. She saved a few thousand dollars. And one night after he beat her up, she took me and we left. I remember we stayed in a hotel where it was really cold, and I remember being very hungry, and she bought me donuts. She was probably scared to death to spend much money.

"I think we hid there for a while, and he never found us, but then she went to talk to him at his office, and she took me with her. Everyone at his office acted like he was a god or something, and he was a big deal at Harvard Medical School. Nobody knew that he used to beat my mother up, or any of it. They just felt sorry for him because of Paddy.

"Mom told him she wanted to go away, and he told her that if she did, he'd never see either of us again, and I could die too for all he cared. He said that if we left, I was no longer his daughter." Her eyes swam in tears again as Jeff continued to squeeze her hand, but said nothing. "That's what he said, I was no longer his daughter. And Mom said we were leaving anyway. He said we were both dead, as we left his office. And I kept waiting to die after we left it. He didn't say good-bye, or kiss me or anything. He acted like he hated us. I guess he hated my mom just then, and in his head, I was all rolled up with it. My mom said he'd change his mind after a while, and I would always be his daughter. She said he was just really sad about Paddy, and acting crazy. And she told me we were going out to California. We came by bus, and every now and then she'd call him, but he'd never talk to her and even hung up on her.

"When we got to L.A., she started writing for television right away. I think she got some lucky breaks, they really liked her stuff. And she told her story to some man at the network one day when I was with her, and he cried while he listened. I think he gave her a lot of work. And about six months after we got here, she met Simon. I was six and a half by then. We left Boston right after my sixth birthday. We had been in the freezing cold hotel on my birthday, and there had been no cake and no presents. Daddy never even said happy birthday or called me. But after everything that had happened to us in the past year, I felt I didn't deserve anything anyway. I felt to blame for everything, but I was never quite sure why. I just figured it was my fault.

"For years I wrote to my father, asking him to forgive us, and he never wrote back to me. And finally he did write and he told me that what my mother had done was disgraceful and unforgivable, that she should never have left him. She had gone to Hollywood like a whore, and abandoned him, and that I was living a life of sin and debauchery in California and he didn't want to know me. I tore the letter up so I wouldn't have to see it. And I cried for weeks. But by then, Simon was like a father to me. And eventually, I just gave up on Charles Stanton." She never referred to him anymore as her father. "He came out to see me, or I guess he happened to be in California, when I was about fifteen, and for some reason he called, and I wanted to see him. And he agreed to see me. I was so curious about him. I wanted to see what he was like then. But it was just more of the same. I had tea with him at the Bel Air. Mom dropped me off, and all he did was say a lot of terrible things about her. He never asked about me, or said he was sorry he hadn't seen me in ten years or that he hadn't written to me. He just said that I was a lot like my mother and he was sorry to see it. He said that she and I had been very unfair to him and we would pay for it one day. It was a horrible afternoon, and I ran all the way home, I didn't even wait for Mom to pick me up. I just wanted to get away from him. And I never heard from him again, until I was stupid enough to invite him to my graduation from college seven years later. And he actually came, to Yale, and he dumped all over me again, but by then I was kind of fed up with the whole thing. I told him I never wanted to see him again after he insulted my mother at the graduation.

"He sent me a Christmas card once, God only knows why, and I wrote and told him I was in law school. And I never heard from him again. He completely abandoned and rejected me. My mom may have left him in Boston, but I was still his daughter. He didn't have to cross me out of his life completely, but he did. And for years, I always had this obsession with wanting to see him, wanting to hear from him, wanting to run after him. But I'm over it now. I don't give a damn anymore. It's over. He's gone, he's not my father. And now my mother wants to put him on our wedding invitation. I can't believe it. But I'm not having my name on the same page as his, I can tell you. He's *not* my father. And he doesn't want to be either. The only decent thing he could have ever done for me was let me go completely and let Simon adopt me, and when I asked him to do that, that day at the Bel Air when I was fifteen, he said that was rude and humiliating and he would never do it. The guy is a completely selfish sonofabitch, and I don't care how respectable he is, or what a good doctor, he's a miserable human being. And he's no longer my father." He had abandoned her emotionally, and she had paid for it for almost twenty-five years. She was not yet ready to forgive him, and she doubted if she ever would be.

"I can see why you feel that way about him, Allie. Why invite him to the wedding? You certainly don't have to." He felt so sorry for her after hearing all of it. Although he knew that she had had a good life and a far happier childhood in the home of Simon Steinberg. But the early loss of her brother, and the rejection of her natural father, had obviously hurt her deeply. And she had looked for rejecting men for years, in order to continue the same story. But at last, after years of help from Dr. Green, she had finally broken the pattern.

"My mother thinks I should include him. Can you believe that? I think she's crazy. She's trying to heap her old guilt, and whatever relationship she may have had with him all those years ago, on me, and she expects me to carry it along. And I'm not going to. I don't care if the bastard dies on my doorstep, I don't want him at our wedding."

"Then don't have him," Jeff said simply.

"Tell Mom. She's driving me nuts over this. She keeps asking if I called him. And I told her, I'm not going to."

"What does Simon say?"

"I haven't asked him, but he's always so obsessed with being fair. That's why I invited my father to my graduation. Simon kept saying that it wasn't fair not to invite him, that he would be so proud of me. But he didn't give a damn. He just came and was rude to everyone, even Sam, and she was only ten years old then. Scott hated him on sight. He never understood who he was. I wouldn't let Mom and Simon tell him. They just said he was an old friend. They know now, but I never used to admit to them that Simon wasn't my father. I was always afraid that it would make me a second-class citizen and they wouldn't love me as much, but the truth is, Simon never treated me any differently than the others. If anything, he treated me better." She smiled, and then sighed, poking at her fish again. And then she looked back at Jeff. "I've been very lucky, except for the early days." But they had obviously traumatized her, and it had taken years to recover. "So what do you think I should do?" she asked Jeff fairly.

"Whatever you like," he stressed again, "this is *our* wedding. You do what *you* want, not what your mother thinks you should do."

"I think she still feels guilty for leaving him sometimes, so she wants to throw him a bone to make him feel better. But I don't owe him that, Jeff. Not with my life. He's never, ever been decent to me."

"You don't owe him anything. I think I'd tell your mother to keep him off the invitations," Jeff said firmly.

"I agree with you," she said, relieved that he at least understood. "And I don't care if it is proper to put him on. How proper has he been to me for the last twenty-four years?"

"He never remarried?" Jeff was curious. It was, in its own way, for all concerned a tragic story. And her brother dying must have devastated them all, to the point that they could no longer recover.

"He never remarried," Allegra confirmed. "Who would want him?"

"He may not be as disturbed as he was then, you know. That all sounds pretty traumatic."

"So was my early childhood." She sat back in her chair with a sigh, relieved that it was all out in the open. "Anyway, now you know all my ugly secrets. I'm really Allegra Charlotte Stanton, except if you ever call me that, I'll kill you. Steinberg suits me just fine," she said bluntly.

"Me too," he said, still thinking about her story. And he came around the table to kiss her.

Neither of them finished their dinner that night, and they went for a long walk on the beach to talk about her father. Allegra felt as though a thousand-pound weight had been lifted from her. She was glad that Jeff knew about her childhood. And, somehow, talking about her father now, as angry as she still was at him in some ways, she didn't really care anymore. She had Jeff, and her own life. At last she was healing.

She sat on his deck afterward for a long time, and it was a beautiful night. She lay against him, as they drank a little wine, and relaxed, and it was after midnight when the phone rang.

"Don't answer it," Jeff begged, but she just couldn't. "Someone's either got hemorrhoids or they're in jail. And either way, they're going to expect you to solve it."

"I can't help it. It's my job, and maybe they really need me." But it wasn't a client, it was Sam, and she asked if the next day she and Allegra could spend some time together.

Allegra was surprised by the call, but not completely. Every now and then, Sam reached out to her, usually when she needed Allegra to convince their parents of something. "Did you have a fight with Mom?" Allegra couldn't help asking with a smile.

"No, she's too busy screaming at everybody about the garden and the kitchen. It's a wonder she doesn't have a heart attack," Sam said, unamused. Her mother had been very difficult lately.

"Not to mention the wedding," Allegra added.

"Yeah, I know," Sam said, sounding more serious again. "Where shall I meet you?"

"What's this about?" Allegra wanted to know ahead of time. "A modeling contract or something?"

"Yeah . . ." Sam said cryptically, "sort of."

"I'll pick you up at twelve o'clock. Jeff is having lunch with

Tony Jacobson, his coproducer. We'll go someplace fun like The Ivy, or Nate 'N Al's."

"Let's go somewhere and talk," Sam said quietly, and Allegra smiled at her younger sister.

"Okay. This sounds serious. It must be love."

"It is," Sam agreed glumly.

"Well, I'm getting better at that, but actually I think I just got lucky. I'll do what I can."

"Thanks, Al," her sister said, and Allegra reiterated her promise to pick her up at noon on Sunday. She was touched that Sam had called her.

"Doesn't anyone call us at normal hours?" Jeff complained, as Allegra told him about Sam's call.

"She sounded upset. She must have a new boyfriend."

"At least she's family," he conceded. That made sense to him at least, a lot more than Malachi O'Donovan calling from some drunk tank.

"Do you mind my having lunch with her tomorrow?" Allegra asked as they went to bed a few minutes later. He had wanted her to join him with Tony. And she liked Tony a lot. He was very Eastern and very smart. He was from New York, and his father was one of the biggest investment bankers on Wall Street. He'd helped them get backers for the film, and given them some great advice. Tony was very different from Jeff, but Allegra genuinely liked him.

"Not at all. I'll meet you afterward. Maybe we can all play some tennis. I understand, and so will Tony. He'll love Sam," he teased, and his fiancée gave him the disapproving look of a much older sister.

"My dad will love that." She glared at him, and then chuckled. Everything was working out fine. And he was right. She didn't need to invite Charles Stanton to their wedding. All she had to do now was tell her mother. And she could do that the next day, after she had lunch with Samantha. She smiled to herself, thinking of Sam's call, and wondered what advice she needed about the new boyfriend. Allegra was certainly no expert, but she was flattered anyway that Sam had called her. Their relationship meant a lot to both of them, although Sam was a brat at times, but even when she was, Allegra loved her.

CHAPTER 14

As promised, Allegra picked her sister up on Sunday on schedule. She thought it might be fun if she took her to lunch at the Ivy. They could cruise through the secondhand shops on North Robertson after that, relax with each other, and have some fun. Lately Sam had been acting fairly bratty, and Allegra was anxious to spend some quality time with her.

But there was nothing bratty about the way she acted today. In fact, she had barely spoken by the time Allegra pulled out of the driveway. Allegra couldn't help wondering what was bothering her. But Sam made it all the way through lunch almost without speaking.

"So what's the deal?" Allegra finally asked, wondering what had prompted her to ask Allegra to come and see her. "A new guy giving you a problem?" She had always had dates in the last two years, but she had never had a steady boyfriend. Unlike Allegra, who, at her age, had always been madly in love with someone.

"Sort of." Sam shrugged noncommittally, and then as her eyes filled with tears, she said, "Not really."

"So what is it then?" Allegra pressed her a little bit as the waiter brought their cappuccinos. Lunch had been delicious, as usual. But Sam had hardly eaten. "Come on, Sam . . . cough it up. . . . Whatever it is, it won't be so bad once you share it." But apparently it was, because she dropped her head in her hands and started crying softly. "Oh, Sam . . ." Allegra rubbed a hand across her shoulders. "Come on, baby, tell me," she whispered. But when her sister raised her face to hers again, Allegra could see the bottomless despair that had overwhelmed her. "Sam, please . . ."

"I'm pregnant." Sam almost choked on the words as she said them. "I'm having a baby. . . ." She just sat there and cried quietly, as Allegra stared at her for an instant and then hugged her.

"Oh, sweetheart . . . oh, God . . . How did that happen . . . ? Who did it?" As though it had been something that had been done to her, and not something she had shared in. But Allegra had never heard her mention anyone's name, and certainly not a steady boyfriend.

"*I* did it," Sam said, taking the full blame upon herself. She looked desolate, as she tossed the shining platinum hair over her shoulders.

"Not all by yourself," Allegra said, "unless things have changed a whole lot lately. Who's the father?" What words for a seventeen-year-old child: *father . . . mother . . .* not just "Who is the boy?" It really brought home the idea that she was having a baby, a child, a living, breathing person.

"It doesn't matter," Sam answered glumly.

"Oh, yes, it does," Allegra insisted. "Are you involved with someone at school?" Without even knowing him, Allegra wanted to kill him, but she was pretending to stay calm, for Sam's sake. Just listening to her, her heart was pounding and her mind was racing. But Sam only shook her head in answer. "Come on, Sam, who is it?"

"I don't want you to do anything about it if I tell you."

"Were you raped?" Allegra asked in a rasping whisper, but Sam shook her head again.

"No, I wasn't. It's my own fault. I did it willingly. I was so impressed with him . . . I thought . . . I don't know," she said, tears flooding her eyes again. "I guess I was flattered. He was so worldly and so grown-up. He was thirty." A thirty-year-old with a seventeen-year-old girl? He should have known better, at least, and he obviously hadn't even had the decency to use protection.

"Were you a virgin?" Allegra asked, overwhelmed with concern for her, and Sam shook her head, and didn't offer further details. Allegra knew she wasn't promiscuous, but she was also almost eighteen years old, and there had obviously been someone before who mattered to her. She didn't want to press her on anything but the present. "How did you meet him?"

"He was the photographer on a shoot I did," she said miserably. "He's French. I thought he was so cool because he was from Paris. He treated me like I was a woman of the world, and he was really handsome."

"Have you told him yet?" Allegra could hardly wait to get her hands on the guy. He'd be lucky if they didn't have him deported. They could have him put in jail for statutory rape. She could just imagine their father. But Sam was looking bereft as she shook her head yet again.

"I don't really want to anyway. But I called the agency and they said he went to Japan or someplace. He was just passing through, and they didn't really know him. He wanted the pictures for his own portfolio before he went to Tokyo. Nobody knows how to find him. It doesn't matter anyway, I never want to see him again. He was okay, but he was kind of a jerk in the end. He offered me some drugs afterward, and when I said I didn't want them, he called me a baby." And now she was having one. "His name was Jean-Luc. But no one even knows his last name."

"Jesus Christ." Allegra was sputtering, she was so mad. "Is that how they run their agency? They ought to be put in jail too if that's how they deal with minors."

"I'm almost eighteen, Al. I should at least be able to handle a modeling gig without having my hand held."

"Apparently not," Allegra said sternly, and then reminded herself that she didn't want to be unduly harsh on her. Sam was in enough misery, and Allegra wanted to help her. That had to remain her focus. And at least her sister had had the guts to come to her with her problem. "I assume you haven't said anything to Mom yet."

"I really don't want to," Sam said, and Allegra nodded. She wouldn't have wanted to at Sam's age either, although their mother was usually incredibly understanding, and some of their friends had always gone to her with problems, rather than their own mothers. But her mother had been so wound up about the wedding and her show lately, that Sam just hadn't been able to bring herself to tell her.

"So what are we going to do about this mess?" Allegra asked, with a sinking heart. As far as she was concerned, at Sam's age, there was only one solution. She couldn't see her sister ruining her life by saddling herself with a baby. "I'll take you to my own doctor tomorrow. Maybe we don't even have to tell Mom. I want to think about this before we decide," Allegra said, thinking it over.

"I can't," Sam said stubbornly, and Allegra looked at her in confusion.

"You can't what?"

"Go to the doctor with you . . . not to get rid of it anyway."

"Why not?" Allegra's face filled with terror. "You're not going to keep it, are you? Sam, you don't even know who the guy is. You can't have this baby all by yourself. It's just plain stupid." Why was she getting sentimental about this? She suddenly thought of Carmen and her acting like it was already born because she'd seen the fetus on a sonogram, and she wondered if that had happened to Sam already too. Bonding.

"I can't get rid of it, Al, not with an abortion anyway."

"Why?" Her family had strong morals, but they were reasonable generally, and they weren't Catholic. Allegra couldn't understand it.

"I'm five months' pregnant."

"*What?*" Allegra almost fell out of her chair when she heard the words. "Why the hell didn't you tell me sooner? What have you been doing for the last five months? Dreaming?"

"I didn't know," Sam said honestly, tears spilling onto her cheeks and from there to the table. "I swear. My periods are so irregular, I just thought that maybe it was from too much exercise or dieting, or exams, or worrying about getting into college . . . I don't know. I never thought I could be pregnant."

"How could you not even suspect? Isn't it moving or something? Does it show?" She glanced at her, but she was rail thin and wore baggy clothes, so Allegra could see nothing.

"I sort of thought I was just gaining weight, and I've had this enormous appetite." And then she looked even more miserable. "It didn't move till last week. And then I felt it. I thought maybe I had cancer and it was exploding inside me or something." The poor kid had no idea. There they were in the civilized world, in one of the most sophisticated cities in the country, and poor Sam thought she had a tumor. Talk about denial. Allegra felt desperately sorry for her, but the problem was so complicated now, it really required some serious thinking.

"You'll have to give it up, I guess." Sam just stared at her, numb. She couldn't even conceive what the "it" was. They had offered to show it to her on a sonogram, and she had refused to see it. She didn't want to know its sex, or know anything about it. She didn't want it to be there.

"What am I going to do, Al? I'll have to run away if I don't tell Mom and Dad soon." That was a frightening thought. The whole situation was a disaster.

"You can't do that."

"I don't know what else to do. I thought of running away all last week, but I wanted to talk to you first." The very thought of it made her shudder.

"We have to tell Mom. If she really has a fit, or they throw you out or something, you can come and stay with me till you have it." She looked up at Sam again then. "When is it due?" This was beyond awful. And this wasn't Carmen. It was her seventeen-year-old sister.

"In August. Al . . . will you help me tell them?" Allegra nodded and the two sisters held hands across the table. And a few minutes later, Allegra noticed two women with buzz cuts smiling at them approvingly. They thought she and Sam were lovers. It was the only thing that had happened so far that actually made her smile, and she mentioned it to Sam as she paid the check finally. It had been some lunch. She had acute indigestion.

"When do you want to tell them?"

"Never," she said honestly. "But I guess I'd better tell them soon, before it starts to show or anything. Mom has looked at me funny a couple of times when I took too many helpings of breakfast. But she's been so busy with the show, and the backyard, and you and everything, I don't think she's really noticed. And Dad doesn't have a clue. He still thinks I'm five years old and should be wearing pigtails." But they both loved that about him. In spite of being worldly-wise in so many ways, there was an innocence about him that really touched them. He believed the best of all of them, and of most of the people he knew. He rarely said anything unkind about anyone. And Sam knew this was going to break his heart. She would have done anything not to tell him, but she knew she couldn't.

"I'll come over tomorrow, and we'll talk to them," Allegra said, as though they were going to the guillotine together. But then what? What was she going to do with it? That was the real question. "What do you want to do, Sam? Do you want to give it up? Keep it?" She had to ask her those questions. The baby was only four months away and she had to face it, but she couldn't.

"Every time I think about it, it just scares me too much. I just want it to go away, and be like it never happened."

"That's not going to happen," her older sister informed her, but as for the rest, Sam wasn't up to making any decisions.

They went for a walk after they left the restaurant, but they didn't go into any of the shops. Neither of them were in the mood. And eventually, Allegra took her home again. She gave her a big hug, and told her to try to stay calm until the following afternoon, and then they'd all deal with it together.

"And no bullshit about running away, you hear!" she said

pointedly. "You can't run away from things like this. We'll face it together."

"Thanks, Al," she said, and really meant it. Her whole body seemed to sag as Allegra watched her walk into the house, but at least nothing showed yet. But Allegra could only begin to imagine her parents' reaction. The next afternoon was not going to be easy. No matter how understanding they were, it was still going to be a terrible blow to them. And it was the kind of problem that could have no happy resolution. If she gave it up, she'd probably regret it to some degree all her life, or at least think of it with pain from time to time, and if she kept it, it could change her life, in a negative way, forever. In fact, Allegra couldn't see any positives to it at all. In Sam's circumstances, it was nothing short of a disaster.

It was so odd to think that to Carmen it was a great joy, and to her, it might have been too, and Jeff was even talking about wanting a baby fairly soon, and yet in someone else's life the same circumstance was a tragedy instead of a blessing. It was all so confusing.

She drove back to Malibu feeling acutely depressed, and she was still sitting on the beach with her arms around her knees when Jeff got home two hours later. His lunch with his coproducer had gone much longer than anticipated. They had so many things to discuss about the movie. But he could tell just from looking at her, when he stepped out on the deck and saw her, that something hadn't gone well that afternoon. She looked completely withdrawn and as though she were in her own private world. He wondered if she had called her father.

"Hi, there," he said, as he sat down on the beach next to her, and she turned her head toward him but didn't answer. "Did you and Sam have a run-in today?" he asked, stroking her long blond hair with gentle fingers.

"No," she said, smiling sadly at him. He was so good to her, and in his own way, so like Simon. It was so odd that for so many years she had had to fight the demons in her soul, and now she had finally put them to rest, and she was free to love someone like him.

"You don't look too happy. Bad news of some kind?"

She nodded, and looked out at the ocean.

"Can I help?" She knew that Sam probably wouldn't have wanted her to tell Jeff yet, but it wasn't going to be a secret for long, not if she was due in August.

"I'm not sure anyone can." She looked him in the eye. "Sam is five months' pregnant."

"Oh, shit," he said succinctly. "Who's the father?" He didn't think she had a boyfriend.

"The father is some thirty-year-old Frenchman with no last name, who passed through here five months ago apparently on his way to Tokyo. The agency has no record of him, and neither does Sam. He just came to town, took some pictures of her, and left her with a baby."

"Great. Can she still have an abortion at five months, or does she even want one?"

"No to either one. It's too late, and she doesn't want one anyway. We're going to tell my parents tomorrow."

"Will she keep it?"

"I don't know. I think she's too shell-shocked to work any of it out just now. But I don't think she should keep it. She's too young, and it'll ruin her life. But I don't have a right to tell her what to do. This is a major life decision."

"It sure is," he said, in awe of what was facing all of them. "If there's anything I can do to help . . ." he said, feeling useless. There was nothing any of them could do now except support her through it.

"I told her that if she has a total blowout with Mom and Dad, she can come and live with me. I could move back to my house for four months," she said, looking depressed over that too, but it was the least she could do for her sister.

"She can stay here with us," Jeff said quickly. "I'll be working on the set all the time pretty soon anyway. I could give her my office as a bedroom."

"You're a nice man," she said, and meant it, as she kissed him.

260

They went for a long walk on the beach after that, and talked late into the night. And the next day, after work, she drove to her parents' house, as she had promised. It was just after five and she and Sam waited for them to come home from work. They were both usually home by six-thirty. The two girls were sitting nervously in the living room when Blaire and Simon walked in within five minutes of each other. They both seemed to be in a good mood, and they were pleased and surprised to see Allegra. But as soon as Blaire saw the way her daughters looked at them, she knew that something had happened, and her heart started pounding. It was Scott. Something had happened to him. She was sure of it—they had called Allegra instead—and her eyes went straight to her older daughter.

"What's wrong?" Allegra knew immediately what she was thinking, and she was quick to reassure her.

"Nothing, Mom. No one's hurt, everyone's fine, we just want to talk to you."

"Oh, God." Blaire sank into a chair, as Simon looked worriedly at all of them. Even he sensed that something serious was in the air, and he was much less of a worrier than Blaire was. "I thought Scott had gotten hurt," Blaire confessed, thinking of Paddy. "It's something about the wedding, isn't it?" she said. Allegra had on that purposeful look she got when something was important to her. She was probably going to demand they cut the numbers back again, but Blaire didn't have the strength to argue with her. "What is it?"

"I need to talk to you, Mom." Sam spoke up with a quavering voice. And her father looked at her with narrowed eyes. She had never looked, or sounded, quite like that.

"Is something wrong?" he asked, as they all sat down.

"Kind of," Sam admitted, and there was a long silence, and then, as her eyes filled with tears, she looked at Allegra. She just couldn't do it.

"Do you want me to tell them, Sam?" Allegra asked in an undervoice, and her younger sister nodded. And Allegra looked at her parents then, and told them the hardest thing she knew she'd ever have to say. But it was better to get it over with, and get it out in the open. "Sam is five months' pregnant," she said very calmly, and Blaire went so pale that Allegra thought her mother might faint. But Simon looked no better.

"What?" was all he said, and the silence in the room was deafening. But they had heard her. "How is that possible? Was this date rape, or something of the kind? Why didn't you tell us?" It was inconceivable to him that she had cooperated in this mess, but she had, and Blaire understood that much as she stared at both of her daughters. It was beyond her to offer any sympathy or comfort just yet, she was in too much shock herself, and she hadn't absorbed it.

"It wasn't date rape, Dad. It was just very stupid," Sam admitted to them, wiping the tears off her face with her hand. She looked awful.

"Is it someone you care about?" her father asked, still trying to fathom what had happened.

"No," Sam said, honest again. "I thought I did, but I was more flattered than anything. He kind of swept me off my feet, and then he was gone."

"Who is he?" her father asked, beginning to glower.

"A photographer I met. And you can't put him in jail. He's gone, Dad. And I can't even find him." Allegra explained the circumstances to them, and Blaire started to cry as she looked at her youngest daughter.

"I can't believe you were so foolish, Sam. And why didn't you tell me?"

"I didn't even know, Mom. I didn't even suspect it till last week, and then I went to the doctor. And after that, I was just too scared to tell anyone. I was going to run away and just disappear, or die, or something. But then I decided to call Allegra."

"Thank God." Her mother shot a grateful look at Allegra, and then went to sit next to Sam and put an arm around her shoulders. And from across the room, Simon was fighting back tears, and Allegra went to put her arms around him and hugged him.

"I love you, Dad," she whispered, and he held her and cried. It was really a disaster, but at least they had each other.

"What are we going to do about this?" he asked, as he blew his nose and wiped away tears, and sat down next to Allegra on the couch opposite Sam and Blaire.

"We don't have much choice," Blaire said practically. She looked at Sam and it broke her heart to think about it. She was so beautiful and so young, and so undaunted by life. But now it was beginning. The first scar. The first major life experience. The first tragedy, or great grief. And there was nothing she could do to protect her from it. "You'll have to have the baby, Sam," she said gently. "It's too late not to."

"I know, Mom," she said, but had no idea what that entailed, for her heart, or her body. So far, it had all been pretty easy. She hadn't been sick, she hadn't been anything. She had just been hungry. And now she was scared. But the rest was still a mystery, and she'd have to discover it herself in the next four months. No one could take this from her.

"And then you'll have to give it up. There's no other way, unless you ruin your life. You don't need a baby to mess up your life at seventeen. You'll be going to UCLA in the fall. When is this baby due?" she asked, her spirit of organization moving into play rapidly. She was sorting it out in her head now.

"August."

"You can have it, and give it up, and be in school on time in September. The only thing you'll have to forfeit, I'm afraid, is possibly the end of the school year, and definitely graduation." But Sam didn't say a word about that. She was thinking about something else now.

"I'll be eighteen when it's born, Mom." She was turning eighteen in July. "Lots of people have babies at that age."

"Most of them are married. And in this case, it would be disastrous. You don't even know who the baby's father is. What will that baby be like? Who will it be?"

"It will be half me, Mom," Sam said, her eyes filling with tears, "and part you . . . and part Dad . . . and part Scott and

Allegra. . . . We can't just give it away like an old pair of boots to the thrift shop." It was suddenly clutching at her heart, and Allegra felt desperately sorry for her.

"No, but you can give it to people who desperately want a baby, who are married and have tried to have one unsuccessfully. There are people out there, waiting for babies like this, whose lives it won't destroy. For them, it will be a blessing."

"What about for us? Maybe it would be a blessing for us too." She was fighting for her life, and her baby's. It was an instinct older than time, which even she didn't understand. But Blaire did. She had given birth to four children.

"Are you telling me you want to keep it?" Blaire looked terrified. "You don't even know who the father is, and now you want to keep this baby, Sam? It's not even a love child, it's a nothing."

"It's not a 'nothing,' it's a baby," she said hotly, and then burst into tears again. The emotions were running too high for all of them, but Blaire was not going to let Sam sway her.

"You have to give this baby up, Sam. We know what's best for you. Trust us. You'll regret it all your life if you saddle yourself with a baby now. It's not the right time," Blaire said calmly, trying to regain their equanimity again. This was just too great an upheaval if Sam had a baby at her age.

"That's not a good enough reason to give up a baby," Sam said, and Allegra finally spoke up. She had to be true to herself, and her sister.

"That's true, Sam," she said quietly. "You have to want to give the baby up. You have to make up your own mind, because you have to live with your decision for the rest of your life. We don't, not the way you do."

"Your sister's right," their father said fairly. "But having said that, I agree with your mother, Sam. You're too young to take on a baby. And we're too old. It wouldn't be fair to the child if we took it on. The whole thing just isn't fair, not to you, or the child. You can give the baby a better chance if you give it up to the right people for adoption." Blaire looked at him gratefully. As always, he said what she had wanted to say, but gently, and better.

"How do we know they'll be nice to it? What if they aren't?" Sam was crying pitifully as she said it.

Allegra stepped in again. "There are attorneys who handle nothing but adoptions like these, Sam. You don't have to go to some state agency. People with lots of money, with good homes, go to attorneys and pay a fortune to find people like you. And you get to choose among them. You can pick the couple *you* like best. You call all the shots. I think you'd feel pretty comfortable about it. It's not a happy thing to do, but as Dad says, there are people out there who would really love it. I have a friend who handles nothing but these adoptions. I can call her tomorrow if you like." In fact, she had already left her a message that morning.

There was an endless pause, and then finally Sam nodded. She had no recourse, no other way to turn, and she trusted them. They were telling her that she owed it to the baby to give it up, and she believed them. The hard thing for her was that she had no one else to talk to, no one else to lean on, or cry with. She didn't want to tell her friends at school; she didn't even have a boyfriend at the moment. All she had were her parents and Allegra, and they were all telling her to give the baby up, and she knew they wanted the best thing for her, and the baby.

Allegra promised to call the attorney the next day, and Sam went to her room to lie down. She felt sick and exhausted. After she left, Blaire started to cry, and Allegra sat and consoled her. Simon looked like someone had died, and the entire house seemed to be under a pall. Even the wedding was forgotten.

"Poor kid," Simon said, and then shook his head miserably. "How could she be so stupid?"

"I'd like to kill the little sonofabitch who did it," Blaire said. "Good for him—he's in Japan, screwing someone else, and her whole life is ruined."

"It doesn't have to be," Allegra reminded her, but her mother knew better.

"She'll never forget this. She'll never forget carrying that baby and giving birth to it, and holding it, and then giving it up forever." It wasn't the same thing, but she was thinking of Paddy. Twenty-five years after his death, she still missed him. She knew she would till her dying day. And Sam would never forget the firstborn she gave up to strangers. "There's just no other way to do it."

"You don't think she should keep it, Mom?" Allegra asked cautiously. In her own mind, she wasn't convinced that giving it up was the perfect answer. As Sam said, other people had babies at eighteen and survived it. Some of them even turned out to be decent parents.

"No, I don't think she should keep it," Blaire said sadly. "I think it would just be compounding the stupidity. And in today's world, where there are so many decent people dying to adopt, with all the infertility there is, I think it's wrong for her to ruin her life, and deprive someone else in the process. How is she supposed to take care of it? Take it to the dorm with her? Not go to school at all? Leave it home with me? What am I supposed to do with a baby at this point in our lives? We're too old to take care of it, and she's too young."

Allegra smiled ruefully. "You haven't been reading the tabloids. Plenty of women your age are getting donor eggs and donor sperm, and in vitro and Lord only knows what else, and having babies. You're not too old, you know."

Blaire almost shuddered. "Some women may be doing all that, but I'm not. I had four kids. I was fortunate. But I'm not going to bring up another baby at my age. I'd be in my seventies when it was in its teens—that would definitely be enough to kill me." They all smiled ruefully, and they all agreed the best solution for all concerned was to give it up, especially for Sam's sake. She needed a clean slate, and then she could go to college in the fall and start over. It was just a shame that she couldn't go to graduation. Blaire said she'd have to go to Sam's school and discuss the situation discreetly with the headmaster. It was certainly not the first time something like it had happened. Sam was a good student, and the school year was almost over. In that way at least, she was lucky.

"I'll call Suzanne Pearlman tomorrow. She's the lawyer I was talking about. We went to law school together, and I see her every once in a while. She's good at this stuff, and she is very picky about her clients. I always give her a bad time about the baby mill she runs. I never thought I'd be calling her as a client. I left her a message today, and I'll call her again tomorrow morning."

"Thanks, Allie," Simon said gratefully. "The sooner we can get this behind us the better. Maybe it's a blessing that she's so far along. In four months it'll be over, and she can forget it." If she ever does, Allegra thought to herself sadly.

It was after nine o'clock when she finally left them and drove back to Malibu where Jeff was waiting to hear how it had gone. He felt desperately sorry for Sam, and he looked sadly at Allegra when she told him everything that had happened.

"Poor thing. She must feel like her life is about to end. What a rotten way to start out. I got a girl pregnant in college once," he said, looking miserable remembering it fifteen years later. "It was awful. She got an abortion, but the whole thing was incredibly traumatic. She was Catholic, from Boston, and her parents didn't know, of course, and she practically had a nervous breakdown over it. We both ended up in counseling, and needless to say, the relationship didn't survive, but we almost didn't either. Maybe what you're doing with Sam is a better way to go. I don't think that girl I knew ever forgave herself for the abortion."

"I'm not sure this is any better," Allegra said. There was a gnawing feeling deep inside her that told her it was almost worse, or that they were both too high a price to pay for a mistake. Any way she went, she would pay for it forever. "I feel so sorry for her," Allegra said, and he agreed. She called her later that night and Sam sounded just awful. She said she had felt sick all night, and for once she couldn't even eat dinner. Allegra urged her to take care of herself and try to calm down. Blaire had already said she was taking her to her doctor the next day, to make sure everything was in order. There was no ignoring it anymore. Now that it was out in the open, Sam had to face the fact that she was having a baby. She was having it and giving it away, and she had to do what everyone else thought was right for her. She felt as though she had given up her life to all of them, but she didn't want to be mean to them and say so. She knew they had her best interests at heart, and all things considered, her family had been incredibly supportive, but she still felt awful.

Allegra called her attorney friend at eight o'clock the next day, and Suzanne agreed to see her at nine before her first appointment.

"Don't tell me you want to adopt," Suzanne said, looking surprised when Allegra arrived at her office. She wasn't wearing a wedding ring, and Suzanne knew she wasn't married, but stranger things had happened.

"No, I'm kind of at the other end of things, I'm afraid." Allegra seemed pained as she looked at her old friend. Suzanne was small and delicate, with short dark hair and a warm smile—all her clients loved her. She also got great results for them, and somehow, through doctors and individuals and other attorneys she knew, babies just seemed to find her. Allegra got right to the point. "My seventeen-year-old sister is pregnant."

"Oh, God. I'm sorry. That's awful. What a miserable decision to have to make. Is it too late for an abortion?"

"Much. She found out last week, and she's five months' pregnant."

"That's not unusual, you know," Suzanne explained, as they sat on the couch in her office. "I guess their periods are often irregular at that age, so they never even seem to suspect until it's too late. And their bodies are in such good shape that nothing shows. I've had kids come in here at seven months, and never suspected they were pregnant. Then, of course, there's always denial. 'This can't be happening to me.' 'It can't happen on the first date,' first time, last date, whatever." She sighed. It was a business built on grief and joy; the secret of her success was knowing how to mix it. "Does she want to give it up?" she asked Allegra very directly.

"I don't think she knows what she wants, to be honest, but she knows it's the best thing to do at her age."

"Not necessarily. I've seen fifteen year olds turn into terrific mothers. And I've seen women our age give them up because they know they just can't take care of anyone else, and don't want to. What does *she* want? That's really the key here."

"I think a part of her would probably like to keep it. That's probably sheer instinct. But I think she also knows she can't take care of it. She's willing to give it up."

"But does she *want* to?"

"Does anyone?" Allegra asked honestly, and Suzanne nodded. She was good at what she did, and Allegra respected her for it. She had always liked her.

"Some. Some women, or even girls, just have no maternal instinct at all. Others do, but make decisions based on practical motives. That's the hard part. I'd want to talk to your sister myself, to make sure that she's committed to giving the baby up. I don't like breaking hearts here. I don't want to offer the baby to some couple who've been trying to get pregnant for ten years, and have finally figured out it won't work for them, and then have your sister, or anyone for that matter, change their mind at the last minute. It happens sometimes, and you can never completely predict how someone will feel when they see their baby, but most of the time you can tell if someone's serious about relinquishing a baby."

"I honestly think she will," Allegra said sincerely. It seemed to be the only answer for her.

"Why don't you bring her in to see me."

They made an appointment for later that week, and Allegra called her mother at the office. She thanked Allegra profusely for taking care of it, and then reminded her that she had to start thinking about things like a wedding dress and bridesmaids.

"Oh, Mom," Allegra said, "from the sublime to the ridiculous. How can you think about that now?"

"We have to. Thank God, the baby business will be behind us by the time you get married. The next few months are going to be a nightmare." Especially for Sam, they both agreed. Her mother wasn't even angry at her, they just felt desperately sorry for her. And then Allegra told her that she was definite, and proper or not, she did not want her father on her wedding invitation. She would agree to let him come to the wedding, if he wanted to, but not announce it. It seemed a fair compromise to both of them, and Allegra promised to go shopping for a wedding dress as soon as she got Sam squared away with the attorney.

Allegra and Sam went to see Suzanne later that week. Blaire couldn't come, she had an appointment at the network. And Sam said she'd rather go with Allegra anyway. She really liked the young attorney. They talked to each other alone for a while, while Allegra waited in the waiting room and made calls on her cellular phone. Eventually Suzanne invited her back in, and announced that Sam had decided to give the baby up for adoption. She explained some of the conditions to both of them, what would be required of her, and what some of the adopting parents would expect of her. But she also told them that Sam would have a choice as to which couple she chose. Suzanne had seven excellent couples waiting at the moment locally, one in Florida, and two in New York, all of whom were candidates she felt sure the Steinbergs would approve of. But to Sam, it was all so confusing, and Allegra noticed that her sister looked a little dazed. Emotionally, it was all too much for her. But she had no choice now, no matter how miserable it made her. She seemed resigned to giving the baby up now, and she didn't ask any more questions about what would happen if she kept it.

After she left the attorney's office, she turned the music up in Allegra's car, and she played it so loud she almost deafened them on the way home. But it was as though she didn't want to hear anything anymore. She'd had all she could stand of real life for the moment. She was on independent study now, so she no longer had to go to school. She just had to send in papers, and do her exams in a special room at school. But she had a feeling that eventually everyone would know why she'd dropped out anyway. She'd only told two of her closest friends, and she'd sworn them to secrecy. But neither of them had come to visit her all week, and no one had called, except Jimmy Mazzoleri, a boy she had known since third grade, and used to go out with, but they were just friends now. Jimmy had called a couple of times, but she hadn't returned his calls. She didn't want to talk to anyone. And Sam and Allegra were both surprised to see him standing in the driveway when they got home. He had just come by to see if she was there, and he was about to leave as Allegra pulled in to drop Sam off.

"I've been calling you all week," he said plaintively. "You have my science book, and they said you weren't coming back," he said, eyeing her cautiously, as Allegra watched them. They were both so young and so innocent. It was heartbreaking that Sam would have to go through so much now. And as Allegra waved and drove away, she realized they reminded her of Alan and her at that age. They seemed to have that kind of comfortable friendship that, in her case, had lasted for sixteen years.

But Sam was looking kind of cool as she answered.

"I was going to send the book back to you," she explained, looking embarrassed suddenly, hoping he hadn't heard why she had dropped out of school. He was a nice boy, and she liked him, but she had no intention of telling him she was pregnant.

"So what happened?"

"I didn't get around to it yet," she said, walking slowly back to her house as he joined her.

"I don't mean the book. I mean why are you out of school for the rest of the year?" She groped for an answer and then thought of a good one.

"Family problems," she said; it was perfect. "My parents are getting divorced. I got really depressed over it, and I have to take a lot of medication . . . you know, like Prozac. My mom was afraid I might kill someone at school or something, she thinks I get pretty erratic on that stuff, and . . ." She had gone too far and he was smiling at her. Even he recognized her tale as nonsense.

"Knock it off, will you please? You don't have to tell me why." Everyone knew, or had guessed anyway. It was the only reason anyone ever dropped out, except to go to rehab. And Sam had never been a druggie. But he didn't tell her what he suspected, and besides, she didn't look it at all, so maybe they were all wrong. Maybe she had some other kind of problem. He had just wanted to be sure that she didn't have anything really awful, like leukemia. They had all lost a friend sophomore year, and he had panicked when he heard she wasn't coming back. That was how it had started with Maria. "Are you okay? That's all I wanted to know," he said gently. He'd been seeing someone for a while, but he'd always had a soft spot for Sam, and she knew it.

"I'm fine," she said, but the sadness in her soul came through her eyes and he saw it.

"Whatever it is, just hang in there. You still going to UCLA in the fall?" They were both going and he was relieved when she nodded.

"I'll get your book. Come on in." He followed her inside, and he waited in the kitchen while she went upstairs. They hadn't gutted it yet, and Simon was still begging Blaire not to. Maybe now she wouldn't.

Sam was back downstairs with his book five minutes later, and as she handed it to him, he reached out and took her hand, and she looked up at him and blushed. She felt so vulnerable these days, and she didn't know why. It never occurred to her that it was because she was pregnant.

"Hey . . . if you need anything, just call . . . okay? . . . We can go out for a ride . . . or get something to eat. Things look different when you talk about them sometimes," he said gently, and she nodded. He was almost eighteen and mature for his age. His father had died two years before, and he had been helping his mother raise his three younger sisters. He was unusually responsible, and very caring.

"There's nothing to talk about," Sam said, looking at the floor and then up at him. And then she shrugged. It was too hard to say anything else, and he understood. He just touched her shoulder and then left. And she stood at the kitchen window, and watched him go in his old Volvo. His family lived in Beverly Hills, and they were comfortable, and respectable, but they didn't have much money. They were still living on the insurance money and what his father had left them. He had a weekend job and he was getting a scholarship to UCLA. And he wanted to be an attorney like his father. She knew he would, too, someday. Among other things, Jimmy had a lot of determination.

And when he was gone, Sam sat down on a chair in the kitchen and just stared into space. There was so much to think about now, so much to decide. Suzanne Pearlman had told her exactly how the adoption worked, and now she had to pick new parents for her baby. It seemed so simple. To everyone but Samantha.

CHAPTER 15

Things almost settled down in the next two weeks, as much as they ever did, especially in the present circumstances. Sam had seen her mother's doctor by then, and she was fine. The baby was a good size, and seemed healthy. She was doing independent study work from school, and she was still very quiet and withdrawn, but she'd had two more meetings with Suzanne, and they had narrowed it down to four couples now, and Sam had more decisions to make over the next month or two, when they would narrow it down further. Suzanne was going to give her as much information as possible to work with. And she didn't want to rush her. She wanted Sam to make the right decision.

Allegra was trying to finish as much work as she could so she could get to New York for the weekend with Jeff to meet his mother. She wasn't exactly looking forward to it; they had spoken on the phone, and Mrs. Hamilton had asked a lot of very pointed questions, as though she were interviewing her for a job and she was not a likely candidate. It seemed funny to Allegra, and also a little insulting, but she didn't say anything to Jeff. She was trying to get everything organized for Bram's tour. He was starting in San Francisco on Monday and she wanted to be there, for the opening night at least. They were following a zigzag course around the country for the next several months, with a Fourth of July appearance at the Great Western Forum in Ingleside, near

L.A., after which they were flying to Japan, and eventually around the world, and ending in Europe. Allegra had said she'd fly in to see him now and then, if she could. The tour was going to earn him a hundred million dollars by the time it was over, a pretty healthy chunk of cash, as Jeff said jokingly when she mentioned it. She would never have quoted the amount except that it had been all over the papers for months, and Bram had foolishly confirmed it.

But everything seemed to be under control right up till the day before Jeff and Allegra were to leave for New York for the weekend. His crew, their itinerary, the promoters had everything arranged. And then at midnight, the night before she was to fly to New York with Jeff, she got the call. The drummer had committed suicide, either intentionally or accidentally, by an overdose of drugs. Everyone was going crazy. The media were all over it, his girlfriend was being held by the police, and the whole tour was on hold until they could line up another drummer.

She was still on the phone with Bram at two A.M. He had just been to the morgue to identify his lifelong friend, and he was deeply upset. But so were the promoters. They had called Allegra ten minutes before Bram did. The phone rang almost constantly until six A.M., and Jeff was in a state by the time they sat down to breakfast. It was impossible to get any sleep with the phone ringing all night, and he had important meetings that morning.

"I'm sorry," she said quietly, pouring him a cup of coffee. She had made a statement for the press about it the night before, and it was already on the front page of the L.A. papers. "It was a rough night for everyone."

"You should have been a cop, or an ambulance driver or something," he said, looking at her ruefully. "You have the right constitution for it. I, on the other hand, do not. I need to get a little sleep every now and then, between phone calls."

"I know. I'm sorry. I couldn't help it. Bram's tour is about to go up in smoke. I have to see what I can do for him today." Her mind had been racing since early that morning. Bram knew of several drummers he could break in, but it would take time, and most of them had other commitments.

"Don't forget that our plane is at six o'clock," Jeff said pointedly.

"I know," she said, feeling jangled. She left for the office half an hour later, and never stopped all day. She actually sat with Bram, and helped him reorganize the tour, and at four o'clock she looked at her watch, and knew that the shit was about to hit the fan. There was no way she could leave Bram. And she had to leave now, if she was going to make the plane. She had told Jeff she would meet him at the airport.

She called him at home, but he had already left, and he didn't believe in car phones, he said they were too California. So there was nothing she could do except page him at the airport. The much-joked-about white courtesy telephone actually came in handy.

She had him paged at five o'clock when they were supposed to check in, and at five-fifteen, he called her at the office. Alice told her he was on the line, and Allegra pounced on it. He didn't sound pleased to hear her.

"Where are you? I guess that's a moot point, since I just called you at the office. What's happening?"

"The promoters are threatening to pull out of the tour on us, they're saying it's breach of contract, and as of this moment, we haven't lined up another drummer. I don't even know how to begin to say this to you, but I can't walk out on him, Jeff. The tour starts on Monday." She had been planning to fly up to San Francisco on Monday, to see him perform at the Oakland Coliseum. But it was out of the question now. They couldn't go anywhere without a drummer.

"Isn't it up to his agent to fix this mess?"

"If he can, but I'm part of it, and they're going to need me to draw up new contracts."

"Can't you fax them from New York?"

She wanted to say yes, she hated to disappoint him, but this was her responsibility and she couldn't just walk out on it. She had to tell him the truth, no matter how mad he got about disappointing his mother. "I really need to be here."

"Okay, I understand," he said quietly, but his voice was like ice, and there was a long silence.

"What are you going to do now?" She was panicking that he would break it all off. What if she lost him? "Will you still go?" she asked, sounding nervous.

"I'm going to introduce you to my mother, Allegra. I already know her," he said coldly.

"I'm sorry," she said, agonizing over letting him down, particularly right in the airport. "I tried to get you at home, but I missed you. Should I call your mother and explain?"

"I'll do it. She'll never understand. I'm going to tell her something outlandish like a death in the family, food poisoning, something. She doesn't know about rock tours."

"Jeff, I'm so sorry."

"I know. You can't help it. How about dinner? Can you manage that? Or are you fasting too?"

"I'd love it," she said, grateful that he was willing to forgive her, or at least feed her. She thought it was a good sign. He was an incredibly decent person.

"It's not your fault, Allegra, I know. It's just a pain in the neck having our plans thrown out the window all the time, for someone else's convenience. Maybe when we get married, you can work on that a little bit. This time it makes sense, even to me, but most of the time, these people just expect you to wipe their asses for them, hold their hands, and make all their decisions for them."

"That's why they pay me."

"I thought it was for legal services."

"That's what they tell you in law school, but like everything else they tell you, it's all a lie. It's for wiping asses." She laughed softly and he smiled at his end.

"I love you, you crazy woman. I'll drive back from the airport and pick you up at the office for drinks, and if Morrison can't spare you for a couple of hours, I'm going to punch him in the nose. And you can tell him I said so."

"I will. Verbatim."

"Everything okay?" Bram Morrison asked her when she got back from talking to Jeff. She actually looked relieved. She'd been terrified he would break the engagement over her failure to fly to New York to meet his mother.

"Yeah," she said with a smile. "I was supposed to go to New York to meet my future mother-in-law this weekend, and I just canceled. Jeff was already at the airport."

"I'm really sorry." He was soft-spoken and kind, and one of the hardest-working men she knew. Like most of the musicians she had worked with, he had done drugs in his youth, but unlike many of them, he had been clean for years. He was a family man, and a real genius with music. And he rarely took advantage of her time except when he really needed her, as he did now. But a star of his magnitude often had sudden and very major problems, like the threats to his kids, and now the death of his drummer.

Bram had long, disheveled hair, and a beard, and he wore little wire glasses, and he looked like a wild man as they pored over the new contracts. Someone had just told him about another drummer they might be able to get their hands on, a truly great one. Things were looking hopeful.

Jeff came by at seven o'clock, and she and Bram broke it up for a few hours. He needed to get on the phone and pursue the drummer anyway, and he told her to take the night off. They were to meet again at nine o'clock the next morning.

She and Jeff went to Pan e Vino for something to eat, and she looked harassed and exhausted, and even Jeff looked a little frayed. His mother had been absolutely furious over their cancellation. She had made reservations at Twenty-One for dinner on Saturday, and she was a person who didn't like her plans changed, especially by some girl she had never met from California.

"What did she say?" Allegra asked nervously, convinced that Mrs. Hamilton would hate her forever.

"She told me to cancel this wedding," he said, straight-faced, and she gasped, and then he laughed. "She told me that ours is an unreliable generation, that you can't count on anyone, and that she's very sorry if your great-aunt did die, but you could have come for a day anyway, just to meet her. I explained that you were far too upset, and the funeral is Sunday. I don't think she believed a word of it, but there's not much she could say. 'Show me the body, send me a mass card'? I called the florist in New York right before they closed, and they promised to send her a huge bunch of flowers from both of us in the morning."

"I don't deserve you," Allegra said sincerely.

"She said that too, but I told her you did. I promised we'd go on Memorial Day weekend, however. That's a big deal to her, because she opens the house in Southampton that weekend. So, come hell or high water, we'll have to go then."

"What about your movie?"

"We won't be working on the holiday weekend." He was starting in three days, which was why they were to have gone this weekend.

But in the end, it worked out for the best. She worked with Bram Morrison all three days, and by Sunday night everything was reorganized and rearranged, and the promoters were satisfied. As usual, Allegra had done a good job, and Bram was pleased. Mission accomplished.

And on Sunday night, Jeff amazed her with a small black suede box that he'd been planning to give her in New York, but they weren't going back there now for another month and he didn't want to wait any longer.

She opened it cautiously, over the dinner they had made. There had been a gorgeous sunset on the beach, and it was their last night of freedom before he started to shoot his movie. Her hands were shaking as she unwrapped the box. It was impossible not to guess what was in it. But when she actually saw it, she gasped. It was a beautiful antique ring, with an emerald as its center stone, surrounded by diamonds.

"Oh, Jeff, it's so beautiful." There were tears in her eyes when she saw it. It wasn't just an ordinary engagement ring, it had a personality of its own, and a beautiful design. She hadn't even minded not having an engagement ring at all. They had never even talked about it.

"I was going to take you shopping with me, but then I saw this, and it looks just like one my grandmother had. I got this one at David Webb, but if you don't like it, we'll take it back, and get something you do like." He was smiling at her, and she kissed him.

"I love it. . . . I don't deserve this. I love you so much."

"Do you like it?"

"I really do." It was perfect, and he slipped it on her finger. It was the right fit too, and she was beaming. She couldn't take her eyes off it, and it looked impressive on her hand, but because it was an old design, despite its size it didn't seem flashy. It was very distinguished.

They sat and talked for hours that night, about their families, their lives, their plans, and the upcoming wedding. The time seemed to be flying past them. It was already the first of May, and the wedding was only four months away now. Allegra still had a thousand things to do, and her mother kept calling her and nagging her about them. She wanted her to hire a wedding consultant to take care of the details, and Allegra thought that was ridiculous, but the fact was that neither she nor her mother had time to organize a wedding. Her mother was busier than ever with the show, and Allegra never seemed to get a moment's breather from her clients.

They went to bed early that night. Jeff wanted to be at the studio at four A.M., to see that everyone arrived, and make sure that every last detail had been taken care of. She reminded him that Tony and the director would be there too, and the responsibility was not all on his shoulders, but it was his book, and his first movie, and he wanted to be there in case there were any problems.

"Who's being compulsive now?" she teased, flashing her ring at him. She couldn't stop staring at it. And she didn't even take it off when they went to bed, incredibly early, since he had to be up by two-thirty.

They were asleep by ten o'clock, and Allegra was completely confused when the phone rang at midnight. She had been deep in sleep by then, and it took her a moment to realize that someone was speaking to her in a foreign language.

"*Mademoiselle Steinberg, on vous appelle de la Suisse, de la part de Madame Alain Carr.*" She had no idea what they were saying, except that she recognized Alan's name at the end of it. She wondered if he was calling collect or something.

"I accept!" she shouted into the phone, and Jeff woke up with a start, and then lay back in bed beside her. "Hello! Hello!" They were losing the connection. Finally, they came back on the line. There was a lot of static, and then, suddenly, she heard Carmen's voice, not Alan's.

"Carmen? What is it? What's going on?" They were nine hours ahead, so for her it was nine o'clock in the morning. But she figured that something must really be wrong for Carmen to call her at midnight. For an instant, there was a tingle down Allegra's spine, wondering if Alan had had an accident while making his movie. And all she could hear at the other end now was Carmen crying. "Come on, dammit." Allegra was losing her patience with her. They had scared her half to death waking her up and now she wanted to know the story. Jeff was wide awake too, he had turned on the light and was listening. "Carmen, what happened?"

There was a long, thin wail at the other end of the phone. "I'm in the hospital. . . ."

"Oh, no. Why?"

"I lost the baby." She burst into tears again, and it was half an hour later before Allegra could calm her down. By then she had moved into the other room so Jeff could go back to sleep, but he was wide awake and couldn't.

Apparently, she hadn't had a fall, nothing dramatic had happened, she had just had a miscarriage. But she'd been on the set with Alan, and she had hemorrhaged pretty badly. They had had to call an ambulance, and she said Alan was terribly upset too. And then Carmen said she didn't want to come home without him, which struck fear in Allegra's heart. They both had contracts.

"Now listen, Carmen," Allegra said, trying to stay calm, "I know this is terrible. But you'll get pregnant again. And Alan *has* to finish that movie. If you talk him into coming home with you, they'll never hire him again. So don't you forget that, and you have to be home on the fifteenth for rehearsals."

"I know, but I'm so miserable. And I don't want to leave him." She cried until one A.M., and Allegra finally got her off the phone, thinking of the ironies of life. Here, she wanted her baby so desperately, and lost it. And Sam's was ruining her life, and hanging in there. Maybe she should have given it to Carmen, she thought, being somewhat flip, as she went back to bed, and saw that Jeff was still awake, and he did not look happy.

"Carmen lost her baby," she said apologetically, slipping into bed beside him.

"I figured out that much, but I'm about to lose my mind. I cannot live in this emergency room atmosphere of midnight phone calls every night, suicides, drug busts, miscarriages, overdoses, divorces, concert tours—for chrissake, Allie, what are you? An attorney or a psychiatric attendant?"

"That's a good question. Look, I know, I'm sorry. She probably miscalculated the time difference."

"Bullshit. She doesn't care. They all do it. They call you at any hour of the day or night. I need my sleep. I have a movie to make. I have a job too, Allegra. You have to tell your clients to stop calling."

"I know, I know. . . . I'm sorry. . . . I swear it won't happen anymore."

"You're a liar," he said, pulling her close to him again and feeling her naked body against his just the way he liked it. "You're going to make me an old man if you don't knock this stuff off."

"I'll tell them. I promise." But they both knew she'd never

do it. It was just the way she was, there for them all the time, whatever their problems.

And two hours later, he left for work, sleepy, and more than a little grouchy. She made him coffee before he left, and went back to bed and called Carmen at the number she'd given her. Alan answered the phone then. He was on a break, and obviously very upset about Carmen and the baby.

"I'm sorry, kid," she told him, and he thanked her, and then he walked the phone into the bathroom and told Allegra that Carmen was in terrible shape. She was deeply depressed about the baby.

"You have to take care of her when she comes home," he pleaded with Allegra.

"I will. I swear. But you stay where you are, and finish your movie."

"I know," he said, sounding harassed. "I told her all that, but she wants me to go with her."

"I'll kill you if you do that. You can't."

"I know that. Just promise me you'll take care of her when she gets back there day after tomorrow."

"I will. Don't worry about a thing," Allegra reassured him, and hung up, thinking about how complicated life was sometimes for all of them. Carmen, Alan, Bram, Jeff, herself. None of them had chosen easy careers. And yet, for different reasons, each of them liked what they were doing. She was particularly aware of that late that night, as she sat, freezing, backstage at the Oakland Coliseum. Bram had sent his own plane for her, and she'd gone up to see him open. The huge arena was entirely sold out, and the crowd went wild when they saw Bram, and they cheered endlessly when he introduced the new drummer. They did a memorial song, and had a moment of silence for the man who had died. And at the end of the show, twenty thousand fans gave them a standing ovation. Allegra had never seen anything like it, not even at one of Bram's other concerts. And the security had their hands full peeling fans off him. In the end, they played seven encores, and Bram was soaked with sweat when he finally came off stage and hugged Allegra.

"You were incredible!" she shouted in the din, and he grinned and nodded his thanks as he put an arm around his wife and kissed her. The crowd was still shouting for him and refusing to leave the arena.

"Thanks for saving us," Bram shouted back at her, and she smiled. They had all saved his concert tour together. This was what she got paid for.

There was a party afterward for him, but Allegra had to get back to L.A. She walked into the house in Malibu at 3 A.M., just in time to make Jeff coffee. She handed it to him just as his alarm clock went off, and he looked up at her sleepily and smiled.

"Great wake-up service. How was it?"

"Fantastic." She leaned over and kissed him. "He's never been better. He was really ready for this tour. I'm glad he pulled it off," she said, as she lay down on the bed next to Jeff, beyond exhausted.

"I'll bet he's glad too." Jeff smiled at her, admiring how beautiful she was, even when she was tired.

"How'd it go yesterday?" she asked, battling a yawn, inquiring about his movie.

"Scary, but fun," Jeff admitted. "It feels incredible being out there, making my first movie. Thank God, Tony knows what he's doing. I sure as hell don't." He grinned. Tony had been doing this for ten years, since grad school, and had won four awards for short features, and considerable acclaim for two long ones. "Come out and see us if you can take a minute or two off. Though God only knows when you'll do that." He hadn't even seen her in the last twenty-four hours, and she only had time for a short nap before she had to pick Carmen up at the airport.

But even Allegra wasn't prepared for the state Carmen was in when Allegra saw her at the airport. She was completely depressed over losing the baby. She was sure she'd never get pregnant again, and she was practically suicidal without Alan. It took every ounce of Allegra's concentration and energy to get her home and convince her that she had to go to rehearsals. For the next week, all Allegra seemed to do was baby-sit Carmen. She hardly even had time to visit Jeff on the set, although she managed it for a few minutes at least daily. And the movie seemed to be going well. Better than Carmen's rehearsals later that week. But at least by then, Bram Morrison was on the road with his concert tour, and so far it was a huge success, and so was the new drummer. Allegra was beginning to feel as though she were carrying all of them around. And Jeff was constantly on edge during the first week of his movie. She visited him on the set several times, and it seemed to be going well, but she hardly had any time to stick around and watch it. On the first weekend after shooting began, Jeff had to rework parts of the script, because two of the actors were uncomfortable with the dialogue. He met with Tony night and day. And Allegra hardly saw him.

Fortunately, Jeff had had to put off visiting his mother himself this time, and the best they could do was promise to go back East shortly. Now Mrs. Hamilton had to take a backseat to his movie, which did not please her.

And by the time Carmen started shooting on the first of June, Allegra was so busy and overwrought, she felt as though she was going to have a nervous breakdown. Carmen was calling her every five minutes to complain about something, the rest of the time she cried, and she swore she'd never work again without Alan in the film with her. She was being completely unreasonable. Allegra lost five pounds in the first week of Carmen's movie. She was getting messages from Bram on tour too, and whenever the group ran into problems somewhere it was up to Allegra to solve them. She felt as though she never saw Jeff anymore. They were never in the house at the same time, unless one of them was sleeping.

Sam was seven months' pregnant by then, but she seemed in slightly better spirits than she had been. And she was working closely with Suzanne Pearlman. And whenever Allegra dropped by to see Sam these days, she noticed that Jimmy Mazzoleri was there too, just hanging around or helping her do homework. She had finally admitted to him that she was pregnant, and he had been surprisingly supportive about it. They didn't have a romance going, but he seemed to be very devoted to Sam. She was wearing maternity clothes now, and the baby had suddenly popped out. And sometimes Jimmy thought it was funny to put his hand on her stomach and feel it kick, but most of the time he just took her for rides to the beach, or to get something to eat, or he helped her do homework. He felt really sorry for her, and he thought she didn't deserve the bad luck that she'd had getting pregnant. She talked to him sometimes about the people who were considering adopting it. She was leaning heavily toward a couple in Santa Barbara. They were in their late thirties and they said they loved kids. And the wife reminded Sam a little of Allegra. She was also an attorney. And he was a doctor. Their qualifications were excellent, and they seemed to have a fair amount of money. Sam didn't want her baby having to struggle, or doing without anything, or not getting a good education. In fact, they said they wanted to adopt more children after they adopted this one. Their names were Katherine and John Whitman.

And in the midst of everything else, Blaire kept reminding Allegra to do something about the wedding. Allegra had ordered the invitations at Cartier, and she had tried on wedding dresses at Saks, I. Magnin, and Neiman's, and none of them had struck her fancy. But the greatest shock of all came when her mother told her she had hired Delilah Williams.

"Who in God's name is that?" Allegra smiled at the name, wondering what her mother was up to.

"She came highly recommended. She's a wedding consultant, and she's going to do everything for us, for the wedding. I told her to call you at the office."

"I can't believe this," Allegra said to Jeff that night, with a look of amusement. But she was in no way prepared for the woman who came to see her in her office three days later. She came armed with albums and photographs, lists and files, and she never seemed to stop talking. She stood well over six feet tall, and when Allegra tried to describe her to Jeff, all she could say was that she looked like a transvestite. She had been wearing a lavender dress with a matching hat, amethysts everywhere, she had dyed blond hair, and her arms were so long that she looked like a large bird ready to take flight off the couch in Allegra's office. Her own office was somewhere in the valley.

"Now, let's reiterate, dear," she said, patting Allegra's hand as Allegra stared at her in total disbelief. She couldn't even begin to imagine her mother hiring this woman. She must have been desperate. "You have to pick your bridesmaids, finalize the dress for them—and for yourself, of course . . . shoes—don't forget shoes . . . We have to talk about the cake . . . the flowers . . . I told your mother we're going to need a tent in the garden . . . menu . . . the band—we can't forget the band . . . photography . . . video . . . long veil or short . . ." She went on ad infinitum while Allegra listened in total horror. The words *Las Vegas* kept ringing in her head, and she couldn't imagine why she and Jeff had decided on a wedding at home with everyone imaginable in attendance.

"We'll meet here again one week from today," Delilah told her, rising from the couch with her giraffelike legs at odd angles, as Allegra tried not to stare at her. "And I want you to promise me you'll do your homework."

"Absolutely," Allegra said solemnly, accepting the album and the books and the checklists. There was even a video to select her cake from.

"You're a dear, now off to go shopping. You have lots of work to do." She waved and was gone like a comic figure in a New York play, and Allegra just stood there, staring. Two minutes later, she walked to her office phone, and dialed her mother. She was in a meeting, as usual, but for once, Allegra told them to get her.

"Allegra? What's wrong?"

"Are you kidding?" Allegra said, sitting down at her desk. She looked shell-shocked.

"About what, dear?"

"That woman. I can't believe you'd do this to me."

"You mean Delilah? Everyone who's ever had her says she's fabulous. I think we'll be glad to have her."

"You *must* be kidding. I can't do this, Mother." But at least Allegra was grinning at the absurdity of it all. The wedding was becoming more ridiculous every day. Maybe she and Jeff should just live together.

"Darling, be patient. She'll help you. You'll like her." Her mother had obviously lost her marbles.

"I've never in my whole life seen anything like her." And all of a sudden, Allegra couldn't stop laughing. She laughed until tears ran down her face, and Blaire started to laugh too. "I can't believe you hired her." Allegra said through convulsive giggles.

"She's very efficient, don't you think?"

"Just wait till Daddy sees her. And Mom"—she really had to laugh at the whole thing—"I just want you to know I love you."

"I love you too. And it's going to be a beautiful wedding." That seemed so insignificant now, in the midst of everything else. All she really cared about was Jeff, not the wedding. And now they had Sam to think about, and her baby. What kind of wedding cake they had, or what color dresses for the bridesmaids, not to mention shoes, as Delilah had said, seemed totally unimportant.

And while she was still laughing over it, the phone on her desk rang again and she picked it up. It was Jeff. "Good news," was the first thing he said.

"I've had a totally insane morning and I think I can use some." She was smiling when she answered.

"I'm free this weekend, Tony says he can hold the fort without me, and I just told my mother we'd fly out to see her. We can fly into Kennedy and go straight to Southampton." Allegra's heart stopped for the briefest of minutes. She had thought she was off the hook indefinitely. He seemed so busy with his movie. "She was really pleased. We've been promising for so long, I don't think she even believed me. You can get away, can't you?" He had noticed her silence; she was trying to adjust again to the idea of having to meet his mother. She wasn't sure why, but she still had the feeling that Mrs. Hamilton didn't like her.

"For once, I don't see a single obstacle," she said, feeling somewhat disappointed. But no one was in crisis. Not even Carmen.

"Don't say that too loud. We're leaving on Friday," he said solemnly. He wanted to introduce her to his mother.

"I'll be there," she said, praying silently that this time nothing would happen to stop them, or his mother would never forgive her. She knew from Jeff how angry his mother had been the last time they canceled. But all Allegra could do was pray that nothing would happen, and steel herself to go with him. If nothing else, it was a weekend away together, and they both needed that desperately. The only problem was that Allegra suspected, long before they left, that nothing about their weekend would be relaxing. All she could think of was the face in the photograph he had shown her in the New York apartment, and the memory of it still scared her.

CHAPTER 16

A llegra felt like she was walking on eggs all week before they
went to meet his mother. She knew that Jeff would be furious
if she couldn't make it. But by Thursday, nothing untoward had
happened, and she heaved a sigh on Thursday night when they
packed, and decided she had been apprehensive for nothing. No
crisis had occurred to interfere with the trip, and she realized that
she was foolish to be so nervous about meeting his mother. That
was also what Jeff said. He told her constantly that his mother was
going to love her.

They were both tired, after long weeks of pressure, but everything seemed to be going well for both of them, and all of
Allegra's clients. Even Carmen had been a little better for the past
few days. Her mind was at least occupied now that she'd started
shooting the film. She was still terribly lonely without Alan, but
she talked to him constantly, mostly on the cellular phone she
carried around in the pocket of her dressing gown. She seemed to
call him at all hours of the day and night. Even more than she
called Allegra. Allegra had finally asked her to at least try not
to call her too much at night. And Carmen had promised. Most of
the time she called Alan instead now.

"I can't believe we're actually going," Jeff said, as he set both
their bags down in the front hall that night. They both had meetings in the morning, and they were leaving right after that.

"Southampton is great this time of year," he told her, but South-ampton wasn't what she was worried about. It was meeting his mother that was still making her edgy, despite his reassurances.

She did her hair and her nails, and she planned to wear a navy linen Givenchy suit for the plane trip. She wanted to look respectable when she met her. She was even planning to tie back her hair. And when they went to bed that night, Jeff smiled at her, and talked about how much he had loved the Hamptons in the summer as a kid, and Vermont where they used to go when his grandmother was alive. They fell asleep like two children whis-pering at a slumber party, and Allegra thought she was dreaming when she heard bells. Something was ringing in the distance, and she had no idea what it was. Maybe church bells in Vermont, she mused as she half listened through the mists of her dreams, and then, suddenly, with a start, she realized it was the phone. She leapt out of bed, as she always did, so Jeff wouldn't hear it, but as usual, he was already awake before she was. And as she picked up the phone, she saw on the clock at her bedside that it was four-thirty in the morning.

"If it's Carmen, tell her I'm going to kill her," Jeff said as he rolled over. "There's absolutely no way to get any sleep in this house, as long as you're here." He was not amused, and Allegra spoke into the phone quietly, sure, as Jeff was, that Carmen would be on the other end.

"Hello? Who is this?" Allegra said, furious for the intrusion at that hour, and terrified it would be something that would keep them from leaving for New York.

"It's Malachi O'Donovan, darlin'," he said with a brogue and a belch. He was roaring drunk.

"Don't call me at this hour, Mal. It's four-thirty in the morning."

"Well, top of the mornin' to you, m'dear. And wouldn't you know that I'm in jail. They said they'd let me call my lawyer. So here I am, and now you be a good girl and come bail me out of jail."

"Oh, for heaven's sake. Another DUI?" He collected Driving Under the Influence charges the way other people did tickets, and she kept warning him that one of these days he'd have to stay in jail. And lose his license. But so far, he had pulled every string he could, and he had been extremely lucky. His frequent stays in rehabs made them overlook his record, but Allegra was sure that this time his license would be pulled. "This is really bullshit," she said.

"I know, I know. I'm sorry." He sounded contrite, but he also expected her to come and bail him out. After all, she was his lawyer.

"Is there anyone else who can come and get you, Mal? I'm in Malibu, and it's the middle of the night." Jeff was right. If she hadn't answered the phone at that hour, he would have just had to wait until the next morning for her to call. But she had answered, and now he expected her to come and get him. It was difficult getting out of it, and he was insistent that he wanted her to come down immediately to bail him out.

"All right," she finally said. "Where are you?" He was in Beverly Hills. He'd been driving on the wrong side of the street down Beverly, and they busted him with an open fifth of Jack Daniel's between his legs, and a bag of grass in the glove compartment of the car. He was just lucky they hadn't found more, but they hadn't looked that hard either. The officers who had arrested him knew who he was. "I'll be there in half an hour." She put down the phone, and looked at Jeff's still form. He looked as though he was asleep again, but she could sense that he wasn't. And as she started tiptoeing out of the room, she discovered that she was right.

"If you don't make that plane today, Allegra, there won't be a wedding," he said calmly from under the covers, and she stopped to look at him with a worried expression.

"Don't threaten me, Jeff. I'm doing the best I can. I'll be there."

"Just see that you are." He didn't say another word then and she went to put on jeans and a white shirt. And as she drove down the Pacific Coast Highway, she was furious with all of them.

Malachi O'Donovan, who thought he could do anything he
wanted, and then expect her to bail him out. And Carmen, who
used her as a crying towel day and night, and Alan, who kept
calling her and asking her to take care of his wife, and even Jeff,
who got so annoyed at all of it sometimes, as if he didn't have his
moments too, between getting up at three A.M. so he could be at
the set before anyone else, or having to rewrite his screenplay
night after night. Everyone expected her to be understanding,
and to do just what they wanted. It was beginning to drive her
crazy, and for some reason she was maddest of all at Jeff. Of
course she would be on the plane . . . she hoped . . . unless
Malachi had really pulled a major stunt. And even now, she'd have
to deal with the tabloids. God, she was getting tired of that too.
They all expected her to get them out of their jams, as though she
had been born to solve their problems.

She slammed her car door when she got to the Beverly Hills
police station, and when she went inside, she saw an officer she
knew. She told him why she was there, and he nodded. He went
inside to check, and a few minutes later he came out with Mal.
She had to post bond for him, which was no problem, and this
time he had to leave his driver's license with them. They gave him
a court date, at which he had to appear, and Allegra was relieved
to see it wasn't for another month, and then, with a stern expression, she drove him home. He reeked of booze, and he kept trying
to kiss her to thank her for getting him out of jail, but she told
him firmly to behave. His wife was asleep when they got to his
house, and Allegra wondered why he hadn't called her. But as
soon as his wife started shrieking at him when she heard what had
happened, Allegra understood why he had called her instead.

Rainbow O'Donovan almost threw him into their bedroom,
and she screamed at him so loudly, she must have woken up the
neighbors. A few minutes later Allegra was on her way, and she
was back at her own house again by seven. Jeff was in the shower,
there was coffee on the stove, and she poured herself a cup, and
sat down on their bed. She was absolutely exhausted, but she had
a lot of nights like that one. That's what Jeff was complaining

about, and she knew he wasn't wrong. But there wasn't much she could do about it either, and she needed him to understand.

He was drying his hair when he came out of the shower, and he was startled when he saw her. He hadn't heard her come in and it was easy to see how tired she was as she sat there.

"How did it go?"

"Great. They took his license away," she said with a soft moan as she lay down on the bed, and he came over and sat next to her.

"I'm sorry I got mad last night. I just get so tired of people pulling at you sometimes. It's as though they want to eat you up. It's not fair."

"It's not fair to you either. I'm going to have to establish better boundaries. I realized when I took him home that he could have called his wife. I think he was afraid to."

"Make them afraid of you," Jeff said, and leaned over and kissed her. He had to be at the studio within the hour, and then they were leaving on a two o'clock flight. "You'll be okay?" he asked as he left.

"I'll be fine," she reassured him.

"I'll pick you up at noon."

"I'll be ready," she promised.

She got to her office at nine o'clock, with their bags in the car, and Alice had a stack of messages and paperwork for her. She got through all of it, and was just putting her files away, when Alice came into her office holding the latest copy of *Chatter*.

"Please don't tell me I'm going to care about what that says," Allegra said, almost cringing. If it was going to upset one of their clients, maybe she'd never get out of town after all.

Alice set it down gingerly on her desk as though it might burn her, and Allegra could see why. The photographs were awful and the headline wasn't pretty. Carmen was going to go wild when she saw it.

"Oh, shit," Allegra said, looking up at her secretary. "I'd better call her." She had the phone in her hand when the operator buzzed her. Miss Connors was on the line. The operator didn't say she was hysterical. But Allegra knew it the minute she heard her. "I just saw it," she said calmly.

"I want to sue them."

"I don't think that's smart." But she could understand how she felt, and she knew Alan would be livid too. The paper said that Carmen Connors, Alan Carr's new wife, had gone to Europe for an abortion. And there were some grim photographs of her leaving the hospital. She looked as though she were sneaking out, but she was actually doubled over.

"They're slandering me. How can they say that?" She was sobbing and Allegra didn't know what to say, but suing the tabloids would only make it worse. They were the vermin of the earth, but they had good lawyers who told them how to protect themselves and they never failed to. "Why do they do this to me?" she wailed, and Allegra felt helpless. There was nothing she could do to change it.

"To sell papers. You know that. Throw it away and forget it."

"What if my grandmother sees this?"

"She'll understand. Nobody believes that garbage."

"She does." Carmen laughed through her tears. "She thinks eighty-seven-year-old women give birth to quintuplets."

"Well, tell her they're a bunch of liars. I'm sorry, Carmen. I really am," Allegra said, and she meant it. She could just imagine how it felt dealing with the lies all the time. It was so painful.

The local paper had the story of Malachi O'Donovan's arrest that day too. It was a high-profile day for some of her clients.

"You'd better warn Alan before someone else tells him," Allegra suggested. "They even read some of that garbage in Europe." But as soon as she hung up, Alan was on the phone from Switzerland. His press agent had called and read it to him.

"I want to sue the bastards," he raged. "The poor kid almost bled to death in the ambulance, and she hasn't stopped crying in six weeks, and they're claiming she had an abortion. I want to kill them. Has she seen it yet?"

"We just hung up," Allegra said, feeling as tired as she

looked. She'd had four hours sleep the night before, and a very long morning. "She wants to sue them too. I'll tell you what I told her. It's not worth it. You'll just sell their paper for them. Fuck 'em." It was rare for her to say that, but in the case of the tabloids, they deserved it. "Just forget about them, don't waste your money on lawyers."

"Some are worth more than others," he said, calming down a little bit. Allegra was always so sensible. That was why he called her. "How are you, by the way?"

"God knows. It's been pretty wild here. And I'm flying to New York in two hours, to meet my future mother-in-law in Southampton."

"Good luck. Tell her what a lucky old broad she is to have you." Allegra laughed at the image.

"When will you be home, by the way?"

"Not till August. But it's going great," he said, and then he sounded worried again. "How's Carmen? She still sounds terrible a lot of the time. I keep telling her there will be more, but she doesn't believe me."

"I know. I tell her the same thing. She's hanging in. I think the movie is keeping her busy at least. But she misses you something awful." It took all of Allegra's powers of persuasion to keep her from running off to Switzerland, and the tabloid story certainly wasn't going to help, but Allegra was sorry she wasn't going to be there over the weekend to talk sense into her and distract her.

"I miss her too," Alan said sadly.

"How's the picture going?" Allegra asked with interest.

"Great. They're letting me do a lot of my own stunt work."

"Don't tell your wife, or she'll be there on the next plane."

They both laughed and he said he'd see her in two months when he got back, but she knew she'd talk to him long before that. As soon as they hung up, Jeff walked into her office.

"Ready to go?" he asked, looking as though he was in a hurry. But she was all set. And this time, nothing would stop her.

"All set." She stood up and he caught a glimpse of the paper on her desk, and the headline.

"That's pretty," he said, glancing over it and shaking his head. There was nothing those people wouldn't stoop to. They had interviewed two nurses, who had probably been paid a pretty penny to sell Carmen's secrets and distort them. "Have they seen it yet?"

"I just spoke to both of them. They wanted to sue and I told them not to. It just sells papers."

"Poor things. I sure would hate to live like that."

"There are other compensations," Allegra said knowingly, but she wondered if they were enough. It was a high price to pay for glory.

They both left their cars in her office garage and took a cab to the airport, and Jeff couldn't believe that this time nothing had happened to stop them. Neither of them had an emergency, a problem, a meeting. They didn't have to cancel again; his mother wouldn't be furious with him.

They actually managed to get on the plane on schedule, and take their seats without a problem. It was amazing.

Jeff looked at her with a grin, as the plane took to the air with the resounding sound of the jets just above them. "I can't believe it. Can you?" They had agreed to fly first class, and they sat back in their seats with a victorious look, as they held hands and ordered champagne and orange juice. "We did it!" he said, and kissed her. "My mother will be so pleased." Allegra was just happy to be with him, and to be going away with him. They still hadn't decided where to go for their honeymoon. They were taking three weeks, and they were talking about Europe. Italy in the fall was glorious, particularly Venice. And after that Paris, and maybe London, to see friends. But Jeff also liked the idea of a beach somewhere, like maybe the Bahamas, or Bora Bora like Carmen and Alan. But Allegra didn't want anything that remote. It was a lively conversation for close to an hour, and a real luxury to even be thinking about it. And then they talked about the wedding. He was thinking about Alan as his best man, and her brother and Tony Jacobson, and the director of his movie, as ushers. And Allegra was having the same problem. She wanted Sam as her maid of honor, and Carmen as a bridesmaid, and she felt as though she should have had more friends stand up for her than that. She had always thought about having her college room-mate from Yale, Nancy Towers, if she ever got married, but she hadn't seen her in five years, and Nancy lived in London.

"Maybe she'd come," Jeff said conversationally, "at least ask her."

And there was another old friend of Allegra's from school, Jessica Farnsworth, who had moved East years before. They never saw each other anymore, but as kids they had been like sisters. She decided to ask both of them after talking to Jeff, and they completed the wedding party. They were going to invite the Weissmans of course, and a lot of people they liked and worked with. Allegra thought Jeff should invite some of his friends from the East, but he doubted that they would come. They were either too poor or working too hard, but he agreed to invite them.

It was an easy flight, and eventually, they both read. He was still jotting down notes on the script, and she had brought an assortment of papers with her in a briefcase. She had brought a new novel too, and Jeff approved of the selection. But before she read the first page, she was fast asleep, with her head on Jeff's shoulder, and he looked down at her tenderly and covered her with a blanket.

"I love you," he whispered as he kissed her.

"Me too," she whispered back, and then drifted off to sleep again until they landed. He had to shake her awake, she was so dead to the world, and she didn't remember where she was at first. She had been completely out, after her exhausting night getting Malachi out of jail, and then dashing to the office.

"You work too hard," Jeff informed her, as they dis-embarked and walked to the carousel to claim their luggage. He had arranged for a limousine to meet them at the airport and take them to Southampton. He wanted the trip to be as pleasant as possible for Allegra so it would be one of the first happy memories they shared of their marriage. There was champagne in an ice bucket waiting in the limousine for them, and it was one of those absurd stretch models that go on forever.

"I didn't know they had those in the East." She laughed when she saw it. "I thought the only people who hired those were rock stars." In spite of his normally unassuming ways, she always teased Bram Morrison because he loved them, the longer the better. He'd even had one with a double bed in it once. That had been quite something.

"Drug dealers rent them here," Jeff explained with a grin, and then commented that they had met in the East five months before, and now here they were, back again, and soon to be married. Their wedding was only two and a half months away. They could hardly believe it.

The ride to Southampton took two hours from Kennedy, and it was a hot June night, but the car was air-conditioned and they were comfortable. Jeff took his jacket off and his tie, and he rolled up the sleeves of his well-starched blue shirt. He always looked immaculate and perfectly pressed and put together, even after a plane ride. The only time he didn't look like that was in his famous sweatshirts and blue jeans in Malibu, but even then he looked intentionally casual, and she teased him because his jeans were always perfectly pressed. It was one of his few obsessions.

"I look a total mess compared to you." Allegra looked nervous as she brushed her hair and tied it back again. But the navy linen suit had suffered badly on the airplane, particularly while she slept on his shoulder. "I should have taken off the skirt," she commented with a grin.

"That would have been a hit," he said, and poured her a glass of champagne and then kissed her.

"That's perfect. I'm going to get drunk before I meet your mother. That'll make a big impression on her."

"Stop worrying. She's going to love you," he said confidently, beaming at his future bride, as she flashed the much-beloved engagement ring at him. And they kissed long and hard as the car made a right turn off the expressway.

It was another half hour to the house, and it was nearly midnight when they rounded the last bend in the road, and she saw a stately old house, with a porch all around it. Even in the dark, she could see antique wicker furniture set in little groups, and there were lovely trees that shaded the house in the daytime. There was a white picket fence that surrounded the property, and the driver drove them right up to the door and then helped them with their bags. Because of the late hour, they all attempted to be quiet. Jeff suspected his mother wouldn't have waited up for them. With the time difference, it was impossible to have gotten there any earlier and still have been able to put in a half day at the office.

He knew where the key was hidden. He paid the driver and gave him a handsome tip, and then let Allegra and himself into the house carefully. There was a note from his mother in the front hall, on a handsome antique English table. The note welcomed them both, and told Jeff he had his own room, and asked that Allegra take the large guest room on the ocean. The message was clear and Jeff smiled at her apologetically.

"I hope you don't mind," he whispered. "My mother is very proper. We can leave your bags in there, and you can sleep with me. Or I can sleep with you, as long as we make it back to our own rooms by morning." She was amused by the proprieties, but perfectly willing to follow the directions.

"Just like college," she grinned, and he pretended to look shocked.

"Is that what you did in college? I had no idea," he said, carrying her bags up the stairs, as she tiptoed behind him. It was kind of fun, being in his house, whispering and trying to find their bedrooms. It was suddenly like an adventure, and she giggled as he walked her past his mother's bedroom. It was a huge, airy room with blue-and-white chintz and a four-poster with heavy curtains. But they couldn't see it that night, the door was firmly closed. In fact, it surprised Allegra that his mother hadn't waited up for them, after they'd come all this way to see her. It was only midnight, and her own mother certainly would have. But she knew Jeff's mother was much older. She was seventy-one, and according to Jeff she always went to bed early.

Jeff led her to the guest room his mother had described, overlooking the Atlantic Ocean, and she could hear the waves lapping against the sand. And on a table next to the bed there was a pitcher of ice water, and a plate of small, thin buttery cookies. Jeff offered her one and she took it, and was surprised at how delicious it was. It melted in her mouth and she loved it.

"Does your mom make these?" she asked, impressed, and he laughed and shook his head.

"The cook does."

The room where they were standing was upholstered in a flowery pink fabric, and there were lace curtains on the window, and it had a big white wrought-iron bed, and hooked rugs on the floor. It looked very New England.

"Where's your room?" Allegra whispered, eating another cookie. She was suddenly starving.

"Down the hall," he pointed, still whispering so his mother didn't hear them. She was a light sleeper. And it reminded him of the summers of his youth, when he'd sneak friends into his house at night and they'd sneak a beer or two. His father was always willing to let them get away with it, and his mother always called him on it the next morning.

Jeff led Allegra down the hall to his own room. There was a dark green bedspread and matching curtains, and a narrow bed with a handsome antique headboard. And on the dressers and desk were mostly pictures of his father. There were several maritime paintings that his father had collected over the years. It was a totally masculine room, and in some ways reminiscent of the Malibu house in that it had a feel of New England and of the ocean, but this was far more austere than the house where she stayed with him. And in spite of the pretty fabrics, and antique furniture, there was something cold about it, like the photographs she'd seen of his mother in the New York apartment.

He went back to her room after he'd left his bags in his own, and he gently closed her door and put a finger to his lips. He had closed his own bedroom door before leaving it, and he didn't want his mother to hear them talking at this end of the house. Allegra understood that. They walked on tiptoe, and never spoke above a whisper, and she looked out the window and wished they could go out on the beach. It looked so pretty in the moonlight.

"I love swimming at night here," he whispered almost inaudibly. "Maybe tomorrow." He didn't want his mother to hear them tonight and they were too tired anyway.

He sat on the bed with her, and they kissed, and after a little while, she brushed her teeth and washed her face, and put on her nightgown. She had brought a frilly one with a dressing gown that looked respectable in case his mother saw her in it. She hadn't been sure what to bring. She'd brought white pants and a brightly colored silk shirt for Saturday, a black linen dress for Saturday night, and a white one just in case something happened to the black one, a bathing suit, shorts and T-shirts, and a seersucker pantsuit for the flight home that looked very Eastern preppie. It all seemed pretty safe. She hadn't known what his mother would be like. She always imagined mothers to be like her own, but not this one. The photographs she had seen of her told their own tale, and she wouldn't have said it to Jeff, but Mrs. Hamilton truly scared her.

He slipped into bed with her, and the sheets were a little damp, as they always were at any beach, and they were of the finest quality and had little white flowers embroidered on them. But Jeff was just happy being there with her. He was afraid to make love to her in the quiet house for fear they would make too much noise, and he just held her until they both fell asleep in the balmy sea air. They slept like children. The only problem was that they didn't wake till morning. He had told himself to wake up with the dawn, but his internal clock must have been set on California time, because he awoke at nine-thirty, and she was still sound asleep and purring. And there was no way to get back to his room without risking that he'd run into his mother.

He peeked into the hall before he went, and then, feeling like a naughty child, he made a dash down the hall, and disappeared into his own room. But he had a feeling he'd made enough noise doing it to let the entire house know that he was escaping from the guest bedroom. And as though to prove it, his mother appeared in the doorway of his room seconds later. He had just put on his dressing gown, and was about to unzip his suitcase.

"Did you sleep well, dear?" she asked, and he jumped a foot, and then turned to see his mother in a flowered blue dress and a sun hat, and for a woman of her years, she looked very handsome. She had been beautiful once, but not in a very long time, and there was nothing warm in her eyes, even when she saw him. She always kept her distance.

"Hi, Mother," he said, and went to hug her. He had all his father's warmth and winning, easy ways. Jeff had always been so much like him. She was far more Yankee. "Sorry we got in so late last night. With the time difference, it's hard to do much better than that, and we both had to work in the morning."

"It's no problem. I didn't hear you come in." She smiled at him, and then glanced at his bed, still perfectly made from the night before. He had forgotten to open it and rumple the sheets and she noticed. "Thank you for making the bed, dear. You're the perfect houseguest."

"Thank you, Mother," he said politely, knowing full well he had been busted by his mother.

"Where's your fiancée?" He was about to say that she'd been sleeping a minute ago, when he left her, but he caught himself. In some ways, it was difficult coming back here. He hadn't stayed with her in a while, and he forgot sometimes how rigid she was. He'd been more used to it when he was younger.

"I don't know. I haven't seen her yet," he answered demurely. "Do you want me to wake her?" It was ten o'clock by then, and he knew his mother disapproved of houseguests who stayed in bed all morning.

He went over and knocked on the door of the pink bedroom, while his mother watched, and a moment later, Allegra appeared in the dressing gown over her lace nightgown. She was barefoot, but she'd brushed her hair, and she looked very young and very pretty. And she immediately came to shake Mrs. Hamilton's hand, and smile at Jeff.

"How do you do, I'm Allegra Steinberg," she introduced herself, and for a long moment his mother said nothing, and then nodded. She made it quite obvious that she was looking Allegra over, and it made her extremely uncomfortable but she tried to be brave about it, and kept smiling.

"It was nice of you to come this time," Mrs. Hamilton said coolly. There was no hug, no kiss, there were no good wishes, or mentions about the wedding.

"We were disappointed to cancel last time," Allegra said clearly. She could play this game too, if she had to. "We couldn't help it."

"So Jeff told me. Well, it's warm today," she said, glancing outside at the ocean. It was clear and bright and very warm, even at that hour of the morning. "Perhaps you'd both like to play tennis at the club before it gets much hotter."

But Jeff wasn't interested. "We can play in California. We came here to be with you. Do you need us to do any errands for you this morning?"

"No, thank you," Mrs. Hamilton said crisply. "Lunch is at noon. I don't imagine you'll want much breakfast at this late hour, Miss . . . Allegra. . . ." She made her point succinctly. "But there's coffee and tea in the kitchen, whenever you're dressed." In other words, please don't wander around my house in your nightgown. Her messages were clear but unspoken. Don't stay in bed all morning. Don't sleep with my son under my roof. Don't be very familiar. Don't come any closer.

"My mother's a little cool at first sometimes," Jeff tried to explain to her as they went downstairs together half an hour later. Allegra was wearing pink shorts and a matching T-shirt, and sneakers. "I don't know if she's shy or just aloof. It takes her a while to get to know people."

"I understand." Allegra smiled at him lovingly. "You're her only child too. It can't be easy for her to be 'losing' you, and see you getting married."

"I would think she'd be relieved," he laughed. "She used to nag me about it. She gave that up a long time ago at least." Allegra wanted to ask him if it was at the same time she gave up laughing and smiling. She looked as though she hadn't cracked a smile since the Spanish Inquisition. And when they went downstairs for coffee, she was in the kitchen, giving the ancient Irish cook instructions. Lizzie had been with her for over forty years, and she made everything exactly the way Mrs. Hamilton wanted, she always explained to anyone who'd listen. Especially the menus.

They were talking about lunch at that exact moment. She had ordered a shrimp salad, and a tomato aspic. There were hot rolls, and floating island for dessert. And just hearing about it sounded very Eastern to Allegra.

"We'll eat in the outside dining room," Mrs. Hamilton explained.

"Don't go to a lot of trouble, Mother," Jeff told her easily. "You don't need to make a lot of fuss for us. We're not guests. We're family." She gave him a chilly look of surprise as he said it, as though she had no idea what he was thinking.

After coffee and muffins, Allegra and Jeff went for a brief walk around the property, and then down the beach, and Allegra tried to get rid of her feeling of tension. Mrs. Hamilton seemed to create an atmosphere of malaise around her, and Jeff seemed completely unaware of it, as though he thought her icy, spartan rigor was normal. Maybe having grown up that way made it seem more tolerable. But Allegra couldn't imagine how he had come to be so loving and affectionate with a mother like an iceberg.

And when they walked back to the house, Mrs. Hamilton was waiting for them on the porch, and there were two pitchers of iced tea and lemonade. There was no wine, and no sign of anything alcoholic, not that Allegra missed it. Allegra sat down in one of the old wicker chairs, and talked to her about the house and how long they'd had it. It had belonged to her husband's aunt and they had inherited it when she died thirty-nine years before, before Jeff was even born. He had come here all his life, she explained, and one day it would be his, she said wistfully, and then her face hardened.

"I'm sure he'll sell it."

"Why would you say that?" He looked hurt that she'd think he was so unsentimental.

"I don't imagine you'll be living in the East again, will you?" she asked coldly. "Now that you're marrying someone in California." It was an accusation, and there were no good wishes attached to it.

"I have no idea where we'll be living," he said diplomatically, not wanting to hurt his mother's feelings. But to Allegra, that looked impossible, she looked as though she were encased in armor. She had never met anyone like her, and she was completely different from Allegra's parents. "I'll be finished with the movie in September, before the wedding. And I'm about to start a new movie. Who knows where we'll wind up?" He smiled vaguely and Allegra stared at him. What was he talking about? She practiced law in California, and her particular brand of entertainment law couldn't be practiced anywhere but in Hollywood, and he knew that. But his mother seemed unimpressed with what he'd said anyway, and a few minutes later they were called in to lunch, and it was a stiff, awkward meal with Lizzie serving and Jeff and Allegra struggling for conversation.

But afterward, as they walked down the beach again, Allegra asked him what he'd meant when he told his mother he didn't know where they'd live.

"What I do is not exactly transportable, you know. I have a very specific kind of practice." He had really worried her with what he'd said and he knew it. But he'd been trying to humor his mother.

"I didn't want my mother to feel that her only son had abandoned her forever. But aside from that, you really could practice in New York if you wanted to. There's Broadway, and certain elements of the music business, and some degree of television."

"Yeah, like news. Jeff, be real. What I do only exists in L.A. I'm a show business attorney."

"I understand that, but you could broaden your horizons if you wanted to." He was sounding stubborn, and she was panicked.

"It wouldn't be broadening, it would be narrowing," she said uncomfortably. "I'd lose more than half my practice."

"And all those two A.M. phone calls. People in New York don't do things like that. They're more businesslike," he said, while she suddenly began to wonder who he had become in Southampton.

"I'm not sure I understand what you're saying to me, but I want you to know that I love my work, and I don't intend to give it up and move to New York. That was never part of the deal with us. What are you talking about suddenly?"

There was a long silence, and he looked at her cautiously. "I know you love your work, and you're good at it. But I'm from the East, and it might be nice to know that one day we could come back here, if we ever decided that that was what we wanted."

"Is that what you want?" He had never said that to her as clearly. "I thought you were trying to adjust to L.A., and you understood that when you married me, we would live there. Is that no longer okay with you? Because if it isn't, maybe we need to talk about that now, before one of us makes a terrible mistake here." She was panicking, listening to him; this was not a fun weekend.

"I understand. I know you feel rooted in L.A., Allegra," he said slowly, and she snapped at him.

"Stop humoring me, dammit. I'm not a child. I get it. But I'm not moving to New York, and if that's the big surprise here, then maybe we need to reconsider what we're doing. Maybe we should just live together for a while, until you figure out how you feel about California."

"I like it very much," he said, looking strained. He had gotten in over his head and he knew it. But this wasn't an easy weekend for him either. He knew how difficult his mother was, and how unwelcoming she was being. "Look, this isn't about you giving up your career. It's about having options. And I didn't want her to feel I would sell this house the minute she died, God forbid. It means a lot to her, and who knows, maybe we could bring our children here in the summers. I'd like that." He looked at her apologetically, and she backed down gracefully, although for a minute she'd had her claws out.

"I'd like that too. I thought you were trying to tell me you expected me to move East as soon as we were married."

"No, let's wait a month or two, okay? Like maybe by November." He chuckled. "I'm sorry, baby. I didn't mean to threaten you. I know how hard you work and what a good job you do. You'll be a senior partner in no time, unless you start your own firm. I don't know . . . old Easterners give it up slowly. I never told myself I was moving away for good. I just told myself, and everyone else, that I was coming out to do one screenplay, and now, maybe another . . . and then I'll write a book there. And one day I'll notice that I've been there for twenty years. But it kind of happens gradually, you don't just throw away your Eastern-ness in five minutes."

"You never will." She kissed him as they headed across the dunes back to the house. She liked the idea of having it for her children one day, especially without his mother. "You still look preppie," she teased him.

"How am I supposed to look?"

"Just the way you do." She kissed him again, and saw his mother watching disapprovingly from the porch. She seemed to have only one speed, and it wasn't happy. And Allegra had noticed that being around her seemed to put a strain on both of them, he because he felt he had to carry the ball for everyone, and she because she thought she had to win Mrs. Hamilton's approval.

"Be careful you don't burn," she warned Allegra, with her fair skin, as they helped themselves to lemonade on the porch.

"Thank you," Allegra said politely. "I use sunscreen."

She watched her son's fiancée as Allegra sat in a comfortable porch swing with the cool drink and sipped it.

"I hear your entire family is in show business . . . Allegra," she said as though she couldn't believe it.

"Except for my brother." She smiled pleasantly at her future mother-in-law. "He's in pre-med at Stanford." It was the first thing that brought a genuine smile to her lips since they'd arrived on Friday.

"My father was a doctor. Actually, almost my entire family, except my mother, of course. They were all physicians."

"Scott wants to be an orthopedic surgeon. The rest of us seem to be trapped in 'show business,' as you put it. My mother writes, directs, and produces. She's enormously talented. My father is a movie producer. And I'm an entertainment lawyer."

"What exactly does that mean?" She stared at her as though Allegra had come from another planet and only appeared to be human.

"It means I hold a lot of hands, and get a lot of phone calls at four in the morning." She looked shocked by what Allegra had said, and aimed her next question at her.

"Is everyone that rude in show business?"

"Only when they get arrested," she said matter-of-factly, enjoying the shock value of what she had just said. Mrs. Hamilton deserved it. She deserved a lot of things, Allegra had decided by then, most of all a good shaking. She was the least hospitable, least pleasant, least warm woman she had ever met. And she felt sorry for Jeff now. Clearly, he had only his father's genes and none of his mother's.

"Do a great many of your clients get arrested?" She was wide-eyed, and even Jeff was amused. But Allegra wasn't.

"Some. That's why they need me. I bail them out of jail, write their wills, do their contracts, reorganize their lives, help them with their problems. It's very interesting and I like it."

"Most of her clients are very big movie stars, Mom. You'd be impressed to know who." But he didn't offer, it seemed more exotic not to.

"I'm sure it's very interesting work. And you have a sister as well?"

Allegra nodded, thinking of poor Sam and her big stomach and the baby she'd have to give up in August. "Yes, she's seventeen. She's still in school," she said, not *and she models occasionally, and gets knocked up*. Allegra almost laughed at that one. "She's going to UCLA in the fall, as a drama major."

"It sounds like an intriguing family." There was a brief silence for a moment then, as the porch swing squeaked, and the next question almost knocked Allegra right off it. She had never expected her to be so blatant. "Tell me, Allegra, are you Jewish?" Jeff looked like he was going to fall right out of his chair as he watched Allegra answer.

"Actually, no," Allegra said coolly. "I'm Episcopalian. But my father is, and I know a lot about it. Did you want to know something about Judaism?" she asked politely, but Mrs. Hamilton wasn't buying. She was a shrewd old cow and she didn't give a damn if Allegra liked her. It was horrifying to Jeff as he listened.

"I didn't think you were"—she compounded matters further with absolutely no concern—"you don't look it."

"Neither do you," Allegra told her calmly. "Are you?" Jeff almost choked, and he had to turn away so his mother couldn't see him laugh. She looked totally shocked, for once. No one had ever asked her that question.

"Of course not. *Hamilton*? Are you mad?"

"I don't think so. Why not?" Allegra seemed totally matter-of-fact, and his mother still didn't get it, but Jeff did. And he was mortified.

"I take it your mother's not Jewish then," she pressed on, relieved at least that her eventual grandchildren wouldn't be tainted. But even at that, she was half Jewish because of her father.

"No, and neither is her father," Jeff stepped in, and decided to put his mother out of her agony, and theirs from listening to her. He felt as though he were betraying Allegra, but for his own sake, he had to. "Allegra's real father is a doctor in Boston named Charles Stanton."

"Why in heaven don't you use his name then?" She stared at Allegra in disapproval.

"Because I hate him. And I haven't seen him in years," Allegra said calmly. Four years of therapy had done something. It was the most disgusting conversation she had ever participated in, and she was about to say so. "Frankly, after what I've seen in my family after all these years, I'd want to bring my children up Jewish. My brother and sister are, and I think it's a wonderful thing for anyone." Jeff thought he was going to have to revive his mother, and he shot Allegra a look, which she gave right back to him. He had sold out just to shut her up, and he knew it. But his eyes said, *okay, okay, but you know I didn't mean it the way it sounded.* But she was going to give him a hard time about it anyway. His mother was not only stiff and unpleasant, with ice water in her veins, she was also anti-Semitic. How in hell had Jeff even turned out human?

"I assume you're joking," she said coldly, and changed the subject, and they both let her. A little while later, Allegra and Jeff went upstairs and changed for dinner. They went to their own rooms, but as soon as he was dressed, and could slip out of his room unobserved, he went to Allegra in the guest room.

"Before you hit me over the head with a chair, I want to apologize. I know I sold out, just to keep her quiet. I always forget how limited she is about things like that. Hell, she belongs to a club where they haven't let Jews in for two hundred years. To her, that's important."

"It was important to Hitler too, and his friends."

"This is different. It's petty and stupid, and 'social.' She thinks it makes her aristocratic to hate everyone who's not like her. It doesn't mean shit. And you know I don't feel that way. I don't care if you bring our kids up Jewish or Buddhist. I love you, whatever your name is. It's going to be Hamilton anyway pretty soon, so why worry about it?" His mother made him desperately uncomfortable, and she could see it. She actually felt sorry for him, and she wasn't nearly as mad as she knew she should be, on Simon's behalf. It was mostly pathetic.

"How did you ever stand it here, Jeff? She's not exactly open or warm, or easy to deal with."

"She used to be," he tried to defend her, "or at least a little bit more anyway. She got all closed up when my father died—she was miserable without him." But Allegra could never imagine her much more open than she was now. She was a viper.

"Weren't you lonely being with her?" Allegra couldn't imagine how he stood it.

"Sometimes. One gets used to it. Her whole family was like that. They're all gone now."

"What did they do when they got together, make ice cubes?"

"She's not as bad as all that," he said, zipping up Allegra's black linen dress, just as his mother knocked, and he knew he shouldn't be there. He slipped into the bathroom after signaling Allegra not to give him away. And she opened the door to his mother, who had come to tell her dinner was served, and perhaps to atone for her earlier comments, she told Allegra she looked very pretty. The truth was she liked her much better now that she knew her real name wasn't Steinberg.

Allegra followed her downstairs to dinner, and Jeff seemed to appear from nowhere. And miraculously, they survived the dinner, mostly by staying on safe subjects, like art, and European travel, and opera. It was the most boring conversation Allegra thought she'd ever had, and fortunately after dinner, Mrs. Hamilton went to bed. That night they went out to the beach and swam, and then they lay on the sand, and he held her.

"You haven't had much fun here, have you?"

She rolled over on her back and sighed in the moonlight. Did he want her to be honest or not? She was quiet while she was deciding.

"It was different." It was the most diplomatic thing she could think of.

"Very different from your family," he acknowledged. He felt guilty now for having brought her, but she did have to meet his mother. "Your family is so warm and affectionate and outgoing.

Everyone's always talking and laughing, and telling some crazy story. I loved being with them from the first moment I met them." He looked ashamed now of his mother. Even he had to admit that she'd been awful to Allegra. But looking at him, seeing how badly he felt, she suddenly didn't mind it.

"She reminds me a lot of my father. I don't mean that nastily. But it's that same Eastern, uptight, upper-class inability to feel or express or give. It's all about constant disapproval. He has never approved of me once in my entire life. And it used to kill me. Now I don't care. And she's the same way. I would have to fight and beg and crawl for her approval, if I wanted it, and I'd probably never get it. All the fun for those people is in the withholding. It's a special art. And she's got it down pat, just like he does."

"She used to be hard on me too, but nothing like she was with you this weekend. I've never seen her like this," he confessed, miserable about how his mother had behaved with his fiancée.

"I'm a big threat," Allegra reminded him. "I've stolen you away from New York, and now from her. She doesn't have much else." It was understandable, but it didn't make Allegra like her any better. "Maybe she'll warm up later," she said, more to cheer Jeff up than because she believed it.

They slept in the pink guest room together again that night, but this time he set his alarm for seven-thirty, and went back to his own bedroom where he showered and dressed and then packed. And then he woke Allegra. Enough was enough. They had done what they came for. He had booked them on an early flight. And after he got Allegra down to breakfast in her seersucker pantsuit, he told both women that they were leaving. He said they had to be on a one-o'clock flight, which meant they had to leave Southampton at ten o'clock that morning. He explained to them that he had called the director and they were having trouble with the movie, so Jeff had to return early.

"What's wrong?" Allegra asked, looking upset for him. She had slept like a baby, and she felt resilient again, and able to take more abuse from his mother. But as soon as she left the room, Jeff whispered to Allegra that they were leaving because they'd been there long enough and they had done their duty. Even he couldn't stand it a moment longer.

"Are you sure?" she whispered, leaning over the cinnamon rolls, and he nodded. She didn't want to tear him away from his mother, but he was far more anxious to leave than she was.

As they left, Jeff gave his mother the wedding date again, and told her they were expecting to see her there. And Jeff hugged her tight, and she almost responded but not quite, and he gave a little bonus to Lizzie, and then Allegra almost fell over laughing when she saw the car come for them. He had ordered the longest limousine they had. It was long and white, and it had a bar, TV, and God only knew what else inside, and Mrs. Hamilton looked as though she wanted to die rather than have it in her driveway. But Jeff looked quite happy about it.

"We use them all the time in California, Mom. We'll try and get you one for the wedding," he said with a straight face as he kissed her good-bye again. He handed their bags to the driver, and then they took off with a last wave, and she stood, looking like a tragic figure in her driveway. Allegra had understood correctly that she was the loneliest woman alive, but she was also the meanest. And to Allegra, she wasn't worth the trouble.

Jeff had a history with her, but Allegra knew she never would. And she also knew that after this weekend Jeff would never push her to it. They had done their best, they had paid their respects, but it was hopeless.

"I was thinking," Jeff said quietly, as they drove back toward the expressway, "maybe we should have yarmulkes at the wedding."

"You're disgusting and irreverent. . . . Will you stop? And how could you get this car?" She laughed at him. "Have you no respect for anything?" She accused, but they were both laughing and he was kissing her, and he was dying to get her home and make love to her. Only his real sense of propriety kept him from making love to her in the outrageous white limo.

But they both acknowledged silently, by the way they clung to each other and the way they cuddled, that it had been a hideous weekend.

"I'm sorry, Allegra. I don't know why I didn't realize what it would be like. I must have had denial. Maybe I should go to Dr. Green for a while, to pay penance."

"I think it's remarkable you survived her for all these years," Allegra said admiringly. Mary Hamilton was the coldest woman she'd ever met. And Jeff was completely different.

"I've never paid a lot of attention to her, and my father was a lot like Simon."

"That must have saved you," she said matter-of-factly.

They talked about other things all the way back, and they both wanted to kneel and kiss the ground when they got back to California, not to mention when they got to Malibu. And the first thing they did was tear each other's clothes off. They never even made it into bed and wound up on the couch in the living room, and he had never made love to her with such fervor. The repressive atmosphere they'd been in for two days had almost driven them crazy. And Allegra had never been as happy in her life, to be home again, to be away from there, and for a while anyway, to have seen the last of his mother.

CHAPTER 17

On Monday morning, after their weekend in New York, Jeff left for the set at three A.M., as usual, and Allegra went through a stack of faxes and papers. They were both in high spirits and happy to be back, especially after the night before. But Allegra frowned when she came across an urgent fax from Carmen's producer. He said that she was so depressed she could barely function on the set. And on Friday, she had gone completely berserk over the story in the tabloids about the abortion.

It was six o'clock by the time Allegra read the fax, and she knew that Carmen would already be on the set by then, or was supposed to be, and Allegra decided to drive over and see her.

She organized her paperwork to take it with her to read on the set, if necessary, and by six-thirty, she was gone. At seven, she was sitting with Carmen. But it was just as the producer said. Carmen was a disaster. She had sat home all weekend and cried over the tabloid story, and she was still in a deep depression about losing the baby.

"You need to see a therapist," Allegra said calmly, as Carmen blew her nose for the thousandth time that morning.

"They can't change anything. My baby's still gone, and these awful people print lies about me."

"They print lies about everyone. You can't let that ruin your life and Alan's. You have to show them you don't care, and you have to show Alan you can take it. Do you think he wants to be stuck with a wimp for the rest of his life, who's buckling at the knees every time someone takes a potshot at you? Carmen, that's pathetic." She gave her a pep talk for hours, and watched her on the set. She was depressed, but she was still doing a good job whenever she was on camera. They had to give her that much.

Allegra was still there at ten o'clock, when someone came to tell her, on the closed set, that there was an urgent call being put through by her office. When she took the call in a soundproof room, it was Alice on the line. She said that she had an emergency call from Delilah Williams, the wedding consultant.

"She's calling me *here*?" Allegra asked in disbelief.

"No, I am," Alice apologized. "But she said it was an emergency of the highest order."

"Is she out of her mind?"

"It sounds like a good possibility. Shall I put her through?"

"All right. As long as I'm here, go ahead, but don't track me down for her again, just take a message."

"Allegra?" The giant crane in purple intoned into the phone, sounding more ominous than anyone Allegra had ever heard. "You haven't answered a single one of my phone calls." Her reproach was that of an irate lover. "I know nothing about the cake, the tent, the music for the church, or the reception, for that matter, nor the color for the bridesmaids." She was clearly outraged. But not nearly so much as Allegra, who was absolutely livid.

"Do you realize that you've called me on a closed set? Do you have any idea how inconvenient, not to mention inappropriate, that is? And the reason I haven't called you is that I've been too busy getting clients out of jail, into concert tours, and up on their feet for their movies. And the *last* thing I need is you bugging me about the bridesmaids."

"Do you even know who they are yet?" She sounded incensed, but Allegra was more so. She had work to do, and clients to take care of. She couldn't be bothered with this nonsense.

"I have chosen the bridesmaids," Allegra conceded to her,

unable to believe that this was their conversation, and it had been considered an "emergency of the highest order." Did that refer to the cake, or the music? "I'll have my secretary send you a list of the bridesmaids' names," Allegra said darkly, furious at having to be bothered.

"We need to know their sizes," Delilah Williams said with equal determination. She was used to dealing with people like Allegra, doctors, lawyers, psychiatrists, celebrities, actresses, none of them capable of putting on a wedding—they all thought they were too busy and important to plan one. But she could do it for them, and make them behave, if she had to. "Do you have their sizes?" she said in a voice that Allegra thought only female impersonators could muster.

"Please have my secretary ask them."

"Certainly," Delilah said, satisfied now with the communication. "I can't believe you haven't found a dress yet, by the way. You'll really have to try harder."

"I'm going back to work," Allegra barked at her, frustrated by how much the woman got on her nerves. She didn't want to be rude to her, but there seemed to be times when there was no option.

As soon as they hung up, she called her mother at the show, and she realized she was trembling when she heard her mother. "If you don't call that woman off, Mom, I'm going to kill her."

"What woman?" The only one she could think of who deserved that, in her mind, was Elizabeth Coleson. But she didn't think Allegra knew about her.

"What do you mean 'what woman?' I mean that buzzard you unleashed on me to plan the wedding. I'd rather hold it in the park and hand out hot dogs and Twinkies than have this woman call me on a closed set to discuss the music and the cake, and the 'color for the bridesmaids.' Mom, you can't do this to me."

"Just trust me, dear. She'll do a beautiful job, and you'll be so happy." It was nearly impossible to imagine, and Allegra rolled her eyes, said good-bye to Blaire, and went back to Carmen.

"Everything okay?" For once, she looked concerned about something other than her own problems.

"You wouldn't believe it," Allegra said, overwhelmed with exasperation.

"Try me."

"The wedding coordinator my mother hired was calling to bug me."

"What?" Carmen looked amused as she changed her makeup. "Wedding coordinator? What's that?"

"What I did when I bought the wigs, and the polyester clothes, and the plastic bouquet for Vegas."

"Is that what she's doing for you?" Carmen looked amused for once and Allegra laughed.

"I hope not. You never know though. You two were so smart to go to Vegas."

"You can too, you know," she said. They had all loved it, and it seemed to make more and more sense for her and Jeff to do it too and avoid the whole wedding.

"It would probably break my mother's heart, if I cheated her out of a wedding." But it would have been worth it, not to see Mary Hamilton again. In some ways, it was a powerful temptation.

In the end, she stayed with Carmen until lunch, and then went back to her office to get organized and sign some documents. She had to be at Suzanne Pearlman's office at two-thirty. They were meeting another set of parents, who had flown in from Chicago. It amazed Allegra now to realize how people flew around the country, looking for babies, interviewing girls who wanted to give their babies up, and being interviewed by them. It seemed to be a major preoccupation. But having seen how obsessed Carmen had been, over a fetus she'd only carried for two months and then lost, Allegra was beginning to understand it. It was an obsession with having, keeping, and acquiring babies.

She had told Sam she'd pick her up at home, and she drove through Bel Air on the way to Suzanne Pearlman's. Allegra was stunned by how much Sam had grown in a few days. She was seven months' pregnant and she really looked enormous. And somehow the odd contrast of it made her seem even younger.

"How've you been?" Allegra asked as Sam got in. She was wearing a short pink dress that accommodated the bulge, and sandals that wound up her legs, her long blond hair in pigtails, and huge sunglasses. She looked like Nabokov's Lolita.

"Okay," Sam answered, with a nod and a kiss for her sister. She was grateful that she was going with her. She had already met several of the couples, and she hated doing it. It was always so awkward and she hadn't liked any of them. Maybe the Whitmans? But they weren't perfect either. "How was New York?"

"Interesting," Allegra answered noncommittally, and Sam laughed. She knew her sister.

"Uh-oh. That doesn't sound good."

"It wasn't."

"Was she a bitch?"

"Yup. Totally. The human iceberg. She was really afraid that I might be Jewish. Can you believe that?"

"Wait till Daddy meets her. He'll love it."

"I can't imagine ever seeing her again, except I know I have to. I don't know how Jeff turned out as normal as he did." It was a total mystery to her after meeting his mother.

"Maybe he's adopted," she said sadly. Despite the banter, she couldn't forget where they were going or why. She was going to meet another set of prospective parents for her baby. And just thinking about it depressed her. She had tried telling Jimmy what it was like the last time she went, and this time he had offered to go with her, but she didn't think he should, and it might confuse them. They might think Jimmy was the baby's father. She was always willing to tell the prospective parents the little she knew of Jean-Luc, though it made her sound pretty flaky. He was tall and good-looking and blond, a photographer, and he was French, and about thirty. Which meant he was foreign, possibly talented, and attractive. Beyond that, she could tell them nothing. Whereabouts: unknown. She had no history to offer.

They arrived at Suzanne's office ten minutes after Allegra picked Sam up, and they rode up in the elevator in silence.

She had a pleasant waiting room with artistic prints all done in cheerful colors, and there were stacks of magazines. There were two kinds: *World of Interiors, Parenting Magazine, Vogue, Connaissance des Arts, Town & Country, Architectural Digest* for the prospective parents, and *Seventeen, Rolling Stone, Elle, Young and Modern,* and even *Mad* for the mothers. But neither Allegra nor Sam chose a magazine, they just sat there and waited. And five minutes later, the receptionist asked them to come in. The couple from Chicago were already with Miss Pearlman.

But as soon as Sam saw them, she knew she didn't like them. They were nervous around her, and they talked a lot about the trips they liked to go on, their skiing, and their last trip to Europe. She was a flight attendant, and he was in insurance, and covered a large block of the Midwest. They didn't have kids, and they had tried in vitro fertilization, but it was too expensive in the long run, and they were tired of trying. They were stories Sam had heard a lot now.

"What are you going to do with the baby when you travel?" Sam asked them with a look of curiosity.

"Leave it with a baby-sitter," the husband said.

"Hire a nanny," the wife offered.

"Why adopt a baby?" Sam went right to the point, not unlike her older sister, and Allegra smiled as she watched her.

"I'm thirty-eight, Janet's thirty-five, we both think it's time," he said, as though they were talking about buying a car. "All our friends have kids, we live in the suburbs." They lived in Naperville, but none of that appeared to be reason enough to Sam to give them her baby. They were anything but appealing.

"But do you really *want* one?" She pressed on, and she could see that they were getting really uncomfortable with her questions.

"If we didn't, we wouldn't be here," Janet said, trying to warm up to the girl, but not getting very far. They didn't like Sam either. She looked like a valley girl to them, and she seemed really pushy with her questions.

"We get free tickets from the airline. We came out here for nothing," Paul said, as Sam looked at Allegra.

"Are there any other questions you'd like to ask?" Suzanne asked Sam. She could see that the interview wasn't going well and that Sam didn't like them.

"No, I think that's fine," Sam said politely, and they went to wait in her other office. A few minutes later Suzanne came in to talk candidly to Sam and Allegra.

"I hate them," Sam said bluntly the minute Suzanne walked into the room.

"No kidding," Suzanne said, and laughed, lightening the moment. "I figured that out myself. Why?" Although she knew that too, but she was just checking.

"They don't want a baby. They should buy a dog. They want to travel all the time, they get free airline tickets, they're going to dump it at the baby-sitter's, and they just want a kid because everyone else in the suburbs has one. Why don't they just move into the city and forget it?" She was sharp. There were a lot of people out there who thought they wanted babies and really didn't. They wanted a sense of completion, or fulfillment; they wanted to put their marriage back together, or feel young again. They wanted a lot of things, but not a baby. And for them, having a baby or adopting one should not be the answer.

"I won't give my baby to them," Sam said definitely, and Allegra flinched as she listened. Sam's pregnancy had suddenly become "her baby." It was far more real now, and she was deeply attached to it, even if she pretended she wasn't.

"I understand that," Suzanne said calmly. "What about the Whitmans in Santa Barbara? They're very interested in you, Sam. They'd really like to pursue it."

"I like them the best so far," she admitted, "but I'm still thinking." It was like trying to put together a major movie deal with a seventeen-year-old producer, sometimes fifteen or even fourteen. Allegra was suddenly glad this wasn't her line of business.

"What are you thinking about?" Suzanne asked her.

"I'm trying to decide if I really like them."

"Why are you hesitating?" This was what Suzanne was so good at. The mix and match of relinquishing mothers and adoptive parents.

"I don't know, they're kind of old," Sam said honestly. They were both in their late thirties and they had never been able to have children.

"They've had a lot of bad luck," Suzanne explained, more for Allegra's sake than Sam's. Sam knew this. She had come alone with her mother last time. Although Allegra usually tried to come with her, Blaire had come twice, and Simon hadn't come at all. He just couldn't do it. The prospect of his baby having one, and then giving it up on top of it, just broke his heart. He didn't want to hear it. Just seeing her right now was hard enough. She looked so swollen, like a little grape, and yet at the same time she was still so pretty, in some ways more so. Her face had filled out a little bit, and there was a softness to it that really made her look lovely.

"The Whitmans are an unusual couple," Suzanne went on to explain in detail. "They've had more bad luck than any adopting couple I've ever heard of. They tried to adopt two babies who were reclaimed by their natural parents before the adoptions were official. That was over ten years ago, and they decided not to try again. And then with the new technologies, they tried to get pregnant again. She's had fourteen miscarriages, and a stillbirth. Now they want to adopt again, and I really have to give them credit. But after all that, they're not quite as young as some of our adopting parents are, Sam. Maybe that's not such a terrible thing. Personally, I really like them. I think they've got an awful lot of spirit." But they were the kind of people Suzanne particularly did not want to play with. She didn't want to offer people like that babies whom mothers might eventually take back. That's why she had asked Allegra, right at the beginning, if Sam was sure about giving up her baby. But Sam was definite about it now. She had

talked to Jimmy about it too. And she felt she had no other
options.

Jimmy was still around a lot these days. But in her current
state, her parents saw no objection to it. Sam needed friends, and
Jimmy was a nice, solid boy who offered her nothing more than
his friendship. He thought it was really sad that she had to give up
the baby, and he said so.

"What about the Whitmans then? Would you like to see
them again?"

"Maybe." Sam was noncommittal. She had her dark glasses
high on her head, and she looked like a chubby little princess. Her
stomach was large and round, her legs and arms were still rail
thin, and despite the bulge, she was still very graceful.

"Katherine Whitman would like to be at the delivery with
you, if you choose them."

"Why?" Sam thought that sounded disgusting.

"Because she wants to see the baby born, and bond with it
immediately. A lot of couples like to do that. Would you object to
having John there too? He said he'd like it, but for him, it's an
option." It made Allegra uncomfortable to listen to all these deals
and conditions. It really was a business.

"I don't want him there. I'll think about her."

"John could be up near your head, where he won't see anything." She pressed just a little too hard and Sam snapped at her.

"No! I don't want him there. I told you."

"Okay. No problem. So who have we narrowed it down to
then?" It exhausted Allegra emotionally just to listen.

"I think just the Whitmans," Sam said sadly. She hated
coming here. It was so depressing. There was just no way out. She
had to give them the baby. The only thing to decide now were the
details.

"Are you going to the doctor regularly?" Suzanne went
down her checklist. Sam hated that part too, but she understood
it. "Taking your vitamins? Not taking drugs? Have you had sex
recently?" Sam glared at her, but answered all the appropriate
questions. She went to the doctor, took her vitamins, had never

taken drugs, did not drink currently, not even beer or wine, and had not had sex since she'd gotten pregnant. She was every adoptive parent's dream. And Suzanne didn't tell her, because she didn't want to pressure her, but the Whitmans were desperate for her baby. She thought there was a better chance of things going well for them, if they played it low-key with Sam. She wasn't the kind of girl who responded well to pressure. Suzanne never pushed her. She let her come to it by herself, and make all her own decisions. And she had told the Whitmans that they had to be patient and wait for Sam's decision. She even encouraged them to pursue some other avenues, and talk to some other girls, so they wouldn't be disappointed if Sam chose other parents. Sam was clearly not enthused at their being older.

"Would you like to see them again?" Suzanne asked one last time, but Sam shook her head.

"Not yet." For the moment, she wanted a breather. And Allegra took her for a milkshake at Johnny Rocket's when they left. She really looked awful. Even thinking about it was a total drain for Sam. It was a hideous decision. And now her doctor wanted her to do Lamaze classes, so the delivery would be easier for her. She had gone for the first time the week before, with Blaire, and they had shown the class a film on childbirth, and she'd almost fainted. She had to go through all that, for someone else. And then give them the baby. It was a lot to ask for. And she certainly couldn't imagine them being there, as Suzanne had suggested. Sam looked as miserable as she felt as she finished her milkshake.

"I wish I were dead," she said unhappily, and Allegra was reminded of Carmen again, who wanted to be dead because she *didn't* have a baby. There were times when life had a strange sense of humor.

"I think that's a little extreme, don't you?" Allegra said calmly, and they looked surprisingly alike as Allegra drank a soda with her. "How about wishing it were all behind you?"

"Yeah, I guess so."

And then Allegra remembered that Sam's graduation ceremony was that week, and she couldn't even go to see it. That was an added blow. She asked Sam how she felt about it.

"Okay, I guess. Jimmy brought me all the stuff. My name is still on the program." And she had gotten her diploma. In spite of her absence these last two months, she had still graduated with honors. "Jimmy said it was kind of boring."

"What's with you and him anyway?" Allegra asked by way of conversation. He was a cute kid, and he hung around the house all the time, especially lately. She had seen him whenever she came by, even in the evening. He seemed to be the only one of her old friends who had stuck by her. It was as though the others were all embarrassed and didn't know what to say, so they just stopped coming, even her girlfriends.

"We're just friends," Sam explained. For the moment, he was her best friend. She told him all her hopes and fears and troubles.

"Alan and I were like that at your age. We started out as boyfriend and girlfriend as sophomores, and then we just got to be like brother and sister. We still are, I guess."

"I haven't seen Alan in ages." Sam smiled. She had always liked him. He loved to tease her. Though for the moment, he didn't even know she was pregnant. He left before Allegra had found out, and she still hadn't told him. He had his own problems in that department, with Carmen.

"He's in Switzerland," Allegra explained, "making a movie."

"How's Carmen?"

"Not so hot. She had a miscarriage in Switzerland. He's still there, working. And she had to come back to do a movie. She's pretty miserable, and she misses him a lot. He won't be back till August."

"Can't she get over to see him?"

"Not unless she wants me to strangle her. She's shooting."

"Oh. That must be hard not being together." Allegra nodded. The miscarriage had actually been harder for her.

Allegra took her back to the house in Bel Air then, and it was too late for her to go back to the office. She had promised to meet Jeff on his set. And Allegra noticed as she drove away that Jimmy was arriving. She wondered if anything serious was happening there. But she doubted it. How serious could it be with Sam seven months' pregnant?

She thought about her all the way to meet Jeff, and it really made her heart ache to think of what she had to go through. And it made her even more uncomfortable when she thought of her giving birth with people standing by, just waiting to snatch the baby from her. It seemed so creepy. She was still thinking of it when she met Jeff, and they talked about it on the way back to Malibu later that evening.

"I hate to see her go through it," Jeff said, shaking his head.

"So do I," Allegra confessed. "Suzanne is doing a good job for her though. I couldn't do it."

"Yes, you could." He leaned over and kissed her, and their conversation finally drifted away from Sam, and on to Carmen. He asked if she had settled down, and Allegra said that things appeared to be quieter for the moment.

And then they forgot the others, and just talked about his movie, and their wedding.

CHAPTER 18

On July first, Allegra finally brought joy to Delilah Williams's heart. Allegra and her mother went shopping at Dior, and they ordered a dress that Mr. Ferre was apparently willing to have slightly readjusted to suit Allegra. It was white piqué, with a white lace overlay. It was short in the front, long in back. And he was going to add a short, high-necked, long-sleeved white lace jacket. It came with a huge white lace picture hat, and it was exactly what Allegra had in mind for her wedding. It was elegant, young, and exciting! Blaire cried when she saw her daughter in it, and Allegra beamed the moment she saw it. They were also going to order white lace shoes. And her mother said she would lend her the fabulous pearl choker Simon had given her on her fiftieth birthday. They wore exactly the same sizes, even in jewelry, which was extremely convenient.

And on the same day, they found a short beige lace dress with short sleeves and a little peplum in the back that was perfect for the bridesmaids. Blaire suggested they have little beige lace hats made for them, like smaller versions of her huge one. And the people at Dior had already promised her miles of white tulle over and trailing behind it. It was going to be absolutely stunning.

"Well, we're all set," Blaire said, going down one of the lists Delilah Williams had sent her.

"Now you can tell her to stop calling me at the office. I don't have time for that nonsense."

"It's not nonsense, dear. It's your wedding."

They had chosen classic wedding music for the ceremony and Beethoven for the recessional through the guests into the formal garden. Her mother had settled the menu for her, and she was going to carry white roses and lily of the valley and philanopsis orchids. The bridesmaids could carry tiny tea-colored cymbidium orchids. They had long since chosen the cake, and they were having dream cake for the guests, in little white boxes with their names and the date engraved on it in silver, like in Europe. The flowers for the tables were yet to be designed, the tent had been ordered months before, and they were having Peter Duchin to play at the reception. The only thing that really remained to do was clean up the garden. The landscape architect was still promising total completion by the first of September and the wedding was only four days later.

They had booked a suite at the Bel Air for Mrs. Hamilton, and smaller rooms for the two bridesmaids coming from New York and London. Blaire had booked the hairdresser for all of them, and a makeup artist for those who wanted it. By July first, everything seemed to be very much in order. There was very little left to do, except plan what Delilah called the "satellite events": the bachelor dinners, and the rehearsal dinner. Normally, that would have been given by Mrs. Hamilton, but coming out from New York, she wouldn't know where to have it. So the Steinbergs were hosting it for her upstairs at the Bistro. It was easy, it would be fun. And they had already booked it.

And Allegra had finally broken down and written to her father. She told him she was getting married, and that although she didn't expect him to come, he was certainly welcome. It cost her a lot emotionally to do it, and she spent a lot of time discussing it with Dr. Green, but writing had been easier than calling. She had written to him in early June, and he still hadn't answered, so she assumed he wasn't coming. She was enormously relieved that he wasn't.

Allegra went back to the office in a good mood, after buying her wedding dress. She and her mother had just been talking about their annual Fourth of July family picnic that weekend. The children always invited a few friends, and Blaire and Simon invited one or two couples. They usually had about twenty people in the backyard, and this year they would be barbecuing on dirt, but the whole family had agreed it didn't matter. The important thing was to be together. This year, Jeff would be with them too. It was his initiation into family tradition, since he had missed Thanksgiving and Christmas. The Steinbergs loved holidays and traditions.

And the morning after she'd bought her wedding dress, Allegra was sitting in her office, describing it to Alice.

"It sounds fabulous," Alice confirmed, and the intercom instantly interrupted. Alice picked it up first, frowned, and then handed the phone to Allegra. There was a long silence as she listened, and then jotted down some hasty notes, and hung up the phone. And when she did, her eyes were blazing.

She flipped through some papers and said not a word, and then dialed an overseas number. It was Alan's hotel in Geneva. She asked for his room, and it answered after four rings, and just as she thought, Carmen answered.

"Just what exactly do you think you're doing over there?" Allegra blazed. "You damn fool, you're giving up your whole movie career to be with him. And they're not going to forget it."

"I couldn't help it," she whined. "I missed him too much." She didn't dare tell Allegra she had come because she was ovulating, and she wanted to get pregnant.

"They said you disappeared yesterday, and they can shoot around you today and tomorrow. But you're costing them a fortune. Starting today, they're docking you for it. After tomorrow, they're going to kick you off the picture. In other words, get your ass back here by tomorrow, or I'll kill you before they do."

"I don't want to come back," she whined again, and Allegra was intentionally hard on her.

"If you don't, then you'd better retire, because after tomorrow, that's what it will amount to. You'll be out of the business, Carmen Connors." And then she thought better of arguing with her and asked for Alan. "Get her ass back here, will you?" she told him in no uncertain terms, and he could hear that she meant it.

"It's not my fault, Al, I swear. I never knew she was coming over. She just showed up. It was great, but I knew you'd be mad as hell. I'll put her back on a plane tomorrow morning. I'll be back in a month anyway," he reminded both of them. "Just take care of her for me in the meantime."

"That's no small job, you know." Allegra was really getting tired of her. She was a spoiled brat, and she whined constantly about how much she missed Alan. "Maybe she's right. Maybe from now on, you two should only work together."

"We'll talk about it when I come home."

"Just send her back tomorrow without fail, or there'll be hell to pay. They're fining her fifty thousand dollars for today, and the same again tomorrow, and she deserves it." He whistled and wagged a scolding finger at Carmen.

"I'll get her back to you right away."

"See that you do it." She hung up and called the producers of Carmen's movie. She apologized profusely for her, said she'd been ill, emotionally overwrought, and needed to see her husband. It wouldn't happen again, and she would gladly pay the fine. And she would be back to work the day after tomorrow. They agreed to forget it had ever happened, as long as she paid the fine and returned to work as promised.

It certainly got her day off to a roaring start. She hardly slept all that night, and the next day she was waiting for Carmen at the airport. She read her the riot act almost the moment she came through customs, and Carmen was apologetic and just kept saying that she had needed to be with Alan. Because of her they were even going to shoot golden time on the Fourth of July, just to catch up on what they'd missed. She wasn't going to get a day off, and Allegra was so mad at her she didn't even think of inviting her to the Steinbergs' Fourth of July picnic.

She made sure that Carmen was on the set by four A.M. the

next day, and she hung around till about nine just to make sure she was behaving. Then she went home to Malibu and climbed into bed with Jeff, and slept till noon, and then they went to her parents' place for the picnic.

The whole family was there, even Scott. He had invited a girl, and Jeff was there, of course. And Sam had invited Jimmy Mazzoleri. He was part of the furniture now, as Simon said good-naturedly. He was at the house all the time. Two of the neighbors had come, and a handful of Scott's friends, but none of Sam's this year. It was a small group, but it was a day they all loved, and they were having a great time, despite the mess in the backyard and the lack of a garden.

The people who hadn't seen Sam recently were shocked at what they saw. She was fully eight months' pregnant, and she looked it. Allegra thought that the saddest thing of all was that no one even mentioned it. It was the most visible thing in the backyard other than the swimming pool, and the least talked about. The subject was completely taboo, and Allegra wondered if that made it harder for Sam. Instead of being the happiest moment in her life, it was the saddest.

Blaire was still going to Lamaze with her, and Allegra had gone once or twice, but most of the time she couldn't make it. And Jimmy had even practiced it a few times with her. It fascinated him to sit and watch the baby moving. It seemed to dash from side to side, moving her stomach like a cartoon with some enormous being in it, like an elephant hiding under a blanket.

"How are you feeling?" Allegra asked as she sat down next to her on a deck chair.

"I'm okay." Sam shrugged. Jimmy was on his way back to her with one of her father's hot dogs. "Sometimes it gets kind of hard to move around now."

"It won't be too much longer," Allegra said, trying to be encouraging, but Sam's eyes filled with tears as she said it, and Allegra wasn't completely sure why, and then Sam told her she'd made a decision.

"I picked the Whitmans in Santa Barbara. Suzanne told

them yesterday. They're kind of weird after all they've been through, but I think they're nice, and they really want the baby." Nobody could want it more than they did. "Suzanne says they were really happy. She just said it was real important that I not change my mind, especially once they get the baby, during the legal waiting period. Because that happened to them twice before and she doesn't think they could take it."

"That's not your responsibility though," Allegra pointed out, and Sam agreed.

"But it still wouldn't be fair to jack them around again. Two girls took their babies back from them before, and Katherine took years to recover from it." Then she took a gulp of air, as though trying to get used to it. Suddenly she wanted to get it over with. The delivery, the legal work, the agony of giving it up, that one hideous moment when she would hand it over to them forever. She could never get past that. She could never figure out what her life would be like from then on. It was all she could think of. "They're really adamant about being at the birth," Sam said, looking uncomfortable again.

"Do what's right for you, Sam," her sister said firmly as their father wandered over to see them.

"What are you two looking so serious about?" he asked, looking down at them with pleasure. There were plenty of serious subjects in the family these days. Sam, of course, and the wedding, which was joyful but fraught with decisions and chaos, and the fact that Blaire's ratings had just dropped again, this time very badly. She was deeply upset about it, though she had scarcely discussed it with Simon. They didn't talk about much these days, but he hadn't wanted to press Blaire about it, for obvious reasons.

"We were just saying that your hot dogs are better than ever this year." Allegra smiled up at him, and then stood up and kissed him. And when she did, Sam almost went flying into the pool, as the deck chair shot up at one end like a seesaw when Allegra got out of it. Her solitary but impressive weight had landed her on the ground and she was laughing. Even Allegra laughed at her, and a few minutes later Jimmy came back again, with another of Simon's hot dogs for Samantha.

"You need this for ballast," he said with a grin, having just seen what had happened. "You'd better be careful, or your sister will catapult you over the wall into the neighbor's garden." They both laughed, and he sat next to her, where Allegra had been, and they chatted and laughed. And then later, when they were alone again, when the others were playing Ping-Pong and horseshoes, she told him about her decision to go with the Whitmans. They had talked about the adoption before, but now she had made a commitment. She could still change her mind, of course, but Suzanne would discourage her from doing that, if possible. And she had up to six months after the baby was born to change her mind later.

"You don't have to do it, you know. I told you that," Jimmy said quietly, so no one else could hear them.

He had offered to marry her, but she didn't want to do that. What would that do? He was already eighteen, and she was turning eighteen in two weeks. Two children taking care of a baby? She knew how helpless they were. They could barely have supported themselves, they couldn't do anything for the baby. And Sam felt Jimmy didn't deserve this burden on his shoulders, since it wasn't even his baby. Samantha liked him too much to do that to him. They'd gotten very close since he'd started hanging out with her, bringing her books, and sharing study sheets and exams with her. They were inseparable now, and when he kissed her, it was very easy to figure out what would happen after the baby. She didn't even want to think about it now. But they kissed a lot, and lately, when they did, it even gave her contractions, which scared her. She half wanted to get it over with, and half wanted it to never come. She just didn't want to have to go through it.

Blaire came and sat next to them for a little while. Sam had been noticing how unhappy she looked ever since her ratings had gone down. She was really upset about it. The show meant a lot to her and she'd worked hard on it for nine years. Seeing it slowly fall apart as she watched was like watching an old friend die of cancer.

And, of course, all day long, they all talked about the wedding, how many people they were going to have, whether or not there would be a tent, who was catering it, whose music they would be dancing to. It seemed like it was all anyone talked about. Then, in the late afternoon, Simon made a point of talking to Jeff alone. He had meant to call him for weeks, but he'd been too busy.

"I've been meaning to talk to you." He finally cornered him near the ice cream. They'd all done nothing but eat all day, and Sam swore to Jimmy that if she ate another thing, she'd have the baby right then and there.

Jeff was eating a last Eskimo bar and looking extremely happy. "Great picnic," he complimented them. He thoroughly enjoyed being part of their family. Not like Allegra's weekend in Southampton with his mother. That had been a fiasco. "You did a great job with the barbecue. You have to teach me your secret, and come out to Malibu to visit us sometime. I'm not the master that you are though," Jeff said warmly, and Simon smiled. He really liked Allegra's future husband. She'd made a wise choice, and he thought they were both very lucky.

"I think you may have other talents than barbecuing," Simon reassured him. "That's what I wanted to talk to you about. I read your second book, and I really liked it. I mean, *really* liked it."

"That's encouraging." Jeff smiled up at him, not expecting anything more than that. It was just nice of Simon to tell him.

"What are you doing about the screenplay?"

"Nothing yet," Jeff said honestly. "I've talked to a couple of people about buying it, but they didn't really suggest anything I wanted. I don't want to produce the next one myself. It's just been too consuming and I want to get back to writing. I'm waiting for the right offer to sell the next movie, and maybe just do the screenplay."

"That's my point," Simon said simply, which was how he

always did business. "I'd like to make you an offer. If you have time this week, why don't we get together and talk." Jeff was beaming at him, unable to believe what he was hearing. Simon was one of the most important producers in Hollywood and he wanted to make Jeff's next movie. And the fact that he was marrying his daughter didn't hurt him any. Or that was what people would say anyway. But Jeff knew Simon well enough now to know that if Simon didn't like Jeff's book, he wouldn't buy it, no matter who he was married to, or how closely related.

"That's the best news I've had in ages." Jeff beamed at him.

"What's that?" Allegra joined them, curious about what they'd been saying.

"Your dad likes my new book. He might want to do something with it," he said humbly. And then he turned to his future wife with a broad grin. "Why don't we keep it in the family? Will you negotiate it for me, Allie?"

"Talk about conflict of interest." She laughed out loud. But she was thrilled for Jeff. She couldn't think of a better business combination than Jeff and her father. They were perfectly suited to each other.

And at the end of the afternoon, Allegra regretfully looked at her watch. They had to get going. They were going to Bram Morrison's Fourth of July concert. It was the high point of his tour before he left for Japan, and although Jeff wasn't crazy about concerts, she had promised they'd go. It was going to be a mob scene. She knew that the promoters had hired eight bodyguards, just to keep the crowd from crawling all over him. Bram had been a huge success on his tour so far, and more and more he was becoming a cult figure for all ages.

"Where are you two off to in such a hurry?" Sam inquired as she saw Jeff and Allegra pick up their things and start to get ready to leave them.

"Bram Morrison's concert at the Great Western Forum."

"Oh, you are so lucky!" Sam said enviously, and Jimmy looked like he would have loved to go. Sam and he had agreed it was too dangerous for her to be in crowds like that in her condition.

"I'll get you a ticket next time," Allegra promised, and a few minutes later they left to dress at her Beverly Hills house. She was going to put it on the market, and they were going to try to buy a bigger one in Malibu than the one Jeff rented.

At six o'clock, she and Jeff were ready. She had rented a limo for them, and the promoters said they'd provide a bodyguard if she needed one, but she doubted they would. It was a benign crowd, just a very big one. The fans loved him, and sometimes they got too close or touched too much. But they were harmless.

She and Jeff were expected backstage before the show, but by the time they arrived, the crowd was so large, they could hardly get there. Even the backstage crowd was bigger than usual. Most of them seemed to get shoved onstage, and during the show they were actually crowding the band, but there was no way to escape it. The number of fans was legendary, it was the biggest concert Allegra had ever heard of.

She and Jeff were buffeted from side to side, and more than once she thought that someone would get rough with them, but they never did. The concert went on for hours. By then, most of the crowd was pretty stoned, some were heavily drugged out, and the rest were fairly mellow. There were fireworks scheduled at eleven, and five minutes before they were due to come on, a guy with a bare chest and a vest, with long hair, got up on the stage and grabbed the mike from the drummer. He started screaming about how much he loved Bram Morrison, and how he had always loved him. How once they had been in Vietnam, and then they both died, and now they were one. It sounded like the lyrics to a song, and the man screamed again and again as security headed toward him, but there were so many gawkers onstage that they couldn't get to him. He was screaming "I love you! I love you!" at the top of his lungs, and then the fireworks came on and distracted everyone, and it was easy for the bodyguards to grab him. They yanked him right off the stage in one fell swoop, still yelling "I love you," but now he was crying and there was a gun in his hands. It looked like a toy, and overhead you could hear the explosions and see the fireworks in the sky. And then Allegra happened to look straight ahead, and she saw Bram on his knees, with blood streaming from him. It was on his head and chest, and running down his arms, and he pitched forward as she lunged and grabbed a bodyguard. She was screaming at him to get help.

"He's hurt!" She pointed at Bram, and then the others saw him. His wife saw him too, and his kids, and suddenly there was a mob surrounding him again, and no one could get through at all. They lifted Bram high over their heads finally, and his music went on, as his blood dripped on the crowd, as his wife held his hand, and his children cried. He was dead before the paramedics ever touched him. And Allegra was kneeling on the ground with them, as his wife held him in her arms and begged him not to leave them. But he was long gone, his spirit high in the sky amidst the brightly colored pinwheels, and his songs playing louder than ever. The crowd didn't even know what happened. The music just went on. And at midnight they told them. They became a wild, seething mass, crying and keening, and still the music went on. It was Bram Morrison's last concert.

The man who had killed him had never seen him before, never met him, never knew him, but God had sent him to save Bram, he said. He had to save him from the people who would hurt him, and bring him back to God. And he had. His mission had been accomplished, he told the police, and now Bram was happy. But surely no one else was.

A single, lone lunatic had killed Bram Morrison, one of rock music's great heroes. And fifty thousand fans went wild, crying, screaming, sobbing. It took until the next morning to clear them from the stands of the Forum. Allegra had been awake for hours by then, her jeans and white shirt still covered in blood, as she held Jeannie's hand and found out what she wanted. She thought they wanted a simple ceremony, but the public would never allow that. In the end they settled for a private burial, and a memorial for a hundred thousand at the Coliseum. The promoters arranged that, and Allegra did the rest. The funeral, the eulogy, the legal arrangements, the untangling of the red tape involving the tour. She did everything including hold Jeannie in her arms and console the children. It was what Bram would have wanted. She had always been fond of him, not like Mal O'Donovan, who was a buffoon of sorts. Bram had been one of the great men of music.

"I can't believe it," she said to Jeff when they went back to Malibu that morning. It was already noon by the time they got home. But she had wanted to go to the beach and see it. "I can't believe he's gone." She just stood there and cried as she thought of him and all that had happened that night, and Jeff held her.

"We live in a crazy world," Jeff said softly, "full of crazy people. People who want to take your soul, or your life or your money, or your reputation, whatever they can get." He was crying too, deeply moved by the senselessness of Bram's death, and the wife and children who would miss him.

A lunatic had taken Bram's life, but not his soul. His soul would be free forever. And Allegra sat on the beach and cried, remembering him and when they had met, and all their quiet, humorous conversations. He had been such an unassuming man, such an undemanding person. And yet he was always being threatened. He was too good, too simple, and too pure. It was an invitation to the crazies.

And later that week when they laid him to rest, and she saw his children in their mother's arms, Allegra knew something she had never felt before. She wanted a child, a baby, a piece of Jeff before fate could strike them down, and he could ever leave her. It was something she had never felt quite like this, if ever. But even more than that, she knew there was something she had to do first, an obligation from her heart. Life was so precious, so short, so easily stolen. It wasn't to be taken, or thrown away, it was to be protected and cherished. She could no longer save him, but there was one small life she could save, and now she knew she was destined to do it. Sam's baby.

She looked quietly at Jeff, and asked him as they drove back home. He was startled at first, and then he wasn't surprised at all. He was only surprised they hadn't thought of it sooner. They were going to be married in a month. It was too soon in Sam's life to have a child, but not in theirs. It was right for them, and it was not right to give it away to strangers.

"I think it's a great idea," Jeff said, looking excited and a little stunned.

"Do you mean it?" she asked wondrously. He really was an extraordinary human being.

"Of course I mean it. Let's tell Sam." They had barely survived Bram's funeral, and the shock of letting him go. And yet in an odd way, this was his last gift to them. It was as though he had suggested it, and they had reached out for this baby, which none of them had dared to reach out to before. It was theirs now.

"I can't believe it," Allegra said, laughing. "We're going to have a baby. . . ." Jeff was smiling too, and she just hoped that Sam would see the sense in it. The only losers in the deal were the adopting parents, the Whitmans. But as Allegra had told Sam before, they owed them nothing at this point. The baby hadn't even been born yet.

And when they talked to Sam later that day, she agreed with them. It was the perfect solution. And Jeff and Allegra would be the perfect parents. They put their arms around her and Sam cried. At least the baby would be near her. It was a blessing for all of them, and the answer to Samantha's prayers.

CHAPTER 19

Apparently, Katherine and John Whitman did not agree with them. They did not feel grateful or blessed, nor did they agree that Jeff and Allegra were the perfect parents. In fact, they were furious about it. Furious didn't even begin to describe their reaction. They had been through too much in the past to even be able to listen to reason. Suzanne Pearlman tried explaining it to them, that there was no contract yet, and that Sam had no obligation. But the Whitmans felt that life owed them more than they'd gotten so far and that they'd had enough cruel jokes played on them, with mothers withdrawing their babies. They were hurting terribly over it, and they were looking to hurt anyone they could now. As far as they were concerned, anyone was fair game. The Steinbergs, Allegra, Jeff, Sam, anyone they could injure in whatever way possible, as long as it was legal. They particularly thought Sam deserved it.

They sold their story to the tabloids for a hundred and fifty thousand dollars, to *What's New* magazine for another seventy-five, and three of the tabloid TV shows for another twenty-five each. All in all, a pretty fair take for the destruction of a family's peace of mind and a young girl's reputation. On her eighteenth birthday, Sam's name was spread everywhere, and none of what they said was pretty. They implied that she was a whore, had slept with half of Hollywood, and that she didn't even know the identity of the father. They supplied the tabloids every detail they'd had and added more. They claimed she'd been on drugs, that she drank, that she had sex with almost anyone, and even propositioned John once or twice when she was eight months' pregnant. It was the kind of story stars have nightmares about, but even more devastating to a girl Sam's age. And because her parents were celebrities, and an argument could be made that Sam was in the public eye because of them, she had absolutely no legal recourse, and they knew it. The tabloids always played it safe, and the destruction of a life or two meant nothing to them. That was their business.

But much to everyone's surprise, she weathered it with dignity and quiet strength. She had been through so much that this almost didn't faze her. She withdrew from public view a bit, took no calls, and seemed oddly peaceful. And as always, her family saw her through, closed ranks and protected her, and so did Jimmy. He was by her side day and night, and the two of them went out for drives or long walks sometimes. They became more inseparable than ever, and he was as strong as she was. They talked about all of it, and what it meant to her. Her feelings were hurt and she was humiliated, and the media was making as much of it as they could, but she knew the truth about herself, and her life, and the baby. She knew better than anyone how stupid she had been with Jean-Luc, but she had never done any of the things the tabloids said she did. And the stories the Whitmans had sold didn't give them a baby. They had done everything they could to torture and humiliate her in revenge for not giving her baby up, but in the end, Sam still had her life, her soul, her integrity, and the baby. She was sorry for them, but after what they did to her, she wasn't sorry she had reneged on the adoption. They were bitter, rotten, vindictive people. The tabloid stories had been going strong for three weeks by the first of August, and her due date was coming closer. The stories about her were still news, and the Whitmans had given another interview, but Sam seemed to be staying calm and close to Jimmy. She had made no comment whatsoever to the press, and Simon had assured her that silence was the wisest course, though often the hardest.

It was the week that Alan came home from Switzerland, and he called Allegra as soon as he got home, hurt that she hadn't told him about Sam sooner. Carmen had called him as soon as the news broke.

"My God, what's been happening? You never said anything when I called you."

"I didn't know what she was going to do. I didn't want to talk about it. It's been kind of rough here. I didn't tell anyone. But now everyone knows, so it's different." *Everyone* was an understatement. The tabloids and TV shows had reached several million people.

"What's she going to do with it?" Alan was sorry for her. She was such a sweet kid and she was so young to have a baby.

"Jeff and I are taking it," Allegra said proudly.

"Talk about jumping the gun. You two aren't even married yet. When's it due?"

"In three days," Allegra said with a laugh. She and Jeff had been running around trying to buy diapers and a crib and tiny little undershirts, and flannel sheets, and washcloths, and bottles and blankets. The equipment was absolutely overwhelming, there was so much of it. It was much more complicated than a wedding. But in some ways a lot more fun, and they were both excited.

And in the midst of it, Jeff was trying to finish his movie, and she was going to the office, trying to settle Bram's estate and take care of all her other clients. She was trying to hire a baby-sitter, just to get her through the wedding and the honeymoon, and then she was also going to take a leave herself, after the wedding if she could, till they all got adjusted.

There was so much to organize. They had put the crib right in the middle of their bedroom. And Jeff had put together a little mobile of sheep and clouds that stood over it. They had musical lambs, and tiny little booties and sweaters, and a mountain of equipment. They had everything. Alan chuckled when she told him all about it. He admitted to them that Carmen was pregnant again too, but they weren't going to tell anyone yet in case she lost it. And she still had another month to do on her picture. They all had their hands full for the moment.

It was the night after Alan had come home, and Jeff and Allegra both had unusually long days, and had gone to bed late and were exhausted. When the phone rang at two A.M., Jeff said that Carmen and Alan were at it again. They'd obviously had a fight and Carmen was calling.

"Don't answer it," Jeff groaned. He needed his sleep desperately, and for once Allegra was tempted to listen to him, but then she thought of her sister.

"What if it's Sam?"

"It can't be," he said miserably. "I'm too tired to have a baby."

In the end, Allegra's conscience won, and she picked it up. It was her mother. Sam's water had broken an hour earlier, and at first nothing had been happening, but all of a sudden she was getting good, hard, regular contractions.

"Are you sure they're not just the fake ones?" Allegra asked nervously, and Jeff groaned.

"I'm too tired for this," he said again, and Allegra laughed and gave him a gentle shove.

"No, you're not. We're having a baby." One day it would be her, waking him up at this hour to have their first child, but for the moment it was Sam, and for them, it was almost as exciting.

"You'd better come," her mother said. "You don't want to miss it." They were already in the hospital, in the labor room, and she was dilating quickly.

"How does she feel?" Allegra asked, worried about her little sister.

"Not too bad," her mother said, still holding the watch she was using to time the contractions. And then she said something that surprised Allegra. "We just called Jimmy."

There was tenderness in her mother's voice, rather than disapproval.

"Are you sure we should?"

"Sam wants him here. He's been coaching her too." And with all she was going through, Blaire felt she had the right to have whomever she wanted with her. She hadn't wanted John Whitman there, and with good reason after all they'd said about her, but oddly enough, she wanted Jimmy.

Before Jeff and Allegra left the house in Malibu, she stood staring at the crib and the mobile for just a moment. By tomorrow, there would be a little person in the crib. It was so exciting it made her smile as they left for the hospital. She had never before realized how much she wanted this baby. It was the most exciting thing that had ever happened to her.

"Exciting, huh?" Jeff said, thinking the same thing, and he put a gentle arm around her. "I'm glad we're doing this." It meant a lot to both of them, even if it was an odd time for them to take on a baby.

"I'm glad too," Allegra said, and then they hurried out to the car, in blue jeans and T-shirts and old sneakers. Allegra was planning to be in the delivery room, and Blaire was too. But when they got to the hospital, Blaire was outside, sitting with Simon.

"What's happening?" Allegra asked, as though a plane were coming in at any moment, and her mother smiled. In some ways, Allegra was less prepared for this than Sam was. Jeff yawned as he sat down next to Simon. They were both half asleep, and their roles seemed the least exciting. All they had to do was remember to tell everyone what a great job they had done when it was over.

"They're checking her," Blaire explained. "She's doing beautifully. It's really getting going now. The nurse thinks it won't take long at all, if she keeps going at this rate."

"Shouldn't we be in there?" Allegra asked, looking worried. She didn't want to let Sam down, or miss the birth of the baby.

"I thought I'd give her a little while alone with Jimmy. They were doing fine together, and he's doing a good job coaching her. I think too many people around will make her panic." They left her alone with him for a while, and then Allegra and her mother tiptoed in to see her. She was sitting up in bed, with wild, frightened eyes, trying to breathe her way through a contraction while

Jimmy talked her through it. He was amazingly calm for an eigh-teen-year-old kid, and when it was over, he gave her ice chips, and mopped her forehead with a cool cloth, as she lay back against the pillows.

"How's it going, Sam?" Allegra asked her gently.

"I don't know," Sam said, looking worried, and clutching for Jimmy's hand. The monitor showed she was having another pain, and they went through the same procedure again, as Allegra watched them. It looked awful to Allegra, but Blaire thought she was doing great, and when the doctor came by a few minutes later, so did he, as he praised her.

"It won't be long," he said cheerfully, patting Sam's leg after he checked her. He was going to deliver the baby right there in the labor bed, when she was ready. "We're halfway there," he said happily, and Sam gave a moan of anguish.

"Halfway . . . I can't do this for much longer." Her eyes filled with tears as she looked at Jimmy.

"You're doing great, Sam," Jimmy whispered, and he didn't look like a boy, he looked like a man, as he held Sam's hand quietly, and waited for the next contraction as he stood at her bedside. Blaire and Allegra felt utterly useless and drifted outside again. Jeff had gone to sleep and was snoring in a chair, and Simon was dozing over a newspaper he'd been reading. The two of them made quite a picture.

"What do you think about Jimmy being so involved with her?" Allegra asked her mother as they strolled down the hall, and stopped to see the babies in the nursery. Some of them were sleeping, but most of them were wailing. Some were newborns, born within the hour, and others were slightly older, very hungry, and waiting for their mothers.

Allegra went to peek at Sam again, and she was sitting on the edge of the bed as Jimmy rubbed her back, sitting just behind her. A nurse was showing them what to do, and he even helped her walk around the room, but she started to cry when the next pain came. Then he lifted her gently back into bed, but she screamed as the pain peaked and he moved her. He was terrific with her, and Allegra was deeply touched by what she saw. And all through the night Sam wrestled with her contractions. At dawn there was still no sign of the baby, but everyone said she was doing great, except Sam, who said she couldn't take anymore. She wanted drugs, she wanted help, she wanted anything. She was clutching Jimmy's arms, and screaming with each contraction, and just when Allegra thought she couldn't take it anymore, the doctor said that Sam could start pushing. Now the real work began, but Sam just looked at them and cried.

"I can't," she said again and again. She was exhausted.

"Yes, you can," Jimmy insisted. "Come on, Sam . . . please . . . you have to do it." They were like two children encouraging each other, except as Blaire watched them she saw something Allegra didn't. These were not two children anymore, they were much more than that. They had grown up overnight. They were a man and a woman. Blaire remembered when her own children had been born, Paddy, and then Allegra, and then the others. It changed your life from that moment on, and the bond you shared with their father. Jimmy was not the baby's father, but he might as well have been. He was totally there for Samantha. And she was unaware of anyone else in the room. The only one she wanted was Jimmy.

They had propped her legs up by then, and she was in horrible pain, begging them to stop, and clutching at Jimmy, while they told her to push and she wouldn't. He helped prop her head and shoulders up then, and finally she began to help them. With Jimmy's help they managed to encourage her, and ever so slowly the baby started moving. Blaire couldn't bear seeing her in so much pain, and she kept leaving the room, as did Allegra. But Jimmy never wavered all night. He was there for her. Shortly before nine, Blaire had just come back into the room again, and everything was frantic. A bassinet was being wheeled in. Two more nurses had arrived, the doctor was bracing her legs for her, and Jimmy was holding her so she could push the baby out. There was a sudden rush of air from Sam, a grunting sound, and she fell back against Jimmy, completely drained, unable to do another thing, and she started to scream again with the next contraction. But this time, no one would allow her to let down, they just kept pushing her until suddenly the room was filled with sound. It was the music of her baby, his little wail, and then a cry, and then her laughter and her tears, mingled with Jimmy's.

"Oh, my God . . . oh, my God . . . He's so beautiful. . . . Is he all right?" Sam was breathless with excitement.

"He's perfect," the doctor told her. Jimmy was completely speechless, but the look in his eyes as he looked down at her said it all. And then, ever so quietly, he took her hand and kissed her.

"I love you, Sam," he whispered. "You were incredible."

"I couldn't have done it without you." She lay back against the pillows and he leaned down beside her as they put the baby next to her, and then she looked up and saw Allegra. She and Jimmy glowed at each other then, and a terrible look passed between them. Allegra and her mother were both in the room by then, and Sam struggled to see them both. Jeff and Simon were there too, admiring the small, healthy boy who was shouting at his mother as loud as he could. It made them all laugh, but Sam looked at Jeff and Allegra, and there was regret in her eyes. She hated to hurt them, but no matter how much she loved them, she knew she had no choice. She had to do this.

"There's something Jimmy and I have to tell you." She took a breath and squeezed his hand. "We got married last week. We're both eighteen, and even if we have to support him all by ourselves, we want to keep the baby. Allegra, I'm so sorry." She started to cry as she touched her sister's hand. She had disappointed so many people. Her parents, the Whitmans, who had wanted to adopt him, and now Allegra and Jeff, but they were looking at her in amazement.

"You want to keep it?" Jeff asked his soon-to-be sister-in-law, and she nodded, unable to say anything more. "That's all right. You worked hard for him," he said, gently patting her hand, and there were tears in his eyes. "We wanted to take him so he would stay in the family, but he belongs with you." He looked at

Jimmy then with a manly smile. "Congratulations." And then he put an arm around Allegra.

"Are you all right with that, Al?" Sam looked at her older sister.

"I think I am," she said sadly. "I think I'm still kind ot stunned by the whole thing." It had all been so much more intense than she expected. "I'm happy for you. I was excited, but I was kind of scared too. It's early for us." But they had wanted him anyway, and giving up the idea of him was an adjustment. Jeff was right though. If at all possible, the baby belonged with his mother. "We'll bring all the stuff we have over to Mom's. You're going to need it." She smiled at them both and there were tears in her eyes too. She had wanted the baby, but a part of her also didn't. Very much like Jeff. They had had mixed emotions, and were trying to do what was best for all of them. Blaire looked at them in disbelief, trying to absorb what had just happened. "No kitchen, a wedding, and now a new baby," she said, lightening the moment, and addressing Sam's announcement. She looked at Jimmy with a slow smile. "And a new son-in-law. I guess we're going to be pretty busy at our house." They would never have turned their back on their daughter, or her son. But she already knew he was worth it.

"I guess so, Mom." Sam smiled, and looked at her baby. He was so beautiful, and she had worked so hard for him.

"You can live with us," Simon said gruffly to the young couple. They'd both be going to the same school in the fall. Sam was thinking of taking the baby with her, for the first few months anyway, so she could nurse him. She and Jimmy had talked about it a lot lately. They were going to try to take some of the same classes.

"Does this mean I can go back to bed now?" Jeff asked with a yawn, and the whole family laughed, and then he looked at his watch. "I guess I missed that part. Time for work."

"You're so silly," Allegra said, "but I love you." They all kissed Sam and Jimmy and the baby, who had no name yet. They were working on it. Sam thought Matthew sounded good with

Mazzoleri. And Blaire realized they were going to have to talk to his mother now that they knew what the two young people had done. They had been very brave, and more than a little foolish, but maybe they could pull it off. Stranger things had happened to other people. Her own grandmother had married at fifteen, and stayed married for seventy-two years to the same man. Maybe Sam would be nearly as lucky.

Allegra drove Jeff to the set, and they talked about not having the baby after all, and how they felt about it.

"Are you very disappointed?" he asked, still trying to sort it all out in his own mind. It had been an emotional night for all of them, and he was worried about Allegra.

"Kind of," she admitted, "but I think part of me is relieved too. I'm not sure yet what I really feel. But I respect Sam's decision." And they both knew it was the right one.

"Neither am I," he confessed, looking sheepish. "I know we'd have loved it, though I'd rather start with our own if we can. But I would have done this for Sam. It never felt right to me for her to give it up for adoption. That just seemed too cruel for all concerned." He had really done it for Allegra and her sister.

Allegra nodded quietly in agreement. And then Jeff looked at her with a broad grin.

"Now we get to try for our own. That could be fun." They smiled as they drove to the far end of town, feeling as though things had turned out right for them. Life had certainly taken some odd turns recently, as it did its little tango.

And in Bel Air, Simon and Blaire had just let themselves into the house. They wandered into their newly mangled kitchen. It was still partially functional, and she made each of them a cup of coffee, and they sat down at the kitchen table. It had been a long night filled with a myriad emotions, and they were both feeling elated, and somewhat drained. It had been difficult for Blaire, watching Sam in so much pain, and they had been ambivalent about the baby. And yet when they saw Sam with him, it all seemed so right. And what they were feeling now was even more confusing. Were they happy or were they sad? Was it a tragedy, as they had first thought, or actually a blessing?

"So what do you think?" Simon asked her with a sigh. "Truthfully, Blaire. Do we approve or not? Just between us." They had already vowed to support Sam and Jimmy in all their efforts.

"I don't know why," she said, rubbing a hand over her eyes and then looking at him again honestly, "and they're so damn young, but I hope it works out for them. The baby is so sweet, no matter how he came into our lives. It's not his fault. And I really like Jimmy. What a good kid he is. He's been wonderful to Sam. This isn't what I'd have wanted for her, if someone had asked me, but maybe in the long run, it will be all right." It was everyone's silent wish for them. And Jimmy had certainly stood by her, both before and while she had the baby. You couldn't have asked for more if he'd been the father. In fact, most men twice his age wouldn't have been half as supportive.

"They're silly kids, getting married like that, without telling us," Simon said, sipping his coffee with a frown. "But you have to give them credit for at least trying to sort this mess out. Jimmy's a nice kid. And the baby is cute too, isn't he?" Simon looked very tender as he remembered their own babies.

"He's adorable," Blaire agreed, and then she smiled sadly. "Do you remember how sweet Scott was when he was born?"

"And Sam," he said wistfully, remembering the wisps of platinum hair and huge dark blue eyes, and then he looked tenderly at Blaire again.

They had come a long way from those memories this year, through no fault of hers. They had just started to drift apart, and he had ventured even farther, but now they both knew that the very fabric of their marriage had been torn. He had thought, stupidly, that she wouldn't notice it if he took some time off. He was still there, officially, but in his heart he had been gone for months. And now he knew how dearly it had cost them.

"I'm sorry, Blaire. I know what a rough year it's been." She didn't answer him at first. She was thinking of the not-so-distant past. She would walk around the house and see photographs sometimes, which reminded her of better days, and just seeing them would catch at her heart. She remembered when he used to look at her like that, when their hugs were tight and their eyes for each other were still excited and alive. Now she felt dead inside. She had never known, never expected, never fathomed, how much he could hurt her. "I've been so stupid," he said in a whisper, with tears in his eyes as he reached out and took her hand. He felt rotten seeing what he had done to her so clearly. Elizabeth had been a breath of new life for him, and she had excited him, but he had never really loved her, not the way he loved Blaire. And he had never wanted her to know about it. It was all so totally wrong. And now it was too late. He could see in the sag of Blaire's shoulders, in the ashes in her eyes when he looked at her, that what they had once shared was gone. It had made her bitter at first, and angry, and frightened. But now she just felt tired, and sad. He could see that. And to him, her sorrow was worse than her anger.

"Those things happen," she said philosophically. They never said Elizabeth's name, but they both knew what they were saying. "I just never expected them to happen to us. That was the hardest part. At first, I just didn't believe it. But after a while, I guess I just figured we were like everyone else, battered, broken, and embittered. It was like losing all our magic," she said, looking at him for the first time in a long time, and he spoke softly and took her hand across the table.

"You never lost your magic, Blaire."

"Yes, I did . . . when we lost ours."

"Maybe we didn't lose it . . . maybe we just misplaced it," he said hopefully, and she smiled at him. She couldn't imagine things ever going back to the way they were. Too much had changed. None of it was on the surface. Superficially, they appeared to be what they had always been, polite, intelligent, creative, happy people with a great family, and a warm, loving life. But inside, she knew different. She had been totally alone for the last year, abandoned for the second time in her life. "It's going to be nice having the baby in the house," he said softly, and Blaire looked sad again and defeated.

"If that's what you want, Simon, you can still have your own. I can't."

"Does that matter to you?" he asked, surprised. He had never even considered that with Elizabeth. Marriage, and certainly children, had never been an issue, just lust and excitement.

But Blaire nodded her head in answer to his question. "Sometimes it matters. Having babies was important to me. Now I feel so old." She had gone through the change of life that year, the same year he had chosen to be unfaithful to her with a woman almost half her age, almost the same age as her older daughter. It hadn't been great timing, to say the least. But there had been nothing she could do to stop it.

"I don't want other children," Simon said firmly. "I've never wanted to be married to anyone but you in my entire life. I never wanted to leave you, Blaire. And I know it was terribly wrong, but I just wanted some time off. I don't know what happened to me, except that I'm old and stupid. She was young, she flattered me, maybe you and I had hit a flat spot in our life. But I've never regretted anything so much in my life." They had paid too high a price for his pleasures. "She doesn't hold a candle to you," he said gently. It was hard to be this honest with her, but he knew it was time. "There's no one in this world who's even half of what you are," he said as he leaned over and kissed her, and for the flicker of an instant, she felt something for him that she hadn't felt all year.

"I'm a grandmother now, you know," she said with a small smile, and she kissed him hesitantly. Just saying it was something of a shock, and they both laughed.

"What does that make me? I feel even older than I am." Elizabeth Coleson had renewed his spirit at first and made him feel half his age. But losing Blaire, emotionally, had suddenly made him feel a thousand years older. "Come on," he said, standing up slowly, and putting an arm around her. "Take this old man upstairs. It's been a long night, I need to lie down." There was mischief in his eyes as he walked up the stairs with her. They were both tired, but he had something in mind for her that he hadn't dared in months, till that morning.

"If you ever do it again . . ." she said, with a spark in her eye he hadn't seen in nearly a year, and it made his heart sing just watching her. Her step was light and her body enticing as she walked quickly upstairs beside him. She turned around at the top to look at him again, and there was murder and mayhem in her eyes. "You won't get away with it twice, Simon Steinberg. There's no mercy for badly behaved old men in this house." But he didn't need to say a word; she could see all his remorse, and love for her, in his eyes. He had come back to her, in spite of everything. It still made her tremble to think she had almost lost him.

"You don't even have to say it," he said to her, as he put his arms around her and kissed her. "It will never happen again."

"No, it won't." She smiled at him as they walked into their bedroom. The sunshine was streaming into the room; it was a beautiful day. "I'll kill you next time." She said it softly. But more likely, she knew it would kill her if she lost him.

"Come here," he said, sounding gruff and sexy. They hadn't made love in months, and he could barely wait to go to bed with her now. They bounced onto the bed like two kids, and she was laughing at him, and then suddenly he was kissing her, and she was remembering everything she had tried so hard to forget about him. How she loved him, how sexy he was, and how much fun they had together. She had never thought she could trust him again, or even love him, but as they lay in the sunshine, on the day their first grandchild was born, they both discovered with relief that nothing had been lost. If anything, their love for each other had grown, and they knew they'd been lucky, and Sam's tiny newborn boy had blessed them.

CHAPTER 20

As August unfurled, all the important things in their lives seemed to be happening the way they were meant to. Jeff's movie was going beautifully. Carmen was still shooting, and behaving herself, and her pregnancy had caused no problems, though Alan managed to show up every time they shot a love scene, and the director had called Allegra and was upset about it. But both movies were going well. And Allegra was helping Jeannie Morrison sell their house in Beverly Hills, and move to their ranch in Colorado. She wanted to get as far away as she could, and she wanted to complete the move before the kids started school in September. They still had bodyguards around the clock, but it appeared that the event that had shattered their lives had been the disturbed, passionate gesture of one random gunman. It had inspired a great outcry among the celebrities in L.A., about the insanity of the public, and the limited protection that was available, given our laws. But Jeannie was beyond lobbying or making speeches. She just wanted to get out of the limelight, and disappear with her children.

Allegra felt terrible for them, and there was to be a memorial concert for Bram in September. It was scheduled for just after her wedding, and she and Jeff had talked about delaying their honeymoon, but Allegra finally realized that she had to understand now where to draw the line. She called and told Jeannie she and Jeff would be on their honeymoon. She understood perfectly—Allegra had already done far too much for them, and she had always been wonderful to Bram.

Sam's baby, Matthew Simon Mazzoleri, was everyone's pride and joy, and he was getting fatter every day. Sam was nursing him, and Jimmy took a thousand photographs and videos of them at all times, having baths, sleeping, at the pool, on the lawn. The baby went everywhere with them, and within two weeks, Sam looked like her old self. She had even regained her slim figure.

The Whitmans were still selling disgruntled stories to the tabloids, and there was another interview on TV with them, after it had been announced that Matthew had been born "to Mr. and Mrs. James Mazzoleri (Samantha Steinberg), a son, Matthew Simon, on August fourth, at Cedars-Sinai, eight pounds, one ounce." The announcements generally included that Mrs. Mazzoleri was the daughter of Simon Steinberg and Blaire Scott. There was a cute picture of Sam and Jimmy and the baby in one L.A. paper, and George Christy mentioned them in the *Hollywood Reporter*, in his column "The Good Life."

The Steinbergs had also had a long meeting with Mrs. Mazzoleri. Although she was somewhat in shock over what Jimmy had done, marrying Sam without telling anyone, she said it was fairly typical of him to try to resolve things by himself. Ever since her husband died, Jimmy had been invaluable to her, but she was worried about what the Steinbergs' expectations of him would be. She wanted him to go to UCLA as planned, but so did they. Blaire and Simon had given them their guest cottage, and it was perfect for them. They would both go to school in the fall, and Simon said he was more than willing to support them both until they finished school. After that, like all his other children, they were on their own. Blaire had already asked her housekeeper to help take care of the baby in the daytime, when they went to college in the fall, and they'd have to work out the rest of it. Mrs. Mazzoleri was very grateful to them for all their help. But on the other hand, Simon said, her son had been fantastic to Sam. And in spite of their age, in the long run, maybe it would all work out.

Things between Simon and Blaire had improved immeasurably. In fact, it was like a honeymoon, now that Sam was living in the guest cottage with Jimmy and little Matt, and her parents were alone in the house. They were surprised, and embarrassed, by how much they enjoyed it.

They had forgotten what it was like to be alone anywhere, and they rapidly established a policy that the kids had to call before they dropped over at the main house. And whenever they did, Simon was amazed at how rapidly they were engulfed in utter chaos: baby seats, high chairs, Portacribs, disposable diapers. The thousand things they needed for Matt seemed to be everywhere; Sam was nursing in every room; and Jimmy was like a big, gangly kid, dashing around all over the house. Simon set up a new basketball net for him in the backyard, and they went out and shot baskets sometimes, just for fun, and to let off some steam and talk. He was pleased by how bright Jimmy was, how determined to get through school and make something of himself. He was definite about going to law school like his dad, and he was trying to talk Sam into going as well. The Steinbergs were not only pleased, but impressed by his devotion as a husband.

The only major upheaval in the house was still the construction everywhere. Dozens of gardeners attacked the backyard every day, and in the kitchen, you could still cook, but they were pulling out all the old tile, and rewiring the ceiling.

The only terrifying thing was that the wedding was only two weeks away. The garden was nowhere near complete, the bridesmaids hadn't had their dresses fitted yet, and Allegra's hadn't even arrived. She was hysterical about that, and a thousand other details, and she tried talking to Jeff about it at night, and he was just too tired. He was trying to finish his movie in the next ten days. He was irritable, and often snapped at her, but the tension on the set was driving him crazy.

"Look, Allegra, I know . . . but can we talk about it some other time?" He seemed to be talking through clenched teeth most of the time. And Delilah Williams was calling them at home day and night, and driving him even more insane than his movie. It had taken them six months to get Carmen and Alan trained, and now Delilah was calling at eleven o'clock at night, to discuss a new "twist" to the cake, or a fabulous little "notion" she'd had for the flowers and the bridesmaids' bouquets. Jeff and Allegra both wanted to kill her.

It had been two weeks of hell for them, and total stress when their phone rang, as usual, late one night. Allegra figured it was probably Delilah again, complaining that Carmen hadn't tried on her dress, and Allegra was going to have to remind her that she'd do it as soon as the picture wrapped. Instead, when she picked up the phone, it was a familiar voice, but at first she didn't register who it was. It was her father, Charles Stanton. He was calling from Boston, in response to the letter she had sent him months before, and he had never answered, inviting him to her wedding.

"Are you still getting married?" he asked cautiously, after asking her how she was. It had been seven years since they last spoke or she'd seen him.

"Of course." Just listening to him, she felt her whole body go tense. Jeff had just walked into the room, and when he saw her face, he couldn't help wondering who had called her. For an odd instant, he wondered if it was Brandon. He had sent her a little note a few weeks before, implying that he would have married her eventually, and making a point of telling her that he'd finally divorced Joanie. He even had the nerve to tell her to call him for lunch sometime, and after showing it to Jeff, she had tossed it in the garbage.

"Something wrong?" he asked, concerned, but she shook her head, and he went back to do some work in his office.

"Do you still want me to come out?" her father asked. She didn't remember asking him, but she knew she probably had in her letter. She thought she had just told him she was getting married.

"I don't imagine it would mean anything to you," she said, explaining her letter to him. "It's not as though we have much contact with each other anymore." It was partially a reproach, and in part just a statement.

"You're still my daughter, Allegra. I'm taking a little time off here, and I was thinking about it the other day. If you'd like me to, I could come out for your wedding." She didn't "like him to," and she couldn't see the point of it, but she had asked him almost three months before. She wished she hadn't. She wished she had never told him at all. And she wanted to ask why he wanted to come to her wedding now. After all these years, after all his criticism of them, all his rejection of her, what difference did it make if she was getting married?

"You're sure it's not too much trouble?" she said awkwardly, feeling years drop away from her. He always made her feel like the rejected child she had been.

"Not at all. It's not every day I get the opportunity to walk my daughter down the aisle. After all, you're my only child." As she listened to him, her mouth almost dropped open. What had she said to him? How could he possibly have interpreted it that way? She had no intention of walking down the aisle with him. He had never been there for her. Ever. And she was walking down the aisle with Simon, who had been.

"I . . . uh . . ." Words failed her, and she couldn't bring herself to tell him that she didn't expect him to walk her down the aisle, but before she could say anything, he told her that he'd be arriving from Boston sometime Friday afternoon, the day of the rehearsal dinner. He was going to stay at the Bel Air. "Shit," she muttered to herself as she hung up, and dialed her mother frantically. The whole wedding ordeal had been an agony and she couldn't believe what had just happened. She had two fathers expecting to walk her down the aisle, one of whom she hated.

Simon answered the phone on the second ring, and he sounded strangely calm. Allegra knew that voice, and it usually meant something was seriously wrong, but she had had her own problems that night, and she didn't pick up on it. She just hastily asked to talk to her mother.

"She's busy just now," he said very quietly. "Can she call you back?"

"No. I need to talk to her right now."

"Allie, she can't," he said, sounding firm, and then suddenly she noticed the tone of his voice. It was scary.

"Is something wrong, Dad? Is she sick?" That was all she needed now, her mother gravely ill before this nightmare wedding they'd forced on her, with that freak, Delilah, flapping around instead of her mother. "Where is she?"

"She's right here," he said, patting his wife's arm. "She's a little upset," he said gently. She'd been crying for the last hour, and he raised an eyebrow at her, asking if it was all right to tell, and she nodded. It would be easier, in fact, for him to tell them all. "We just got a call from Tony Garcia at the network an hour ago. They're going to cancel your mother's show. They're going to do a big finale and run it in a few weeks, and then they're off the air." After nearly ten years, it was a huge blow to Blaire. She felt as though she had lost an old friend, and she had been crying since she heard it.

"Poor Mom," Allegra said. "How's she taking it?"

"Pretty hard." Simon was honest.

"Can I talk to her?" she asked hesitantly, but when he consulted with Blaire, she said she'd call Allegra later.

Allegra hung up, looking pensive, and thinking of her mother. She had worked so hard, and had had so many victories with that show. It had been a real accomplishment for a long time, and now it was over. She could just imagine how her mother felt, and her heart went out to her.

"Something wrong?" Jeff had drifted by and seen the look on her face. She looked like she'd had bad news, and he stopped to ask her about it.

"They just canceled my mother's show." It was a somber announcement, and in some ways it hadn't sunk in yet. *Buddies* was so much a part of her mother's life, she couldn't even imagine her without it. And now she would have to rush to make the last episode. It was terrible timing, with Allegra's wedding.

"I'm sorry to hear that," Jeff said sympathetically. "She's looked preoccupied for a while; I wonder if she knew."

"It's funny," Allegra said. "I thought she looked better for the past few weeks." And in fact she had, since her rapprochement with Simon. She seemed happier and less distracted. "Maybe she wasn't feeling well. Anyway, Dad says she's really taking it hard. Maybe I should go over to see her." And then she told him about the call from her father, about his unexpected appearance at her wedding. She hadn't even expected to hear from him anymore. She had forgotten all about her letter. "He's actually expecting to walk me down the aisle. Can you believe that? After all these years, he really thinks I'd let him do that. He must think I'm incredibly stupid."

"Maybe he thinks that's what you expect of him. Maybe he doesn't know how to act with you anymore either. It could be that he's changed. You should give him a chance, and at least talk to him while he's out here." Like Simon, Jeff always tried to be fair, but Allegra was outraged by his suggestion.

"Are you kidding? When do you think I'm going to have time for a talk like that, two days before our wedding?"

"Maybe it's worth it for you to make time. He had a major impact on your life, Allegra." And in a way, on their marriage. Jeff thought acknowledging that was important.

"It's not worth my while even seeing him, Jeff. I'm sorry I ever wrote him." She was steaming at Jeff for suggesting she should give him a chance, and at her father for being so presumptuous.

"You're awfully hard on the guy," Jeff said quietly. "He is coming out, and you invited him. It sounds like he's trying."

"Trying to do what? It's too late anyway. I'm thirty years old, and I don't need a father."

"You must, or you wouldn't have written to him in the first place. Don't you think it's time you resolved things between you? I think this is as good a time as any, kind of an end and a beginning."

"You don't know anything about it," she exploded at him,

storming across the room as she paced. She couldn't believe he was telling her to give her father a chance, after he'd always been a bastard to her. "You have no idea what it was like after my brother died, the way he drank, the way he slapped my mother around, the way he treated us after we left and came to California. He never forgave my mother for leaving him, and he took it out on me all my life. He hated me. He was probably sorry I didn't die instead of Patrick. Paddy would probably have been a doctor like him." She was sobbing as he came to her, all her fears and inadequacies and terrors hanging all over her, like laundry on a clothesline.

"Maybe that's what you need to talk to him about," Jeff suggested gently as he approached her. "What was he like *before* your brother died, if you can remember?"

"Okay, but he was always kind of cold, and he was very busy. He reminds me a lot of your mother, unable to open up and reach out and relate to anyone else, not very human," she said candidly, and then looked at him in embarrassment. Although they both acknowledged that the weekend in Southampton had been horrible, she had never openly criticized his mother to him.

"What's all that supposed to mean? My mother is very reserved, but she's perfectly human, Allegra." He sounded chilly.

"I'm sure she is." Allegra was trying to back off, but she was annoyed that he had taken her father's part, and was so willing to be compassionate toward him. "Except if you're Jewish," she added hastily, and Jeff suddenly backed away from her as though she were radioactive.

"That's a rotten thing to say about her. The poor woman is seventy-one years old, and she's a product of another generation."

"The same generation that put the Jews in Auschwitz. I didn't exactly feel like she was a warm and caring person while we were there. And what exactly would she have said if you hadn't told her my 'real' name is Stanton, and not Steinberg? You know, that was a pretty shitty thing to do. Downright cowardly in fact."

She glared at him from across the room, and he was trembling with rage over the things she had said about his mother.

"So is refusing to talk to your father. The poor guy has probably paid his dues for the last twenty years. He lost a son too, not just your mother. She's had other kids, she has another life, another family, another husband. What has he got? According to you, he has absolutely nothing."

"Why are you so fucking sympathetic to him, for chrissake? Maybe all he deserves is nothing. Maybe it was his fault Paddy died. Maybe if he hadn't been treating him himself, or wasn't such a drunk, maybe he could have saved him."

"Is that what you think?" He looked appalled. They were the demons that had trailed her for twenty years, dancing all over their living room, and even she looked frightened. "You think he killed your brother?" He looked horrified. It was a terrible thing to say about anyone, especially her father.

"I don't know what I think," she said hoarsely, but he was still bristling. He hardly recognized her in the things she had said that night and he didn't like her. It was the first real fight they'd ever had, and it was a lulu. It was almost worthy of Carmen and Alan.

"I think you owe me an apology for the things you said about my mother. She never did anything to hurt you. She was just shy when she met you."

"*Shy?*" Allegra screamed at him from across the room again. "You call that *shy?* I call it vicious."

"She was *never* vicious to you!" He was shouting now too, and neither of them liked it.

"She hates Jews!" was the only retort Allegra could come up with.

"You're not Jewish, so what do you care?" He threw back at her ineptly.

She slammed out of the house, and got into her car. She didn't know where she was going, but she knew she wanted to get away from him, and as far as she was concerned, he could take his wedding and stuff it. She wasn't going to marry him if he was the last human being alive, no matter who organized the wedding, or who walked her down the aisle. They could have the whole god-damn mess for all she cared.

She drove down the Pacific Coast Highway going eighty-five and was at her parents' house in forty minutes. She opened the front door with her key, forgetting their new rule to call them first, and she slammed the front door so hard she almost broke the picture window. Her parents were sitting in the living room, and her mother jumped when she heard her.

"Good God, what happened to you?" Blaire looked at her. She looked like a wild, rumpled mess. She was wearing shorts and a T-shirt, bare feet, and she had her hair piled high on her head and stuck through with a pencil. "Are you all right?"

"No, I'm not," Allegra said, looking like a madwoman. "I'm canceling the wedding."

"Now?" Her mother asked, horrified. "It's less than two weeks away. What happened?"

"I hate him."

Simon turned away to conceal a smile, and her mother stared at her, unable to believe she would do this. All she could think of now were the endless preparations. All for nothing. "Did you have an argument?"

"That's beside the point. His mother is a monster, and he thinks I really ought to give Charles Stanton a chance after all these years. 'The poor man has had so many problems.' That's disgusting." She looked irate as she said it.

"How did Charles get into this?" Blaire looked totally confused. She hadn't seen him herself in seven years, and he hadn't crossed her mind since she'd told Allegra to at least invite him to the wedding.

"He called tonight. He thinks he's walking me down the aisle. Can you beat that? He wants to come to my wedding."

"That's all right, dear," her mother said calmly, forgetting her own woes and disappointments, and concentrating on her daughter. "Maybe Jeff is right. Maybe it's time to make peace with him." But Allegra only got angrier when she heard it.

"Are you all nuts? The man abandoned me emotionally twenty-five years ago and you all think we should be pals? Are you all out of your minds?"

"No. But it's not worth hating him for all these years, Allegra," she said wisely. "There were a lot of things back then that you weren't old enough to understand, about grief, and what happened to him. He just couldn't handle it when Paddy died. He cracked for a while. I think he actually lost his mind, partially—emotionally in any case. And I'm not sure he ever completely regained it. I'm sure he's quite sane technically, or at least I assume he is. But he was never able to get the pieces put back together after that, to have a personal life, or maybe not until now. But you ought to at least listen to what he has to say." As her mother spoke to her, there was the insistent sound of their doorbell. Simon looked surprised and went to answer it. It was like living in an airport, or on a sitcom. But much to everyone's amazement, it was Jeff, and he looked almost as disheveled and angry as Allegra.

"How dare you walk out on me like that!" he shouted at her, and Simon and Blaire exchanged a look, and walked quietly upstairs. Allegra and Jeff were so furious, they never even noticed that her parents had left, and they stood in the living room and shouted at each other for an hour, as Blaire tiptoed around upstairs wondering if they were still going to have a wedding.

"Well, they certainly sound well matched," Simon said with a small smile. It was more excitement than they'd seen in their house in years, if ever. And a few minutes later, Samantha called. With the windows open, on a warm night, they could hear Jeff and Allegra's argument all the way to the guest house.

"Are you and Mom having some kind of a fight?" she asked, sounding worried. She had just nursed Matt and put him back to bed, and she had never heard so much fighting in her life. Jimmy thought she had better call to make sure they were all right, and Simon laughed at the question.

"No, but your sister is," he said simply.

"With Mom?" Sam looked surprised. Allegra had never fought with their mother like that, or with anyone for that matter.

"No, with your future brother-in-law, that is, if the wedding's still on." He couldn't help but laugh. It was a soap opera of the first order. "We'll ask them when it's all over."

"When did they get here?" Sam was intrigued by what was happening, but the fight was still raging on from what they could all hear. The floodgates had finally opened. They had lived with tension for months, with clients, and movies and screenplays; Allegra had dealt with death threats and miscarriages, and one of her favorite clients being gunned down and murdered, her sister's pregnancy, and nearly giving the baby up, and then nearly adopting it herself, and then the disappointment of giving it back to Sam, and all the stress of getting married, and meeting her new mother-in-law, and all the expectations and hopes and plans that went with getting married. It was enough to make anyone hysterical, and Jeff and Allegra certainly sounded as though they both were.

"They got here a little while ago. I'm sure they'll leave soon, if they survive," he said, and a little while later, he and Blaire went down to see if they could lend a hand and stop the war before there were no survivors. Allegra was crying softly in the living room by then, and Jeff was looking as though he wanted to kill someone or die, whichever happened first. This was clearly not the moment to ask them if they were still getting married. There was no question that both of them were ready to toss the whole wedding right out the window.

"How are you two doing down here?" Simon asked calmly, pouring four glasses of wine, and handing the first to Jeff, who looked as though he needed it very badly. He took it with a nod, and then sat down, far across the room from Allegra.

"We're fine," she said between sobs, in answer to her father's question.

"I'm not sure I believe you," he said, and Blaire went and sat next to her. She had the best suggestion anyone had made to them in months.

"I think you two need to get away for the weekend. This may be your last chance before the wedding." She looked at Jeff. "I think if they can spare you from the set for two days, you ought to try." He nodded, looking at her. Even he knew it was a wise suggestion.

"I was sorry to hear about the show," he said sympatheti-cally, and then glanced over at Allegra.

"So am I, Mom," she said, and blew her nose again. No one had ever been as unfair to her as Jeff had just been. He said she was being rude about his mother, and she wasn't giving her father a chance, and it all seemed like the end of the world to Allegra. That and having to finish up everything on her desk, and get everything done before their wedding. It was almost inhuman.

"Thank you," Blaire said quietly. She had done her share of crying that night too, but this was so much more real to her. She knew it wasn't serious, but it was their lives, not just a lot of pretend nonsense on television. Fortunately, she knew the differ-ence.

"I think your mom's right," Jeff said as he finished the wine. "Maybe we need to get away for the weekend." Allegra wanted to tell him she wouldn't go anywhere with him, not after the things he'd said to her, but she didn't dare do that in front of her par-ents. Instead, she agreed to go away with him, to Santa Barbara, for just two days. At Simon's suggestion they were going to stay at San Ysidro.

It took another two hours, but they left finally, in separate cars, with their own thoughts and fears and regrets and terrors. Allegra thought about him all the way home, and how cold his mother had been to her. She thought of her own father too, and the anguish caused by him over the years, but she thought too of how different Simon had been, and how different Jeff was. None of it looked quite as monumental when she got back to Malibu and Jeff apologized for the things he'd said about her. He hadn't really meant to say most of those things, but he was so upset about what she'd said, and so wound up over the end of his movie. They said a thousand things to each other that night, but mostly they just lay in bed and talked, and laughed at how stupid they had been and apologized for the vicious things they'd said. When it was all said and done, they lay in each other's arms and slept, and in Bel Air, Simon and Blaire went to bed too, still awake and talking about them.

"I'm not so sure I'd want to be that young again," Blaire whispered to Simon. They had talked about them for hours after they left, and how frantic both of them had been. It had been exhausting just watching and listening to them.

"It might be fun to get that wound up and stomp around and scream. Allegra certainly got excited anyway. You never shouted at me like that." He looked amused and she laughed.

"Is that a complaint? I could learn, I guess. I've got lots of time on my hands now." She still felt bad about that. She was going to miss her show so much, and she didn't know what to do now. She didn't want to just stay home and take care of her grandchild. She was fifty-five, and there was still plenty of life in her, but she no longer had a job, except for one last episode. She still couldn't believe it.

"I had an idea tonight. I don't know what you'd think of it," he said pensively, as they lay side by side in the dark, comfortable again. The specter of Elizabeth Coleson had finally disappeared between them. He rolled over on his side and propped himself up on one elbow so he could look at her in the moonlight. "I've been wanting to add a coproducer to my staff for a while. I'm tired of doing everything alone. I get all the glory, but it drives me crazy sometimes, and you're so much better on the creative details than I am. I'm better at the broad strokes. What do you say we try a collaboration on my next picture? Maybe Jeff's? What do you think of that?" She thought about it and smiled at him.

"What are we calling it? *Family Business*?" She thought he was being charitable, or just kidding.

"I'm serious. I've wanted to do something like that for years, but you never had the time. You're too good for television any- way. Why don't you at least try it?" He loved the idea of working with her. They were a good team in many ways, and their professional skills were compatible. She was smiling at him, thinking about it.

"We could try, I suppose. I don't have anything else to do. I'll be free in three weeks, right after Allegra's wedding." She actually liked the idea, and she kissed her husband to thank him.

"Is the wedding still on, by the way?" he teased. "I didn't dare ask them before they left."

"I hope so," Blaire said with a sigh, as she lay down again. She liked the idea of working with Simon.

"So what do you think?" He was prodding her for an answer.

"I'll have to call my agent," she said coyly, and he laughed.

"You Hollywood types, you're all the same. Go ahead, call your agent. I'm calling my attorney." He chuckled and kissed her on the neck, and she snuggled closer to him. For a day that had been disastrous for a while, it had taken a definite turn by the end of it. She was still sad to lose her show, but the idea of a partnership with Simon had a lot of appeal to her. She wanted to talk to Allegra about it in the morning. And when she turned to Simon again, he was sound asleep. It was very late, and they'd had a long night, and a lot of excitement. She smiled to herself, looking at him. He was such a good man, and after all the pain he'd caused her in the past year, she felt as though she'd found him again, and maybe some of the pain had been worth it.

CHAPTER 21

A llegra thought that her parents working together was a great
idea, particularly on her husband's movie.

"Talk about keeping it in the family," she said, and laughed.
"Can I have a starring role?" she teased her mother.

She talked about it after she and Jeff got back from San
Ysidro, and by then everything had calmed down with them
again. Everything had returned to normal, as normal as it was
going to be with her wedding in six days. As Delilah Williams
said, the final countdown had started.

The dress had come, the hats had finally arrived, the veil had
been made. And the landscape gardener swore that the garden
would be finished by the weekend.

Both of Allegra's bridesmaids who were coming from out of
town were arriving in two days, one from London, the other from
New York. Jeff's mother was arriving the day after that, and
staying at the Bel Air. And worse yet, her father was arriving on
Friday.

"Do you think we'll survive it, Mom?" she asked her
mother, looking terrified. She was trying to finish out the week at
work, and Jeff was wrapping his movie on Wednesday. It was all
very tightly scheduled, and poised like a house of cards. She had
even sold her house, and the closing was in two days. And wherever she looked, there were a thousand details.

After her bridesmaids arrived on Tuesday night, they were having a last-minute fitting of the dresses on Wednesday morning and any necessary adjustments could be made. But Nancy and Jessica had willingly supplied their sizes, and there was no reason to think there would be a problem.

"I'm so scared," Allegra whispered to Blaire as she visited her on Monday night. Jeff was working late, and she had come to see Sam and the baby.

"Of what, sweetheart?" Her mother was trying to calm her.

"Of everything. What if it doesn't work, like you and . . . you know . . . Charles . . . ?" Her original father. She refused to call him "Daddy."

"It can happen, but those circumstances were very unusual and I was much younger than you are when we got married. You and Jeff are a lot smarter than we were and you're going to be just fine. I know it." They were intelligent and young, and they had entered into it with much thought. Dr. Green felt really good about the way Allegra was handling all her old fears and feelings. But there were still no guarantees, they could lose their jobs, their lives, their limbs, their children could die, as her mother's had, their life's dreams could be shattered by a bolt of lightning at any moment. "There are no guarantees in life. You just have to do your best, and be there for each other no matter what," Blaire said wisely, as she smiled at Allegra.

"Yeah, and never run out of Häagen-Dazs or frozen pizza," Sam added her marital advice. Feeding Jimmy was like keeping the Green Bay Packers supplied, but she had never been as happy in her life, and they were loving the baby. He was asleep in her arms, and he nursed all the time. He was a month old and he weighed twelve pounds. And Sam looked as though she had been born for the life that she was leading. She loved being with Jimmy all the time, and he was wonderful at helping her with the baby. His little sisters came to visit them all the time, and they played in the Steinbergs' backyard. All of a sudden, Blaire felt as though she had a house full of children. It was like turning the clock back for her, except that in a nice way, it also wasn't. She and Simon had their own life, and they were free for the first time in years, except when they wanted to see Jimmy and Sam, or Allegra came by, or Scott came back from Stanford, which was rare now. They had time for each other; they were making plans for their new collaboration as soon as she did her last show. They were even talking about going to Europe for a while before his next movie. It was the most time they'd had for each other in years, and Simon really enjoyed it. He even came home for lunch now sometimes, and they seemed to spend more time in bed than they ever had when they were younger.

"Maybe getting old *isn't* so bad," Blaire had teased him only that morning, as he pulled her out of the shower and dragged her back to bed to make love, complaining that she had gotten up too fast that morning. She had still been dripping wet, and her hair was piled on top of her head. He had left for the office afterward, half an hour late for an appointment.

But they were at the end, or getting closer to it. Allegra and Jeff were all the way at the beginning, like Jimmy and Sam, when love was still young, and there were mountains to be climbed, before children, before real life, before victories and defeats, and all the things that make you who you are. In some ways Blaire envied them; in other ways she didn't. She had already been there, and she liked the valleys now. The mountains had gotten just a little bit too rugged.

"Just relax and try to get through this week," was the best advice Blaire could give her. "This is probably the hardest part."

"I'm glad I didn't have to do all this stuff." Sam laughed, putting Matthew back on her breast again, and gently touching his velvety cheek with her finger. But Blaire was still sorry that Sam had missed it. She had skipped right over the window dressing, and gone for the brass ring. But for the moment, it looked like she had a good hold on it. And poor Allegra was still riding the carousel, and her head was spinning.

Both of her bridesmaids called her when they got in on Tuesday night. They were both staying at the Bel Air, and Allegra had had Alice send flowers to their rooms, and magazines and chocolates. Their dresses were hanging in the closet, waiting for them, along with beige lace shoes in the sizes that Allegra had been given. Absolutely every last detail was in order.

Allegra was meeting them for lunch at the hotel on Wednesday with the fitter. She had booked an enormous suite and she was going to bring Sam. Carmen was meeting them there for her fitting too. And Allegra had to go to the title company before that to sign papers for the sale of her house. It was truly a whirlwind week. She was dizzy from all that she was trying to accomplish.

The best part of it was that she hadn't seen Nancy Towers in five years, when she moved to New York and then to London, or Jessica Farnsworth since law school. It had been a long time, but they had been dear friends, and it meant something to her to have them take part in her wedding.

When Allegra got to the hotel with Sam, she was helping her carry Matthew's bag, and a swing that would keep him happy while they tried on their dresses and had lunch. Allegra had reserved a big suite so they'd have privacy and could get everything done. The hairdresser wanted to meet them too, and he was bringing the makeup artist with him, and there were going to be a few informal pictures.

Blaire had decided not to come. She said she didn't want to intrude on the younger women. And no amount of arguing with her would persuade her, even though Delilah Williams said she really "had" to come. She wanted to meet *all* the girls, not just one or two of them, and see how divine they looked in their pretty dresses. Allegra had made such a good choice with the beige lace, and since they obviously all had such good figures, the fitting wasn't going to be a problem.

But, evidently, the gods had been drinking that day. When Sam and Allegra arrived, first the suite wasn't ready, and then it started to rain. They got soaked as they ran past the swans, trying to juggle all of Matthew's belongings and entertainment. Carmen was already there waiting for them. She was drinking Coke, nibbling on a box of chocolates, and talking to her agent on the phone. She was swinging one long leg over the other in a legendary pose, but as soon as she stood up, Allegra knew they were going to have a problem. She hadn't seen Carmen in a month, and she was only two and a half months' pregnant, but Allegra thought she must be having twins. She had doubled the size of her waist, and her hips were even bigger than that. She had to be wearing a size twelve dress. Allegra cringed, remembering the size of the dress they had ordered for her.

"What happened to you?" Allegra said in an undertone. They were good enough friends that she could be honest. "How much weight have you gained?"

"Twenty pounds," Carmen said without a blink. "Thank God, we finished the movie."

"How could you gain so much so fast? Sam only gained twenty-five the whole time," Allegra scolded. There was no way they were going to get her into the dress. They'd have to leave it open and have her whole behind hanging out, and there certainly seemed to be a lot of that. She was going to be very sorry later. But she was so happy to be pregnant again, she was doing nothing but staying home and sleeping and eating.

"Your sister is only ten years old," she hissed back. "No wonder she weighs eighty pounds."

"She has a little self-control," Allegra clucked, and then they all sat around and admired Matthew.

In the end, Sam tried her dress on first, and she had actually lost weight since before she got pregnant. She was five nine and weighed a hundred and twelve pounds, and the zipper started up at full speed, and then stopped halfway up her back, and it was easy to see why. Nobody had taken into account the fact that she was nursing.

"What size bra are you wearing these days?" Allegra asked, looking panicked.

"Thirty-eight D," she said proudly.

"Oh, my God, do they make them that size?" her sister asked, and Carmen rolled her eyes.

"I can hardly wait," Carmen said cheerfully.

"Didn't it occur to you that maybe you should tell me?"

Allegra asked her sister. "You went from a thirty-two A to a thirty-eight D and you didn't think it would make any difference?"

"I forgot." Sam apologized, but the fitter said she could take enough fabric from elsewhere to make up for it. Carmen's was another matter. They frantically called Valentino, and they said they had one more dress, in a size fourteen. Would that be too large?

"I'm afraid not," Allegra said with a sigh of relief, ready to kill Carmen. Two down, and two to go, and with that, Nancy Towers arrived, all excited to see her again. Nancy had gotten married and divorced, was thinking of moving back to New York, was trying to start a magazine, had dyed her hair, and then dyed it back, and had been having an affair with a divine man in Munich. She had a very international life, and Allegra was exhausted by the time she'd heard it all, or most of it, and there always seemed to be more. But there was also more of her than there had once been. She had claimed to wear a four, and was more like a ten now. She had gotten a little bit roly-poly. But the dress Carmen had outgrown could be altered to fit her, and they were saved once again from the jaws of disaster.

"I don't think my nerves are going to hold out," Allegra said as she sat down and looked at Sam.

"Relax, you're going to be fine," her suddenly mature sister said calmly as she held her baby.

"You sound just like Mom." Allegra smiled, thinking she even looked like Blaire, and she leaned over and kissed her. "You're a good kid. Did I ever tell you that?" She'd felt closer to her ever since the birth of the baby.

"Not lately, but I figured it out. You're a pretty terrific older sister." And then she lowered her voice. "But your friends are getting a little fat." The two sisters laughed, and then Jessica arrived, but no one had warned Allegra of how much her life had changed in the past five or six years. She arrived wearing short hair, no makeup, and a beautiful Armani suit she had bought in Milan. She worked in publishing, but she had a lot of friends in fashion, and she had a spare, austere look that was very fashion-able in Europe and on the East Coast, but there was more to it than that. There was a quality about Jessica that had never been there before, and Allegra couldn't help noticing that Jessica had glanced with particular interest at Carmen. And then, as she looked at her more carefully, Allegra realized what had changed since they last met. She was openly gay now, when for years she had been in the closet.

Jessica, now "Jess," talked about her lover over lunch. She talked about her life, and the fact that she felt that the lesbian movement had gained momentum in the West, but not enough in the East. Carmen just stared at her and told her there were no lesbians in Portland.

"Well, there sure are in London," Nancy said, laughing. She laughed at everything and everyone. She had a great time wher-ever she was, even if she did drink a little too much. But she was the life of the party.

"Have you ever had a homosexual experience?" Jess asked Nancy casually, and Nancy paused, thinking about it, while Car-men blushed, and Sam looked pointedly at her older sister, who was trying to remain calm. She was convinced now that she was never going to survive her wedding.

"Actually," Nancy finally answered Jess. "I don't recall that I have," she said nonchalantly.

"Oh, you'd remember it." And then Jessica agreed to try the dress. She took off her shirt and the Armani suit, and she was wearing silk Jockey shorts, and nothing else, and Allegra had to admit that she had a fabulous body. But it was not one that appealed to her, and just knowing what her interests were made Allegra faintly uncomfortable. And later as the waiter poured champagne, Jessica teased her about making a big mistake mar-rying a man, she should have been marrying a woman. She no-ticed then that Jess was wearing a narrow gold wedding band, and she explained that she'd lived with the same woman for two years now. She was a fashion designer from Japan, and they traveled all over Europe and the Far East whenever they got the chance, for pleasure and business. She led an interesting life, but had made some very different choices from Allegra.

But at least the dress fit, and when Delilah arrived, everything appeared to be in fairly good order. The shoes fit almost comfortably, the hats were fine, the photographer took some informal pictures, and by then Nancy had had a little too much to drink, and Jess had decided to play games and, more for the fun of it, appeared to be in hot pursuit of Carmen.

"I'm pregnant, for God's sake," she snapped, when Jess put a tantalizing finger down her neck as a joke, but Carmen was not amused by it.

"It's all right, I don't mind," Jess said, and a little while later she was chatting seriously to Sam and holding the baby. She was a nice woman, and over the past several years she had come out of the closet, and she was completely unashamed of who she was, and at times she was unabashedly outrageous. In some ways, Allegra still loved that about her, but she needed to readjust her thinking about her a little.

"Why didn't you tell me?" Allegra asked, later that afternoon.

"I don't know. I didn't know you that well anymore. It's a hard thing to explain sometimes. I didn't think you'd understand."

"I probably wouldn't have," Allegra said honestly. And after that, they talked about the impact of AIDS on our culture, and all the friends they'd lost, particularly in Hollywood, or creative fields in London and Paris. They all had.

And finally, at five o'clock, they gave up the room and left. The two women from out of town had plans to see friends. And they were all getting together with Allegra again the next night for her bachelor dinner. The rehearsal dinner was the night after that. And then, finally, the wedding.

"If I survive it," Allegra said as she dropped off Sam and the baby in Bel Air. It had been an exhausting but amusing afternoon. She wasn't even sure if she liked her old friends anymore, but they were part of her life, and her history, and they were there to be part of her wedding. She was still a little taken aback by Jess. She was thinking about her as she stopped off at her office, to pick up her messages and some work on her way to pick up Jeff on the set. It was a big day for him. This was it. The final hour. The end of his first movie.

She walked quietly onto the set and watched the last take of the final scene, and heard the victory yell as the director said the magic words, "It's a wrap, folks." And Jeff and Tony shook hands and then hugged. It was an emotional moment for them and the entire cast. And when Jeff turned and saw Allegra, he was beaming. Tony came over and hugged her too. He was short and wiry and blond, and as different from Jeff as two men could be. But they both knew they'd done a fine job and were proud of what they'd accomplished. Producing the movie had been hard work, but full of rewards and private visions. They had a party that night, and Allegra stayed. By the time they got back to Malibu, Allegra was absolutely exhausted.

"How was your day?" Jeff finally asked, focusing on her again as they got home. It had been such a big day for him. The movie was finally over. Now they had to deal with postproduction, but the problems were more likely to be smaller. The stars would have gone home, and the cast and crew. The rest was up to editors, the director, and him and Tony.

"My day was strange," Allegra answered with a grin, and told him about Nancy and Jess. The odd thing was, she had nothing in common with either one of them anymore. They were old friends, but they had become strangers.

"That's why I didn't want a lot of my old school buddies coming out from New York. After a while, you have nothing in common. The only one I still care about is Tony."

"You were smarter than I was."

They sat and talked about it for a while, and then finally went to bed. He still had some loose ends to tie up the next day, and at noon, he had to pick up his mother.

Allegra would have gone too, but she had to go over some final details for the wedding with her mother, and Blaire wanted

Allegra to help with the seating for the rehearsal dinner. It all seemed so out of control. It always reminded her of how much smarter Carmen had been to go to Las Vegas. Not to mention Sam, who had gone nowhere at all, but that was different.

She agreed to meet Jeff and his mother for tea at the Bel Air that afternoon. And this time, she was bringing reinforcements. She had asked her mother to join them. Blaire had promised to come, no matter how busy she was. But even Allegra's warnings hadn't prepared her.

Mrs. Hamilton was wearing a dark suit and a white silk blouse as she walked stiffly around the gardens of the Bel Air when Allegra first saw her.

"Hello, Mrs. Hamilton. How was the trip?"

"Fine, thank you, Allegra," she said formally, with no invitation to call her anything else. Certainly not Mary, or Mom, or Mother.

They went into the dining room to sit down, and Blaire went quietly to work on her, and by the end of an hour, they were not fast friends, but there was a certain mutual respect there, and the two mothers were quite cordial. Jeff was particularly grateful to his future mother-in-law for her efforts. She knew just how to handle Mrs. Hamilton, and although she certainly wasn't easy, Blaire told Allegra later, she could be managed.

Mrs. Hamilton told Jeff, as he escorted her back to her room to lie down, that for a woman in show business, Mrs. Steinberg was extremely intelligent, and surprisingly distinguished. All of which he reported to Allegra the minute he got back to her in the lobby.

"She likes your mom," he translated into simple English.

"Mom likes her too."

"What about you? You holding up okay?" He remembered their hideous argument two weeks before, and their appalling insults about each other's families, particularly his mother. He felt an obligation to defend her, but he also knew that some of what Allegra had said was true. Mary Hamilton was far from easy. But she wasn't young, she wasn't of the modern world, she was prejudiced and biased, and limited in her own way. And Jeff was her only child. You had to give her a break for some of it. But Jeff also sympathized with Allegra.

"I'm fine. I'm just nervous."

"Who isn't?" He grinned. They had their bachelor dinners to get through that night. To Allegra, much of what she was doing seemed to be about survival. It wasn't relaxing, it wasn't fun. You just had to get through it. Even their wedding gifts weren't as much fun as she would have liked them to be. After the first one, a pair of crystal candlesticks from Cartier, there had been ten more pairs like them. And everything they got had to be listed, cataloged, inventoried, computerized, and thanked for. It was all work, and no fun. All the little details just became a headache. She wanted to tell people to wait and send them things later, but of course she didn't.

"What's on your agenda for your bachelor party tonight?" Jeff asked as he drove her home to change. She was hardly getting anything done at the office, but she hadn't really expected to anyway. And Alice was trying to cover all her bases.

"We're having dinner at Spago," she said, lying back against the seat with a yawn.

"We're going to The Troy."

"That sounds pretty civilized. Hopefully nobody will show up with half a dozen hookers." Those stories of bachelor parties had never amused her. It did not seem to be any way to start a marriage, and she would have been furious with whoever brought them, and even more so with Jeff if he used them.

But as it turned out, his bachelor party was far more chaste than hers, thanks to some of her colleagues, whom Carmen had invited. At Jeff's, there was the required stripper—but she came and left without incident—a series of bawdy songs and limericks and stories, and the only unexpected visitor was brought by Alan Carr. He had brought an alligator, heavily drugged, on a leash, with its trainer, and it was wearing a little sign around its neck that said ALLEGRA. The guys thought it was hysterical, but Allegra was happy no one had brought it for her. She would have been terrified. The guys, on the other hand, loved it.

A male stripper showed up at Spago for her, which Jess said was *very* boring. She had a good sense of humor about things, and she teased the other girls a lot, and somehow made the whole gay issue very unthreatening, and at times very funny. The girls all gave Allegra outrageous gifts, dirty movies and vibrators, and there were X-rated party favors, crotchless underwear for all, with pasties and G-strings, and gifts of "marital aids" for Allegra. It was funny for a while, but it got tiresome by the end, and all she wanted to do when she got home was climb into bed and go to sleep and forget the wedding.

"It's like being in the Olympics," she muttered as she fell asleep next to him, wondering if they were doing the right thing. Why was everyone else so sure? Carmen . . . Sam . . . why was it so easy for them, and hard for her? Was she afraid of the wedding, or him? She couldn't remember any of the answers, but she fell into a deep sleep immediately, and spent the rest of the night having nightmares.

CHAPTER 22

Friday was the hardest day of all for her. It was her last day at work, and she wrapped up everything. Her house had already been sold, and escrow was closed. She seemed to be doing nothing anymore except tying up loose ends. And there was one last big one for her to deal with. Her father was flying in that afternoon, and she had agreed to meet him at the Belage for coffee.

She had been dreading it for weeks, and had nightmares about it all night. This had nothing to do with Jeff, or the wedding. It had to do with her, and her life, and her memories, and freedom, and she knew it. She had been waiting twenty-five years for this moment.

What she hated most about what was happening these days was that she seemed to be losing Jeff in the midst of all the preparations. Everything was about hats and shoes and veils and videos and photographs and wedding cakes and bridesmaids. It had nothing to do with him and what had brought them together in the first place. It was almost as though they had to get through it now, like a maze, in order to find each other again, and she could hardly wait to see him.

She had left the house that morning before he got up, and called him after he'd left for God knows where—he had his own arrangements to make for the ushers. They'd wanted to have lunch, but never hooked up, and now she had to meet with her father, Charles Stanton.

The rehearsal would be late that afternoon, and she'd see Jeff then, and then they would lose each other again at the rehearsal dinner. And that night she was staying at her parents', just for tradition's sake, so she wouldn't see him before the wedding, and she no longer had her own house to go to. But she was looking forward to staying with them, and maybe chatting with Sam until late at night, if she came to visit from the cottage.

But in the meantime, Allegra had work to do. She had to see her father. She had talked about it with Sam, and about how reluctant she was to go down the aisle with him, and Simon had scolded her. "You make it sound like a kidnapping."

"In his case, it is," Allegra had said, and all she could think of as she went to the hotel was that she had to tell him he was a guest at the wedding, and not her father. "The part of the father will be played tonight by Simon Steinberg, *not* Charles Stanton." She was still thinking of it as she walked into the lobby, and walked right into him, and didn't know it.

She excused herself and went to the desk, and then when she got there, she turned and looked. He looked familiar, but so much older. He was watching her too, and he walked over slowly.

"Allegra?" he asked cautiously, and she nodded, holding her breath. It was him. Her father.

"Hi," she said, bereft of words, as he suggested they go to the bar, but when they sat down, he ordered a Coca-Cola, and she was glad to see it. At least he wasn't drinking. Those were her worst memories of him, when he was drunk and had beaten her mother.

They chatted about nonentities for a while, California, Boston, her work, the weather. He didn't ask about Blaire, and Allegra sensed that he probably still had a lot of animosity against her. He had never forgiven her for leaving. She told him that Jeff was from New York, and that two of his grandfathers had been physicians.

"How did he escape?" Charles Stanton said, trying to warm

up to her, and not finding it easy. There was a wall between them. And she was surprised by how old and frail he looked. Her mother said he would be seventy-five; she had never realized that he was that much older than her mother.

"He's a writer," Allegra said about Jeff, and told him about both books, and his movie. "He's very talented," she explained, but she couldn't concentrate on what she was saying. All she really wanted to know was why he had hated her so much, why he had never seen her, never called her, never loved her. She wanted to ask him what had happened when her brother died, but just sitting there with him like that, she couldn't. All her anger just sat in a little pool, like oil, with nowhere to go unless someone lit a match and let it burst into flame. But at last he did it. He asked about her mother, and his tone of voice said it all as Allegra bristled.

"Why do you sound that way when you ask about her?" Allegra asked, suddenly astonished by her own question. It had come out of some dark recess of her heart, with no warning whatsoever.

"What do you mean?" He looked uncomfortable, and sipped his Coca-Cola. He was the master of passive aggression. "I have no animosity toward your mother." He lied, and his eyes said so. He hated her even more than he had hated Allegra. In Allegra's case he just seemed not to care. In Blaire's, he had old scores to settle.

"Yes, you do have animosity toward Mom." Allegra stared him down. "But that's understandable, she left you."

"What do you know of all that?" he said, sounding irritated and cranky. "That was a long time ago. You were a child then."

"I still remember it. . . . I still remember the fights . . . the screaming . . . the things you both said. . . ."

"How could you?" He looked down into his drink, remembering it as well. "You were barely more than a baby."

"I was five years old, six when we left. It was awful." He nodded, unable to deny it, afraid she did remember the times he had hit Blaire, and all the rest. He knew himself that he'd been crazy then. And then Allegra decided to brave the deepest waters. She knew it was the only way to reach the opposite shore again, and this time she knew she had to. She might never see him again. It might be her only chance to free herself, and him. "The worst part," she said, "was when Paddy died." But as she said it, he winced, as though she had hit him.

"There was no help for that," he said brusquely. "He had a form of leukemia that could not be cured, by anyone. Not in those days. Perhaps not even now," he said sadly.

"I believe you," she said softly, and she did. Her mother had told her that years later. But she also knew that her father thought he should have saved him, and had never forgiven himself for failing. It was why he drank, and why he lost them. "But I do remember him . . . he was always so sweet to me. . . ." In some ways, he was like Jeff. He was so gentle, and giving, and took such good care of her. "I loved him so much."

Her father closed his eyes and looked away from her. "There's no point talking about that now." As he said it, she remembered that he had no other children, and for just an instant, she felt sorry for him. He was tired and alone, and sick probably, and he had nothing. She had Jeff and her parents, Sam, and Scott, and even Jimmy and Matthew. All Charles Stanton had were regrets, and ghosts, one child he had loved and lost, and another he had abandoned.

"Why didn't you ever want to see me?" she said quietly. "After that, I mean? Why didn't you ever call, or answer my letters?"

"I was very angry at your mother," he said, unhappy to be asked about it so many years later. But it was not an explanation that satisfied Allegra.

"You were my father."

"She had deserted me, and so had you, as far as I was concerned, and hanging on to you was just too painful. I knew I'd never win you back, either of you. It was simpler to just let go and forget you." Was that what he had done then? He had forced her from his head, refused her? Buried her like Paddy? Cut her off? Severed the tie that bound them?

"But why?" Allegra pressed him. "Why didn't you answer my letters, or at least talk to me? And when I did talk to you, you were so angry, and so mean." She came right out and said it, but she had to.

He said something very strange then. "I didn't want you in my life, Allegra. I didn't want you to love me. Perhaps that sounds strange to you. But I loved you very much, both of you, and when I lost you, I gave up. It was like losing Patrick all over again. I knew I couldn't fight the distance, or your new life here. Within a year after you left, you had a stepfather, three years later, a new brother, and I knew there would be more after that. She had a new life, so did you. It would have been cruel to try to hold on to you, for both of us. It was kinder to you to simply let go, to let the tides sweep you away to your new life. This way, you had nothing to look back at. You had no past, only a future."

"But I took it all with me," she said sadly. "I took you and Paddy everywhere. I never understood why you stopped loving me," she said with tears in her eyes. "I needed to know why. I always thought you hated me," she said, looking deep into his eyes, needing affirmation.

"I never hated you," he said, smiling sadly, and he barely dared to touch her fingers. "But I had nothing to give you then. I was broken. I hated your mother for a while, but even that dissipated after a time. I had my own demons to live with." And then he sighed and looked at her. "I tried an experimental treatment on your brother, Allegra. He would have died anyway, but I was sure that it would help him. It didn't—in fact, I always feared it had shortened his life, perhaps not by much, but by something. Your mother always said that I killed him." He looked beaten again as he said it.

"She didn't say that to me when we talked about it. She never has."

"Perhaps she's forgiven me," he said sadly.

"She did that a long time ago," Allegra said quietly. There

were no easy answers. There was no way of truly understanding what had made him let go of her, but at least she knew now that it had been his own demons, his own guilt, his own terrors, his own inadequacies that had convinced him it was the right decision. He simply had nothing to give her. It was what Dr. Green had always told her, and she had never believed, but at least now she had heard him say it.

"I loved you very much," he said quietly. They were the words she had waited most of her lifetime to hear. "I suppose I didn't know how then. I still love you, that's why I came out here. I'm beginning to understand that time is a luxury, and sometimes it's better to spend it. Sometimes I think of the things I would say to you, of the times I should have called you, like on your birthday. I always remember it, yours and Paddy's, and hers . . . but I've never called you. I thought about it for a long time when you wrote to me. I wasn't going to answer you. And then I realized I didn't want to miss your wedding." There were tears in his eyes when he said it. This was important to him, even more than he could tell Allegra.

"Thank you," she said, as tears slid down her cheeks. She was thanking him for his words, his honesty, her freedom. "I'm glad you came," she said, kissing his hand, and he smiled at her, not daring to respond more than he already had. As before, he was bound by his own limitations, as we all are.

"I'm glad I came too," he said softly, still shaken by their conversation.

They had another Coca-Cola then, and talked about the wedding for a while, and she said nothing to him about who would walk her down the aisle. She was thinking of having Delilah tell him. But she was so relieved about the things he had said, that he had cared, and thought about her, and had even remembered her birthdays. It was unimportant in a way, he still hadn't called her in the end, yet to Allegra, it made a tremendous difference.

When she stood up, she offered to drive him to the rehearsal. They were holding it in the same place as the rehearsal dinner itself, which was easier than going all the way back to Bel Air to the Steinbergs' garden, especially while the gardeners were still frantically working. The wedding was at five o'clock the next day. They had exactly twenty-three hours left in which to do it.

On the drive over, he astounded her, by admitting that he was nervous about seeing Blaire. It seemed so strange to her. Her mother had been married to Simon for twenty-three years; this man had no part in her life at all. Except he did. Historically. They had been married for eleven years, and she had borne him two children. It was hard to imagine it, he looked so gray and tired and old. He was so restrained and reserved and conservative. So unlike the beautiful, expansive, youthful, lively woman she knew as her mother. She seemed in no way related to Charles Stanton. And in fact, now, she wasn't.

They arrived at the Bistro promptly at six o'clock, and the rest of the wedding party was starting to arrive. The minister and Delilah were conferring in a corner, while waitresses served champagne, and at exactly seven o'clock, Delilah brought everyone to order. Allegra's whole family was there, her bridesmaids, her friends, the minister, and both her fathers. Jeff's mother was standing next to him, in a severe black dress with her hair pulled back, and she looked terribly serious, but Allegra thought she actually looked pretty, all things considered.

Alan was telling Simon all about the film in Switzerland, while Carmen chatted with Sam about the baby. For once, Sam had left Matthew at home with a baby-sitter. She had nursed him right before she left, and she had told Jimmy she didn't want to stay too long, it was the first time she had ever left the baby. But it felt great to be out again, and Jimmy had been admiring his wife's luxurious figure.

They were a handsome group, and the tabloids would have been well satisfied with the names that were represented, as the minister explained exactly what the drill would be the next day, who would go where, who would do what first, and Charles Stanton looked confused about what his role was, and Simon saw it. He drew him quietly aside, introduced himself, and shook his hand, and told him he had an unusual suggestion. Allegra had heard the beginning of it, but then they moved away from her, and she couldn't hear what they were discussing.

It was all very exciting suddenly. It was happening. All the pieces of the puzzle fit. It was coming together. Her oldest friends were there, and her family. And her father had even admitted to her that he loved her. He had been confused and frail and misguided in what he'd done to her, but she had not been abandoned through any fault of her own, or perhaps even of his. She had always known that, and been told by experts, but at last she had been able to hear it from her father.

She had introduced him to a few of her friends as they came in, and if one narrowed one's eyes very carefully, one could see a small resemblance, but it was Blaire she really looked like, and Simon that she loved as a father. But this man was still part of her, of her history, her ancestry, her past, and her future. He simply was, just as she was a part of Matthew.

She had introduced her father to Mrs. Hamilton too, but after the minister had explained everything and the group had gone back to chatting again, Charles slowly made his way over to Allegra and her mother. They had been standing together, discussing the garden.

"Hello, Blaire." If he had been any younger, he might have blushed. As it was, he simply stared at her. She looked so unchanged, so youthful. For him, it was like turning the clock back. And the memories were bittersweet as they washed over him, and he remembered when Paddy and Allegra were children. "You look very well," he said softly.

"So do you," she said, not knowing what else to say to him, as their eyes met. They shared the same memories, the same pain, the same dashed hopes, and once upon a time they had shared the same joys and laughter. It was hard to remember those days now. Only the tragedies remained: Paddy's death, and their departure. He had come here to add one last memory to their albums.

"It was nice of you to come," Blaire said, as Allegra went to greet Tony Jacobson, *and Jeff's director*. And as she moved away, she noticed that Nancy Towers was in hot pursuit of her brother, and Scott didn't seem to mind it. She had already had a little too much to drink, and her hand kept wandering across his thigh. Scott's eyes met Allegra's and she nodded.

"She looks so much like you," Charles said to Blaire, watching Allegra fly across the room, laughing, her hair moving just as Blaire's had. She was so tall, and young and graceful. "She gave me a start at first . . . I thought it was you. . . . We had a good talk this afternoon at the hotel."

"So she said," Blaire said, wanting to reach out to him, to comfort him, to tell him how sorry she was all these years later. "Is everything all right, Charles?" she said, trying not to remember when they were young and she had called him Charlie.

"My life is very quiet," he said, but he seemed to accept it. "You have a lovely family," he said, looking around. It was easy to spot them. All of her children looked like her. And he had liked his brief conversation with Simon. Maybe she had gotten what she deserved. She hadn't deserved the pain he'd given her. But he couldn't help it. He hoped she knew that. He wished he could say to her the things he had said to Allegra that afternoon, but they both knew this was different.

"I'm glad you're here, Charles," she said, and he understood her. His eyes were full of tears as he touched her hand and walked away. He couldn't be near her any longer. It was just too painful. He went to talk to Mary Hamilton instead, and found that they not only had several mutual friends in Boston, but he had known her father, who had been one of his professors in medical school. They were talking animatedly when Blaire urged them all to sit down to dinner.

There were several toasts that night, and Jeff and Allegra actually got to sit together and talk and laugh, and be with their friends. And the following night they'd be at the Bel Air Hotel, and the next morning off to Europe. It was hard to believe that the moment had come, the day had arrived—almost. It was another twenty hours till their wedding.

Simon toasted them that night, and Jeff toasted her, and

Blaire said how proud she was of all her children. And Allegra saw Charles Stanton watching her more than once, but he was getting on very well with Jeff's mother, and she seemed to be a lot friendlier than Allegra had ever seen her, as she responded. Charles Stanton and Mrs. Hamilton were fast friends by the end of the evening, and Charles was escorting her back to the Bel Air when Allegra last saw them.

"I think my ex-father is chasing your mother." She laughed as she told Jeff before he left to drive back to Malibu, "I'm going to miss you tonight." Suddenly it seemed such a stupid old tradition, to not see the bride before the wedding. In those days, it hadn't been a matter of people living together and forfeiting one night before the honeymoon, it had been far more serious than it was now. This was only token deprivation.

"How did it go with him today, by the way?" Jeff asked cautiously. He had never had a chance to ask her at dinner.

"Pretty well," she said with a small smile. "I think I got some of the insights I needed. He's kind of a sad person actually. He must be very lonely."

"Maybe he's more comfortable that way. I can't imagine your mother with him. They're as different as night and day."

"They are, aren't they? Thank God for Simon."

"Are you all straightened out about who's walking you down the aisle?" Jeff was smiling at her; he hated to leave her.

"Simon said he took care of it, not to worry. Thank God." She breathed a sigh of relief. She had made peace with her father for the first time in more than twenty years, but she still wanted to walk down the aisle with Simon.

Outside the Bistro, they all got into separate cars. Sam had already left with Jimmy an hour before, with breasts like bowling balls, to nurse her baby. And Allegra kept reminding Jeff of where her suitcases were for the honeymoon. She was afraid he'd forget them.

"Don't forget my suitcases," she shouted out the window after him as they left.

"I'll try not to!" he shouted back, following Alan and Carmen in their car, who were going to Malibu too. They stayed there most of the time now.

Ten minutes later, she was back at her parents' house in Bel Air. Simon and Blaire were checking some details, and the lights were burning bright in the cottage. Allegra was dying to visit them, but she didn't want to intrude. She would have loved to see Scott, but he had disappeared after dinner with Nancy, and Allegra had a feeling he wouldn't be back till the morning.

"You'd better get some sleep," Blaire warned, as Allegra roamed around the house, looking restless.

"I'm not tired," she said, sounding like a little kid, and her mother smiled.

"You will be tomorrow."

In the end, there was nothing else for her to do, and she went upstairs to her old room, got undressed and into bed, and lay there. She called Jeff, he had just gotten home, and they talked about what a nice evening it had been, how funny some of their friends were, and how excited they were about the wedding.

"I love you so much," he said, and meant every word of it. It was the happiest time he could remember.

"I love you too," she answered him, and after they hung up, she lay awake for hours, thinking of him, and how lucky she was. She had found exactly the man she wanted. More importantly, he was the man she needed. And just as she had dreamed, in some ways, he reminded her of Simon.

She slept peacefully that night, and there were no dreams. She had taken care of everything. Her work, her life, her past, her future, and her father.

CHAPTER 23

On Saturday, September fifth, the weather in Los Angeles was brilliantly sunny. There was no haze, no smog. There was the smallest breeze, and a bright blue sky, and at five o'clock, it was still beautiful and the sun was shining.

Allegra was standing in her bedroom then. The dress fit her exquisitely, the hat was spectacular, and the long, full veil swept over it, and made her look like a fairy princess. Her hair was gently upswept under her hat, and she looked incredible with the lace skirt at her knees in front and long in the back, and her mother handed her the fragrant bouquet David Jones had designed for her.

"Oh, my God, Allegra . . ." her mother said, as tears filled her eyes. She'd never seen a bride as lovely as her daughter. She looked absolutely regal in the dress Gianfranco Ferre had designed for Dior, and when Simon saw her walking down the stairs to him, tears filled his eyes too. There was no way to stop them.

"Oh, sweetheart," he said. There was absolutely no doubt in either of their minds that she was his daughter. And he knew, as he looked at her, that neither of them would ever forget this.

The music was playing softly outside; the guests were waiting for them. And Delilah was flapping around the living room like an ostrich, rounding up her chickens. The bridesmaids were already lined up, and everything was ready to go as Simon came up to Allegra.

"I did something yesterday, Allie. I talked to Charles. I had an idea. . . . Now, don't get mad at me," he said, and she started to get nervous. "It's sort of a compromise." He whispered in her ear, she considered for a moment, then smiled at him and nodded. And almost as soon as she did, Charles Stanton appeared in his morning coat and striped pants. He looked very distinguished and somewhat stiff. But Simon looked absolutely movie-star gorgeous.

"All right, ladies, let's go quietly," Delilah said, pretending to clap her hands silently, and suddenly Allegra giggled. It was all so silly. They had spent months on this, and it was all a big show, with a thousand ridiculous details. "Quietly and slowly! . . . quietly and slowly!" Delilah was whispering, demonstrating the solemn pace to them.

Nancy went first, having spent an unforgettable night with Scott in her room at the Bel Air, and Jess came right after her, looking extremely ladylike in her beige lace dress and beige organza picture hat. She winked at Allegra just before she stepped out into the garden, and the bride laughed irreverently. It was the happiest day of her life, and in ten minutes she would be married to Jeff . . . forever.

Carmen was the next in line. They had purposely placed her third so she wouldn't steal the show, but even with her expanded waistline it was hard for her not to. She had the kind of looks that took people's breath away, and there were lots of whispers as she glided down the aisle to the flowered altar. And then came Sam, so young, so pure, so striking with her tall, lithe figure that was so like Blaire's and Allegra's. Jimmy was an usher, and he was up ahead waiting for her with the others at the altar.

Then there was a long pause as everyone waited for the bride, and at last she came, every bit as beautiful as everyone had hoped she would be. She came toward them on her father's arm, with measured steps, and eyes cast down beneath her veil, and she could feel him tremble beside her. He had come back to her at just the right time in her life, time for her to leave him this time, and not be left. And this time, they would sail on, neither of them abandoned.

And as they came halfway down the aisle, Charles Stanton stopped, and turned to look at her with a small smile. He lifted her hand to his lips and kissed it, as he gave her his blessing.

"Godspeed, my child . . . I love you," he whispered, and she looked at him in amazement. He'd said it. He stepped aside just as Simon stepped smoothly beside her, tucked her hand in his arm, and guided her toward the altar, just as he had through life. They had led her as they had through her nearly thirty years, Charles Stanton through her very early years, and Simon after. And then, holding tightly to her, Simon looked down at his first child, the little girl Blaire had brought to him, so hungry for love, so frightened. "I love you," he said through tears, and she stood on tiptoe to kiss him. And then she left him, as she had all others, forsaking them in just the way she had loved them before, and taking on a new role as Jeff's wife. As Simon went to sit beside Blaire, Allegra turned wide, trusting eyes filled with love to her husband. She had come far for him, and together they would go farther. They had each waited a long time for the other.

"You look so beautiful," Jeff whispered as she squeezed his hand.

"I love you so much," she whispered back, and he looked down at her, so proud, so young, so tall, so hopeful, as the people who had loved her cried, wishing her a peaceful future.

They pledged their love, and troth, and promised to forsake all others, and then at last Jeff kissed her for a long, long time, as the assembled guests applauded.

The minister pronounced them man and wife, and they hurried down the aisle hand in hand, while the guests threw rose petals at them. It was a happy time, a happy day; it was the culmination of a lifetime.

The guests swore she was the prettiest bride they'd ever seen, and she and Jeff greeted everyone, and at last Peter Duchin played "Fascination" for them, and they began a slow waltz around the dance floor. Everyone stood in rapt admiration. They were the best-looking couple they'd ever seen. And then Allegra dutifully danced with Charles, who seemed quite overcome by emotion, and at last with Simon, who guided her easily around the dance floor, making her laugh at all the absurdities, and the fun of her wedding, just as always. He had a light touch, and a heart that had engulfed hers long since. And after her father, she danced with Alan, and then her brother, and her new brother-in-law, then Tony, Art, and their friends, and Jeff again. She danced for hours, and at last they finally had dinner. And she danced some more, and thanked her mother and Simon for the splendid wedding, and she told them they'd been right all along. They had two hundred and fifty guests and it was perfect. And even Mary Hamilton seemed to be having a good time. Charles Stanton hadn't left her side all evening.

Then, at last, while Allegra changed into a white silk Valentino suit, Simon danced slowly with Blaire, savoring the last moments of the wedding. Jimmy and Sam were dancing nearby, and as Blaire looked at them she suddenly felt terrible and looked up at Simon.

"Do you realize the poor thing has had a baby and gotten married in the last month and a half, and she never even had a wedding? Maybe we should do something for them after we put the kitchen back," Blaire mused, looking up at him. Suddenly it all seemed so simple, but he was laughing and shaking his head.

"Don't you dare. I'd rather give them a check and send them on a honeymoon. Don't you dare plan another wedding," he said firmly, and then looked at his youngest child, so happy in her husband's arms, and then back at his wife. Sam still looked so innocent and so trusting. "Unless she really wants one. Maybe you should ask her. . . ." He hated to cheat her out of a wedding after all she'd been through.

"We could do something for her at Christmastime . . . or next spring . . ." Blaire was already planning: a Christmas party for Sam . . . a renewal of their vows . . . little Christmas trees all over the garden . . . a tent . . . a younger band than Peter's, something the kids would like. . . .

"Stop," Simon said, laughing at her. "Why don't we get married again? That might really be fun." And in their case, perhaps appropriate. Since Matthew had been born, they had had a renewal of their marriage. "I love you, you silly girl. . . . Stop planning Sam's wedding for five minutes. I just want you to know I think you're terrific."

"I think you are too. I thought that was a stroke of genius, what you did about Allegra coming down the aisle with Charles. It gave everyone a chance, and in some ways, it was so symbolic. . . ."

"It comes from working with actors for forty years . . . compromise and creativity. It works every time."

"I'll have to remember that when I come to work with you next week," she teased, as they danced to "New York, New York." And then Allegra appeared in her white Valentino. She stood on the stage with the band, and turned her back to the crowd, and threw her bouquet high above and behind her, and it flew through the air and landed in Jess's arms, who shook her head and tossed it away again like a hand grenade ready to go off, and this time Samantha caught it. Sam and her sister laughed over it, and as Allegra kissed her good-bye, she whispered to her that their mother wanted to give her a wedding over Christmas.

"Oh, no," Sam squealed, like a kid facing spinach. "I couldn't. . . . Jimmy would kill me. . . . I'd die. . . ." She meant it sincerely. Allegra's wedding had been beautiful, but in Sam's opinion, way too much trouble.

"Tell Mom," Allegra said, waving at everyone as they got into the car to leave for the hotel. It had been the perfect wedding.

Blaire and Simon watched her go. She had come to kiss them good-bye and thank them, and Jeff had thanked them too. They'd be back in three weeks from Europe, and as they drove away, Jimmy pulled Sam onto the dance floor to dance with him, Scott disappeared to his room with Nancy, and Simon pulled his wife tightly into his arms and kissed her.